The Captive Girl

Book 3 in the Dan Stone Series

A Novel

David Nees

The Captive Girl: Book Three in the Dan Stone Series, is a work of fiction and should be construed as nothing but. All characters, locales, and incidents portrayed in the novel are products of the author's imagination or have been used fictitiously. Any resemblance to any person, living or dead, is entirely coincidental.

To keep up with my new releases, please visit my website at *www.davidnees.com.* You can sign up for my reader updates. Just Scroll down to the bottom of the landing page to join.

You can also click "Follow" under my picture on the Amazon book page and Amazon will let you know when I release a new work.

ISBN 9781790386864

Manufactured in the United States

For Carla

My greatest fan and encourager. You give me strength when the going gets hard.

Many thanks go to my beta readers, Ed, Chris, and Eric. Without your help this story would remain crude and unpolished. Thank you for the generous amount of time you gave to my endeavor.

Thank you, Catherine for your sharp-eyed proofreading. You found so many things I missed.

Thanks also to Onur Aksoy for his great cover design. He is talented and works diligently with sometimes conflicting directions to produce great covers. His website is, www.onegraphica.com

The Captive Girl

The soul that has conceived one wickedness can nurse no good thereafter. —Sophocles,

When justice is done, it brings joy to the righteous but terror to evildoers. —Proverbs 21:15

Chapter 1

The girl stuffed a change of clothes into her book bag. She grabbed her jacket and opened her bedroom door. Holding back tears, not allowing herself to call up the images that threatened to surface and destroy her composure, she tiptoed down the hall to the stairs. There was inside security in the mansion along with guards who patrolled the surrounding grounds. She knew their pattern having lived with this security all her life. When the guard walked past the entrance foyer, where the grand staircase ended, Evangeline noiselessly descended.

She went around to a side hallway and opened a door to another set of stairs that led down to the basement. She paused at the top of the stairs to gather her courage. The basement held terrors. There were things that went on down there that she didn't want to know about. Her mother, who had died that very night, had been subjected to the terrors in her sacrifices to protect her child. Now, with her gone, Evangeline knew she had to run away. To where she didn't know.

With a deep breath, she descended the steps and hurried through the corridors, past storerooms which held an elaborate variety of foods including a large wine collection, past other rooms, locked, that Evangeline suspected were the location of the ravages her mother experienced.

She came to a door near the end of the corridor. She had a key, given to her by her mother some time ago for just such a critical moment. They had once before explored the tunnel behind the door. It was an escape route for her father, Jan Luis Aebischer. It would allow him to leave the mansion undetected if there were ever a break in or attack. Herr Aebischer had reason to be cautious. He dealt in large sums of money and he moved them around, hiding them from authorities as needed. Money was not only hidden for his wealthy, tax-avoiding clients, money was also hidden for underworld figures as well as terrorists. Herr Aebischer did not discriminate; for a proper fee he would handle your money. His interest in what you did with it only extended to his desire to protect himself.

At the end of the tunnel was a set of steep steps, almost a ladder. It stopped at a plate. Evangeline turned the wheel that locked the plate in place like a ship's hatch. It was heavy. She and her mother never actually opened the hatch, but her mother wanted Evangeline to know about it, for this very purpose, to escape should anything happen to her.

Panic arose as the hatch at first refused to budge. Once it cracked open, she knew an alarm would be sent. She had to get it all the way open, get out, and move fast to not be captured. For she was sure the guards would capture her at their master's command. They were always polite, but she knew to whom they answered.

She braced herself and put her shoulder against the metal plate. She took a deep breath and, using her legs, pushed with all her might. A sharp screeching sound of metal on metal resounded in the stillness of the tunnel; the hatch slowly gave way. With one last push it flopped open.

Rain poured in on Evangeline. She dropped back down, grabbed her bag, and climbed back up the steps and out into the shrubs at the edge of the grounds. The cold rain pelted her. It was late September in Zürich and the weather already showing hints of the cold to come. Now it was rain, soon it would be snow.

She didn't hesitate, but ran to the fence, threw her bag over, and climbed after it. On the other side, she took a quick look around. The street was empty. The airport and downtown Zürich lay to the south. She set out on a run through the rain, a run to freedom and an uncertain future.

Chapter 2

Rashid al-Din Said, the son of a successful Saudi businessman and successor to his father's wealth and empire, had been able to grow his father's companies and double their worth in the ten years since he had taken over the reins of power. He was now numbered among the world's billionaires, albeit one with a very private persona. There were few pictures of him and his name was rarely mentioned in reports on his companies. He controlled construction, finance, and resource exploration operations world-wide.

The success provided ample wealth for his family. His younger brother, flamboyant and charismatic, served as the public face of the firms under Rashid's ownership. He was happy to let him play that role. His brother was good at it and it kept the spotlight away from Rashid.

He had just landed at the Frankfort airport in his private Gulfstream jet. His agent was there to greet him at the private hanger. Rashid was dressed as a western businessman, forgoing his fine robes. The western suits seemed so confining, but worked well in the colder climate. He was privately processed through customs and sat back in the large Mercedes while the driver slipped out of the airport. The authorities knew who he was and how many deals he made around the world, sometimes with German partners. Although he didn't like the country, Rashid was a regular and welcome guest in Germany.

"Can we drive around the perimeter without anyone noticing?" He asked as they exited the airport.

"Yes *Sayyid*. Later I can show you detail photos but it will help for you to see the area yourself."

Rashid looked out of the window as the Mercedes drove along the *Airportring Strasse*. The road circled the airport and its runways, giving a view of the take-off and landing activities. There was a convenient place along the road for plane watchers to park. Frankfort was one of the busiest airports in the world and possibly the second busiest in Europe after Heathrow in London. He would be inspecting that as well on this trip.

Later he reviewed all the pictures and approved the reconnaissance work done by his Frankfort office. That afternoon he took off for London. He was a jet-setting businessman inspecting his empire on a whirlwind tour. In London his agent repeated the actions that occurred in Frankfort. That evening he departed for Paris and spent the night in a penthouse suite at the Mandarin Oriental. The next morning Rashid drove to Gare du Nord, one of Paris's largest train stations. After sitting and watching the throngs of travelers coming and going, he drove to Charles de Gaulle airport to inspect it as he had done at Frankfurt. Later he was briefed on the Amsterdam airport.

On his evening flight home Rashid went over the tour in his head. He had observed the lineup of planes, the crush of travelers at the airports and the Paris train station. He smiled. His idea was bold. It would take everyone by surprise.

He had been disappointed by the failure of his plans to insert sixty terrorists into the U.S. under Tariq Basara's supervision. The result had been the death of all the terrorists. Rashid's subsequent investigation indicated that a very small operation, possibly the work of a single person, had thwarted his insertion plans and led to the death of the sixty jihadists. It was a major setback.

For now, Rashid would turn his attention to Europe with bold moves that would sow terror among the capitals. It was to be a coordinated attack. Citizens would be unnerved, governments would topple or be compromised, and enclaves of Muslims in Europe's large cities would rise up to support the fighters. The message would be to cast the attacks as reprisals for actions against the Muslim faithful. Europe would grant ever more accommodation, hoping for peace and stability, thereby advancing the inevitable victory over the continent.

Christianity was dying in Europe. The western culture was in decline along with birthrates. His terror operations would cause the population and governments to cower in the face of Islamic strength. Then he would let birthrate demographics do the rest and turn his attention back to the U.S.

The explosives would be placed on major rail lines of the French TGV bullet trains. These high-speed trains, traveling at over one hundred miles per hour were a marvel of luxury and sophistication. They linked the major cities of Europe and were prized as engineering marvels. The explosions would be timed to create disastrous derailments. Teams of infiltrators would insert themselves onto the ground near the runways of the Frankfort, Amsterdam, Charles de Gaulle, and Heathrow airports. In a coordinated attack, they would fire Panzerfaust 3 launchers sending rockets into the waiting planes lined up to take off. They would target not only the cabin but the wing tanks to trigger engulfing fires. Meanwhile, gunmen armed with their automatic weapons would assault the terminals of those airports. Other assault groups would attack at the Gare du Nord railway station.

Chapter 3

Pietro Conti had a problem. His boss, Jan Luis Aebischer, had directed him to hire someone to find and rescue his daughter, Evangeline, and kill the man who had taken her. She had run away two years ago and her father had recently learned that she was working for a Croatian pornographer. Working was not the correct word for it as Pietro had learned. The man kept a stable of women under his control using a combination of drugs and intimidation. The girl was not free to leave, he was certain.

His problem was not the task, he was not squeamish about such an operation; it was the instructions that he was not to hire a hitman connected to the underworld. Herr Aebischer didn't want any trailing liability from this operation and he didn't want to be blackmailed for more money after the fact.

Pietro had few options. Herr Aebischer had forbidden him to hire a man they called "the bookseller". This was the man Pietro usually contacted if there was any dirty work to be done, work that one didn't want any connection to. Besides the man didn't do people rescues. He handled an assortment of thieves and assassins, and Aebischer didn't want those men connected to his daughter.

In his search Pietro had come across rumors that a minor arms dealer, Guzim Lazami, had been marked for elimination. He was trying to make a play and strike out on his own, using his own connections and not going through the established hierarchy of dealers. Some criminal bosses were not happy and the betting on the street was that Guzim might soon be eliminated. He certainly was acting like his life was under threat.

Pietro's long shot was to follow Guzim around and hope to hire whoever could get close enough to kill the gun dealer. Anyone who could get close to Lazami and kill him would have to be very good at what he did. Pietro knew that the man loved dance clubs. It was one of his passions and therefore a possible weakness to exploit. That idea brought him to the Lightspeed Dance Club of Milan. It was holding its largest rave of the year and Pietro, knowing Guzim was a fan, hoped he would be in attendance. Maybe, just maybe, someone would try to take him out.

Dan had been stalking Guzim Lazami, an Albanian-Italian, for almost a month now. He had spent countless hours on many rooftops and hills, waiting for the shot that didn't materialize. Jane, Dan's handler back at CIA headquarters and the woman who had recruited him, had noted Guzim had recently escalated his security, perhaps because he was striking out on his own and knew others might object. He was certainly careful. He rarely went out and when he did, he minimized his exposure, getting into armored cars while in garages and running with bodyguards covering him when he had to step out in the open to get from car to building or the reverse.

As a sniper, Dan's instinct was to strike from afar. Distance was his friend; the more between him and his target the less likely he would be discovered or engaged by the enemy. The safer his strike would be. Guzim's cautious nature was making it hard for Dan. The hit would have to be done at close range even though that was against all of Dan's training and instinct. But where?

The only chink in Guzim's defenses was his enthusiasm for dance clubs, especially the wilder ones that held marathon raves. This attraction, with the attendant crowds, created an opportunity, but Dan would have to do the job at close range and then make his escape. One of the hottest clubs was the Lightspeed Dance Club in Milan. It was listed as a "must see" on all the guidebooks for dance club enthusiasts. It attracted a young, energetic crowd that would rave the night away with the club spilling out customers in the early morning hours.

When reconnoitering the club earlier in the week Dan had noticed metal detectors at the entrance. So, the day before, early in the morning when the club would be closed, Dan pried open the bathroom window and climbed in. He taped his double-barrel .22 caliber derringer along with a stun grenade to the back of a toilet water tank.

Once he was near the club entrance, Dan found a spot to wait. He had to mark Guzim's arrival. He didn't want to be hunting for him inside, not knowing for sure if he had shown up. Sure enough, at about 10:30 pm, an SUV, pulled up and three men piled out. They formed a perimeter around the curbside back door of the vehicle. Then Guzim stepped out and the group quickly shuffled into the club, bypassing the line waiting to get in. When Guzim had disappeared inside, Dan strolled up to the doorman and, after flashing a one hundred Euro bill, was passed through, leaving the bill in the doorman's hand.

Stepping inside, the music assaulted Dan's senses. He had to fight off an immediate sense of disorientation. The heavy beat pounded away at him, vibrating his bones. Lights flashed and spun around the room like droplets of water, some of the light was split by mirrored balls hung from the ceiling, scattering the light like broken crystal around the room. Dan wandered through the space to get acclimated and to locate Guzim. There were two bars made of Plexiglas at either side of the room with islands of booths placed around the dance floor. At one end of the room, on an elevated platform, the DJ was busy at his turntables.

People danced with their arms in the air, often seeming to just jump up and down to Dan's untutored eye. The kaleidoscope of lights made it hard to see clearly. There was a background of ultraviolet light that made white shirts shine brightly and cause day glow colors to come alive. Many females had the glowing colors painted on their arms and face. The result was a surreal tribal look. Most everyone had glow sticks wrapped around their necks. The effect of it all was very synthetic and futuristic.

Why would you subject yourself to this abuse? Dan found it hard to relate to the scene and wondered why Guzim, who was around forty liked this atmosphere. *Trying to hold on to his youth?*

The arms dealer was sitting in a booth reserved for VIPs near the dance floor with his guards around him. There were three good looking women sitting with him as well. People came and went greeting and glad handing him. Other women came up, but it looked like Guzim had picked his bevy for the night. The body guards spent their time scanning the clubbers that swirled around the table. *Wouldn't want their job, especially tonight.* Most of those who came by the booth were oblivious to Guzim's true identity and only knew that he was wealthy and connected.

The action grew increasingly heated as the music grew louder. The beat was insistent, overpowering you and forcing you to move. Dan tried to tune it out, but it was impossible. Two hours later, Guzim was acting much looser from the mix of drinks and drugs that he had been sharing with the women in his booth. The same could be said for most of the dancers on the floor.

Dan left the dance floor at a short break in the music, abandoning his dance partner. It didn't matter to her, or anyone else. Dance partners came and went as people milled around on the floor engaging one another and then turning off, focusing inward, only to connect with another dancer for a few minutes before repeating the pattern. The only difference was that those who came in groups tended to remain connected to one another. He headed to the men's room.

Now in the restroom, he waited for the correct stall to open and went in, locking the door behind him. He retrieved his weapons and put them in his coat pocket. Then he washed his hands and headed back out to the dance floor.

Upon leaving the relative quiet of the men's room the music again assaulted him with an almost physical wave of sound. His chest vibrated with the ever-driving beat. The sound was impossible to tune out. He maintained the stance of a partygoer but, like a predator, he narrowed his focus to the arms dealer bouncing around on the dance floor with his hands in the air, surrounded by his women. Dan gave an occasional glance to the body guards. The guards were trying to keep Guzim in sight while he was being swallowed up by the crowd. One of the guards seemed to have given up and was drinking and flirting with another girl that had stopped by their table. Dan had not come to their attention; he still blended in.

Guzim was deep in the midst of the ravers with his three young women, all with the neon stripes on their clothes and faces that lit up in the ultraviolet light, dancing with him in a semi-circle. Dan maneuvered himself slowly towards Guzim. He used the surge of the crowd to bring him closer so he would not stand out. When the surge moved away from his target, Dan resisted the flow. And so, minute by minute, he "danced" himself closer to Guzim.

Then he was within reach, just like dozens of other ravers had been throughout the evening. When the crowd shifted, blocking the view of the bodyguards for a moment, Dan slipped the pistol out of his pocket. While still dancing he extended his arm towards Guzim, the pistol almost touching the back of his neck, and pulled the trigger twice in quick succession.

You could not hear the sound over the music. Guzim's head flung forward and his body collapsed to the floor in a heap. The two bullets had stuck him at the base of his skull destroying his brain stem and shutting his body down immediately. He never felt the shots. One of the guards seeing Guzim disappear jumped up and started towards the dance floor. Dan pulled the flash-bang grenade from his pocket and threw it in the direction of the guards.

After throwing the grenade, Dan dropped to the floor, closed his eyes, and covered his ears. The grenade went off with a flash of nearly seven million candlepower and a bang of over one hundred, seventy decibels. Those within ten feet were all knocked to the ground from the blast energy and many would suffer long-term hearing loss. The advancing body guard was knocked to the floor. The brightness blinded everyone not covering their eyes. People couldn't see for some five seconds and the flash produced an after image on their retina that interfered with one's sight for minutes afterward. The loudness not only produced temporary hearing loss but loss of balance. The combined effects caused severe disorientation within fifty feet of the blast.

Dan got up after the blast and started for the door. The crowd panicked, first in the vicinity of the explosion and then spreading through the club. People surged towards the doors thinking the club was under attack. The grenade halted the advance of the body guards and when they began to recover, the panic of the crowd made it impossible for them to make any coordinated advance. They only made it to Guzim's body as Dan was leaving the club.

He maneuvered his way out of the stream of panicked ravers that spilled out of the doors. People were running, some were screaming, there was chaos at the door and in the street beyond. Dan turned to separate himself from the crowd and began to walk casually away towards some darker alleys.

Pietro sat across the street and watched the patrons rushing out of the club. He knew what had happened. The assassin would be coming out. He would not be panicked. Pietro expected the man would be acting in a calm, purposeful manner, wanting to fade away into the side streets before the police could respond. Out of the crush of people, he noticed a man, all alone, walking calmly away from the action. Pietro took a deep breath. This might be the man. It could be lethal to try to connect, but this could be the one chance to satisfy his boss. Besides, the assassin would not want to create a second scene; he would want to leave quietly. He got up to follow.

After making two turns through tight pedestrian walkways, Dan realized someone was following him, someone not too adept at hiding his movements.

He sank into the dark of a doorway after turning a corner and waited. The man following him came around the corner. Dan grabbed him around the neck with his arm and pushed the reloaded .22 caliber pistol into his back.

"Don't turn around," he said in Italian. "If you do, you die." He pulled the man back into the deeper dark of the doorway. "You're following me, why?"

"I need to talk to you," the man said. His voice was low and harsh.

"You don't know me. Why would you need to speak with me?"

"My employer wants to hire you. There's a card in my jacket pocket. Take it and call the number. There's a million Euros in it for you."

"You are very close to being dead. This pistol I'm holding can't be heard, especially over the sirens and noise coming from the club. So I can easily eliminate you."

"Just take the card and call me. We can talk later. Here—"

"Don't move!"

"My jacket pocket, the card's in there. You can reach for it yourself. It's worth a million Euros."

Dan pulled the card out of the pocket. "If this has a microdot tracer or transmitter on it, I'll find it and I'll use it to find you and kill you."

"No no, the card is clean. We want to hire you. Call me and I'll explain the details."

"Okay. Now you are going to turn around and walk back from where you came. You are not going to look at me. If you do, I will shoot you on the spot. I'm going to watch to see that you walk all the way down the alley. If you try to follow me, I'll kill you."

With that Dan turned the man around and shoved him forward. He watched him trudge back down the narrow alley and then turned and sprinted away. Upon reaching his car, he got in and moved into the traffic. After driving around Milan for twenty minutes to assure himself he was not being followed, Dan set out east on the A4 towards Venice, about three hours away.

Chapter 4

After arriving in Europe, Dan needed a home base for his operations. His public persona was that of a security consultant for corporations throughout Europe. He represented an American company, SecureTech, which if anyone checked, had a website and looked legitimate, courtesy of the CIA. You could contact them, inquire about bids for work, and even seek employment.

He wanted the comfort of a home, not an apartment, and so had purchased a modest villa located in the Marghera district just outside of Venice. It was an incongruous home. A once luxurious residence left in place as the surrounding area had evolved into an industrial zone with canals for freighter ships coming in to unload their cargos. Apparently, the owners didn't want to abandon the property and sell out. They had held on, trying to rent the property with little success. The location didn't bother Dan; he liked the isolation it presented and offered a hefty price that changed the owners' mind.

Dan had chosen Venice because it was generally a safe city with little crime. Most of the activities involved pickpockets preying on tourists. Even walking around in the city proper at night was considered safe and violent crime was quite unusual. In order to get to know his surroundings, he spent a few weeks walking the streets of the Marghera district, watching the activity.

Since his anonymity might be compromised at any time, Dan knew he had to have some local help to alert him if any strangers came around asking questions. It was a risk to connect with locals, but one he needed to take. He set out to identify any local street criminals he could enlist to help him. He was determined to find someone or some group and get them on his side.

After two weeks, he had identified a loose group of pickpockets and scam artists. They worked mostly in Venice proper and did little in the suburb outside where they lived. Dan was able to locate a bar in the neighborhood where the group hung out.

He walked into the bar late one evening after all the activity in Venice had died down. The young men slowly stopped talking and stared at Dan, obviously not a local, as he sat the bar and ordered a beer. Dan could see, as he scanned the room, that he was the subject of hushed conversation. *Wondering who I am, why I'm here.* Finally, someone, probably the leader, approached Dan and sat down next to him.

"Buonasera," the man said as he placed his drink on the bar.

Dan nodded.

"Parla italiano?"

"Sì," Dan replied.

"Are you a tourist?" the man asked.

"No. I live in the area."

"Where are you from?"

"I'm from here," Dan said as he turned to look at the young man for the first time.

"I mean before you came here."

"It is not important. This is my home now."

The man thought about that for a moment. "So you stop in this local bar and expect to be treated like a local?"

"No, I'm looking for someone," Dan said keeping his gaze fixed on the man.

"Who are you looking for?"

"I think I'm looking for you."

The man opened his eyes further. Dan's gaze never wavered. His look was the look of a serious person, a hard man. Dan could tell the young local was evaluating what to do next. Was Dan a threat? How tough might he be?

"You don't know me," the man finally answered. "Why would you be looking for me?"

"I think you have some influence on the hustlers that work the streets."

The man started to stand up. "I think you had better go before you get hurt."

Dan put his hand on the man's arm. His grip was vise-like. "You want to hear me out. You don't want to do anything stupid."

The man looked at Dan's hand squeezing his arm so tight it cut off his circulation. He sat back down.

"I want to hire you to keep an eye out on my house. I need to know if any strangers come around or show any unusual interest in the place."

"You are hiding from someone?" Dan had released his grip and he could tell the young man wanted to rub his arm but didn't want to give Dan the satisfaction of seeing him do it.

"That's of no interest to you. I just want you to arrange for what I just described."

"We're not going to get in trouble with this? You're not in trouble with the *piedipiatti*?" He used the slang word for cops.

Dan shook his head.

"The mafia?"

Again, Dan shook his head. "I just don't like strangers nosing around my home or my business. *Capiche?*"

"Sì. How much do you pay for this work?"

"One hundred Euro a week."

The young man thought that over and then shook his head. "Too low, make it two hundred a week."

"I'll give you one-fifty, and after I see how well you do the job, I'll raise it to two hundred. Deal?"

The man considered the offer and nodded; they shook hands.

"What's your name?" Dan asked.

"Marco, Marco Favero. What's yours?"

"Steve."

"Okay, where do you live?"

Dan gave him the address. "How do I find you to pay you?"

"Cash in advance. You can leave it here with Bruno, the bartender."

"One hundred fifty Euros. You'll get an envelope once a week. Use as few guys as you can. I don't want a lot of attention drawn to me about this."

Dan pulled out his wallet and handed Marco the first week's fee. "Can I buy you a beer?" He asked.

"No. I have to be going." Marco stood up. *"Ciao."*

Later, two of the hustlers that Marco recruited argued they should shake Dan down for more money by threatening to expose him. Marco shut that idea down firmly. Even though Dan was older he could see he was someone not to be fooled with. Dan was probably involved in much more serious things than the street hustles Marco played with and he didn't want to get on the wrong side of him. If he wanted to be anonymous, then Marco would help. Maybe there would be more rewards along the way.

After all the hectic work of moving in, the purchasing of furniture, the setting up of the security systems, the furnishing of the kitchen and bathrooms, Dan finally had time to sit back. He now had something that had been missing for some years in his life, a home. But it was still incomplete.

Chapter 5

Dan sat in the breakfast room off of the kitchen late one morning. It had east-facing windows which allowed the morning sun to stream in. He nursed a cup of strong, Italian coffee. He couldn't shake a feeling of emptiness, a loneliness that surrounded him and followed him through all the rooms of his new house.

Rita was not present. Rita, his high school sweetheart, the woman he had married and who had been pregnant with their first child, was gone. She had been killed, burned alive in a fire in the restaurant she and Dan had opened in Brooklyn. Their lives had been going so well. And then it had all come undone.

After getting out of the Army where Dan had served as a sniper in Iraq for two tours, he had come back to Brooklyn. The two of them took some savings and started the restaurant. They worked hard at it and were successful; life was good. The only off note was that the mob wanted protection money. Dan and Rita knew some of the mob members from high school and refused to pay. They just wanted to be left alone. But it didn't work that way in Brooklyn. The mob torched the restaurant to teach them a lesson. Tragically Rita was there late that night, working on the books. She was caught in the conflagration and died along with their unborn child.

Dan was devastated. His parents were gone having died just before he enlisted in the Army. His only relation was his sister, Lisa, who lived in Montana. After the funeral he left Brooklyn to get away from the memories and hit the road, not knowing where he was going, finally winding up at his sister's ranch. During that time, Dan had decided to bring retribution, payback, to the mob. That had led to his recruitment by the CIA. Now he sat, alone, in Italy, in a nice villa, but no one to share it with.

Wonder how Lisa would like the place? Probably too urban for her. He smiled at the thought. Lisa had been transformed from an Easterner, a city girl, into a western, ranch girl. She had married a cattleman, Bob Jackson, from Montana and learned to love his western lifestyle. She was comfortable working with cattle and pitching hay in the barn. Hunting elk and other game now came naturally to her as well. He and his sister were close, or had been. Bob and Lisa were the only family he had. While she had a husband and his family, she was still protective of her younger brother.

Do you wonder what's happened to me? After his vendetta ended, Dan had told Lisa very little, just that he had been offered a job and a way out of New York. He was vague on the details and not sure whether Lisa understood what that meant. How would Lisa take knowing her brother was a professional assassin? His reflections only sharpened his sense of isolation. There was so much he could not tell Lisa. And Rita, the love of his life, was gone forever.

He still talked to Rita and sometimes thought he could hear her respond when he was in that state between sleep and wakefulness. The shaman he had met in Mexico had spoken of Rita. His name was Tlayolotl, and he had not only saved Dan's life but introduced him to the spirit world from which Dan had learned to draw strength and assistance in his mission. *What did Tlayolotl say? 'She has a strong spirit and spoke loudly.'*

Dan stood up and headed for the kitchen with his now empty coffee cup. *Big house. Too big for one person to rattle around in. How in the world would I fill it? And with whom?*

Just then the phone rang in the other room. It was his secure phone.

"Jane here," the voice said after Dan answered. Jane Tanner was Dan's boss back at the CIA. She had recruited Dan after he came to her attention while carrying out his vendetta on the Brooklyn mob. His attacks had been so effective that he had taken down a prominent capo of the Brooklyn family boss.

"When are you coming over to visit? I have a very nice villa and it's pretty empty with just me in it. It's in the industrial section of Venice."

"Sounds like a mismatch."

"It is a bit odd, but it works. The boat is an hour away in Porto Santo Margherita. If you come over, we could go out for a week; sail down to the Dalmatian coast...get away from it all."

"Not sure I could be gone that long. Besides, Henry might not like me fraternizing with employees."

"So I'm just an 'employee' now? Where's my medical and dental plan? How many days of vacation do I get? I don't remember reading any of that in the employee manual. In fact, I don't remember *any* employee manual."

"Don't be a smartass. You know what I mean."

"I know we have a good relationship, even if you get upset at my improvising out in the field sometimes."

"It's the relationship. Things could go too far if we let them and I don't think that would be good for the mission…or that Henry would approve."

"Let's not tell Henry. It'll be our secret."

"Damn. You must be lonely. I'm flattered and I do admit it's tempting, but we have important business to deal with."

Dan sighed. "I *am* lonely, to tell the truth. You're my only connection to a normal world and you're not that normal."

"But you like me that way."

"I guess I do. Okay, what do you have? I'm beginning to get bored since I finished moving in."

"Guzim Lazami, he's an arms dealer, mid-level. He's Albanian-Italian and has contacts in the Balkans. He's not a kingpin type, but he's made inroads into terrorist groups in Europe. We understand he's orchestrating a deal for some heavy weapons, rocket launchers and explosives. It goes beyond the usual assault rifles."

"Don't we want to get to the larger players? Won't just watching him lead you to them? It would be more efficient to take them out rather than a mid-level guy like this."

"Maybe, but Henry's worried. Lazami seems to have developed his own connections and Henry thinks there's a pending heavy weapons deal going down outside of the normal channels. Lazami may be striking out on his own. He wants to stop it before it gets into full swing."

"If I take Guzim out will it stop the deal?"

"Pretty much. He doesn't have a large organization behind him. If he's gone, the deal falls apart."

"Or so you hope."

"It's the best we can do. I've sent a sealed packet to the Consulate General office in Milan. You'll be able to pick it up tomorrow. Use the Steve Johnson alias."

"At least I don't have to drive to Rome."

"Trying to be helpful. Call me after you've gone through the material."

"Okay, but, seriously, plan on coming over sometime soon. I've got a nice set up and in this business I'm not sure how long it will last."

"I'll work on it. Take care of yourself. I'll be in touch." With that Jane hung up.

After killing Lazami and returning to the Venice area from Milan, Dan called Jane. "Mission complete," he said after she answered. "The job was done in Milan, so you'll probably hear about it from the Consulate General office. It had to be done up close, which is not the way I want to do business, but the man was very careful about exposing himself."

"You tried other ways?"

"For a month. I got nothing, so I decided to go to the one place where he would be exposed."

"Where was that?"

"He was a rave fan. It was the one weakness in his security, but I guess the man needed an outlet for tension."

"You did it at a rave?"

"The biggest one of the season in Milan. I figured it was one Guzim wouldn't miss and I was right."

Dan proceeded to give Jane a run down on the night's events. It was delivered in a matter-of-fact tone. Guzim was a bad guy. He sold guns to terrorists and didn't care who they used them on. And he lived a decadent life style from the profits, including a yacht and lots of women along with his two homes, one in south eastern Italy and one in the northern lake country. And now he had upped the ante and decided to supply even heavier weapons to the bad guys, all to kill innocents. Dan didn't resent his wealth. He knew there were people who would pay well for his services. But he also didn't lament the man's death or have any second thoughts about his causing it; Guzim knew the risks he took. And this was what Dan had signed up to do when he joined Jane and the CIA. *If I take out more of them, the enablers as well as the terrorists, they'll all start to keep their heads down.*

Chapter 6

Dan enjoyed living near the old city of Venice. A short drive would get him over the causeway and into a parking garage where he would shed his car for the unique methods of travel in the city of canals. The standard way to get around for most was the *vaporetti*, the water buses. You could purchase a multiple-trip pass and go all over the city with the ticket. The routes were shown prominently throughout and the "bus stops" were easy to spot, being covered stands set out into the canals.

Dan would start out in the morning and ride a *vaporetto* into the city, get off near some destination he had marked out before, a church, museum, special district, or one of the outlying islands like Murano where the glass makers created their marvels. Then he would tramp the "streets" all populated by pedestrians. He enjoyed almost getting lost, challenging his sense of direction among the narrow, winding walkways, practicing his counter surveillance skills.

The "streets" always fascinated Dan. They were for pedestrians only. They were narrow and dark, in perpetual shadow, and had an air of mystery about them. During his walks, he would find a small restaurant that catered to locals, not tourists. He enjoyed trying the *cicchetti* at such places, the Venetian version of *tapas*.

This day he had spent a morning at the Guggenheim Museum on the Grand Canal. Afterward, he took a *vaporetto* to *Piazza San Marco*. He intended to sip a coffee outside one of the restaurants and watch the tourists. He enjoyed people watching. Maybe it was an unconscious expression of his loneliness, but tourists sometimes provided good entertainment. Since taking out Lazami, Dan had been unoccupied and starting to feel restless.

Watching tourists should be a warning. You need a hobby or you should go sailing. He berated himself for becoming a slacker and promised himself to go on a ten - mile run that evening. After finishing his coffee, Dan got up and started off across the piazza, away from the water and towards the labyrinth of narrow walkways branching off from it. As was his habit, he casually scanned the people as he walked.

His eyes passed over a woman selling T-shirts and scarves from a kiosk in the middle of the square. It was her gaze that caught him; he'd seen it before in Mexico City. It was a penetrating gaze that captured you; that looked into and through you, singling you out. There was no mistaking it for random eye contact; you were the subject of her gaze.

The woman turned to a young girl and spoke to her. Then she looked back at Dan again and started to walk, past the basilica, towards the edge of the square. Dan knew he should follow. He was cautious but he had been in this scenario before so was less reluctant. The woman entered one of the side streets. A block off the square she looked back to check on Dan, then she turned right into an even narrower street. Dan followed. His eyes adjusted to the dimmer light in the narrow passageways that were in perpetual shadows. The woman stopped at a door, and with a last look back at him, entered.

Something's up.

In Mexico he had been told that there were special people—the shaman, Tlayolotl, had called them Watchers—all over the world. They had the gift of being able to see the spirit dimension to reality as well as the physical. The revelation had disrupted Dan's western world view, but he had seen the truth of what the shaman had spoken about played out. Tlayolotl had saved his life in the Chihuahuan desert and his guidance had helped Dan create major disruption to the drug cartels. The old native mystic had said Watchers would contact him to help in his mission. Dan followed the woman into the house.

Inside the light was soft, filtered through curtains and aided by gentle lighting placed on the walls. He was in a tight hallway leading back into the house. The woman was at the back of the hallway. She motioned for him to hurry. Dan followed her into the kitchen where she directed him to sit him at a table.

"You are a Watcher, aren't you?" Dan asked.

She nodded. She was of medium height with black, wavy hair that threatened to burst free of her scarf. Her complexion was dark but she didn't have a Roma or gypsy look about her.

"I hope you don't have foolish questions. My daughter and I clean houses as well as sell scarves. The owners of this house will be back soon and we must be gone before then. This is a safe place to talk to you."

Dan shook his head. "No foolish questions. But I'm not on any mission right now."

"You have been given an offer."

Dan thought for a moment. “Someone gave me their business card and said I should call them. How did you—”

The woman put her finger to her lips. “No foolish. No time for that.”

Dan nodded and blushed. These encounters, as few as he had, were full of surprises.

“I decided not to follow up on it. I don’t want to do outside work.”

“There is a greater darkness than the one you scattered in Milan. The man who wants to hire you...the darkness is thick behind him. I cannot penetrate it. He wants you to rescue a girl and she holds the key.”

“The key to what?”

The woman gave him a scathing look as if he were a child who refused to get his sums correct.

“A larger darkness.” Her voice was full of condescension.

“You want me to take the job? It wasn’t assigned to me.”

She nodded. “I know. The woman in the U.S., the one who directs you, she doesn’t know of this but we have seen it. We don’t know what it is. We can’t penetrate it to see. It is too thick, too dangerous.”

“How does the girl play into this?”

“We only know she is the key. She will show you if you rescue her. But her heart is not clear and will not be truthful.”

“How does she help me? Give me the key you say she holds?”

“Rescue her, change her heart.”

“Rescue her from what?”

“You must call the man. He is a messenger. He will give you the information for your task. Beyond that he should not be trusted.”

"So, I can't trust him and the girl isn't truthful. That doesn't seem like much help for me to fight this greater evil you refer to."

"You can find a way, use your gift."

"My gift from Tlayolotl? I don't even know what it is."

"But you are finding it. You may not be aware, but it is emerging. Look for it. It will help you with the girl."

"What do I tell Jane, my boss, as you pointed out?"

She shook her head. Her hair fell loose around her face. "No foolish questions."

She indicated that Dan should go. He stood up. The woman reached out and touched his arm.

"Trust no one. Rely on your gift."

Dan started to speak, but she pushed him out of the kitchen. He walked down the hall and let himself out of the house. Outside in the dim street he scanned the pedestrians. There were few people about and nothing looked suspicious. Dan sighed and headed back to *Piazza San Marco.*

This gift! It's a mystery and now I have to depend on it. Anger began to rise in him. He liked things under control and this certainly didn't fit that category. Jane was not going to like this idea either. She had been skeptical when Dan walked her through all he had experienced in Mexico. She had reluctantly accepted that there were mystics in the world. But she remained unconvinced they would play a significant part in Dan's further missions, contrary to what Tlayolotl said about expanding her world view. And now he had to tell her he was going to free-lance a job on the suggestion of one of these Watchers. That wouldn't go over well. He cut short his plans for walking around and headed back to the car park. When he got home, he would go for that run and try to sort out how to proceed.

After getting back to his villa, he changed into his running shorts and shirt. Strapped to his upper arm was a small case that bulged more than it should because it had the two-shot .22 derringer stuffed inside. Lacing up his running shoes he set out along the canal. He pushed himself along, forcing his pace, making himself pay for the week of leisure he had enjoyed. His mind went over the woman repeatedly, but there was no help in that. Gradually he let his thoughts go and focused on his run.

He got back to the villa in sixty-seven minutes, sweat covering his body. It was a good pace. He knew it was not one he could keep up for a full marathon, but he could force it for ten miles. After stretching and cooling down he went up to his bedroom where he stripped and got in the shower. He let the water sooth his body. After, he began to get dressed and on the chest of drawers he saw the business card from the man who followed him in Milan. It read, "Pietro Conti, Investment Banking Assistant" with an address and a phone number. He sat down and studied the card. There was no mention of who employed Mr. Conti.

Chapter 7

Pietro Conti was a short, solid man. He affected a refined manner but it could not hide his working-class roots. The key to his success was that, unlike many street hooligans who inhabited the fringes of the underworld, Pietro was smart. When he met his boss, Pietro realized that becoming indispensable to him would get him off the streets and into a more comfortable, and safer, life. It was better to be part of pulling the strings rather than being pulled by them. His encounter with Dan had been uncomfortable. Following an assassin had seemed a foolish idea. He had hoped the man's interest in putting distance between himself and the rave club would work to Pietro's advantage, and so it had played out. Now he had to wait. That evening his phone rang.

"Conti here," he said upon answering.

"*Signore* Conti, this is the man you spoke to outside of the dance club in Milan."

"*Sì*. I'm glad you called." Pietro smiled. He would not have to go looking for another hired gun.

"First of all, you don't know me. How did you find me?" Dan was concerned about blown cover.

"I found you by chance. My employer wants me to hire someone to do a very special job, one that requires a certain skill. Pietro took a deep breath and continued. "There was word on the street that Guzim Lazami had been targeted. We know he's an arms dealer. I figured the best way to find someone with the right skills was to shadow Guzim and try to connect with whoever killed him."

"That story sounds made up."

"It's the truth. I know it sounds crazy, but my employer doesn't want anyone off the streets. He wanted me to find someone extremely good and those people are hard to find let alone to connect with."

"And you were able to pick me out? How?"

"I spent the evening watching from outside…in case anything was to happen that night. When the crowd poured out, I knew something had happened inside. You were the only one exiting the club that didn't look panicked. You looked purposeful, especially when you walked away. I figured it was a good bet to follow you and try to contact you when you had put some distance between you and the club."

It registered on Dan that he had dropped his persona too soon and gave himself away to the most unlikely of observers.

"Do you know how dangerous, or stupid that sounds?"

"*Sì*. I thought it was, but I had nothing else to go on. I knew a hit on Guzim might be imminent so I decided to follow him around. The dance club presented a good opportunity for an assassin…and I was right."

Dan couldn't believe how foolhardy the man sounded but decided to move the conversation forward. "What does your employer want?"

Pietro exhaled as if he had been holding his breath. "My employer has an eighteen-year-old daughter who ran away two years ago. He's finally tracked her down. She apparently became addicted to drugs and is working in the porn industry for a Feriz Sadiković. He produces a lot of videos and has a stable of women, all of whom are addicts at some level. He keeps them under his control. They are not free to come and go. My employer wants you to rescue her and kill this bastard."

Dan thought for a moment. The job was outside of his mission and it didn't sound like it would be a clean operation. Yet the woman in St. Mark's Plaza, the Watcher, said he should take the job. But his instincts kept warning him away.

"I don't take work off the streets," he said.

"He's willing to pay one million euros for the job. And I was right to try to find you the way I did. You pulled off what no one had been able to do."

"You may think you have found me, but you don't know who I am or where I come from. If you did, you would be dead now." Dan's Italian, while clearly not native, gave no hint as to his true nationality.

"But you are the only one that can do this job," the man protested. "Feriz stays in his compound with his women and production crew. He is harder to reach than Guzim. And a regular assassin wouldn't find the girl."

Dan thought, *what the hell is a 'regular' assassin?* It was a strange idea that there might be an archetype of the profession, if one could call it that.

"It doesn't matter. This is not my problem." Dan was not going to agree quickly. He hoped his reticence would generate more information.

"My employer is desperate and wants his daughter back. Can you imagine his pain knowing his daughter is addicted to drugs and is now forced to make porn movies? It breaks his heart."

"With the price he's offering, I assume he's wealthy. You should have little trouble to hiring a good hit man."

"Maybe, but they would all be connected to gangs...or the mafia. That connection could create a trailing liability for my employer, an entanglement he would like to avoid. He's very respectable."

"And I would be different?"

"I don't think you are connected to any mafia or gang. I think you work for other people."

"I think you speculate too much for your health." Dan's voice carried a hint of threat in it.

"I don't want to know who you are or who you work for, I only want to hire you and pay you a million Euros."

The Watcher said to take the job. Dan trusted her. He'd seen others like her in action.

"We need to meet. I have some questions and need some information. If I get the right answers, I'll take the job. Where are you?"

"I am in Rome right now."

"You live there?"

"No, but I will be here for the week. I leave on Friday. Of course," he quickly added, "I can arrange my schedule to accommodate you."

"Today is Tuesday. I will meet you on Thursday. Go to the *Parco Fabio Montagna*. It's on the *via Della Rustica* near the ring road, east of the *Coloseo*. Sit on one of the benches near the highway. A dark blue car will stop at the curb and a door will open. Walk over to the car and get in. And bring half of the money as a deposit...in cash."

"That's quite a large amount of cash to assemble."

"Be at the park at 10 a.m. Wait for half an hour. If the car doesn't come, you can leave. But don't be late."

With that admonishment, Dan hung up.

Pietro put his cell phone down. He smiled. The gamble had paid off. He sensed this was an assassin, an *assassino*, of exceptional skills. His employer, Jan Luis Aebischer had burdened him with this assignment and had just put the first part of the job behind him.

It was a bit over five hours to drive from Venice to Rome. Dan decided he would take the train to Milan and rent a car there under one of his aliases. He'd drive from Milan to Rome and back. There would be nothing to connect him to Venice. He went into his study. In the room, he reached under the center area of his desk. Attached to the underside was a keyboard. He had memorized the physical locations of the proper buttons and punched five in the correct order. A panel on the wall swung open to reveal a closet. In the closet was his weapons collection. Dan grabbed his 9mm. He took two magazines out of a drawer and checked to see that they were fully loaded. After putting one in the weapon and one in his pocket he stepped out of the room and closed the panel. It locked with a solid clunk. Without the code it would take hours to break through to the closet, if one even realized what was there behind the panel.

Next, he went into his dressing room. There he spent the next hour putting on a disguise. When he left, he would have dark, slicked down hair, a van dyke style beard, blue eyes, a protruding chin, and heavy eyebrows. It was a sinister look, but Dan figured Mr. Conti would expect that. He would try to give him the look of a hitman. Dark slacks, solid shoes and a loose, black jacket over a lighter blue shirt completed his look. The jacket effectively hid the 9mm he would carry.

The next day, Dan boarded the train to Milan. There he rented a car and drove to Rome. Once in Rome, he checked into a Novotel hotel near the meeting point. It was large, convenient, and anonymous with an easy entrance and exit to and from the ring road.

The day of the meeting, Dan got up at dawn and drove over to the park area. He found a three-story apartment building with a vacancy. He drove around to the back, parked, and picked the lock on the door. After getting in, he went up to the top floor and found a roof access hatch. It was locked. Dan spent a frustrating five minutes working to open it. The lock finally yielded to his efforts and he went out on the roof. He found a spot and settled down to wait and watch. It was routine sniper practice to survey the area of operation and to make sure Pietro wasn't being followed.

Just before ten Pietro appeared in the park, walking to the benches where he had been instructed to wait. After a final check of the area, Dan slipped off the roof and left the apartment building. No one would ever know he had been inside. He made sure the alley was clear when he exited and a minute later, he was on the street driving around to approach Pietro.

He stopped at the side of the road and, as instructed, Pietro got up and walked over to the car after Dan opened the door. He had a briefcase in his hand. The man got in and sat still with his case on his lap. He didn't appear to be intimidated but didn't look directly at Dan. *He remembers I told him that he could get killed if he saw my face.*

"You bring the money?"

"*Sì*. It's in my briefcase."

Dan pulled away from the curb and drove down the road. He had a car park picked out from the day before. It was five levels high and, since it was attached to a shopping area, was free with no attendant.

After pulling up to the top level, Dan parked with the car aimed directly at the down ramp.

"Open it," he said to Pietro.

Pietro opened the case and swiveled it towards Dan, still not looking at him. It was filled with one and two hundred-euro bills.

"I didn't put in the five hundred bills because they are sometimes hard to use and draw attention."

"Thoughtful of you. Now give me the details of this job."

"Don't you want to write them down?"

"No. Just go through the points carefully."

"Feriz owns a hundred acres in the mountains east of Gračac, Croatia. It's set up almost like a fortified retreat." Pietro handed Dan a photograph. "Here's a picture of the man."

"Why didn't your boss go to the authorities? The daughter was a minor when she ran away. That has to be illegal in Croatia, it's part of the EU."

"He didn't know where she was for most of two years. When he finally located her, she was eighteen. Plus, Sadiković pays off the authorities and spreads a lot of money around the local villages. He's practically untouchable, even for someone like my employer—"

"Who has a lot of money."

"*Sì.*"

"Just who is your employer? I'm not sure I want to work for someone so secretive."

Pietro shook his head. "No, I'm sorry I can't reveal his identity. That is why he wanted someone like you, not a common criminal. He has to not be connected to this in any way."

Dan gave that some thought. All his instincts were telling him to drop this like a hot rock and move on, but for the woman in St. Mark's; she said this was what he should be doing. *It's got to be important and it's got to fit in with what Jane wants me to do...somehow.* He was not looking forward to that conversation.

"*Va bene,*" okay, he said. "I can understand his desire. Now tell me about the girl. I have to be able to identify her."

"Her name is Evangeline. She was called Evie at home." Pietro handed Dan another picture. "This is the last photo before she ran away. It's two years old now." It showed a beautiful girl, with the full face of youth. She had long blond hair, more white than yellow and blue eyes with long lashes. She was standing on a large lawn that looked like it might be part of a fancy estate. Her countenance was almost ethereal, but there was something about her eyes. They had a sad, almost lost look to them.

Next, he handed Dan some stills from a movie. "As embarrassing as this is these might be most helpful." They showed quite a different looking girl. Her hair, while still blonde, was cut much shorter in almost a punk fashion. Her face had lost its child-like softness. It was now sharper, harder. She still looked beautiful, but had a more angular look now; the soft edges of youth were gone.

"She has a birthmark, a dark spot on her abdomen. You can see it in one of the photos."

Dan shuffled the pictures until he found the right one. "I'm supposed to take time to examine all the girls' abdomens? Do you have one of her movies? I'm not being prurient, but seeing her in action, how she moves, will help me to identify her."

"I told my employer you might want that. He is upset that she is exposed like this, but I told him it might help."

"It's not like I'll be the first to see her in action."

Pietro took a DVD out of his pocket and handed it to Dan. "There are two movies which have her in them on the disk."

"Okay. Now I can't tell you when this will happen and so I can't tell you when the daughter will be returned. When I contact you again we will meet, me with the girl and you with the other half of the fee."

"I will wait to hear from you."

"Have the money prepared the same way as today. And Mr. Conti," the man turned to Dan, "don't think about doing anything to interfere with a smooth transfer. That will be a dangerous time for you. If I sense anything wrong, you could die on the spot. *Capiche?*"

"*Sì, sì*. Nothing will go wrong."

Dan dropped Pietro back at the park. He then wound his way through some side streets and onto the ring road. After determining no one was following him, he headed for Milan.

Chapter 8

Feriz Sadiković's compound was located east of Gračac near the Dalmatian coast. It was secluded and his guards kept anyone from wandering onto his property. According to Pietro Conti, there was only one road leading to his mansion. It went up over a mountain and was barely maintained. It was essentially a long driveway since there was only one small farm on the other side of the pass, on the western slope. The driveway turned off the road and crossed a ten-foot chasm through which ran a mountain stream. The stream would dry out to a trickle in the late summer but ran wild through the fall and spring. After crossing the bridge and passing through the guard house, you drove a quarter mile to the grand complex.

With his stable of girls, his drugs, and a constant stream of guests, Feriz rarely left his compound. Occasionally he would attend an awards ceremony where he usually won an award for some piece of dubious work. At these times he would be accompanied by one or more of his glamorous "stars" who had gotten sober enough for the event. He had begun to think of himself as a true artist of the post-modern, anything goes age. If it feels good, do it; if it feels good it's okay and no one should interfere. The soft morals and lack of principles espoused in modern culture fit perfectly into Feriz's work. And his work made him a great deal of money.

After getting home, Dan checked in with Marco who now saw his role almost as caretaker of Dan's property. He had done so well, using only two of his closest companions, that Dan had increased his pay to two hundred and fifty Euros a week. That amount gave Marco a sizeable boost to his income with enough left over for his two helpers. He let Marco know that he would be gone for a few weeks and would contact him if he was going to be away longer.

There was nothing left now but to pack and head out to Gračac. He assembled some changes of clothing, including what he referred to as "civilian" outfits as well as his tactical clothes. A ghillie camouflage suit which allowed him to weave local vegetation onto it was added to the pile. After pondering his selection of long guns, which included an M16 and M4 military assault rifles, an MP5 submachine gun, a reworked civilian Remington 700 SPS chambered for .300 Win Mag, and an M110 semi-automatic sniper rifle also chambered in .300 Win Mag. In that caliber, Dan had sub-sonic and supersonic loads. The Remington was bolt action with a five-round magazine. The M110, being semi-automatic and equipped with a twenty-round magazine, was more versatile than a bolt action, having the ability to put a large number of rounds down range rapidly in a fire fight. One drawback was that the cartridges were ejected with some force and were often flung far away, making them hard to retrieve when the shooter wanted to clean up his site. There were arguments among shooters about decreased accuracy, but Dan had sent the M110 out to be blueprinted and had tested its performance to his satisfaction.

He selected the M110 with a suppressor and supersonic rounds along with the M4. He included his CZ75 9mm with a sixteen-round magazine. The gun was steel and absorbed recoil better than some lighter weight models. The barrel was set a bit lower which reduced the flip that occurred with each round and increased rapid-fire accuracy. Three weapons, each one geared for a certain job, each one proven and reliable. The collection required three different calibers of ammunition but they were the right tools for each job. After some consideration, he put a few other assault items in the bag along with a combat first aid kit and zipped it up.

I'll take the Range Rover. Better choice if I have to use bad roads going in or out of the area. Dan owned the SUV as well as a Peugeot 607 Executive Sedan. The Peugeot was a plain looking business sedan that Dan had modified with custom suspension, brakes, and a supercharger added to the V-6 engine. The result was a boring looking car that didn't stand out but would outrun most anything on the road including the powerful and flashier S500 Mercedes. The Range Rover had a compartment built in underneath the rear seat. After releasing a hidden latch, you could fold the seat forward to access a space large enough to hide an adult. It was useful for any hidden cargo he might need to transport. There was no issue within the EU but going beyond those countries involved border crossings with varying degrees of security checks. Dan put his mission gear, ropes, tape, first aid kit, rations, weapons, and ammunition, into two packs, separating the weapons from the rescue and first aid gear. They would go in the hidden compartment when he left. The CZ would be kept closer at hand, under his seat.

Dan's villa and grounds were equipped with sophisticated security including normal and infrared cameras mounted outside. Inside he had installed cameras throughout the house so any intruder could be tracked through the rooms. Along with reinforced doors and windows, he placed low-tech monitor strings across each entrance, almost invisible lines that would indicate if anyone had opened a door. The cameras would tell the tale, but if they failed, or were defeated, the filaments of line would give evidence of any intrusion. Dan could remotely monitor the cameras to check on the property both inside and outside. He mentioned his security in a general sense to Marco to forestall any idea he might have of going into his home while Dan was gone.

Dan knew Marco had already noticed the array of outside cameras and must have concluded the house was well monitored. His cover story about being a security consultant would explain much of the gear, but Dan guessed Marco thought he was something more than what he claimed to be.

He was ready to go. But there was one more thing he had to do and he didn't look forward to it.

Chapter 9

Dan sat down on his couch, poured himself two fingers of bourbon, Knob Creek Limited Edition. Jane had introduced it to him at the safe house in New York. After taking a sip, he punched the speed dial for Jane's number on his secure phone.

"Are you back home?" Jane asked when she picked up the phone.

"Yep. Did you get much blowback from the operation?"

"No, not like Mexico. Some people think it was a mob hit because he was striking out on his own. All in all a good operation, even if it had to be at close range."

"Are things more settled now at HQ?"

"If you mean regarding our work…yes."

"Well, something's come up here that I want to let you know about."

"I'm listening."

"I'm going on an assignment—"

"I haven't given you one. What are you talking about?"

"It involves rescuing a teenager from a porno ring."

There was a long silence on the other end. Finally Jane spoke, "Are you freelancing? That isn't going to work. We talked about that."

"Not exactly freelancing."

"If I didn't assign the mission, it's freelancing. You can't be doing that."

"Hear me out. There are extenuating circumstances."

"Like you're being paid a lot of money?"

"More than that."

"So, you *are* being paid a lot of money. How much?"

Dan took a breath. This was not going to sound good.

"Let's just say it's a lot. But that's not why I took the job. In fact, I wasn't planning on taking it at first."

"Then they upped the offer? Is that how it worked?"

"No, Jane. And I don't like the assumption behind your question. Will you let me explain?"

Jane was silent. Dan took a sip of his whiskey.

"I'm all ears," she finally said.

Dan proceeded to tell her how the man, Pietro Conti, had approached him and that he decided he wasn't interested.

"Then a woman in Venice connected with me. She's a Watcher, like Tlayolotl and the woman in Mexico City. She found me in St. Mark's Plaza. Don't know how. I know this sounds unreal but she knew of the man and his offer. She knew about the girl. She said it was important that I take the assignment as there was a greater darkness to uncover and attack. In short, this job fits into our overall mission, even if it isn't on your radar yet."

There was a moment of silence before Jane spoke.

"You're going off on some wild rescue which doesn't contain a hint of fighting terrorists. Dan this isn't about forces of darkness and light, this is about killing the bad guys, the terrorists and their helpers, in order to cripple their efforts before they strike."

"That's just how the watchers speak about what we do. Tlayolotl spoke of it. I told you he said we were a part of a larger battle going on and you needed to understand that, broaden your thinking."

"It's just mumbo jumbo the way—"

"Damn it, Jane! It's not. I saw it, I experienced it. I'm alive because of it."

"Exactly what 'it' are you talking about?"

"The existence of a spirit world and people who can see that dimension. These people can help to guide us. I need you to see that. I thought I had shown you how they helped me survive in Mexico. Just the fact that I survived should give some credence to it."

Jane sighed. Dan could hear it over the phone. "I believe you experienced what you spoke about. I'm just not ready to assign the terms to it that you do. I think of our mission in more concrete ways. We find bad actors, we take them out."

"And that's my point. I'm running into these people everywhere. First in Mexico, now in Italy and they seem to be able to help me...want to help me, want to help us, target the bad actors. Isn't it worth a try? They helped before, they can help again."

"What do I tell Henry? He's less convinced about all of this than I am."

"Hell, I don't know. But I'm going to rescue someone caught up in drugs and pornography, someone young with their whole life ahead of them. Right off, that's a good thing. And the woman said it would lead me to identify a greater darkness and destroy it. That's a good thing as well."

"But there's so much risk in what you do. An unplanned job like this will only increase that risk. I don't want to lose you to a side job."

"I appreciate your concern, really I do, but most of the jobs are barely planned. I always have to freelance in the sense of making plans as I go along. This won't be any worse."

"You've been speaking about this as if you've already decided. Is this a done deal?"

"I have decided, but I want you to know...and I want your blessing on it."

"Cover for you with Henry?"

"That too."

Jane swore softly. "Damn, I don't like this. I can keep Henry from going ballistic. He kind of understands your independence." She paused for a moment. "But can you promise to check in and keep me informed? We didn't hear from you for long stretches in Mexico."

"I can do that, but I can't promise a strict schedule."

"All right, where's the girl?"

"Somewhere in the Balkans. I have to find her."

"Who's the pornographer? Do you have a name?"

Dan stiffened and hesitated. "Feriz Sadiković, but don't you let anyone interfere and screw up the operation. That will only endanger me and them."

"I'll keep clear, but I want Fred to find out everything he can about him."

Fred Burke was one of two assistants working for Jane. He was a meticulous researcher and could tease useful information out of the massive stream of data that flowed over the internet. Warren Thomas was the other assistant. He was a technical wizard, a true geek who could get past almost any security set up without leaving a trace.

"Thank you," Dan said. "I don't think the woman, the Watcher, meant Feriz is going to be connected to the more important characters. I think the path lies through the girl."

"Good luck dealing with a teenage girl, who's also an addict."

"Yeah. That's uncharted territory for me."

"Be careful, Dan. I don't have a good feeling about this."

"I didn't know you were psychic," he said with a smile.

"I'm not. And don't be cute. But this job worries me, and not because I didn't arrange it. You go from a dangerous rescue to some greater, unknown danger, probably without proper information."

"I'll be careful. It's how I'm going to survive in this game. That's also a reason to listen to these Watchers. It may improve my odds. You and I still have a sailing date to make happen."

"You finish this and I'll fly over. We'll go sailing."

"Now you're talking. It's a date."

With that Dan turned off the phone.

After his meeting with the assassin, Pietro reported his success to his employer, Jan Luis Aebischer in Zürich. Herr Aebischer was in his seventies. He was a solidly built man still trim and fit from a lifelong daily exercise regimen. He stood five feet ten inches tall with a thinning head of silver hair. His face was angular with a strong jaw and clear, blue eyes of piercing intensity. One could easily call his visage patrician. He had an aristocratic appearance that fit with his wealth and status. The effect was that even people who didn't know him gave him deference in public. Herr Aebischer however was not a very public man, preferring the privacy of his office or mansion in Zürich.

Today like most days, Herr Aebischer was working from home. Pietro Conti stood in front of desk in his office.

"Send two men to Gračac to keep an eye on this assassin you hired. I want them to retrieve Evangeline after he completes his assignment."

"I'm not sure that's a good idea, Sir," Pietro said. He was caught off guard. He didn't often oppose his employer, but this seemed to be a rash idea.

"You're not?" The banker raised his eyebrows and for the first time looked directly at Pietro.

"No Sir." Pietro took a breath and continued. "First of all, we won't have the final payment and second, it is not according to the plan he set up."

"But you work for me, so you follow my plan...do you not?" The man eyed Pietro with his stern gaze.

"Yes Sir. But this is a dangerous man. I don't think we should risk your daughter any more than we have to."

"I'm not going to leave my daughter in the hands of an assassin, someone who could run off with her and blackmail me for more money. And who knows what might happen to her while she's in his control?"

Pietro stood his ground. "But he could cause us trouble afterward."

"I've thought of that. This assassin could be a trailing liability for me. He should not survive the operation. Send two men, the best ones we have. That will close down the trail and save me half a million Euros."

Pietro stood there. Aebischer looked up at him.

"Did you hear me?"

"Yes. But I have to tell you this is not a good idea. He is not someone I would want to cross."

"Pietro," Aebischer said leaning back in his chair, "I pay you well. You do lots of things for me and offer advice, but in the end I expect that you obey me. This is my decision. Now you are to make it happen. Do not overstep your bounds."

Pietro nodded and retreated from the office.

Chapter 10

The next morning, Dan was on his way. He followed the A4 roadway which ran around the top of the Adriatic Sea through flat, productive farm fields. It was visually not very stimulating. He would be nowhere near the water until he started heading south. Past Sistiana he drove along the coast and two and a half hours after leaving Venice, he stopped in Trieste for lunch.

From Trieste, it was another four hours to Gračac, Croatia. There he checked into a medium-priced hotel under a little used identity, Bob Joseph. He had put on his disguise before departing: mustache, nicely trimmed beard, and dark hair and eyebrows. He also had enlarged his nose to be more prominent, with a decided lump in it, as if it had been broken once before. Someone trying to describe him later would focus on the nose, which did not look anything like Dan's regular shaped appendage.

The village was small with a few quaint buildings mixed in with the plain, functional structures. It was an easily dismissed farm village but the place had a small reputation among bicyclers and so catered to this tiny segment of the tourist industry. He rented a room for the night at *Apartman Odmor* on the east side of the village.

It was going to be hard to get any information without tweaking the interest of the locals. He would have to rely on his disguise to protect his identity. In the aftermath of his mission, which Dan didn't think would take place quietly, his name and visage would come up and be relayed to the authorities. The alias would be blown and could never be used again.

That night he ate in a small restaurant, not really set up for tourists. His plate of rice and vegetables was sufficiently good to hold his attention. After finishing his meal, he asked in purposely halting Italian whether the proprietor knew where the famous movie maker, Feriz Sadiković lived. The man looked at him with suspicion.

"I heard he makes lots of movies and has lots of beautiful women at his house. Someone said he holds very entertaining parties," Dan said.

The man shook his head. "I don't know where he is." His Italian was worse than Dan was making his own out to be. "He is very private."

"That is a shame. I promised to drive by the mansion and take at least one picture for a friend of mine."

"No. I not know where he lives." He paused for a moment before plowing on with his limited Italian. "You come for that?"

"No. I'm planning a bicycle trip with my friends, but we wanted to go past the famous movie maker's house. We will ride through the *Nacionalni Park Paklenica* and then to the seashore."

"Ah, *Park Paklenica, molto bello*. You will enjoy. The man seemed happy to change the subject.

Dan thanked him, paid his bill, and left to walk the streets. There were a few pedestrians about. Out of habit, he scanned the people as he walked along. A few gave him furtive looks which Dan registered. He wrote those off to being a stranger in a small village. Two men, however, stood out. They were dressed better than most of the locals. Both were solidly built. But it was the shoes that stood out to Dan; they were expensive-looking dress shoes, something he did not expect to see in this small town. The two men were distinctly taking notice of him and turned away as soon as he looked at them. Dan made a mental note of their faces in case he ran into them again.

He hoped to find someone younger who would not be so suspicious about his questions. There was a coffee shop in town, an attempt at a modern establishment that would attract the small but growing group of adventure tourists. Dan decided to give the shop a try. The help were all younger, sporting elements of the hip styles of the modern culture. A young man at the counter could speak Italian. Dan tried the direct approach.

"I'm bringing some friends here next month to cycle the area. I heard about a Croatian movie maker who has a large compound around here. We thought we'd cycle past it on our way to the national park. Do you know where it is?"

The kid laughed. His Italian was better than the older restaurant owner. "Not many people want to talk about him. They're a little embarrassed by him."

Dan gave the kid a quizzical look.

"He's a pornographer. He makes porno movies."

"Ohhh." Dan feigned surprise. "That's why I was getting a cold response."

The kid nodded, still chuckling.

"And that's why we heard about his outrageous parties."

"But he never invites the locals," the young man said, still smiling.

"So, do you know how to find the place?"

The barista nodded. He gave Dan the directions, where to turn off the main road leaving town and approximately how far up the road to go. The property entrance was before the road went over the pass and down the western slope of the mountain.

"I wouldn't hang around the turnoff to the driveway. The place is guarded and someone may confront you."

"Thanks for your help. It will add some color to our cycle trip." Dan handed the kid a twenty Euro note and left. He'd head out tomorrow and find a place to set up his base of operations.

Chapter 11

Dan found the road going over the mountain just as the barista told him. It was gravel. The surface got rougher as the road climbed higher but the Range Rover handled it well. In a high valley before reaching the pass, Dan passed the turnoff into Feriz's compound on his left. He continued without stopping. A half of a mile below the ridge, Dan found an old two-track trail heading off the road in the same direction. He stopped. The trail showed no signs of being used recently. There were no tire imprints, nothing to disturb the leaves that had accumulated over many seasons, almost obscuring the signs of the trail. Dan turned the Rover onto the two-track and followed it until he was sure he could not be seen or heard from the road. He pulled off the trail and placed the vehicle under the trees poised for a rapid exit if one was needed.

After parking the SUV, Dan immediately went to work setting up his encampment. He draped camouflage netting over the vehicle and gathered brush from the surrounding woods which he put over the netting. Although not fully camouflaged, it would be overlooked by someone using the trail unless they were looking for a vehicle. He would sleep in the vehicle which to Dan marked a huge improvement over his usual accommodations when scouting a shot. Next, he took out his ghillie suit and proceeded to weave the local vegetation into the netting.

The forest had a dense canopy of aspen, oak, and beech trees mixed with spruce evergreens, along with numerous rocky outcroppings. These were older growth trees and beneath the canopy the forest floor was open and easily navigated.

It was afternoon when he was finished. *No time like now to get a look at the compound.* Dan gathered his M110, field glasses, night vision goggles, put on his suit, now covered with leafed-out branches, and set out in the direction of the mansion. The compound was down-slope. It would take some hiking around to find it and set up some good spotting and shooting sites. Dan was looking for an overlook that would give him a clear field of vision and fire. A half hour of hiking brought him to a point where he could see the cleared valley below. He spotted the buildings, but his sight lines were not clear. Another half hour of careful hiking around brought him to a ridge outcropping. Near the edge of the rocky clearing the increased sunlight stimulated the smaller bushes which could find purchase in the rocky soil. Dan crawled up to the edge in the brush. He was just another bush in the undergrowth. He would not be spotted even by someone using binoculars.

He was positioned about seven hundred feet above the cleared grounds. Below him there was a large and impressive mansion. It had soaring roof lines that indicated many wings and partitions inside. Behind it was a pool that meandered around landscaped grounds. Dan could see a swim-up bar, multiple lounging and sunning areas, and four diving boards for the adventurous. The area was equipped with a convertible roof that could be unrolled to cover part of the area in inclement weather. Off to one side were grassy fields for volleyball and soccer.

Next to the pool was what looked like a large, wood-heated sauna that could probably hold twenty people. It was a short dash from the sauna to the pool. Beyond the pool was another large building which Dan guessed housed the studios where Feriz produced his pornography: explicit movies that were short on plot and long on skin and sexual activity. Pietro also spoke of an S&M dungeon in the basement for his more hard-core production work. Some of the films looked like they had been produced in the mansion proper to take advantage of its more glamorous setting.

Dan was facing east with the sun was behind him. It called for an afternoon shot, if he was going to shoot from a distance. His eye followed the long driveway to his left where it crossed the bridge before intersecting the road over which he had driven earlier. A plan began to form in Dan's mind, a bit loose and vague on details, but he hoped more scouting would improve it on that score.

He turned his focus back to the mansion area. There were a few girls around the pool, most topless, a few with no clothes, and no one fully dressed. There was some activity in the back building with men and women coming and going. *Making a new movie?* It was a Thursday. Dan had some time to watch and refine his budding plan. The weekend might bring a party which would ensure most of the girls would be at the compound. His thinking still didn't include an exact plan on how he would take out Feriz, nor how he would find the girl.

After watching for an hour, Dan slipped back from the outcropping. The vantage point was not too far away to shoot from, but Dan needed a spot where he could get to the compound more quickly. It would take a half an hour of thrashing his way downhill through the woods before he could emerge in the clearing around the buildings. Whatever plan he came up with, it had to include getting onto the grounds and finding the girl. Then he had to get her out of there. *Have to neutralize the guards, if I can identify all of them. Don't want to have to shoot my way out carrying a drug addled girl.* He shuddered at the thought. So much could go wrong in that scenario.

He began working his way down the hill. He was under the cover of the forest, but it was treacherous going, with gentle slopes transitioning into steep drop-offs which he slid down. At about three hundred feet above the valley floor, Dan worked his way to another overlook. The people could be seen more in detail but the buildings hid some of the view of the grounds. *This might be a good place to try to locate Evangeline. If I can identify her in her current look, it'll be easier to find her when I go in.* After watching for over an hour but not seeing anyone that looked close to the pictures he had of the girl, Dan called it quits.

He started the long climb back to the SUV. It took over an hour. The sun went down behind the ridge and the woods began to darken. He ate a camping meal in a pouch. It was lasagna which he heated over a camp stove. *I should explore the grounds tonight.* He didn't mind sleuthing around, confident in his skills, but he wasn't looking forward to the long climb back up the slope. *Getting soft, buddy,* he chided himself. The ghillie suit would not be of much help on the cleared, landscaped grounds, so he opted for his dark tactical pants, shirt, and jacket. The air was beginning to chill as the heat of the day dissipated.

Finishing his meal, he stretched and gathered his gear. He took his night vision goggles and his M4 with the suppressor attached. On his belt he carried his CZ75 pistol, also with a suppressor attached. This was a scouting mission. Dan didn't anticipate any contact or need for weapons, but he would not penetrate the compound without a way to defend himself if discovered. *Better to compromise the mission and be alive than to compromise it and be dead.* He assumed there would be external security around the compound. It could be ultrasonic or infrared. Before leaving Dan decided to bring a thermal blanket which he had painted in a camouflage pattern on the outside. He also brought a can of silicone spray which would blind an infrared sensor. After a look around, he set out down the slope, for the compound.

Chapter 12

After an hour of hiking and sliding down the mountainside, Dan reached the edge of the clearing. He was in the woods to the west of the mansion. Away from the buildings, near the trees, the grass was allowed to grow higher. There was no fence. As one approached the mansion, the grass was cut more carefully, kept short and neat. Thankfully where the grooming improved there were landscape plantings which could provide Dan some cover. The driveway down to the guard house and bridge was lined with mature trees. He could not see around to the back of the house from his current position. Dan took out his binoculars and studied the guard house for a while. There were two guards stationed there. No one came or went. *Probably do three or four-hour shifts.* They had to have some communication with the main house, either by wire or wireless.

After a half hour, Dan slipped back into the cover of the woods and moved to his right. He walked easily through a grove of beech trees; the area was almost park-like. He wanted to get a look at the back area of the property from ground level. The pool area was brightly lit and people were still hanging around it. Infrared heat lamps had been placed around. After the sun went down the warm air rose and was displaced by cooler air sliding down from the ridge above and settling on the grounds. No one was using the pool. The activity seemed to be about eating and drinking. Dan could hear laughing and talking but couldn't make out the conversations.

He backed up from the clearing and unslung his M4. He set it on the ground next to him and sat back against a large beech tree trunk. He would wait until everyone went inside. He wanted to see what the late-night security involved. He yawned. It would be a long night for him including the climb back to his camp.

Around eleven that night the sounds coming from the pool area died down. People were drifting into the mansion. Dan crawled closer to the edge of the forest. The last few feet, thick with bushes from the increased sunlight, presented a green wall of concealment hiding the interior of the woods from view. The thick brush, while not easy to squirm through, allowed Dan good cover from which to watch the compound.

He made himself comfortable. The lights were turned down around the pool. Dan put on his goggles and waited. Within ten minutes he spotted a figure coming around from the front of the house. The man was armed but in the greenish light of the night vision goggles, Dan couldn't identify the weapon. *Probably a submachine gun, like an MP5*. The man walked back along the side of the mansion, outside of the foundation plantings. He passed the pool area and finally disappeared around the back of the studio building. A few minutes later he reappeared, retracing the same route. *Must have two guards, each working one side of the building*. That made things more difficult. They probably met at the back of the studio and if one didn't show, an alarm would be triggered. Dan watched through two more cycles to get the timing established. If he was going to get to the mansion, he would have only ten minutes after the guard passed before he would be returning. And that meant moving across the cleared area, almost a lawn, while the man was walking towards the rear building.

If there are motion sensors, I'm screwed. Dan could see light fixtures along the side of the building. He could only assume there might be motion detectors mounted as well. But they must be turned off to allow the guards to move around. *Feriz must think active guards are better security than passive detectors.* He lay in the brush and thought about the situation. *Take out Feriz, get into the compound, find the girl, and get out. In that order?* Dan's mind swirled with all the possibilities of how that could and probably would go wrong. If the job was to assassinate Feriz, that would be relatively easy. Just identify him, take a long-range shot, and disappear back into the forest. He'd be over the mountain pass and on his way home before anyone figured out where the shot came from. But the rescue? That made the job infinitely more difficult.

Dan took a deep breath. *Got to work this out. It's what you do. I should see what's out front and figure out how often the guards change.* He reluctantly put down him M4 and dug into the ground. He dug down through the mulch layered on the forest floor until he found some dirt. He rubbed it all over his face and hands. Then, with just his CZ and tactical knife, he began to crawl out onto the lawn. He had his night vision goggles in a side pocket of his vest.

He crawled slowly out onto the field, staying flat against the grass. From his ground level vantage point, he could not see much. He followed every dip in the ground. The ground was not completely flat and even a depression of a few inches would help conceal him from the guards. He moved slowly so as to not trigger an alert if anyone was monitoring the cameras. Each time the guard passed, going to the rear, or coming back, Dan pressed himself to the ground and lay still. He only looked through slitted eyes, not wanting even the whites of his eyes to show in the dark.

It took an hour to cover the seventy yards from the edge of the woods to the house. As he got to the shorter grass, he used bushes and flower beds that were part of the landscaping to provide cover when the guard passed. When he got to within twenty yards of the building, Dan waited until the guard went by and crawled the last yards to the wall. Now he was hidden by the shrubbery planted along the building foundation. He sat still and composed himself. The guard walked by on his return not twenty feet from where Dan hid.

After he went by, Dan started crawling towards the front of the mansion. He wanted to see what went on at the front. Did the guards meet there? Were more of them hanging out there? How often did the shifts change? Once he had the information he needed, he then would have to make his way back to the woods without detection. Dan moved flat against the dirt under the bulk of the bushes that grew up against the walls. His elbows dug into the soil and the dirt scrapped along the front of his body.

When he reached the corner of the house, he found a well concealed spot to sit while he watched the activity. He forced his breathing to slow and made sure he couldn't be heard. He was hidden not more than ten feet away from the men. Not a muscle moved. He was a shadow. The guards met after their separate walks to the rear of the building and back. They spoke little.

One of them, stopped next to Dan. Only a bush separated them. Dan held his breath. No sound could come from him, no smell either. The man looked towards the guard house near the bridge, then up to the sky which was partially obscured by clouds.

"We going to get rain?" He said in what sounded like the standardized version of the Serbo-Croatian language used throughout the Balkans.

"No, this will pass," said the other guard.

The man started forward and Dan slowly released his breath.

"How do you know?" the first man asked.

"My grandmother. She says her joints don't hurt enough for rain."

"She's better than the forecasters?"

"Everyone in the village relies on her," came the reply.

"She should get paid," the first man said and laughed.

They seemed more alert and professional than the guards he had encountered in Mexico, but they suffered from what all sentries suffer from, boredom. The same routine every night, with nothing to show for their work, tended to make even the most professional hired gun complacent. Dan would have to count on that.

No one came out to check on them throughout their patrol cycles. The only time others came out of the house was when the guard changed. It was a three-hour shift. There was his opening. If he could take both guards out early in their shift, he would have two or more hours to work without alarms being raised. He still wasn't sure what he'd do, but now he saw how to create a stealthy window in which to operate.

After the guard set out again, Dan moved back around the corner to the side of the building. After the guard had walked past the second time and was down by the pool area, Dan slowly stood up. He pressed his back to the wall and moved along it until he was under one of the light fixtures. The cameras wouldn't be triggered while he was up close to the wall; they were aimed further out into the yard. He studied it. There were flood lights mounted with the camera. The cameras didn't look to be infrared. *Relying on the guards outside?* Dan shuffled back to his arrival point. He'd have to be patient and just reverse his path. He made it once, he could do it again. *Move slowly so no one watching notices.* He knew that while lying still, he would be an indistinguishable shadow on the ground and once in the taller grass, never be seen.

An hour later he was into the woods. It took a few minutes of casting about to find where he had left his pack and carbine. It was 2 am. *One more thing to do tonight.* Dan took a drink from his water bottle. *No rest for the weary.* He gathered his gear and began to walk towards the rear of the compound, keeping inside the cover of the woods. The green "fencing" at the edge provided effective screening; he just needed to not make any noise.

The woods curled around the back of the property with a smaller cleared area beyond the last building. This meant Dan would be closer and have less open ground to cover. There were a few plantings, but not much landscaping attention had been paid to an area that few people saw. Dan watched from the edge of the woods. The guards arrived at slightly different times. He waited through two cycles. What he learned was that they passed each other and actually made a circumference of the compound rather than retracing their steps. On one of the rounds, they stopped for a smoke.

Satisfied he'd seen enough; Dan headed back through the woods and began his long climb back to his camp. It was 4:40 in the morning when he got back to the SUV. He washed his hands and face, ate a power bar, and drank some water. Then he lay down on the back seat of the SUV and fell asleep. Images of explosions, people shouting, screaming and a young girl running raced through his confused dreams.

Chapter 13

Jane Tanner walked into Henry's office. She was not looking forward to the exchange about to take place. Henry was her boss. He worked in the Psychological Operations subsection of the Special Activities Division or SAD. With Jane he had begun the black ops program that had identified Dan and set him up to hunt down and kill terrorists and their enablers. Henry's boss was an old friend and the Director of SAD. He provided cover for Henry and Jane to pursue their program in the climate of an increasingly timid and politically correct agency. The work required a large amount of secrecy in order to not generate opposition from congress or come under the scrutiny of the Office of the Inspector General.

"What do you want to tell me about?" Henry asked as Jane entered. He motioned her to sit down in front of his desk.

"Dan's gone on another operation." She paused.

"Okay."

"It's not one I assigned him."

Henry sat back in his chair and gave Jane a long, hard look. He was an even-tempered guy. His unruly, white hair, glasses, and slightly rumpled clothes gave him an absent-minded professor look but underneath he was serious about operations and striking out against the enemies of the U.S. He didn't like rogue operations or rogue agents.

"You'd better elaborate," was all he said.

Jane proceeded to recount her conversation with Dan, emphasizing how the operation would at least save a young girl from a life in pornography or worse, and at best lead Dan to larger players in the underworld; people which they might want to find.

"So, he freelances and justifies it with some mystical mumbo jumbo? Is that what you're telling me?"

Jane nodded.

"And you didn't stop him? You allowed this?"

"Henry, I tried, but Dan had made up his mind. You know he's a bit headstrong. In the end, I don't think it will hurt."

"I don't find your assurance all that comforting. This could be the beginning of a rogue agent carrying out his own agenda. And you know what we have to do then."

Jane shuddered inwardly, not allowing her feelings to show. He was referring to sending an agent to take Dan out, an assassin to kill an assassin.

"That won't be necessary. It won't happen. I did some research on this Feriz Sadiković. He's pretty disreputable. He started off recruiting poor girls across the Balkans to work in night clubs. Only when they arrived, he prostituted them. He paid recruiters to comb the region, preying on the impoverished. The girls who resisted disappeared. The rest were forced into prostitution and most of them became addicts. You can imagine how bad the life was and how they would turn to drugs to escape it, even if only for a short time.

"He soon figured out he could make as much creating pornography and it was safer, not really being illegal.

Apparently, he's moved to more and more hard-core fare to keep up with customer tastes. And now, with so much of that stuff being free on the internet, he's going to be looking for other activities to keep up his income and life style. It doesn't take a genius to imagine him getting into drugs or gun running." She paused. "And that puts him on our list of targets."

Henry was still staring at her, sitting back in his chair. Over the years of running operations, it had been up to him to order the elimination of an agent that had gone rogue or become unreliable. He didn't like it, but he wouldn't allow those issues to jeopardize a mission.

"Your justification, then, is that this guy might become a problem for us in the future."

"It may not be so far in the future. We just eliminated Guzim Lazami. He had connections in the Balkans. Feriz must know those people. These rats all run through the same gutters. He could easily move in to fill that vacuum."

"All right, you make a point." Henry leaned forward. "But I'm not convinced that Dan isn't a liability. When this is over, if he survives it, I want you to go over there and get him under control. I promise you, if this keeps up, I'll have him taken out, as much as I like him. And you'll be looking for another assassin."

Jane nodded.

"Do not misread me on this, Jane. I support you one hundred percent. But I'm supporting you and the mission, not some free-lancing cowboy."

Jane was about to say something in Dan's defense, but kept her mouth shut. She had gotten Henry to sit on the sidelines and not act. That was enough for now. And she definitely would visit Dan in Venice when this was all over.

Chapter 14

Dan spent the next day watching the compound. He wanted to try to identify Evangeline ahead of time to make finding her easier when he went in. His plan was beginning to take shape, but it still had so many cloudy parts to it that he really couldn't yet call it an action plan.

Dan had pictures of Feriz that Jane had sent him. One showed him in a tux at some award or party event. There were a series of telephoto shots of the man entering and exiting a restaurant. He looked to be about five feet eight inches tall and on the heavy side. His hair was thin and brown with a severe widow's peak. He had a tan complexion and narrow set eyes with a protruding nose. He was not bad looking, but not someone one would call handsome. However, money makes everyone more attractive.

Dan scrambled down the hill again to his observation position. After an hour he had identified three girls that could be Evangeline. He marked them in his mind. *Better three than fifteen or twenty.* There was no shortage of females at the compound. He saw Feriz coming and going from the back building where there must have been filming going on. It was Friday and the work activity seemed to stop after the lunch break. Finally, he had seen enough. He knew what his first move would be.

Dan hiked back up the slope and got something to eat and drink. He rummaged through his weapons bag until he came to the brick of C-4 explosive and the detonators he had brought. He cut the brick in half. With the explosives, Dan had brought a transmitter and receiver which worked in line-of-sight mode and could remotely trigger the blasting caps which would be inserted into the half bricks of C-4. He had taken the system in case there was no cell reception in the area. It proved to be a good decision.

Dan went over his nascent plan. *First thing is to take out Feriz. That will cause panic among the guests. Next, I have to isolate the compound.* He had noticed a rooftop satellite dish for communications. There was no cell service in the valley, so Feriz must have had his own connection installed through the dish antenna. He had checked and found a wi-fi system that was password secured. He would disable the connection with the M110. *Then no one can be allowed to leave. Can't have people rushing out and miss getting Evangeline.* That's where the C-4 came in. Dan would plant charges under the bridge. Without the bridge, no one could get across the ravine with its stream. *I'll plant the charges and receiver tonight.*

When it got dark, Dan collected the explosives and started down the slope. He would set up at the lower vantage point. It had a clear sight line to the bridge and was closer than the outcropping further up the slope. After double checking the visual to the bridge, Dan took the charges and receiver in his pack and headed through the woods past the front of the mansion. He would get close to the stream and then work his way towards the bridge. The guards would not be paying much attention, their job being mostly to stop cars and make sure the visitors were invited. There should be few cars arriving late at night.

He waited at the edge of the woods until past midnight. Cars had rolled in during the evening but arrivals had trickled off and none had appeared in the last half hour. *Most are probably staying the night.* Shortly after midnight Dan crept out from the woods and crawled to the stream. He slipped down the steep bank and worked his way along the stream bed using his night vision goggles to navigate the rocky terrain. He could not be seen from the guard house. The water was icy cold but Dan steeled himself to it and kept moving. He expected the noise of the flowing water, rushing over the rocks, would mask his work under the bridge.

Twenty minutes later he was under the bridge. The bridge had two longitudinal beams carrying the load of the decking. The beams were supported by concrete piers on either side of the stream. There were cross beams of thick six by four timbers bolted to the beams forming the planking of the one lane roadbed. He took the two charges and placed them on the support beams in the middle of the span. If they were blown and torn apart, the decking would go with them and the bridge would be impassable, locking everyone inside. No cars would drive over the bridge for weeks.

After sticking the charges to the beams, Dan had to position the receiver so it could be seen from the outlook. He had marked the spot with some ribbon before he had left for the bridge. Now Dan crawled to the top of the bank, next to the concrete pier supporting the bridge on the mansion side of the ravine. He was close enough to hear conversation coming from the guard house. It was unintelligible over the sound of the rushing water filling the air. His head was a dark lump just above the bank of the ravine. Dan searched with his goggles to find the ribbon.

He had to keep down a rising concern at not being able to find it. *If you can't, you just have to go back and reset it and try again. It's a pain in the ass, but not disastrous, just more work.* After fifteen minutes of scanning, he found the ribbon barely visible and only noticed by its fluttering in the gentle night breeze. *Okay. Now to mount the receiver.* Dan had some putty-like plastic that would hold the receiver in place. It just had to not be seen by the guards. He was relying on them not being too interested in the bridge. A close inspection of the beams would reveal the receiver stuck on the outside. He spent ten minutes carefully aiming the receiver at the ribbon. He would check the alignment when he returned to the outlook. If he couldn't get the receiver in the transmitter's sights, he'd just have to go back and readjust. He hoped it wouldn't be a long night.

When he was satisfied with the aiming, he dropped back into the stream. He made his way back upstream and when reaching the woods, climbed up the bank. Back at the outlook, Dan took the transmitter, which had a simple notch and post sight on the top, and aimed it at the bridge. Using the goggles, he was able to finally see the receiver. *If I can see it, the signal can be received.* It would all work better in the daylight.

Pietro Conti was worried. He rarely offered dissent to his employer. Herr Aebischer, while stern, was a generous man. Conti was paid well to be his assistant, handling day-to-day details, and cleaning up loose ends. The work sometimes involved Herr Aebischer meeting with unsavory characters, men who appeared to be either dangerous or devious. His employer managed funds for these men or the groups they represented. Their histories were mostly obscure and their work was murky, sometimes in the extreme. Pietro didn't look too deeply. There was much he didn't want to know. His role sometimes involved action that would be considered illicit or morally questionable. But the work paid well. Enormous fees went into the coffers of his employer, some of which were channeled to Pietro allowing him to fund a lifestyle of modest luxury in Zürich, a very expensive place to live.

While he purposely didn't know all the details of most of his employer's work, he was observant and reasonably intelligent. Herr Aebischer's ability at making the funds untraceable to their owners was his value to the clients. It didn't take a genius to guess that the reason for the secrecy might be more than just clients wanting to avoid taxes. It might have to do with funding activities that were outside of the law. It didn't bother Pietro. He would do his job and was happy to not know too much. Ignorance of the activities seemed to equal safety.

But Herr Aebischer's actions regarding his daughter worried Pietro. He understood rescuing her, he even understood the desire to strike back at the pornographer, but he didn't understand going so far as to arrange for the man's killing using an obviously dangerous professional. And that professional was someone other than a low-level, underworld hitman. There was something different about him, something that set him apart, as if he was involved in a greater purpose or mission beyond killing people. Herr Aebischer's plan to double cross the man seemed fool hardy and out of character from his employer's normally well-considered actions. He was risking his daughter's life in order to clean his trail. If there was a shootout, the daughter could get killed. And if the assassin survived an attempt on his life, there would be hell to pay. He struck Pietro as a man who would come looking for revenge.

The two men with the dress shoes had followed Dan's route into the mountains. They had found the compound and turned around like lost tourists, not waiting around to cause any undue interest by the guards. They had driven out of sight and had parked their BMW sedan just off the gravel road. They waited all day, not knowing when Dan would appear. When night fell, they returned to the village with the plan to set out the next morning. There was a discussion about whether Dan would come down the road after pulling the girl out where they could wait to ambush him or would he drive over the pass to the west. In the end, they figured they would hear shots during the operation and if the assassin didn't come their way, they would drive up the mountain and catch him from behind. Their instructions were clear and they were prepared to do what was necessary to carry them out.

Chapter 15

Dan lay back in the Land Rover and tried to relax. It was 3:00 am. Sleep wouldn't come. His mind raced over tomorrow's sequence of events. He knew the start, how he would begin the operation, but it all got fuzzy from that point onward. There were so many variables he couldn't box them in with solutions. Killing Feriz would not be a problem if the man showed himself anywhere around the pool. It was dealing with the guards, the number of which he still wasn't sure about. And then finding and taking the girl who might not want to be taken; who might view him as an attacker.

And always, he came back to the guards. How many were there? He had counted two at the gatehouse, three sets of two walking the grounds, but how many more were stationed inside? Dan didn't fear a shootout, even though eight or more to one were not good odds. It was the girl that worried him. *Your thwarted urges of fatherhood kicking in?* He wondered if that frustration, triggered by the death of his pregnant wife, Rita, applied to teenage girls. Slowly, his body relaxed. *Think it through in the morning. Perhaps it will all seem more clear.*

When dawn came, Dan roused himself and stretched. He got out of the SUV and began a series of exercises to loosen up his body. After the calisthenics, he ate something from his camping rations and drank a full bottle of water. *Going to be a busy day, got to stay hydrated.* Getting ready for an operation was a bit like getting ready to play football. Only this contest had more deadly outcomes, and failure on his part was permanent.

First Feriz, then communications, isolation, and recovery. The formula was simple; all except for the last part, recovery. Reviewing the steps again in his mind brought no new insights. His best option was to sow as much confusion and terror as he could. He even might not be noticed at first if there was enough panicked activity among the guests. He would try to fit in as much as someone wielding an M4 automatic assault weapon could, and take out as many guards as possible. His best hope was that the guards would not get themselves organized and so would be running around singly or in pairs.

Dan was in no hurry. The morning sun would be in his eyes and also reflect off of his scope, exposing his position.

As it neared noon, Dan gathered his gear. He'd take the kill shot with the M110 and then use his M4 carbine with its suppressor when he went on the grounds. He kept his CZ75 holstered to his side. His clothes: boots, black tactical pants, dark T-shirt, with a tactical vest didn't fully match the outfit of the guards, but came close. He hoped it would delay any response from them, especially if they saw him from a distance. He carried only one ten-round magazine in the M110. The M4 was equipped with a thirty-round magazine. In his vest, Dan carried two extra loaded mags. He had an extra magazine for the CZ as well. If ninety M4 rounds and thirty-two 9mm rounds weren't enough there was no hope for him. He couldn't afford a long-term stand-off fire fight. The operation had to be violent and quick. A furious attack that would shock and disorient and then a quick retreat and escape. A couple of water bottles, power bars, duct tape, and some zip ties completed his gear.

He headed down the slope to the lower outlook position where he had aimed his receiver. He watched the poolside activity through his binoculars. There seemed to be no filming going on, everyone was getting into party mode. The girls were all scantily clad or topless, the men hung about in tight pants and shirts or swim trunks. Drinks were set up on two portable bars. It took Dan a few minutes to spot Feriz. He was surrounded by people and seemed to be holding court with everyone paying attention to what he said and seeming to laugh a lot. *The man paying the bills always gets a laugh with his jokes.* Dan waited.

As the sun slipped past its zenith, he switched from the binoculars to the scope on his M110. He was about two hundred and fifty feet above the pool level and three hundred feet away. This computed to a shot of three hundred and ninety feet. Not far. Dan checked his notebook and adjusted the scope for the distance. He had done a similar computation on the satellite dish and could quickly adjust his aim for that shot. It was a well-practiced, familiar routine.

Dan settled himself and slipped the muzzle of the M110 with its suppressor through the bushes. There would be no dust signature and no flash. The sound that would be heard would be the sonic boom of the round which would offer no hint of the direction of the shot. Someone who knew about these things, about shooting, would know the direction from the response of Feriz's body after the hit, but most would not have a clue.

Dan lay in the brush, concealed with only the muzzle showing its deadly presence. He slowed his breathing.

Things would move fast after the first shot, but now it was only Dan, the rifle, and the target, all locked in a deadly connection. His heart rate slowed. Dan kept the rifle centered on Feriz's head which came in and out of view with the people around him. Then there was a clear moment, the woman standing in between Feriz and Dan stepped aside to pick up her drink. And in between beats of his heart, Dan closed the circuit on his connection. The gun fired with a muffled *whoomp* and a solid kick in his shoulder.

Feriz pitched to one side as the bullet entered his right temple and exploded the left side of his head. People started screaming and confusion spread throughout the pool area. Dan didn't watch but turned his rifle immediately to the dish antenna. He sent a series of rounds into the dish and the base, causing the antenna to tip over on its side.

That done, Dan laid the rifle aside and took out his transmitter. He pointed it at the bridge and squeezed the trigger on the instrument. Nothing. He moved his aim slightly and squeezed again. Nothing. There was no panic, he knew it might be hit or miss. He continued to move the aim of the transmitter inches along the side beam of the bridge, squeezing the trigger. On the sixth squeeze the bridge erupted. One of the guards had come out of the guard house, looking towards the mansion when he heard the shooting and screaming. The other one was inside on the phone.

The blast pressure wave flung a section of the six by four timbers making up the roadbed against the guard's head knocking him to the ground in a fatal blow. In addition, his body suffered pulmonary lung contusion which probably would have killed him if the wooden beam hadn't. The guard inside was hit by a shard of broken window glass in the neck as the blast pressure knocked him unconscious. He bled out on the floor of the guard house.

Dan slipped back inside the screening. He placed the M110 against a tree and grabbed his M4 and scrambled down the slope. After a quick look around, he burst onto the lawn and raced towards the building. He reached the side of the mansion while the guards at the house were all running towards the pool. One of them came around the corner and Dan pointed to the woods, indicating where the shot came from. In the flurry of action, the man failed to notice that Dan was not one of the guards. He started towards the woods gesturing for Dan to come with him. Dan raised the M4 and dropped him with one shot.

He ran to the corner of the pool area. Some people were milling around the body and being shoved by three guards to keep them away. Others were heading into the mansion, looking to get under cover or leave. Dan scanned the crowd around Feriz. He didn't see Evangeline. He slipped into the group rushing inside without any guards seeing him.

One guard from inside the mansion, rushing towards the pool, focused on Dan. Not recognizing him, he shouted, "*Stanite!*" Stop! Dan didn't hesitate but brought the M4 up from the low ready position and shot him center mass. People close to Dan screamed and some dropped to the ground. Further away the crowd couldn't understand what had happened, but they had heard the screaming. It only panicked them more. *Three at the pool, two down, at least three unaccounted for*. Dan rushed forward with the crowd while scanning for Evangeline. *Got to find her quick before this gets much worse.* Many of the guests were headed upstairs when they got to the front foyer of the mansion. There were two guards in the foyer, one talking on his com speaker. Dan hit both of them with an automatic burst. They collapsed like rag dolls. The gunfire only accelerated the flight up the staircase. He followed. *Were there other guards? Would the ones at the pool be coming back into the mansion?*

There were multiple rooms upstairs and the guests were scrambling off to them. *Bedrooms? Getting dressed?* Dan began to open the doors. *She has to be in one of the rooms, she wasn't out at the pool.* He began throwing open the doors and entering with his M4 at ready in case there was a guard inside. The guests inside screamed when they saw him. When a quick glance around didn't show anyone close to Evangeline's description, he backed out and went to the next door.

As he backed out of the third door, someone shouted stop again. That proved to be a fatal mistake. Dan dropped and turned as a round passed over his head with a sharp whistle. In the same motion he swung the M4 up and loosed several rounds on automatic fire. The man fell back down the stairs.

Dan ran to the edge of the stairs, dropped to the floor, and peeked around the corner. Two guards below fired their MP5s with the rounds going over his head. They had been aiming at the height of a standing man. Dan's prone position gave him the extra moment to respond with his own automatic fire, dropping the two men. The magazine was empty, Dan ejected it and slammed in another one. *Seven down out of eight? Or maybe more.*

He moved down the hall. At the next room Dan found one of the three girls he had identified the day before. He grabbed her and pulled up her shirt. She started flailing away at him. He ignored the blows and looked for the birth mark. She didn't have it. He shoved her away from him and backed out of the room.

In the next room was the jackpot. The girl had the birthmark. She looked dazed. Dan grabbed her and in Italian told her to come with him.

"*Vieni con me. Ti salverò.*" Come with me. I'll save you, he said in a harsh voice.

She looked at him, her eyes wide in panic, but also without understanding. *She's high*, Dan thought in disgust. This just made his job harder.

"*Vieni, vieni!*" He said louder now, gesturing with his hands. "*Komen Sie, komen Sie!*" Dan switched to German.

The girl finally stepped forward a bit unsteadily. She was dressed in a pullover T-shirt and jeans. She had sneaker-style shoes on her feet. Dan grabbed her hand. Others in the room began to shout to her not to go with him. He turned and swept his eyes over the girls in the room and they fell silent, some diving behind the bed. Dan crouched and opened the door. The hall was filled with guests now running downstairs. Dan pulled Evangeline behind him and joined the crowd.

Part of the way down the stairs two more guards, probably from the pool area stopped at the foot of the stairs. They saw Dan in the crowd and shouldered their automatic weapons shouting at him to drop his weapon. Dan shoved Evangeline down as others began to drop to the steps.

The staircase was built in a grand curve. The two men were standing on the outside of the curve where it reached the foyer. Dan leapt over the banister on the inside of the curve. In that move, he protected himself from their line of fire for a moment. A moment was all he needed. He threw himself forward and poked the M4 over a stair step, forward from where he had disappeared. He opened up on full automatic and sprayed bullets across the foyer in front of the stairs. The rounds caught the men as they were moving to the side of the staircase to fire at him. They flopped back to the floor with their weapons flying out of their hands. One burst of automatic fire went off into the ceiling as one of the guards went down.

Without a moment's hesitation Dan jumped up and ran to the stairs. He pushed his way against the panicked guests both male and female until he reached Evangeline. She was standing and looking disoriented. Now she resisted Dan's urgings to come with him. He grabbed her arm, not allowing her to pull away and dragged her through the front door.

As Dan and Evangeline exited the front door, two more guards were struggling through the hallway from the pool area, against the crowd. Some of the guests were running out the front door and some back towards the pool to where the cars were parked. Dan slung his M4 over his shoulder and grabbed the girl under his arm and started running for the woods. She began to scream. Her understanding of what was happening grew, causing her to panic. He didn't have the breath to speak but just kept running. He had to reach the woods before any guards came out of the house. As he crashed through the thick brush at the edge of the woods, he heard shots from the mansion. Bullets whistled their ominous, sharp sound of death as they flew past. Some hit trees with a solid *thunk*, causing chips to fly.

Dan ran back up the hill to where he had left his backpack and M110. He dropped the girl and crouched in front of her.

"*Parla Italiano?*" The girl stared at him wide-eyed.

"*Sprechen Sie deutsch?*" The girl nodded.

In German Dan told her he was not going to hurt her but he had to get her away from the men coming after them. He lied and told her they wanted to hurt her. If she was confused by drugs, he didn't see any reason not to give her a story that would put him on her side.

"*Verstehen Sie?*" He had to say it twice before she nodded.

"We have to run now, uphill. Come with me." He grabbed her hand again and set out up the slope. The guards might follow but they would be at a disadvantage; Dan would have the high ground and the experience in the woods.

Chapter 16

The two men waiting in their car down the road from the compound heard the loud blast of the bridge going up. They looked at one another but didn't speak. They were patient, not wanting to get in the middle of whatever mayhem was going on. Listening more carefully, they could hear the gunfire, some of it sporadic, some of it obviously automatic fire. Still, they waited.

Before reaching the Range Rover, Dan heard the pursuit behind him. Some of the remaining guards were following and closing in on him as he struggled with the girl. She had concluded that she didn't want to go with Dan. She started to resist and pull back. He had to drag her onward. She began to shout and scream for help. He heard the footfalls and the crack of branches close behind, soon the bullets would fly and might find his back...or hers.

He reached a large oak tree and threw himself and the girl behind it just a burst of gunfire whistled past them. The trunk was almost three feet in diameter. Bullets now flew around the trunk on both sides. He pushed her flat to the ground. His face was set in a rage, his eyes bright with anger.

"You see? They will kill you as easily as me. They don't care. Shut up and stay still. You move from this tree, you are dead."

The girl now lay still, her eyes wide with fear. Dan turned and jiggled the brush to the right of the tree. A long burst of automatic fire followed. He switched the M4 to his left shoulder and swung it around the other side of the tree and let loose on full automatic. One guard fell back like a rag doll. The other threw himself into the bushes but Dan saw him get pitched back from a round. The 5.56 round fired by the M4 would take out a man with a hit anywhere, even an extremity. It delivered a massive amount of energy to the target. The man might not be dead, but he was going to be out of action.

Dan grabbed the girl and they slid back from the tree, keeping the large oak tree between them and where he saw the second guard go down. When they had gotten enough distance and could not be seen, He pulled her to her feet and they continued up the slope with Dan pulling, half-dragging the girl along.

When they reached the SUV, Dan turned the girl to face him.

In German he told her, "You almost got both of us killed back there. I'm trying to save you."

She had a more rebellious look in her eye now that the shooting seemed to be over. "I don't want to go with you. You kidnapped me."

"You're coming whether or not you want to. I'll tie you up if I have to."

"I'll scream. The police will stop us and catch you. Leave me alone." This last she delivered almost as a plea.

"You're high right now. You can't think, so I'm not going to listen to you."

"I can think enough to know I don't want to go with you." She glared at him. "What did you do back there? At the mansion? We were all having a good time. It was going to be a fun afternoon and evening, then you came."

Dan thought for a moment. This was not the time and certainly not the place to argue with a teenager on drugs.

"We'll talk later, when you're straight. Right now, you will come with me."

He grabbed her. She screamed again. He pulled her arms behind her back and zip tied her wrists.

"Stop it you pervert!" She shouted.

There was more shouting with hearty and vulgar epithets as Dan wrestled her to the passenger door and shoved her inside. After throwing his gear in the back, Dan put a fresh magazine in his M4 and placed it on the floor under his seat. He climbed in and started the engine.

When the gunshots died down the men got restless. they heard only a few ever-fainter reports. The passenger nodded to the driver and they started the car. They drove up the hill carefully, watching ahead for any sign of a descending vehicle. When they got to the compound, they stopped and looked at the blown-out bridge. The driver grabbed a pair of binoculars from the dash and trained them on the bridge and then the mansion further away. The passenger reached over into the back seat and opened a bag on the floor. He pulled out an AK-47 and set it in front of him. The driver nodded and they began to drive upward.

Further up the road they heard the sound of an engine coming from the woods. They stopped. Then the Range Rover appeared, coming out from a side trail. The passenger reached for the binoculars as the SUV reached the road and slid sideways. He called out the license number as the vehicle started up the hill in a shower of gravel. "*EP865CP*".

Dan saw the car in the rearview mirror. *What's that?* He had no illusions that it was a random encounter. He pressed the accelerator and the Land Rover hurtled up the winding road. The sedan accelerated, following him.

The car was no match for the Rover on the gravel road. Dan had the advantage of four-wheel drive. He threw the four thousand plus pound machine sideways into the corners and floored the throttle, causing the tires to claw their way ahead accelerating the machine out of each turn. The sedan driver, even while ignoring the pounding his car was taking on the bumpy surface, saw that he was losing ground. He could enter the corners faster but with only two-wheel drive the car struggled to accelerate on exiting.

With every turn, the BMW lost more and more ground. The passenger looked over at the driver but didn't say a word. He knew the disadvantage they had. When they got to a paved road that would be over and the powerful BMW could reel in the Range Rover. It was fast, but not as fast as the car. And he had the license plate number in his head.

"Slow down, you're going to wreck. You'll kill us!" the girl shouted.

Dan ignored her in his concentration. She threw herself against him almost causing the Land Rover to go off the road. Dan shoved an elbow at her, throwing her back into her seat. He was losing them, but he had to gain enough ground that they couldn't see where he turned when he started north. *Who are they?* The car didn't come from Feriz's compound. And a late party arrival would not be chasing him. Partygoers had no stomach for this action. He shook his head.

"Why are you doing this?" Evangeline asked.

Dan glanced over at her for a moment. Her short hair was disheveled. She had a fearful look in her eyes. She needed an explanation but he had no time to give it to her and doubted she was in any condition to understand it.

After cresting the pass, the road snaked downhill on the other side as it had done going uphill. It was even harder to go fast downhill than it was going uphill. You didn't have gravity helping you brake into each corner. He worked his brakes hard but had to be careful. They could easily get burned out trying to stop the heavy machine at which point the pursuing car would catch him. The BMW now had the advantage. Dan could only hope the four-wheel drive traction would still keep him ahead. He started throwing the big SUV sideways just before entering the turn to help scrub off speed and set the car up in a rally-style drift through the corner. The Land Rover responded gallantly for such a large, tall vehicle. As long as Dan didn't ask too much of it, he could slide into the corners. The girl had put her head down in abject fear. Going downhill frightened her more than the race uphill.

Part of the way down from the ridge the road turned north to follow a narrow valley. It was flatter, still full of curves but with long straight sections where Dan could let the Land Rover stretch its legs. The sedan could not go as fast on the rough surface without tearing itself apart. The rough, loose gravel was still favoring the SUV. He was a half mile ahead when he came to the E71 route. It was the main road he had taken to get down into Croatia.

He turned right onto the highway just before it went into a long tunnel. Dan slotted in with the traffic. He could not pass and had to drive in line knowing pursuit was somewhere behind him. But the pursuers also could not pass and would have to remain in place in the traffic stream.

Dan's plan was to get to Zagreb and then drive through Slovenia and into Austria if he could shake the car following him. He had rented a remote chalet in anticipation of spending a day or two there, getting his charge ready for delivery while he arranged the drop off.

Now that they were at normal speed, the girl spoke up. "Where are you taking me?"

"We're going to Austria for a day or two and then on to Italy."

"Who are you and what do you want with me? You're not going to hurt me, are you?"

Dan shook his head. "*Nein.*" I'm going to buy you some new clothes and let you get sober."

"Why?"

"You're Evangeline. I'm taking you back to your father. He sent me to rescue you from the porno guy."

Dan looked sideways at her and saw the blood drain from her face. "No, no!" she almost screamed. "I won't go back. *Nie und nimmer!* No, never!"

Dan was taken aback at her ferocity. "He's worried about you and wants you back. Can you imagine how bad he felt when you ran away?"

"He's a monster. I'd rather die than go back. You won't get me to Austria let alone Italy."

The Land Rover had tinted windows which helped. No one looking at them as they drove along would notice that Evangeline's hands were tied behind her.

"My hands hurt. Will you untie them?" she asked plaintively.

"I don't think I can trust you. I'm sorry but I'll have to leave you tied up until we can figure out how we're going to make this trip together. Because we *will* make the trip."

"What about the car following us?"

"I'm trying to figure that out. Why they would be following me and who would know I'm here?"

Jane might know. They could be agency assets sent to keep an eye on him. If so, he'd had a driving adventure for nothing. But he had told her to keep others away. The only other person who knew about his mission was Pietro Conti. And if he sent people, Dan had to wonder why. Too many unknowns He'd have to try to give them the slip.

After the tunnel, Dan took a chance and opened the Land Rover up. It could do one hundred and forty miles an hour. He hoped he wouldn't have to go that fast. It would only be a matter of time before he ran into the Croatian police. It was a crap shoot. His problem was there were so few routes going north. Dan thought hard about his options.

Chapter 17

"Here's what we're going to do," he said to Evangeline. "I'm going to pull off where I can hide the Rover. The car following us will go past. They think we're going back to Italy so they'll head to Trieste while we go north to Zagreb. By the time they figure out we're not on our way to Italy, we'll be long gone."

"But you don't know who they are, do you?"

"There's only two possibilities and neither choice calls for me letting them get involved. For whatever reason they're following, I don't want them around."

"Are you going to hurt me?" She asked again.

"No. I told I wouldn't. My job is to deliver you to your father."

Evangeline shuddered. "Please don't do that. I'd rather die."

"Why is that?"

"I can't tell you. But please don't do this."

"We can talk about it. We're not going back right away, not in the condition you're in."

"I'm not high now."

It was true. Dan noticed that she was making more sense, but he also noticed that she had begun to rapidly shake her legs, flexing them on her feet in a nervous manner.

"Are you cold?" he asked.

She shook her head.

"Do you have to pee?"

She nodded.

"After we pull over and give the BMW the slip."

He drifted the Land Rover around a gentle bend at a hundred miles per hour, passing slower cars like they were standing still. A short distance up the road was a gas stop. There was a small forest of lorries parked in the back. Dan pushed hard on the brakes and swung into the lot pulling around to the back and nestling among the trucks so he wouldn't be seen.

He kept the engine running for a quick getaway in case the BMW pulled in after him. After ten minutes had gone by, Dan assumed they had passed.

"Twenty-five kilometers up the road, if you're going to Trieste you turn left on E65, along the coast. The road we're on goes northeast to Zagreb. We have a choice. We can go to Zagreb before turning north or turn north before the city and head to Ljubljana in Slovenia. If they backtrack, they have only a fifty percent chance of going the right way."

"Don't say 'we'. I don't have a choice in this. You're kidnapping me and if I get a chance, I'll see you arrested."

Dan didn't answer. The girl's mood was deteriorating. He would try to get some food and fluid in her. He looked around. There was no one about in the maze of trucks.

Dan turned to Evangeline, "I'm going to let you pee here. If you try to scream or yell, I'll clamp your mouth immediately and put you back in the car and you'll pee in your pants. *Verstehen Sie?*"

She nodded.

"Don't test me." He gave her a hard stare until she looked away, now frightened again.

He got out and walked around to the passenger door. After opening the door, he helped her out.

"I'm going to pull your jeans and underpants down, you can squat here by the SUV and pee. Then I'll get us some water and food from the back."

"No privacy?" she asked.

Dan shook his head. "I don't think you've been very private from what I've seen in your pictures."

"You're a pig," came her reply. "And a murderer."

He ignored her and pulled her jeans and panties down. She squatted with her back against the SUV while Dan stood over her. When she was done, he yanked her upright and pulled her underpants and jeans back up. Then he put her back in the vehicle.

In the back he found some power bars and water bottles and brought them up front.

"Do you want to eat something?"

She shook her head.

"Here, drink some water. I don't want you to get dehydrated."

She shook her head again, but Dan grabbed her jaw and squeezed it until she opened her mouth. He poured some water into her and put his hand over her lips. She spluttered and coughed but swallowed the liquid.

"One more and we can go. Want to do it voluntarily?"

This time Evangeline nodded and Dan gently poured her a drink from the bottle.

Two hours later the two men, on the road to Trieste, concluded the Range Rover had given them the slip. They couldn't be sure, but aggressive speeding had not overtaken the SUV. It could also be going very fast so they may not have gained on it. But the two men did not want to spend the night in jail for excessive speeding.

The passenger punched a number on his cell phone. When the call connected, in Swiss accented German, he spoke to the other party.

"We may have lost him. We've been pushing hard but haven't caught up yet. He has an Italian license number." He repeated the number that he had memorized.

The man at the other end of the call, Pietro Conti, also spoke in German. "We'll get a track on him from the plates."

"It's a Land Rover," the man said.

"Understood. Head to Milan. If you don't see him, call me for further instructions." The phone went dead.

Pietro Conti sat back. *Now it is going to get more complicated.* This was what he had hoped would not happen. He had resources to call and could get a lead on the vehicle, but things were getting more complicated with each additional effort required to do what Herr Aebischer demanded.

Dan pulled back out on the highway and proceeded towards Zagreb at a more legal speed, keeping pace with the traffic flow. It wouldn't do to get pulled over. Evangeline would scream and get him arrested regardless of what might happen to her. How was he going to get to Austria with a rebellious passenger? *I could drug her and stick her in the secret compartment under the rear seat.* The thought had crossed his mind a couple of times, but he was loath to subject her to that treatment. *Maybe use it as a threat to gain cooperation?*

"Here's your choice. Are you listening?"

Evangeline didn't say anything.

"Evangeline, are you listening? You have a choice to make."

"Yes," she mumbled.

"You can agree to cooperate while we drive to Austria. I'm not going to take you back right away. Or I will put you to sleep and stick you in a hidden compartment that is under the rear seat. You'll be tied up and you'll stay there for the rest of the trip."

"I'll scream until someone hears me. They'll lock you away for a long time. I'll tell them you were going to rape me."

"No one will hear you because you'll be gagged. Believe me it's not pleasant."

Evangeline tried a different track. "Why are we going to Austria?"

"I told you, to a chalet I've rented. There'll be time for you to detoxify, get the drugs out of your system. We can talk about why you don't want to go back. I'll listen, but you have to cooperate now. If you don't, I probably won't listen and stick you back under the seat and take you to Italy where I'll drop you off in your father's hands."

She shuddered again. "*Nein, nein,*" she mumbled almost to herself. Looking at Dan, she pleaded, "Promise me you won't take me back."

"I can't now. But I'll listen to what you have to say."

"I can't tell you except that he's a monster."

"Your father?"

She nodded.

"If you want me to help you, if you want me to understand, you have to work with me."

"I don't think I can," her words came softly, almost a whisper.

She began to shake and her legs were now fluttering even more rapidly. It was not due to her bladder. Dan turned on the heater even though the temperature was in the seventies. The Land Rover began to heat up. Evangeline put her head down and started moaning.

"I don't feel good," she said.

"Will you cooperate so I don't have to put you under the seat?"

She nodded.

The day was fading. Dan figured when it got dark, he would stop and fill the Rover's gas tank. It would hold enough gas to get him into Austria without another stop. The dark would hide Evangeline's presence.

Dan picked an uncrowded station. Evangeline was quiet, even nodding off at times while he filled the tank. He pulled a blanket and pillow from the back before getting in. After filling the tank, he drove ahead to a dark area of the lot.

"I'm going to free your hands. I'll rope your left hand to my seat belt anchor so you can't jump out of the car, but your right hand will be free."

He tied her left hand with some slack; she could move it around so it wouldn't go numb, but there wasn't enough line for her to exit the vehicle. Then he gave her a pillow so she could rest her head against the door and put the blanket over her. Evangeline pulled the cover tightly around her and tried to curl up on the seat. She was shivering strongly now. Dan needed to get her to the chalet so he could help her through withdrawal. He didn't know what drugs she was on but guessed her addiction involved cocaine and possibly heroin. She had no needle marks on her arms, so she probably was snorting the drugs. That was a slim positive in an otherwise depressing picture of this pretty girl, pasty skinned with a poor complexion, dark circles around her eyes, looking ten years older than she was, and now getting sick.

Evangeline stayed curled up in the passenger seat. "I'm sick," she said. Her voice barely audible. "This is all your fault. You've ruined my life."

"I can't help you right now...when we get to the chalet it will be better."

She didn't answer. There was just an occasional whimper and cough from her. The girl seemed to have slipped into her own world of misery. Dan asked her if she wanted water now and then. She just shook her head. He didn't press the issue. Stopping to force her to drink didn't seem to be a way to help the situation.

He drove to Zagreb before heading north into Slovenia. It was past midnight when he turned off the main road, E59, just outside of Graz, Austria to head northwest on more local roads. Before his turnoff point, traffic was slowed by a lane closure. Evangeline was now asleep, thankfully. They crept along in the backup and passed the flashing lights of the *polizei*. Dan was unaware that one of the officers noted the Land Rover and wrote down the license number.

Dan followed winding secondary roads to a small town named Baierdorf. From there he turned onto an even smaller, but well paved road, Erzherzog Johann Strasse, on the way to Sankt Nikolai. The road climbed into the mountains following the gorges that snaked through the peaks.

The houses and yards in Sankt Nikolai were all neatly trimmed. The steeply pitched roofs with their large overhangs were covered in wood shakes, all to deal with abundant snow falls. There were flower boxes under most of the windows. It was a tidy, quaint town. The village was nestled in the Carinthian-Styrian Alps and looked like it should be featured on a picture postcard.

Dan saw little of this as he drove through the village an hour before dawn. Just outside of the village, he found the unpaved road heading up from the valley floor and followed it. There were two chalets at lower levels and nothing beyond except the one he had rented. It was another three miles of slow travel along the serpentine route needed for the road to scale the increasingly steep slope. Five hundred feet below the summit of the hill the chalet came into view. It was placed on a small, flat area that had been graded out from the slope. The mountain, covered in conifers, rose steeply behind the house. There was a gravel clearing at the side where Dan could park.

The chalet could not be seen from below; a large shoulder of the mountain blocked direct views to the village. There was a magnificent view eastward along the valley which promised bright morning sunshine. The road seemed to give up when it reached the chalet. There was no barrier, but the two-track beyond was definitely four-wheel drive terrain.

Dan pulled into the drive and parked the Land Rover. He unlocked the door which led into a mud room. Beyond it was a game room with table tennis and various bar games in it. A set of stairs took one up a flight to the main floor. There was a mezzanine above that served as a sleeping loft with three separate rooms. They looked out over the open-plan main floor with kitchen, eating and living space. At one end was a generous, open fireplace. A large deck faced eastward to take advantage of the views. At the rear, the windows looked out at the hillside almost within touching distance as it rose up from behind the house. Underneath the deck was a concrete pad where the firewood was stacked to keep it dry. You could get to it from the mud room without going out from under the cover of the deck and eaves.

Dan gently lifted Evangeline and carried her into the chalet and up to one of the sleep rooms. He locked the bedroom door behind him and proceeded to unload the SUV. Then he sat down in the kitchen and poured himself a whiskey from the liquor cabinet. He had done it. What had seemed almost impossible a day ago was finished. His body ached from all the stress and exertion. He sipped the whiskey and slowly let his body relax from the tension of the day and the long drive.

The only off note to his achievement, was Evangeline's intimations that her father was a monster. The level of her fear and anxiety at returning made it hard for him to dismiss the situation as teenage rebellion. Still, he had gotten over the main hurdle, by getting her away from Feriz. Or so he hoped.

Chapter 18

Dan grabbed his secure phone from his pack and stretched his legs out as he sat back on the couch. He punched in Jane's number. The sun was just breaking over the mountains to the east.

"Do you know what time it is here?" Jane asked when she picked up the phone.

"Early, the sun is just coming up where I am."

"And where is that?"

"Later. First tell me, did you send anyone to shadow me when I went to rescue the girl?"

"No, I didn't send anyone. I told you I wouldn't do that."

"But you told Henry? Was he okay with the operation?"

"Not fully, that's something we need to talk about."

"Did he know where I was going? Gračac?"

"No. I just told him you were headed to Croatia. He didn't care about the specifics. He's more concerned about whether you're going rogue on him."

"And no one but you knew."

"Right. What's this all about?"

"Some people were there, at Feriz's compound. They followed me, pretty aggressively."

"You know who they are?"

"No. But if you didn't send them, I have a good idea who did...but I don't know why and that bothers me."

"But you're safe now?"

"Yeah. I lost them and no one knows where we are."

"Can you tell me?"

"I'm in Austria."

"Why there? What's that got to do with the mission?"

"The girl is in bad shape. She's an addict and I need a place for her to detox."

"Then you're going to return her to her father?"

Dan hesitated. That was the plan but the girl's reactions gave him some concern. "I think so. She's terrified about it. Says her father is a monster. She won't tell me why, but I told her I would listen if she can explain herself."

"That's why she ran away."

"What do you mean?"

"If a daughter has that extreme of a reaction to her father, there's probably some reason for it. Something beyond teenage anger over too many restrictions."

"Aren't you the psychologist."

"I'm a female. What you're describing sounds like there may be something serious behind it. Do you know anything about the father?"

"No. My only contact is some underling. I'll have to rely on the girl. You probably should be talking to her, but we don't have time for you to come over."

"I couldn't anyway. You can do this, but don't be forceful. Be sensitive and listen, listen intently, like the way you shoot, with full concentration."

Dan sighed and stretched again. The fatigue of driving all night was catching up with him now that they were safe in the chalet. He wished this time was going to be a peaceful interlude, but there was a teenager going through withdrawal upstairs and she had issues with her father. It was going to be a turbulent week.

"You tired?" Jane asked.

"Drove all night."

"Well so am I, so let's both go back to sleep. But first tell me what happens next."

"Looks like I play counselor and nurse while Evangeline, that's her name, works the drugs out of her system and then we talk about her father. If I return her, I'll be heading back to Italy. Otherwise, I don't know what I'll be doing."

"Improvising. It's what you do well. Are you seriously thinking about not returning her?"

"Jane, I don't know. The woman in St. Marks Plaza said the girl was the key but she would not be truthful. I had to use my gift, the one Tlayolotl gave me. Only problem is I don't know what that is. It's something I have to discover."

"Jesus, Dan. These mystics have got your head turned around. You don't sound like you're thinking straight."

"If Evangeline was a guy, I'd get the truth out of him...her. But she's not. And you said to be gentle, so I'm floundering a bit here."

"You'll need some way to sort the truth from the lies."

"That's all there is to it. Thanks for that insight."

"I'm sorry. I wish I could help, but I can't. I understand you are way out of your comfort zone. But when you were in Mexico you held on to your sanity and figured out what to do. In the end some good came out of it. The drug lord's wife is making a life for herself. I checked up on her."

"Yeah, I know." Dan sighed again. "I'm going to try to get a couple of hours of sleep before I have to start playing nurse. Thanks for your advice."

He ended the call and swung his legs up on the couch. After pulling a throw cover over him, he lay back and fell asleep.

Pietro Conti received a call from Zürich. An Austrian federal policeman had made a call to his local station. The station commander relayed the message to the state command headquarters, to a *Chefinspektor*. The *Chefinspektor* then made a call to a number in Switzerland and passed on the information.

Pietro sat back. The assassin was in Austria. It was a neat, tidy country, very orderly. The assassin would stand out, especially with what was probably a traumatized teenage girl. He could assume an arc of one hundred miles swinging to the east, north, and west from the sighting. That would be a large enough area to check. The assassin probably wouldn't go much farther. The man certainly wasn't headed south from where he was spotted. It could be done. He might not risk taking the girl into a larger city but strangers stood out, especially in small towns. He sent some emails to the staff in Zürich. Next, he made a call to the two men in the BMW and told them to drive to Graz and wait for further instructions.

Two hours later Dan was awakened by the sound of retching coming from the mezzanine. He jumped up and ran up the stairs. Unlocking the bedroom door, he found Evangeline leaning over the edge of the bed convulsed in dry heaves. There was some bile on the floor, but nothing was coming up. Dan went over to her and held her head with one hand while he gently rubbed her back with his right hand. She leaned against him for support. The heaving gradually subsided.

"I'll get you some water," he said.

She shook her head. “No, I’ll just throw it up.”

“Just rinse out your mouth.” Dan left her and went to the bathroom at the end of the loft. He returned with a hand towel and a small glass of water. “Rinse. You can spit it in the trash can.” He brought over the can and placed it under her. She rinsed a couple of times and lay back shivering.

“I’m cold,” she said.

Dan pulled the covers over her. I’ll get you a sweater. I noticed one in the closet. Put it on and get back under the covers. It’s not that cold, but you’re going through withdrawal.”

“I need something. My stomach is in knots and my head is splitting. I ache all over.”

“Those symptoms will pass.”

“Can you get me a drink at least?” Mucous ran down from her nose onto her lips. She swiped the sheet across her face.

“No. That will only make things worse, lengthen your misery. Let me get you the sweater and then just lie back.”

“I can’t sleep. Shit, I can’t do a thing. I’m dying.” She lay back and turned on her side, moaning.

Dan got up and retrieved the sweater. He helped her sit up and put it around her, then laid her back and pulled the covers over her.

“You’re killing me,” she said in between moans. “You’re a pig. I hate you.”

Dan didn’t answer. He grabbed a chair and sat in the corner, watching. Evangeline turned away and buried herself under the covers. Dan could see the shivering decrease. She didn’t seem to be asleep but was uncommunicative.

During his vigil, she began to shove the covers off of her.

"I'm boiling," she mumbled half asleep.

Dan helped pull the covers away. She struggled out of the sweater. He brought a wash cloth over and wiped her arms to help cool her. Fifteen minutes later the shivering started again.

She groaned. "Please get me something. I'm freezing and hurt all over."

Dan didn't answer. It would only trigger an outburst. He placed the sweater over her and pulled the covers back up as she curled up into a tight ball and then retreated to his chair in the corner.

Chapter 19

It went like that for the whole day; going from chills to sweats and back to chills. She really didn't sleep but lay in bed not able to get up and walk around. Dan insisted strongly enough to get her to drink some water. She kept some of it down. Food would have to come later.

By evening, Dan was exhausted. He'd had only three hours of sleep. He needed to get some food in the chalet. The kitchen came equipped with utensils for cooking, along with a stocked liquor cabinet, but there was no food in the house except for coffee and tea and cooking staples. He made up a list and, after checking on Evangeline, he locked her bedroom door and left the house. He told her he was getting some supplies and would be back quickly. He hoped she was too sick to try to escape.

Down in the village of Sankt Nikolai, Dan found a butcher. He purchased various cuts of beef and then went to the vegetable grocer where he got a collection of carrots, potatoes, beets, onions, along with celery and two types of lettuce. The dry grocer had pasta, Muesli, bread, and other cereals. He also was able to purchase milk, cream, eggs, cheese, and juice.

"You are stocking up. Staying long?" a lady at the counter asked him. The stores were cramped and the customers all seemed to know one another. It was a small village. Dan knew he stood out.

"For the week. Going to do some hiking and relaxing," he replied in his High German.

"You speak German well, but you're not a native. Where are you from?"

"I work all over the continent," Dan replied ignoring the 'where from' part of her question. He figured he'd give her a little info to pass on to everyone she talked to for the next few days. "I work for a company that sells corporate security systems. They keep me busy and moving all around the continent. It's a treat to come to such a beautiful place and relax."

The woman smiled at Dan's acknowledgement of how lovely her home town was. "We get to live here all year around, but you only get a week. It's a pity."

"I'll be back whenever I can," Dan said as he left the shop. He stopped to fill the Land Rover's tank before heading back up to the chalet.

There was no helping the fact that his stay in Sankt Nikolai was not going to be stealthy. A stranger, a foreigner, in a small town; the word would get around. He only hoped it stayed in the village and he would be just a local point of interest.

Dan slept little that night. He stayed in the chair and was there to help cool Evangeline when she overheated and bundle her up when she began shivering. The second day brought more of the same.

By the end of the third day, they were both exhausted but Evangeline was starting to feel better. She had some tea and toast. Then came a soft-boiled egg with some juice. After eating she was able to shower; later Dan brushed her hair. It was short but tangled. He gently worked at it.

"Don't pull so hard," she complained. "It feels like you're tearing my hair out."

"I'm trying to get these knots out. Your hair is pretty short, how the hell did it get so knotted?"

"It's your fault. You abused me and kept me tied up. Here, let me do it." She reached for the brush.

"Just relax. I'm trying to be nice to you."

"Well, you aren't helping." She grabbed at the brush again. "Just leave me alone and let me brush my own hair."

Dan relinquished the brush and stood up. "Okay, you do it. If you don't want my help, that's fine. I'll just feed you and nursemaid you back to health...oh, but you said you didn't want my help. Shall I stop helping altogether?"

"Just let me brush my hair. I can do some of this on my own."

Dan headed for the bedroom door.

"And this wouldn't be happening if you hadn't kidnapped me. Remember that." She shouted after him as he closed the door.

Dan felt his anger ebb. He realized he shouldn't have lost his cool. This was a traumatized young girl who was also recovering from withdrawal symptoms. He needed to not respond when she lashed out at him.

An hour later she came down to the main floor. She went to the kitchen and put the kettle on to boil some water.

"Making some tea?"

"What does it look like," she said. Her tone was full of sarcasm.

"How about making me a cup?"

Evangeline didn't answer but she did pull a second cup from the cupboard. With the tea made, she sat down on a chair across from the couch where Dan was sitting. She avoided eye contact with him and stared out of the window. The afternoon light bathed the mountains to the east in a yellow glow. It looked like they were lit up by floodlights. They sipped their tea in silence, both taking in the view.

"You ready to talk about your father?"

The girl seemed to shrink in her chair and shook her head.

"We need to talk at some point. You're getting healthy again. I could take you back now, but I want to hear your story."

"You'll have to kill me. I won't go back. I'd rather die."

"That's kind of what you were doing to yourself with the drugs and the pornography, committing a slow suicide."

"What do you know about it? You've seen me? So now you judge me? You're just as bad as those assholes who pay to watch."

"People pay to watch?"

"You are so stupid. They pay to watch the scenes being filmed. We put on S&M shows while making the films. Feriz makes money in production and in distribution. He's got it figured out."

"Not anymore."

"You killed him. And some of the guards. How many others did you kill?"

"He was not your friend. He got you hooked. He's enslaved other girls with the drugs and then used them to make his movies. Have you ever thought about what he does with them after he's used them up?"

She looked over at him.

"Did you see any of the girls disappear? Not be around anymore? Ever wonder where they went? Did they just decide to leave and live a normal life?"

She shook her head obviously not wanting to acknowledge the truth of what Dan was saying.

"They didn't come to a good end. I can assure you of that. Either he prostituted them or put them into more violent films where they may have been injured or worse. There's a market for that sick stuff and don't act like you don't know it. You've seen the dark side of men, but it can get even darker."

Evangeline shrank back from Dan's words. "I don't know what went on."

"But whether or not you knew it, you were headed in that direction. If your addiction got too bad or when your good looks faded with the abuse and the drugs you were going to wind up in a similar scenario."

She stood up and glared at him. "You don't know. Those are just words. What I know is that you kidnapped me and now you're going to put me back in hell. I'd rather die!"

She stomped up the stairs and back into her room.

Dan sat there. *Going too fast. But how do I get her to open up so I can listen the way Jane told me to do?* He got up and put his cup on the sink. *First, she has to talk.*

That evening was more peaceful. Evangeline apologized to Dan and Dan said he was sorry for speaking harshly to her.

"I might have been headed in the wrong direction. I know that. But I can't go back and I can't live with what I know."

"Tell me. It will help you to talk about whatever is bothering you."

She gave him a sardonic smile. "'Bothering you'. Such a gentle phrase. It doesn't begin to describe what I know.

I can't speak of it. It's a something that should never see the light of day."

"If you keep it to yourself, it will fester. It will devour you from the inside out."

"It already has," she said sadly. She got up. "I'm going to lie down and hope I can sleep through the night."

The sky was clouding up and a storm was brewing. Dan could see the rain coming down to the east. It moved towards them and would soon climb the slopes and wash over them. It would be a noisy night with rain thrumming on the roof and lightning and thunder cracking overhead.

Maybe their conversations were making progress. Dan couldn't really tell, but if they were, it was slow, maybe too slow. He didn't want to stay too long and he had a decision to make.

Two hours later, Dan opened the door to Evangeline's room to say goodnight. She was asleep, wrapped up in her covers. The rain had started and the pounding on the roof was louder in the bedrooms than down on the main floor. He was glad she could sleep. That was a good sign. Hopefully he could as well.

He locked her door and went into his bedroom. An hour later he was asleep.

Chapter 20

Around 2:00 am an especially loud clap of thunder woke Dan. He got up and went to the bathroom. On the way back, he unlocked Evangeline's door and peaked in. There was a lump in the bed like she was hidden under the covers but something didn't look right to Dan. The window was open. He stepped over to the bed and gently pulled back the blankets. There were only pillows underneath.

Evangeline had pretended to be sound asleep when she heard Dan open her door to check in on her. She lay in the bed for another two hours. The storm increased in intensity and noise. Around midnight, she got up and put on her clothes. She only had her jeans and T-shirt, both of which Dan had washed. The sweater was in her room. She put it on. Then she went to the window and opened it. The rain was coming down hard, but the steep hillside protected the back of the chalet from the onslaught of the wind. She climbed through the window. The slope rose up so her drop was not three stories, more about ten feet. She slid down the side of the cottage, holding on to the rim of the window.

When she was fully stretched out, she took a deep breath and let go. In a moment she hit the ground. She was facing the wall and her feet flew out from under her and she slammed back against the hillside. The wind was knocked out of her. She just lay there with the rain drenching her face. After getting her breath back she got up and slithered down to the foundation and made her way around the wall to the opposite side of the cabin from where the car was parked.

She was limping. Her left foot had twisted when she hit the ground. It would be all right. She only had to go downhill to the village. Once there, she could get some help and be safe from Dan taking her back. He had been gentle with her, but he could scare her as well. She saw how lethal he was, yet so solicitous of her well-being. It didn't matter. She brushed any friendly thoughts out of her mind. He was going to deliver her to her father and that would be like delivering her to her death. She'd get help. Maybe the authorities would capture him and arrest him, maybe he would get away. Evangeline didn't care. She only cared that she not be sent back to Zürich and her father. She'd disappear again and this time she'd avoid the pornography industry.

The fastest way downhill was to cut through the forest and fields, going straight down rather than following the road which snaked back and forth. The woods seemed safer than the road as well as faster. She slipped and slid across the field in front of the chalet. Once she'd reached the evergreen trees with no one seeing her, she breathed easier. From there on, she'd be out of sight. The rain beat down. It quickly soaked the thick wool sweater which became very heavy. Still, it was better than just a T-shirt. It was a cold night up on the mountain.

In the woods there was some protection from the downpour although large drops of water would fall after building up on the fir needles until they couldn't hold the water. They would hit her in the head and shoulders with loud, wet splats. The sweater, already large for her, stretched and hung loosely around her. It repeatedly snagged on the stiff dead branches sticking out from the lower parts of the trees. The snags held her up and she pulled and ripped herself free numerous times. Emerging from one swath of woods, she walked through a waist-high hay field. Out in the open she was pummeled by the wind and rain. She tripped and fell, sliding ten yards down-hill. She picked herself up. Her clothes were now muddy. The sweater hung limply from her arms and slipped off her shoulder. Her hair was matted down, some of it sticking to her face. She kept wiping her face and eyes with the back of her hand which was covered by the wool sweater. She trudged on and crossed the road to go into another field.

The next section of woods was tighter going, but the wind and rain were less intense under the trees. She twisted through the conifers; one branch grabbed her so hard she was stopped in her tracks. She angrily jerked forward and the sweater was ripped off, the buttons pulling through the water-stretched eyelets. Evangeline grabbed at the sweater but it stubbornly remained hooked by the branch. She swore and set off without it.

She crossed the road again and gained the next lower field. The rain lashed her arms, now exposed. She stumbled forward, slipping down into a muddy ditch on her back. She lay there and caught her breath. Then she started up the bank of the ditch only to slip and fall face-forward into the mud and slide back down. A string of curse words erupted from her. She again crawled up the muddy bank. At the top, covered in mud, she got up and staggered forward. She began shivering intensely. *How far is it to the bottom?*

Her strength, not fully returned from her withdrawal, began to fail her. *Got to make it to town.* After crossing the road again, she walked over the shoulder of the hill. The ground fell away in the steep drop, her feet slipped in the wet field, and she went tumbling and rolling down the slope. It was steep enough to be difficult to walk in the dry and now impossible in the wet. When she finally stopped, she was face down against the ground. The hay smelled fresh in the wet but provided no comfort.

With a groan, Evangeline got up and started off again. Finally, she reached another patch of the forest and entered it with some relief. The branches now scratched at her torso and arms as she stumbled along in the dark, guided by the slope, always downhill.

Ahead, the darkness lessened as she neared the end of the woods. She stumbled forward, on the sloped ground, trying not to trip over fallen branches. Stepping out of the woods, too late she saw that she was at the top of a bank cut into the hillside to make a bench for the road below. The wet ground gave way under her feet and she went tumbling down twelve feet of dirt and rocks banging to a stop in a ditch next to the road. She didn't move.

When Dan saw the open window and confirmed Evangeline's absence from the bed he ran to get dressed and went out to the Land Rover. *She'd go downhill, try to get to the village.* He stopped for a moment. *Did she go straight down, across the fields and woods or keep to the road?* He didn't know how much head start she had but it could be as much as two hours. He grabbed his flashlight and went back around the house. She'd go around the chalet away from the car area. He went there and then started straight across the field.

He moved fast with the benefit of the flashlight. When he reached the woods, he slowed his pace to look for signs of her passing, freshly broken branches, or footprints. He didn't see anything but kept going. *She would go down, that would be her frame of reference, always downhill.*

He crossed the road and continued through the next field. In the next section of woods, he thought he could see freshly broken branches but could not be sure. Coming out of the woods, he crossed the road again. He jogged down the hill on the far side of the road, his boots giving him some traction. His light exposed a ditch ahead and Dan slowed down. Evangeline, with no light would not have seen the ditch. There was a good chance she would fall into it. He started off parallel to the ditch and went fifty yards, his flashlight playing along it, looking for signs of her passing. Seeing nothing, he turned around and retraced his steps, going fifty yards in the other direction. There he found the marks, the signs of her slipping, of her crawling up the opposite side.

With a swelling of relief in his chest, Dan crossed the bank and headed downhill. He now had her trail. She would not vary her path from downhill and he would do the same. He crossed the road again and entered the lower field. His flashlight picked out the shoulder where the hill dropped away. Dan slowed his pace and shone his flashlight around. He suspected that the drop-off might catch Evangeline out and she might fall. The waist-high grass should show him evidence of that if it happened. Sure enough, he found a swath where the grass had been disturbed, partially knocked down. It was wider than if someone walked down. She rolled down the slope. *I hope she's all right.* He slid his way down the hill on his heels and butt.

He entered the next woods section. He was still on her trail. *How far ahead was she?* Dan guessed he had to be moving faster than her with his light and boots. He pushed through the woods, trying to go faster. He didn't need to go slow, looking for signs, he was on her trail, like a hound homing in. Up ahead the flashlight showed horizon. There was a drop off. He slowed his pace and carefully approached the lip of the cut bank. He played the light along the bottom of the bank and there, in the ditch, he saw her lying face down.

Chapter 21

She was barely conscious. Her body was cold. Icy water ran down the ditch sluicing around her body, chilling her even further. Dan looked around. Further up the road the bank tapered off as the shoulder leveled out. He picked her up and carried her up the road. When he was beyond the bank, he trudged up the hill and back into the woods. There was no dry place to be found, but the rain and wind were less fierce inside the pines. He laid her down on a thick bed of needles and took off his coat to cover her. She moaned and shivered but didn't regain full consciousness.

That done Dan went back to the road and started running back up to the chalet. He was a little over a mile away by road. He settled his body into a quick jog. This was going to be as bad as any training run, over a mile uphill in hiking boots in the rain and wind. His lungs began to burn, as his forceful breathing kept pumping cold air in and out of his lungs. He sounded like a steam-driven locomotive with each explosive exhale. The legs began to feel heavy but he wouldn't slow, pumping his arms ever harder to help thrust his body forward.

The picture of Evangeline lying in the ditch drove him forward. He picked up his pace and just as he had done in training runs, shut his mind to everything but the image of his goal, the parking area with the Land Rover.

Finally, the chalet came in sight and with a new burst of energy Dan hammered across the gravel and grabbed the door of the SUV. He got in and raced back to where he had left Evangeline. He ran up into the woods. It took a few minutes of circling around to find her. She was shivering uncontrollably. Dan picked her up and carried her down to the SUV. He put her in the back, turned around and drove back to the chalet.

He brought her up to the bedroom and stripped off her wet clothes. She lay naked on the floor.

After toweling her dry, he picked her up and placed her on the bed and pulled the covers over her. Then he went to get more blankets. She was semi-conscious but couldn't talk, her body racked with violent shivers. *Got to get her warm. Build a fire? No time.* Dan's mind raced over his options. He checked the closets and found a down comforter which he put that over her. *Her body's not going to reheat by itself.* Without an additional heat source, she could just get colder until her body shut down. After running through questionable options, Dan took off his clothes, grabbed a towel and violently rubbed his body until it became red. He wanted blood near the surface of his skin.

With only his underpants on he slipped into bed with Evangeline and pulled her to him. He was nestled up against her back, maximizing the skin-to-skin connection. His arms wrapped around her and pressed her back to him. Her shivering continued. Dan could feel how cold she was. He started rubbing her arms and legs with his hands and moving his body against hers, trying to transfer heat into her.

With the addition of his body heat, the cocoon under the covers began to get warmer. Slowly her shivering diminished. When her shivering lost some of its intensity, Dan got up and went down the hall to the bathroom. He filled the tub, warm to start. When the tub was full, he went back and carried Evangeline to the bath. He slid her into the water and then began adding hot water to the mix, gradually increasing the temperature so as to not shock her system.

After ten minutes she looked up at him. “You found me.”

Dan nodded. “You scared me. It’s a cold night. You could have died out there.”

“I wanted to get away. I don’t want to go back. You saved my life...but you’ll end it if you send me back.”

Dan could see she was trying to process all that had happened.

“Don’t talk now, just get warm.”

He stood up.

“You’re not dressed,” she said. “Were you taking advantage of me?”

He couldn’t read her expression, whether or not she was kidding him. Then she lowered her gaze to his crotch. Feeling suddenly embarrassed, Dan turned towards the door. “I’ll get you something warm to drink now that you’re conscious. Don’t get out of the water yet.”

When Dan returned, he had his clothes on. He handed Evangeline a mug of hot tea with honey in it.

“Drink this, it will warm you and give some energy.”

“No fair. You’re dressed and I’m naked,” Evangeline said. Her complaint was accompanied by a sly smile.

Dan turned his head. “You’re right. I’ll get you a bathrobe. Your clothes are too wet and dirty to put on.

Later, after she got out of the bath, Evangeline came down to the main floor wrapped in a terry cloth robe.

"This is cozy," she said.

Dan didn't say anything. He was unsure of how to respond to what were now pleasant comments. Hours ago, she was desperate enough to run away into the storm, now she seemed oddly friendly.

It was getting brighter outside, but there would be no sunrise this morning. The skies were still laden with clouds and the rain and wind continued, although more intermittent now.

"Are you hungry?" Dan asked.

She shook her head and put her mug on the counter.

"I'm tired. I need to sleep."

"So am I," Dan replied.

"Would you do me a favor?" Evangeline asked, turning to him.

"What is it?"

"Would you sleep with me?"

"What? I can't do that, you're just a teenager," Dan responded. He was taken aback by her request. He had not expected anything like that, especially since she'd been so angry at him.

"Not like that. More like cuddling, like you did to help warm me up. I don't want to be alone." She looked over at him with plaintive eyes.

"I guess I could...I mean if you really want me to." He thought for a moment then blurted out, "But you don't have any underwear. It's dirty and wet. I can't lie down with you when you're naked."

Evangeline almost laughed. She smiled back at him.

"It's okay. Give me one of your shirts. I'll use it as a nightgown. I'll get in bed first and then you just slide in behind me. I hope I'm not repulsive to you."

"It's not that and you know it. You're quite beautiful, even with your bad haircut."

She gave him a sad smile. "Maybe. Sometimes I don't feel so pretty...most times, I guess."

"Why is that?" Dan asked.

Evangeline just shook her head. "So, will you do it? Please?"

"Okay,"

She smiled again, stretched, and yawned. "Good. I'm exhausted. I'm going up now. You get a shirt for me and follow."

"Let me close up the chalet and turn off the lights. I'll be up shortly."

He hoped that she would be asleep when he got there. He didn't know what, if anything, she might have in mind but she was acting different since he rescued her from the storm.

Ten minutes later he slipped into her bed and drew himself up close to her. She pushed herself back into him and reached behind her to pull his arm over her body. She placed his arm and hand on her stomach. She put her hand over his and snuggled down, sighing contentedly.

"I've never had a man hold me when it wasn't sexual...and usually it was headed towards something harsh and kinky. This is nice."

Dan kissed her on the top of her head.

"I'm sorry for that. It's okay now. Relax and go to sleep."

"It feels nice, being close with no agenda, no demands. Thank you."

"Shhh. Sleep now."

She wriggled again and Dan could feel her body relax into him as sleep overcame her. He was planning to leave when she fell asleep but fatigue overcame him. They were out of the storm. She was safe; they both were safe for now. He let his mind relax. There was no need to worry today. Let the day be one of peacefulness and the chalet a place of refuge. They had made a connection. It was enough for now. He fell asleep next to this girl who had begun to burrow her way into his life.

Chapter 22

That afternoon, Dan awoke first, dressed, and went down to the kitchen. He put on a pot of coffee and began working on a simple egg and cheese omelet. Evangeline came down the stairs a few minutes later. She had the bathrobe wrapped around her.

"The coffee smells good," she said.

Dan watched her. There was no mention of the cuddling last night but her demeanor seemed friendlier to him.

"How do you feel? Are you hurt from falling?" he asked.

"I sprained my ankle and have some bruises on my arms and ribs, but I'm okay."

"Are you hungry?"

She nodded her head vigorously. "I'm famished."

"You didn't eat much while detoxing. It looks like you're doing much better." He gave her a critical look-over. "I think you lost a lot of weight. Your face is a bit gaunt, so it will be good to put some weight back on."

"You really know how to compliment a girl, don't you?"

"What did I say? Last night I told you that you were beautiful, even in your condition. Getting off the drugs will only enhance that."

The coffee maker finished its job and Dan went over and poured two cups.

"Just a half cup for me," Evangeline said.

He handed her a cup and she filled the remaining amount with cream and sugar.

"That looks like dessert, not coffee," Dan risked a comment. He wanted to stay off how she looked which seemed to be a sensitive subject.

"It's the way I like it. I suppose you drink it black like some macho man."

"You found me out." Dan nodded to her and took a sip of his black coffee. "I'm making a cheese omelet. Would you like that?"

"Ja...bitte und danke."

When Dan neared finishing, Evangeline put some bread in the toaster and took out the jar of elderberry-plum jam from the cupboard.

They ate in silence, both enjoying the meal. Evangeline ate a full plate with three slices of buttered toast and jam along with a glass of juice and a second cup of coffee and cream.

The two men waited in Graz as they had been instructed. They spent their time sitting in a hotel room watching television. They didn't talk much. Neither wanted to go out. They didn't want to be seen much. The call would come. It was only a matter of time. There would be instructions, they would carry them out and then go back to Zürich. There was one unspoken worry that stuck in both of their minds. They had not completed the job back in Croatia. And the man in charge didn't abide failure.

After their brunch, Dan and Evangeline sat down. The storm outside was beginning to pass. Clouds were lifting and the sun was beginning to break through. They could see the bright patches of sunshine down in the valley. It looked like spots of light running across the fields. The change promised a sunny end and a clear, bright day tomorrow.

They both sat and watched the growing sunlight play across the valley floor. Neither spoke. Dan tried to figure out how to broach the subject of Evangeline's father without triggering her defenses or panic. She was friendly to him and there was a comfortable atmosphere between them that he was loath to disturb.

"You know, I don't even know your name," she finally said, breaking the silence.

"It's Steve," he said, using his alias. "But my name really isn't important."

"Well, I don't want to just call out 'hey you' every time we talk." She smiled at him, a genuinely friendly, attractive smile. "And I think I should know the name of the man who saved my life."

"I was scared I couldn't find you in the dark and the storm. I guessed you would go straight downhill and not follow the road, so that's what I did."

"How *did* you find me? In the dark like that, I could have veered off in any direction."

"I've had some training in tracking. It helped. When I came to a ditch, I figured you might have slipped into it. It was impossible to see in the dark, but I had a flashlight."

He went on to describe how he discovered her trail and all the events leading to getting her back to the chalet. They were sitting in two chairs facing the large windows overlooking the deck. When Dan finished, Evangeline got up and leaned over to him and kissed him on the cheek.

The kiss lingered a moment longer than a perfunctory peck of thanks.

"You're welcome," he said smiling at her. She smiled back.

"Do you think we can talk about your father now? I can see that you're serious about not wanting to go back. Why?"

Her face darkened. "I can't speak of it. Why ruin a nice afternoon? I want to think of you as someone who saved my life, not someone who will end it."

Dan leaned towards her in his chair. "That's why I want to know, so I can understand your anxiety, your fear."

She lowered her head and shook it back and forth. "*Nein, nein*. It is not something to talk about." She looked up at Dan. Her eyes full of dread. "I ran away when I was sixteen. Something happened and I knew I had to leave."

"What happened?"

"My," she hesitated, then stammered, m-m-my m-m-mother died."

"And that caused you to run away?"

She nodded, looking at the floor.

This was a crack in the wall she had put up. Dan tried to pry it open a bit more. "How did your mother die?"

Now Evangeline started to choke back sobs. "She...she killed herself."

"Oh my dear girl. I'm so sorry," Dan said.

"Are you?" Her eyes flashed. She looked at him, now angry again. "You who will take me back to hell? You want to dig open my wounds so you can understand? Or just to satisfy your curiosity? You're not going to change your mind, are you?"

She jumped up crying and ran for the stairs.

"Evangeline, I'm sorry," Dan called out as she ran up the steps and disappeared into her room.

"Hell," he mumbled to himself. "I really fucked that up." He started to follow her but then thought better of it. He sat back down. Was he just picking open an old wound? Yes. Did he have to? Dan wasn't sure. He had taken the job to rescue her from the pornographer and to kill him. The man was just another low life who would fill the vacuum and get into the gun and drug business Dan had created by killing Guzim. He was glad to have eliminated him before he could do more damage.

But returning the girl now filled him with conflict. Jane was right. Dan sensed there was something serious in her fear and loathing about being returned. He needed to understand what it was. Or was he just being stubborn? He wished Jane were here to help. This was not going all that well.

After a half hour, Dan got up and climbed the stairs. He opened Evangeline's door and gently stepped into her room. She was face down on the bed. He sat on the edge and touched her head.

"I'm sorry. I know the subject is hard for you. But now I have a little more information. I truly want to help—"

"Do you?" she said into her pillow. "Or is your mind made up? Maybe you still have part of your fee to earn." She turned to him. "How much did he offer you to bring me back?"

Dan's face must have reflected his pain.

"It was a lot, wasn't it? He's very wealthy."

"The amount isn't important. I turned him down at first."

"Then what changed your mind, more money?"

Dan shook his head. "There were two things that changed my mind." He paused. How would he explain the Watcher? Jane still didn't buy the whole idea. "First there was a young girl to save from a ruined life in pornography and drugs. Believe me, that was important. But the other thing was a woman I ran into."

Dan gave her a shortened version of his encounter with the woman in St. Marks Plaza, leaving out the location.

"She told me to rescue you. She said that you would lead me to uncover a greater evil to destroy. But she also said you would not be truthful."

Evangeline kept staring at him, but her fierce look began to soften.

"So, I'm in a quandary," Dan continued, "I need you to tell me things, but I don't know if you'll tell me the truth."

"Truth? I don't want to talk with you or anybody." She turned her head to the wall. "Once I left, I vowed never to talk about him again. And I haven't until now."

"Your father?"

She nodded.

"Do you even know his name? she asked."

"I don't. A *Signore* Conti was my contact. He said his employer wanted to remain anonymous."

"I don't wonder. Didn't he think I'd tell you?"

"Maybe not. Maybe he thought I'd deliver you right away and we wouldn't have any conversations."

Evangeline seemed to ponder this information. "*Signore* Conti is a flunky for Herr Aebischer, Jan Luis Aebischer." Her words were bitter.

"And he's your father?"

She nodded looking at him with fear and pain in her face.

"Evangeline, I can't fully understand the hurt you feel at losing your mother, but I understand pain and anguish. I lost my wife, not to illness or accident. She was killed...murdered by some evil men, along with our unborn baby."

Evangeline looked at him now without so much anger and defensiveness in her eyes.

"And so you became a murderer?"

Dan stared back at her with a hardened look on his face. "I made those responsible pay...with their lives."

Evangeline looked away. "Maybe you *can* understand. I don't know, but for now please go away. I'm tired and want to take a nap."

Dan stood up. "Okay, I'll leave you alone. Again, thank you for telling me as much as you did. I'll make us a big dinner. Do you think you'd like to eat something later?"

She nodded and then turned away. Dan left the room.

He went back to the kitchen. Before he started on supper, he took his secure phone out and called Jane.

"At least it's a more reasonable time of day. How are you doing?"

"Jan Luis Aebischer."

"Who's that?"

"That's what I want you to find out. He's Evangeline's father, the one she abhors."

"Sounds like you're making progress."

"A little. It would be easier if you were here. Can you get Fred on it? Knowing something about him may help me understand her fear."

Fred Burke, the researcher, and Warren Thomas, the hacker, were able to get into almost any system and not be traced. Together they made a formidable information gathering team.

"So, she hasn't told you yet," Jane said.

"Only a little. I need more information."

"I'll get right on it. Keep going, sounds like you're doing well."

Around dinner time Evangeline came downstairs dressed in her jeans and shirt that Dan had washed and dried. She had brushed her hair and put on some makeup that had been in her pockets. Dan stopped turned from the stove and looked at her. She smiled at him.

"Wow. You look beautiful. Where'd you get the makeup?"

"I had some lipstick and mascara in my pockets."

"Just that? You look like you're glowing, so much better than before..." He paused. "How do you feel?"

"I feel good, physically."

She didn't say more and Dan didn't probe.

After they had eaten a robust dinner of ham, potatoes and salad, Dan pulled the couch around to face the deck. They sat down and watched the light fade in the valley.

As it got darker, Evangeline moved close to Dan and snuggled up to him. She put her head against his chest. He sat still with his arm around her.

"We get along pretty well, don't we?" she said after a while.

"It seems were getting along better now, for sure."

"I could be a good companion to you." She looked up from his chest. "Why don't we just go away together? Forget about my father. I'd be good to you. You'd never get bored. And I'll learn how to cook and clean. I could make life more comfortable."

She stared up into his face. Dan looked down at her. He didn't know what to say. The obvious answer was "no", but he had to be careful. She seemed fragile and her ploy to get him to change his plans was obvious.

"I don't think that would work. My job doesn't really lend itself to having a partner."

"I could be more than a partner. Believe me, I'd make you happy."

Dan smiled. “I’m sure you could, but I don’t think I could make *you* happy. I lead a pretty monastic style of life.”

“Do you kill people for a living?”

Dan shook his head. “I don’t talk about my work. I’m a security consultant for corporations. There’s lots of secrets in that job.”

“Sure you are. And I’m really a fairy princess.”

“We’ll talk more about this tomorrow. I have to start thinking about us leaving here.”

“I can’t go back. I’ve told you.”

“Well we can’t stay here much longer. We’ll talk tomorrow. I want to listen to anything you have to tell me. But for now, let’s leave this subject alone.”

Dan hoped she would not try seduction on him. It would only lead to hurt feelings and possibly closing off their burgeoning relationship.

Chapter 23

The call the men were waiting for finally came. Pietro Conti had quizzed many local polizei who had asked around their villages in their areas of jurisdiction about a stranger driving a Land Rover, possibly with a young girl. The request was couched in doing a low -key search in a possible abduction, something that had to be kept discrete. He struck gold when the local police office in Sankt Nikolai reported some merchants seeing a foreigner purchasing supplies. He drove a Land Rover similar to the one described.

After the call, the two men packed up their gear and checked out. It was the middle of the afternoon. They would arrive in Sankt Nikolai that evening which is what they wanted. A search of house rentals had come up with the chalet high on the mountainside above the village. They would approach it at night, late at night.

Evangeline looked at Dan. She was still sitting close to him, trying to make a connection with her body.

“Now it’s you who doesn’t want to talk. That’s a switch. Why do we have to wait to talk about you and me? Let’s talk about it now.”

“There’s nothing to talk about,” Dan replied.

"Yes there is. You saved my life, maybe twice. And now you want to throw it away. You don't want to consider that I can be a good partner, a good mate to you. I'm not that young and you're not that old." She put her hand on his chest. "You've not taken advantage of me and that shows you have character. I don't think you would send me back if you knew what I was running away from."

Dan looked back into her eyes. "And that's what I want to know. Why won't you tell me?"

Evangeline looked down and shook her head. "I told you. It's too painful. It should never be revealed, not be talked about." She looked back into his eyes. They were eyes that could be hard like a killer's or glow with understanding. She had seen both in him. "You have to trust me."

Dan sighed.

They talked late into the night, always working their way around the subject. Dan kept refusing to entertain Evangeline's idea of them living together. It wasn't at all tenable but she was like a bulldog and would not let the idea go. Perhaps it was due to her horror at being returned. Dan had by now decided that her father must have abused her, but he needed to penetrate the darkness that lurked behind the story. He needed Evangeline to tell him. That was what the Watcher had said.

The two men stopped below the chalet. They had been told it was the last one on the road, the third one. After passing the second cottage they killed the headlights and drove slowly upward. They were a couple of hundred yards below the chalet when they stopped. The passenger reached back for the satchel lying on the back seat. He took out a short barrel AK-47 with a folding stock. The driver took out an MP5 chambered in 9mm. Both weapons could be fired in automatic mode; the MP5 could fire 800 rounds per minute, the AK47 600 rounds. Both men had semi-automatic hand guns holstered to their belts. They didn't plan on leaving the kidnapper alive when they grabbed the girl. With a nod to each other, they exited the BMW and started walking up hill towards the chalet.

It was midnight. Dan and Evangeline had talked and talked. She snuggled against him, partly to use her sexuality to convince him and partly just to enjoy the pleasure of his tenderness without any expectations. For his part, Dan just relaxed and tried to hold his ground. Now they were both at the edge of sleep, sinking further into the couch and each other.

As Dan was drifting off, he heard a click downstairs. Instantly he was awake, his eyes open in the now darkened main room, his ears intently probing the chalet for unusual noises. There was another click.

Dan jostled Evangeline.

"What is it?" she asked, still half asleep.

"Shhh." Dan leaned close to her ear. "Someone is downstairs."

She opened her eyes wide now and looked at him. She started to speak but Dan put his hand to her mouth and shook his head. He leaned close to her ear again.

"Get up and go to the back window. If you can slide it open, do it and go outside. If the window starts to squeak, stop. Do not make any loud noise. Understand?"

She nodded and got up. Dan rose from the couch. His hand gun and other weapons were up in his bedroom. There was no time to retrieve them. He had no shoes, only socks on his feet. He quietly padded over to the island counter in the kitchen area. He slipped a large knife from the wooden holding block. It had a ten-inch tapered blade that started at three inches across. It was stiff and strong. He grabbed the knife in his fist like he was going to stab it into a table. He went over to the edge of the stairs.

Whoever entered had to come up the stairs to get into the rest of the chalet. He'd meet them at the top of the stairs. Dan figured he had one chance. His back was against the wall; his right hand holding the knife was positioned across his abdomen. When the intruder stepped beyond the door frame Dan would fling his arm in an arc slamming the blade into the person's neck, one chance, one blow to take them out. There could be no time to check on who it was. These were not friendlies coming in the middle of the night, picking the door lock; this was a hostile intrusion.

His senses, now heightened, could detect footfalls on the stairs. Was there more than one person? Dan wasn't sure. He slowed his breathing and readied himself. He had the element of surprise but only for one moment. After that he would be unarmed facing someone whom he could be sure was armed.

Dan spared one glance across the room. Evangeline had pushed open the window and was crawling through it. He hoped she wouldn't use the moment to run again. He dismissed any further thought of her and turned back to the moment at hand. The furtive steps were coming closer.

Dan tensed. A figure showed in the door frame and Dan exploded. His arm flung across his body at the intruder. The blade glanced off the clavicle and sank into the man's lower throat. He jerked back pulling Dan forward. Dan's feet slipped on the floor and he crashed against the intruder. The man's right hand held an MP5 which went off as his reflexes pulled the trigger. The gun sprayed bullets across the room and into the stairwell ceiling as he fell back down the stairs, carrying Dan with him.

The MP5 fell away. Dan tried to stay on top of the man, but the intruder's shoulder dug into a step and he flipped over, throwing Dan ahead of him. There was another man, falling with them. He had been right behind the one Dan stabbed. When they crashed at the bottom, Dan shoved the injured intruder aside and scrambled to his feet. The second man was uninjured and armed. Dan could see the short assault rifle. He had to close on him before he could bring the weapon into action.

He leapt forward. The second man was getting to his feet and bringing up his weapon. He was taller than Dan and thicker; built like a linebacker. Dan threw himself at the man with all the force he could muster, as if tackling a runner in football. As the weapon came up, Dan swung his left arm at it to deflect it.

The gun fired an automatic burst. Dan felt a searing pain in his left side. The breath was almost knocked out of him. He let out a loud grunt as he slammed into the larger man. One of the rounds had hit him. He had to disable his opponent quickly before the man could bring the weapon into action again.

As Dan's head slammed into the man's chest, he also swung his right fist towards his throat. The blow missed the throat, hitting the man in the side of his neck. It was not a disabling blow but contributed to stunning him along with getting some of the wind knocked out of him. His grip on the weapon slipped and the machine gun fell behind him.

Dan spun to the right, crying out at the pain in his side. The man threw a right hook at Dan's head with a meaty fist. The blow hit him in the temple but its impact was diminished by Dan's moving away from the punch. Dan used his momentum going to his right to throw a right hand into the man's kidneys. He was rewarded with a solid grunt from his opponent. Now, though, the intruder squared up to Dan and threw a left at his head. Dan raised his left to block it and the man threw his right into Dan injured ribs.

Dan let out a yell and fell back against the wall. The pain almost blinded him. The man closed on him, his right hand reaching to unholster his pistol. Dan was running out of options. As the man was pulling out his pistol, Dan flung his right leg up and hit the man in the groin. He followed through like a field goal kicker. The intruder let out a howl. His knees buckled with the pain of smashed testicles. As he fell, he tried to pull his gun out. Dan stepped up and placed another kick under the man's chin which snapped his head back. He hit the ground. His head flopped back on the concrete floor with a loud splat that spelled a cracked skull and concussion.

The gun dropped from his limp hand. Dan kicked it away. It was too painful to reach down to retrieve it. He sagged back against the wall and put his right hand to his left rib cage. It came away wet with blood. A careful exploration around the wound indicated that the bullet had not penetrated, but skimmed across his side, gouging out a channel and probably cracking a rib. The pain was severe but the wound was not life threatening.

Chapter 24

Dan went over to look at the man he had stabbed in the throat. He was choking on his blood. He would not last much longer. The other man was still unconscious.

"Steve?"

He heard Evangeline call from outside the door.

"I'm okay," he shouted to her. "Don't come in."

The door opened as he finished saying those words. She gasped at the two figures lying on the concrete floor. Then she looked at Dan.

"You're hurt," she exclaimed going over to him.

"I'm okay. The bullet only grazed me but I think I have a cracked rib." He winced as he spoke.

"It hurts," she said.

Dan nodded. "Do you know these men?"

Evangeline looked at the unconscious man first and then the one stabbed in the neck. She shuddered at the sight of his last choking gasps.

"Can you help him?" she asked.

Dan shook his head. "I can't save him. Remember they tried to kill me. And who knows what they would have done with you."

"They would have brought me to Aebischer," she said. "I recognize them. They visited the mansion a few times. They work for Aebischer."

"Why wouldn't he just wait to have me return you? That's what the arrangement was supposed to have been."

Evangeline looked Dan in the eyes. "Maybe he wants you dead. He's a very cautious man. With no witnesses he can lock me away and no one will know."

Dan thought about that for a moment. "Go upstairs and gather some food and any extra clothes you can find. We have to leave."

Evangeline just stood there.

"Go now!" Dan shouted. "I have to take care of things down here."

She turned and climbed the stairs. When she was gone Dan went to the utility sink in the corner of the room and filled a can with cold water. He splashed it into the face of the unconscious man. He stirred. Dan squatted down close to him.

"*Für wen arbeitest Sie?*" Who do you work for?

The man stared at Dan. He repeated the question adding "Herr Aebischer?" There was a flash of recognition on the man's face which told Dan the answer was "yes".

"Did Pietro Conti send you?"

The man didn't answer but just looked at Dan. Then he turned to look at his partner.

"He's dead or dying," Dan said. "Do you want to join him?"

The man just looked back at Dan without answering. His eyes were the cold eyes of a trained killer. One who knew how the game was played. You win, someone else dies. You lose, you die.

"Pietro Conti, did he send you?" Dan asked again.

"*Macht nichts*," came the response.

He was not going to get any more information out of him. It didn't matter. He knew who had sent them. Dan stood up, walked over to the man's discarded 9mm, picked it up and put a round in the man's forehead. He then went over to the man he had stabbed and did the same.

Evangeline opened the door at the top of the stairs. "Are you alright?"

"I'm okay, stay up there."

Dan didn't relish his next chore but it would give them extra time before any pursuit began. He took the doormat and placed it under the first man. Then grabbed him by the legs and pulled him through the basement game room to the rear door. He would put the bodies in the woods. They would be found without much work, but they could gain a few precious hours before any alarms were raised.

When he was done, he climbed the stairs back to the main floor. His side was searing in pain. Dan tried to ignore it.

"Let's get going," he said.

"Why? You're injured. You need to bandage that wound." She bent down to examine his side. "Look, you're still bleeding. We need to stop that and then you need to rest."

Dan shook his head. "You don't understand. These men were sent to kill me and, at best, take you back to your father. I don't know if there are more of them. If so, they may be coming. And, we have two dead men here. We don't want to be around when the *polizei* show up."

"But your wounds—"

"Out in the Rover I have an emergency first aid kit. I'm going to get it and you can help bandage the wound. Then we must go. Finish gathering any food and clothing you find. We didn't get a chance to buy you some new clothes and it's too cold for just your T-shirt."

He turned and went back down the stairs to retrieve the first aid kit.

Evangeline washed the wound with soap and water. After, he had her pour some clotting powder on the gash and then place some pads over it. She finished by wrapping gauze around his mid-section to hold the pads in place. When she was done, Dan climbed the mezzanine stairs and packed his gear. He had Evangeline help him carry the bags down to the main level. She had packed some food and drinks. She had also found a jacket in the main floor closet which she put on over her T-shirt.

With a last look around, they both headed down the stairway and out into the yard. Dan started the engine and then just sat there.

"Are we going?" Evangeline asked.

He nodded. "I'm wondering if the track goes over this hilltop or just ends further up. I don't want to go back down towards the village for obvious reasons."

"These alpine trails are used to get to higher pastures either for grazing or growing," Evangeline said with some authority. "If it's a high mountain, they end at the highest pasture or field the farmers can clear. If it's a lower hill, they often go over and down the other side."

"Which one is this?"

"My guess is it's a lower hill, like the ones we can see across the valley."

"I hope you're right," Dan replied. "We'll give it a try." He didn't relish backtracking but Evangeline seemed sure about how the geography worked and it was far better than going back down to Sankt Nikolai. Someone in the town must have given him up. He didn't want anyone watching them depart and triggering a pursuit. He put the Range Rover in neutral and selected Mud & Ruts from the

Terrain Response menu. The Rover rose up on its suspension. He drove out of the yard and turned uphill.

Chapter 25

The Range Rover was an expensive luxury SUV but it came with a strong off-road heritage. Behind the Terrain Response menu selection was a wonder of electronic wizardry. The result was increased ground clearance and the vehicle's electronics monitoring wheel spin and directing drive through the differentials to the wheels that had traction. With the technology working behind the scene, the Range Rover picked its way up the muddy, rocky two-track steadily. The driver just needed to guide it away from any deep holes or ruts.

They drove upward in silence. When in the forest, Dan used the headlights. Out in the open he drove nearly blind with no lights showing. He did not want to signal the vehicle's presence to anyone down in the valley. Evangeline kept looking back over her shoulder, obviously worried about pursuit.

"Did you kill the two men downstairs?" she asked. "I heard two shots."

"I helped complete the process. They were going to die within minutes, or at the longest, an hour."

"Why do that? Do you enjoy that?"

"Don't be silly. They tried to kill me. I had a hand-to-hand fight with one of them. Had I lost I would be dead and you'd be in their hands…for whatever they had planned."

"But they were going to die."

"Yes. And they might have been able to call someone, or someone might have shown up to save them or get some information from them. I couldn't take that chance. It made no difference in their ultimate fate."

"I don't understand you. You can be so kind and tender, and the next moment so cold."

"I live in a dangerous world. You have no idea about my life."

Evangeline didn't say anything. She seemed to be processing what Dan had told her. Finally, she changed the subject.

"Where are we going?"

"Whoever is behind this will know we've escaped, probably within a day. We can count only on a day's head start. They'll find the bodies soon enough and that could set off a hunt for our vehicle. I'm thinking they may have our plate number, but it doesn't matter. It wouldn't be hard to stop every Land Rover they come across."

"How do we escape, then?"

"They'll expect us to head to Italy. At least that is what I'm going to assume. We'll go south to Slovenia instead. Once in that country we should be safe from police patrols."

"Do you know how to get there?"

"Not in detail. Look it up on the navigation system and see if you can figure it out."

Evangeline bent over the Rover's GPS system and began to work on it. They continued their slow, steady pace up the mountain. Finally, they rolled out onto an open field that sloped away in three directions. The two-track went up and over it into the next valley.

"Just as you said," Dan remarked. "We'll use the paved roads when we get to the valley and make more time.

Evangeline looked up after working with the nav system for another ten minutes.

"I've got it figured out…I think. If we head directly south, we'll hit two big lakes, Ossiarcher See and Wörthersee." She paused for a moment to think. "Do we want to stay away from large towns?"

He played it out in his head. He could race for the border and hope to cross before anyone became aware of what went on at the chalet. Or he could assume that there might be an alert out for them this very morning. In which case, if they used the main roads, there was a high probability they would be stopped either on the road or at one of the larger towns. Did he trade off time, staying longer in Austria for stealth, or make a quick run for it?

Stealth won out. He had no idea how quickly their escape would be discovered and the men found and he didn't want to bet on what he didn't know. He did know using the back roads gave him a good chance to get into Slovenia where they would not be pursued. He did not anticipate an all-Euro alert.

"Yeah. Larger towns will be more dangerous after word gets out about us."

Evangeline went back to the nav map and began fiddling again. Finally, she looked up.

"There are big towns around both those lakes. We'll have to backtrack to the southeast. It will be longer, but we can avoid large towns."

"We can't go back to Graz."

"No. We go more south. We'll head to the south of Wolfsberg and cross at a little village named Pfarrdorf."

She looked over at Dan beaming at her accomplishment.

"Great job. You're quite the navigator."

"See, we make a good team," she said still smiling at her display of usefulness.

When they reached the paved road, Evangeline directed Dan. She used the navigation system as a map source since it kept trying to route them on the main routes. They stayed on the secondary ones which, thankfully, were well paved and smooth. With the Terrain Response menu in pavement selection, he could maintain a fast pace even along the winding roads.

By dawn they had put many twisting miles between them and the chalet. The GPS system indicated a trip length of two and a half hours by using the main roads. Dan figured it would take five hours, double the time, by staying on the back roads.

The sun rose higher. Dan had Evangeline retrieve something to eat and drink from the back seats. They ate some rolls and cheese and drank some juice. Dan kept up his pace, driving with one hand most of the time.

"You're going to get us killed, driving like this," Evangeline said. "Why don't we stop and eat."

"No. We're already going the longer and slower way south. I don't want to add extra time. Don't worry, I'm not anywhere near my driving limits."

She snorted in a very unlady-like fashion. "All men think they're great drivers. Most aren't worth a crap at it."

"But you saw me in action before, so you know."

"I wasn't in much shape to pay close attention. I only know we didn't get killed. But it seemed like we came close a lot."

"Well, I'm not planning to crash. If everything goes well, we'll be in Slovenia by noon."

Dan sensed his relationship with Evangeline was getting stronger. Maybe this afternoon they'd have time to talk more deeply and he could get to the truth that was somewhere hidden inside of her.

The heavy SUV barreled down the twisting roads, following the valleys, occasionally climbing over hills to drop into another valley. He slowed down to a serene pace to pass through each village or cluster of houses at a crossroads. He didn't want to cause anyone to take notice them.

The Range Rover did its best to deliver what Dan asked of it but it was no match for a high-performance sedan even with its top speed. Still, Dan coaxed what he could while protecting the brakes and tires as they struggled to handle the two-ton load. Evangeline complained now and again as the machine lurched around corners causing her to push the wrong buttons on the GPS system.

They picked up a main road, the A2, south of Wolfsberg. Dan was tense. They had to follow it for ten miles before Evangeline said they could veer off on another back road. It was 11:00 am when they picked up the road running into Pfarrdorf. It was a small village on the Drava River. They had to cross the river at Pfarrdorf and then continue another fifteen miles to the border of Slovenia.

Evangeline turned off the GPS system and sat up craning her neck around to watch in every direction. The traffic was light. Both kept an eye out for the *polizei* but Dan wasn't sure what he'd do if they were spotted and stopped. Running would just cause a general alert that could spread to Slovenia. Right now, if they made it across the border, Dan felt the danger would dissipate.

A half hour later they passed the abandoned customs building, hardly more than a large box and crossed into Slovenia. Evangeline let out her breath as if she had been holding it since Pfarrdorf. They high-fived each other in a spontaneous gesture of success. From the border, Dan headed southwest towards the Adriatic coast with the intent of bypassing north of Ljubljana. He slowed his pace which made for a more comfortable ride.

"Anything more to eal in thc back?" he asked.

Evangeline turned back in her seat and rooted around in the bags she had brought.

"Some cheese, ham, and bread," she reported.

"Something to drink?"

"Same as before, juice and some water. Can we stop and eat? I need to stretch and I have to pee," Evangeline said.

Chapter 26

Dan found a pull-off where the Rover would not be right next to the road. He didn't anticipate much traffic but still wanted to be discrete. He pulled a blanket out of the SUV and spread it on the ground away from the road; the vehicle would shield them from being seen. They ate in silence, savoring both the food and their escape.

After eating, Evangeline went over to Dan. "Let me look at your wound," she said.

He pulled up his shirt which had a blood stain on it.

"It's bleeding a little. Should we change the bandage?"

"No, we'll wait until tonight or tomorrow. I don't have a lot of supplies and there's not a lot of blood."

"Does it hurt?"

"Hurts like hell. I think I have a cracked rib. A couple of inches to the inside and I would have been in serious trouble."

Dan pulled his shirt back down. Evangeline leaned back and looked at him.

"Have you been shot before?"

He nodded.

"How often?"

"A couple of times. It's not something I want to record and memorialize."

"But any one of those could have killed you."

He nodded. "I told you, I live a dangerous life."

She changed the subject.

"What happens now? Where do we go?"

With the immediate threat of the two men gone, Dan could see she was now beginning to worry again about his ultimate plan. Would he return her to her father?

"Those men were sent by Conti. I'm trying to understand why he'd do that."

"I told you. Aebischer wants to eliminate any trail back to him. You don't know what he's capable of doing."

"I wish you'd tell me."

She leaned forward so he would look at her. "Are you going to deliver me to Conti?"

"I don't know." He looked across the field full of grain. "What I do know is that the Watcher said you were the key. You could expose the greater evil that I need to attack." Dan turned to look into her eyes. He held them with his sharp stare. "I need you to tell me. Tell me the truth or I can't help you."

She dropped her gaze and began to shake her head. Dan grabbed her chin in his hand and turned her face back to him.

"Don't look away and shake your head. There's no more time for that. I need to know and if I know, I can help you. Tell me what's going on. Why did you run away?"

She gave him a helpless look. There was terror in her eyes. They filled with tears.

"It's too painful...too hard—"

"I'll listen. I won't judge. But I have to know." Dan held her chin and forced her to keep looking at him.

Evangeline was shaking, her breath coming in gasps.

"Take a deep breath, take a couple if you need to, and just start telling me the story."

She took a few breaths and began in a timorous voice.

"I ran away when my muh…muh…mother died."

Dan nodded. She had said that before.

"Aebischer's wife."

Evangeline shook her head violently, breaking Dan's hold on her chin.

"*Nein*. His wife died before I was born."

"Your step-mother?"

She shook her head again.

"He didn't marry again then?"

She shook her head once more.

"My sister raised me. She died and I ran away."

"Evangeline, tell me the truth. Don't try to confuse me. You said you ran away when your mother died, but Aebischer didn't remarry. Did he have a mistress?"

"*Nein*."

"And then you say you ran away when your sister died. Did both of them die? What happened?"

"My sister and my mother died."

"Both of them? Together?"

She nodded.

"What happened?"

"They said it was suicide, that she hung herself."

"Your mother or your sister?"

"Both. I ran away the night she hung herself."

Dan clenched his fists in frustration. "Which person? Evangeline, you said there were two people who died."

"No," she said in a voice so quiet he could hardly hear it. "One person…my sister…and my mother."

Her body shook with sobs as she turned her head away from Dan but not before he saw the look of abject horror in her face.

"Oh my God, Evangeline!" Dan exclaimed as the reality of what she said flooded over him. He reached out to her but she pulled away. His head swirled with emotions. What could he say? Was there anything *to* say? He sat stunned by the revelation.

"I'm a freak. I'm not good for anything. I buried all of this until you came along. Damn you!" She broke down into more sobs.

No words came to Dan. He grabbed her and pulled her close even as she tried to pull away. The horror of what she felt flooded over him; the self-loathing that accompanied the fact of her existence. When he leaned close to her, he could almost see the scenes in his head. His body was filled with her anguish, how she didn't feel normal. He understood the word she used, "freak". Her alienation from being normal, her shame, the pain over her mother/sister dying washed over him. He moaned with the burden she felt as he rocked her in his arms.

When her sobs quieted, she looked up at Dan. She seemed comforted by his embrace.

"You, you understand. You can feel what I've felt. I sense that. How?"

"I don't know. The Indian shaman said he had given me a gift. Maybe it was one of empathy or understanding. But this was more. I *felt* the pain you felt, the shame and anguish. But I also felt the love, your mother's love for you and yours for her. You had something precious. She protected you, somehow."

Evangeline nodded. "*Ja*, she protected me. He wanted to take me, but she placed herself in between. She gave herself up to him and his twisted urges in order to protect me."

"What I'm feeling is that she was strong for you. I don't get the feeling that she would leave you...kill herself."

"If I go back, Aebischer will lock me away. He suspects I know too much."

"What do you know?" Dan asked with trepidation. He could sense the story was going to get darker than even what he'd heard so far.

Evangeline shuddered. She took a deep breath. "Sophia, that's her name, let him do unspeakable things to her. But she began to fight back when he showed a desire to take me. She threatened to expose him, not only for the incest but his business dealings as well." She paused to gather herself together. "The night she died he had tied her to his bed. After he had used her, he placed a pillow over her head and smothered her." Her words now tumbled out in rapid succession, like a dam that had held flood waters back too long and finally burst.

"I was watching. After she was dead, he carried her to her room and took a rope and put it around her neck. He...he...pulled her up by her neck and hung her! Like a rag doll! In her bedroom! I ran back to my room and barricaded myself in. But he didn't come. The monster was satiated for the night. I lost one of my slippers that night. I dropped it outside of my mother's bedroom. I'm sure he found it. That night I slipped out while he was asleep.

"I ran. I went to Italy. Feriz found me. I was doing tricks to survive. He promised a better life making movies. He gave me drugs. They helped me to forget. And then you found me."

She looked at him, her face full of accusation.

"I can't go back. He killed his daughter, my sister and mother. He'll kill me. He's a monster."

Dan's face was gray. He had felt everything Evangeline described, as if he had been watching it happen. How could a man do such evil, with his own children?

"We should go to the police—"

"*Nein!* Don't you understand? He's rich and powerful. He'll just get me declared insane and have me locked away. Out of the goodness of his heart, he'll rescue me from a sanitarium and keep me locked up in his mansion. Then he can protect his secrets. If he doesn't kill me, he'll abuse me until he gets bored. No! I can't go back and I can't go to the police."

She composed herself and said in a calmer voice, "It goes deeper yet. Sophia found some documents. Aebischer is involved in money laundering for evil men, terrorists and Neo Nazi's. I know where the documents are hidden in the mansion. He'd kill me just for that, if nothing else."

"He's involved with terrorists?"

"*Ja.* His father was a Nazi sympathizer. He's an anti-Semite but more than that, he is getting rich from money laundering and arranging payments through shell companies to fund terrorists. He doesn't care. It's all about making money to him, even if innocent people are killed."

Was this the darker evil the Watcher referred to? Dan now knew where he had to strike. But how?

Chapter 27

The computer showed an incoming email. It was sent to an address that handled fully encrypted emails. Only the receiver and a few customers knew the code. The message stated that a Saudi businessman, Rashid al-Din Said, would be arriving the next day to talk about money matters. Jan Aebischer smiled a thin smile. Rashid was a cautious man. He didn't like giving out information, even on a secure email system. The unencrypted emails could be printed and left lying around for someone to find. Better to talk in person, even if that meant traveling from the mid-East to Zürich.

Rashid would fly in his private jet. He would dress in a western business suit. He would look like a typical Arab millionaire doing business and managing his money. In short, he would not attract any undue attention in a place like Zürich. Aebischer knew that whatever Rashid was asking it would involve a large fee for his services. Over the past five years, Rashid had grown increasingly active moving money around in the shell companies that Herr Aebischer had set up, and funneling them to drug dealers, gun brokers, and sometimes, directly to terrorists. The world was going crazy, but Aebischer felt safe from the growing violence in Zürich. The terrorists didn't touch Switzerland; it was an important nexus for transferring money. And Aebischer wanted to make his share from the insanity. Who knew how long it would last?

Aebischer kept a ninety-foot yacht in Villefranche sur Mer just east of Nice. The marina was a half hour drive from the airport. The boat was a converted Russian ice breaker. Aebischer had purchased it at a bargain price when the Soviet Union collapsed and state assets were being sold off cheap. He had spent millions to have it towed to the Black Sea, and refitted into a first-class luxury yacht. What Aebischer liked about the vessel was how strong it was. He could go anywhere in the world with it. If things ever got too crazy, Aebischer would close his business, retreat to his yacht, and depart for distant ports.

He had his world under control except for one thing: his daughter. Some affection faintly stirred within when he thought about Evangeline. She was so beautiful. How well she turned out being the daughter of her sister. In his mind the stirrings of affection mixed with the stirrings of desire for her. He lamented losing Sophia, but that had been necessary. She had become unstable and could have brought the wrong attention to him. His clients would have stepped back, distancing themselves from a man with a scandal erupting. He couldn't let that happen even as much as he had enjoyed her.

He picked up his phone.

Pietro Conti had not received any word from the two men. It was now mid-morning. They had set out yesterday from Graz. They told him the job would be completed that evening. Yet there was no call. Something had gone wrong. Pietro knew to trust his instincts. The men were punctual and not checking in indicated something was amiss. If the job had gone well, he would have heard. Even if it had not gone well, they would have alerted him. Pietro had to assume the worst. They were either dead or compromised so they couldn't communicate.

He started calling his connections in Austria. Within an hour the polizei around the country were told to keep an eye out for a Land Rover with a certain Italian license plate. He sat back. It was now getting worse, more complicated. He didn't like complications and neither did his employer.

When his phone rang, Pietro picked it up, hopeful that the caller was giving him news of the Land Rover.

"Conti here," he said.

"Pietro," Herr Aebischer said. "How is the recovery going?"

Pietro swallowed. "We haven't found them yet."

"But you said you knew where they were...Austria. We have contacts there. They haven't found them yet?"

Pietro had learned long ago to not leave anything out when report to his employer. Herr Aebischer had ways of finding out what went on without going through Pietro. He would learn what happened, whether or not Pietro told him.

"We located a vehicle meeting the description in Sankt Nikolai. I sent our two best men to finish the job last night. I haven't heard back from them so I have to assume the worst. I've sent out another call to find the SUV. They'll be on the run if anything happened in the chalet."

"Where are they headed?"

"My guess is Italy. That's where I contacted the assassin and that's where I said we'd make the transfer."

"He'll go back to Italy? After your men may have tried to kill him? Unsuccessfully?"

“Where else is he going to go? I think he lives somewhere in Italy.”

“You think he’ll take Evangeline to his home?”

“Herr Aebischer, I just don’t know. He could kill her and just disappear. He could attempt to transfer her to me. There is a half million Euros still in it for him. If he goes to ground, I don’t know if we’ll ever find him. If he comes to drop her off, we can get Evangeline back and maybe tie up the loose end.”

“I want my daughter back and I want this loose end tied up. I don’t like loose ends. You eventually trip over them.”

“*Jawohl mein herr.*”

Pietro hung up. If the Land Rover wasn’t found his only play was the half million. He wasn’t sure the assassin would be motivated by the money; he had not seemed to be so at the start. Maybe now with more time invested he would want the full payoff. It was his only play at this point...aside from waiting.

He began to plan for the final exchange.

Chapter 28

After their lunch, Dan went into the hidden compartment under the rear seat and pulled out a second set of license plates from Germany registered to the Land Rover. He replaced the Italian plates with the alternate ones and put the correct documents in the glove box. When he was done they got into the vehicle and drove off. Dan pulled out his secure phone and called Jane.

"I've got some information for you on Aebischer," she said after answering. "Fred and Warren have done their usual good work. How are things on your end?"

"It's why I called. We're on the move. My contact seems to have set me up. Two men came to eliminate me last night. I dealt with it and we had to leave. This guy, Aebischer and his assistant have a long reach. They found me in Austria. Maybe they had the plate numbers but maybe they found me just from the vehicle description. In any case it was quite an impressive achievement."

"Are you and the girl okay?"

"She's okay. I'm sore. I think I've got a cracked rib or two, nothing life threatening."

"What's next? Are you headed home?"

"No. But I'm not taking her back. Her father may kill her or have her locked away because of what she knows about him."

"Did she say what that was?"

"Yeah. He's involved with terrorists. He funnels money around for them, hiding it in shell companies, keeping it from being traced. It also sounds like he's central to getting funds to gun dealers, drug dealers, and terrorists directly."

"That's the suspicions we came up with. But the boys couldn't uncover any smoking gun. The man has strong walls built up around his activities. They couldn't penetrate them except to learn he works through a lot of companies, most of which probably don't do any real business. They couldn't find anything to pin him to illicit activities."

"He runs a tight ship. Try Pietro Conti. He's the one who arranged this job for me. He's Italian but I don't think he lives in Italy. Aebischer lives in Zürich. I suspect Conti does as well."

"If you're not going back to Venice, where are you going?"

"I'm thinking about meeting Conti under the guise of returning Evangeline."

"Why would you do that if he tried to double cross you?"

"Doesn't make sense, right? Except for the half million yet to get paid. He might think I'd risk meeting him for that final payout."

"He'll be setting you up again—"

"I'm counting on it."

Evangeline put her hand on Dan's shoulder when he said he wasn't taking her back. He turned to her and she smiled at him.

"Jane, can you come over? I need to drop Evangeline somewhere safe. You could talk to her, get all the info you can about Aebischer while I take care of Conti."

"I'll talk to Henry and get back to you."

"You can stay in a safe house. I assume you have some in Italy."

"We have them all over. I'll call you back. Where are you?"

"On the road heading to Italy right now. I'll wait for your call before contacting Conti."

"Thank you," Evangeline said after Dan hung up. "You have lifted a huge weight off of me."

Dan nodded in acknowledgement.

"I don't think you work for a security firm, going around selling systems to corporations."

"That is all I can admit to, officially," Dan replied with a smile.

"You are a good man."

She was quiet for a few miles.

"Do you think I'm a freak? I know I'm not normal. I didn't have a normal mother."

"I don't think you're a freak. I think you are a beautiful girl with a good head on her shoulders. Someone anyone would love to know and be close to. Your mother was a brave woman. She defended you so you could have a chance in life. In the end she gave her life for you. Now you're getting your life back. You should be proud of your mother. She didn't think of you as a freak. She considered you special. What you've been through could have destroyed most people. It almost did with you, but you survived. You are strong and can do some good in this world."

"Quite a speech. But thank you. No one's said kind things like that to me." She took a deep breath and went on. "I know you aren't going to send me back, but I still think we'd make a good team. You're the only man I've ever met that I can trust."

"Evangeline," Dan turned to her while driving, "I'm just the first man you met that you can trust. They'll be more and you have the insight to figure out which ones are and which ones aren't. You just have to keep remembering how special you are and the legacy your mother left you. Be proud of her...and yourself."

"But my father, the man whose genes I carry..."

"He's a bad man, and his father might also have been a bad man, but I don't think those get carried through one's genes. They come from decisions you make, from what you learn and absorb." He reached over and touched her arm. "Focus on the lessons from your mother, lessons of courage and commitment and sacrifice."

She shook her head. "I hear you, but there's so much pain. I ran from all of that when I escaped. I wanted to bury it. I felt tainted, like there was something wrong with me and I shouldn't live. But now...now maybe there is."

She leaned over and kissed Dan on the cheek. "Thank you."

Late in the afternoon, they approached the village of Branik. Dan slowed down. He was looking for any small homemade signs that had the word *osmica* on it.

"What is it?" Evangeline asked.

"It's an open-door event. The local farms twice a year get to act as restaurants. You can go there and enjoy, literally, the fruits of their labor. There's local meats and vegetables and some great local wine that never gets exported. It's an old custom, some say going back to the days of Charlemagne."

Evangeline gave him a confused look.

"You don't know who Charlemagne was?"

She shook her head. Dan turned back to the road wondering about her education.

"Do you know where to go?" she asked.

"No, that's why we have to look for the signs. They're not all on the same day, so we must watch for the signs. They'll be homemade so look sharp."

On the way out of town, Evangeline spotted a sign and called it out with excitement.

"Good eyes," Dan said.

"I'm not only a good navigator, but a good lookout as well," she said with pride in her voice.

Dan turned onto the small road that soon led to a neat farm with pastures and vineyards around it. They pulled in and were greeted with a smiling welcome. The common language was Slovene but the country had been part of so many other empires in the past that many of its people could get along in either halting Italian or German.

Slovenia had been under the Hapsburg Monarchy and the Republic of Venice at one time. It was part of the Austria-Hungary Empire until 1918, and more recently Yugoslavia, until that country's breakup and the country achieved its independence.

A long row of tables was set in a courtyard protected from the wind. The evening set in, overhead lights were turned on to give a festive atmosphere to the space. The rich odors of the evening mingled with the aroma of good food. There was a stew and casserole with a charcuterie of sausages, ham, and steaks along with a variety of potatoes, plump tomatoes, and the local red and yellow wines of the region. On his previous visits to Slovenia, Dan always enjoyed their surprising taste, always a bit different at each farm. The host's and other guest's conviviality relaxed both Dan and Evangeline. For the evening their troubles were put aside under the balm of friendly hosts and guests. It was like sitting in on a large family reunion, an experience new to Evangeline but one that brought a bright smile to her face.

It was after 10:00 pm when they finally bade their hosts goodbye and strolled back to the Range Rover. Evangeline slipped her hand into Dan's. When they got to the SUV, she turned and kissed him full on the mouth, wrapping her arms around his neck.

"Whoa girl," Dan said when she pulled back. "Let's not get carried away."

Her smile started to fade as she stared up at him.

"I think the wine is making you feel a bit more amorous than you should."

"You don't like me? You don't like my kiss? I thought you said I was beautiful."

"I do and I did. But it doesn't have to lead to something more."

"It's okay. I can handle it."

"Maybe you can but I'm not sure I can."

She tilted her head to one side.

"Look you're very beautiful. More so since you've gotten healthy. Your smile is like a thousand-watt light shining in my eyes—"

"It sounds like you're attracted to me."

"That's my point. I don't trust myself to get too physical with you."

"So you keep me at arm's length. You want to keep your emotions bottled up? Didn't you work on my emotions...to get me to open up? But you give yourself a different standard. That's not right."

Dan smiled and took a deep breath. "Maybe you're right, but let's just be close friends tonight. We had a good time and let's enjoy that with no other agenda. Like when we snuggled. Can we do that?"

She exhaled forcefully. "You are so frustrating." She tried to glare at him but it didn't work. "Okay. It's been a lovely evening. I have never experienced one like it in my life, so thank you."

She patted his cheek.

"Are we going to do more driving tonight?"

Dan shook his head.

"I'm not ready for that. Too much wine. Let's drive down the road and find a secluded spot to pull over. We'll sleep in the Rover tonight if that's all right with you. There will be no record of our passing through."

"Some way to end a date. You sure know how to impress a girl."

She smiled at him and got into the Rover.

Dan planned to sleep outside the SUV while Evangeline slept in the back seat. He'd wrap himself in the thermal blanket for the night. Before bedding down, he walked off from the vehicle and called Jane.

"Are you coming?" he asked.

"Flying out tonight. I'll land in Rome tomorrow. Where do you want to meet?"

Let's meet in Rome. I'll drop my vehicle off in Venice and take the train to Milan. I'll rent a car there and drive down. We can be there late tomorrow."

"We can talk more after we get together. There's not much on Conti as well."

"I'll get something out of him. After you take Evangeline, I can get to work on arranging my meeting with him."

"To collect the money?"

"No, to collect *Signore* Conti."

Chapter 29

The meeting with Rashid was held at Aebischer's mansion. Increasingly, he worked from there to avoid the public. They sat in a large library in comfortable leather chairs. Tea had been served along with some cheese, fruit, and sweets. There was wine on a side table but Aebischer knew Rashid would not avail himself of it. Still, Aebischer kept it ready as a token of hospitality. They spoke in English.

"I need twenty million Euros transferred next week." Rashid took out a sheet of paper and pushed it across the coffee table to Aebischer. "It is to go to those recipients in those amounts."

The banker looked at the list. There were five names on it. Bulat Zakayev was the first name on the list. Next was one he recognized as a person who dealt in explosives and finally, three mid-Eastern names attached to what he guessed were front companies.

"Who is this first name? I don't recognize it."

"You recognize the others?"

"Most. It's my business to know these things."

"He replaces Guzim Lazami who was assassinated a month ago."

Aebischer nodded that he understood. "He was getting ready to complete a large order, for heavy weapons as I remember."

Rashid looked steadily at Aebischer. He didn't know how much the man knew about his activities and Aebischer always insisted on not wanting to know too much. Rashid felt that was a convenient front. The banker wanted to know all that was going on around him. He sensed a kindred spirit of wanting to control everything he touched.

"That was your order?" Aebischer asked.

Rashid just smiled.

"That's a Chechen name," Aebischer continued. "His company is located there? It may raise notice to move six million to a bank in Chechnya."

"I will have him open an account here in Zürich."

"And one in Lichtenstein and one in Malta. I need to run the money through more than one account."

"It will be done. You are planning something large? I have heard things and Guzim was preparing a large shipment when he was killed."

"I didn't think you wanted to know what was going on." Rashid smiled at the banker. He understood him but liked to try to disturb his sense of control. It was better for those Rashid dealt with to always be wary of him. It made them more careful and less likely to try to double cross him.

"I don't want to know details, but it is helpful to be aware of what will be going on around me." He paused for a moment, then continued, "This second name, Yevgeni Kuznetsov, is a person who has access to explosives as well as weapons. And he is with the Russian mafia."

"You are correct. We have had to change some sources. We have had setbacks in our struggle against those who support the Zionists. Guzim was the most recent. But we persevere. We cannot be stopped in the end."

Aebischer nodded. Rashid knew appealing to his anti-Semitism was always useful. His father had had close ties to the Arab world as well as the Vatican and had used them to help Nazis after the war.

"These last three companies I don't recognize. I assume there are other accounts the funds can flow to. Stopping here will allow a trace back to you...and we don't want that," Aebischer advised.

"Go through some of the companies that you set up for me. Create the invoices for the appropriate goods and services as you usually do. When it hits those accounts, I will make sure the funds get passed further along before they reach their destination."

"My fee will be twenty percent for this work. It is very large and requires much care on my part."

Rashid looked steadily at the banker. Aebischer looked calm, as if he felt in control. Rashid sensed he needed to feel a little more vulnerable.

"You should not get too greedy. The large funds are put to immediate use. Those who I fund perform for me, sometimes paying with their lives. They are not trying to get rich off me. I find you useful to my cause, but don't become a burden."

Aebischer didn't flinch. "I trust you respect the careful work I do to insulate you from outsiders. Intelligence agents try to penetrate my network regularly. I spend large amounts of money to keep everything secret. I thought you understood that."

Rashid kept his eyes on Aebischer. "I do understand that. I also understand greed and overreaching. I'm pointing out that such behavior would damage our relationship. And there are serious repercussions to such damage."

Rashid stood. "I will be going now. I think we both understand each other. Let me know when all this has been completed."

"How quickly do you want to put your plans into operation?"

"Let me know when the money has been fully dispersed. That is all you have to do."

"As soon as I receive my fee, I'll begin. Everything will be ready ahead of time."

Rashid nodded. He would pay the fee this time, but he would not allow this infidel banker to dig larger and larger fees out of him. The man had an impressive security record, but Rashid could send a message to him; a message advising him to not disturb their relationship.

He reached out his hand for Aebischer to shake and then turned to leave.

After Rashid's departure, Jan Luis Aebischer sat down and thought. The Arab was clear in his threat. But he didn't say no to the fee. He picked up his phone.

"Pietro, have you found the assassin?"

"No Herr Aebischer. He has gone to ground. I don't think he is in Austria any more or we would have found him by now."

"And he hasn't contacted you?"

"*Nein mein Herr*."

Aebischer considered this. He was not happy. Evangeline knew too much. She was unstable and now she was in the hands of a capable killer who felt he had been double crossed. This was a dangerous situation and Aebischer didn't like his lack of control over events. It made him feel vulnerable.

"Pietro, I want you to find out everything you can on Bulat Zakayev. He's a Chechen arms dealer. Also find out more about Yevgeni Kuznetsov, the Russian arms broker. I want to know what Rashid is planning. It's something large, and explosives will be involved."

"Is that a good idea? To get that much information?"

"Do not question me." The words came out slow and ominous. Aebischer was getting angry. "We have an uncontrollable situation because your men failed. I do not want another uncontrolled situation developing. What Rashid is planning might be rash and place us in some danger. I need to know so we can be properly shielded."

Chapter 30

Dan awoke early. He slowly unwrapped himself from his blanket. Stiffness had set in and he struggled to get upright. He spent some time moving his body, a little at first and then more as the complaining muscled began to unwind.

He rolled up his blanket and then stopped. There was the sound of soft crying coming from the Rover. He walked around and opened the rear passenger door. Evangeline was lying on the bench seat sniffling and whimpering, still half asleep. Dan reached out his hand and touched her head.

"What's wrong Evangeline?"

"I don't know," she said in between quiet sobs.

He raised her head up and scooted into the seat. He cradled her head and upper body in his arms as she lay across the seat.

"We had a nice evening and we're going to have a better day today, one without threats or danger."

"That's just it," she said. "Last night was so nice. I started to miss my mother. We never got to share anything nice like that...and we never will."

Her sobs became stronger, racking her body as she buried her face in Dan's chest. All he could do was hold her and rock her gently back and forth while she cried and cried. Her tears flowed; it was as if a dam holding years of grief had burst and the flood waters of anguish were rushing out.

"It's all right; I've got you. You're grieving for your mother. It's normal. It has to come out at some point."

"I have never let myself go there," she said between sobs. "It seemed too dangerous, like I would get lost."

"Maybe it was, but you're safe now, so you can let it out."

Some minutes later she calmed down, spent. She wiped her nose on the blanket.

She looked at him. "I miss her so much."

"You kept all of that emotion bottled up. Maybe you were too scared. Now it can come out; now that you're in a better place."

"But it's so painful," she said in an agonized voice. "She was my best friend. She was only fourteen when she had me. We were like sisters...we were sisters...in a perverted way..."

"In a good way as well. The relationship between the two of you was special, not only due to the circumstances but also to how strong your mother was. It's okay to be sad but don't be afraid to enjoy the good things now. I lost my wife and she isn't here to enjoy last night's experience. That's something she and I will never share. It's what I have to live with. But I know she wants me to enjoy life. I just hold her in my heart and never let her go."

Evangeline reached up to stroke Dan's cheek and slide her arm around his neck. "How can you understand so well?"

"The gift...from the Shaman. It seems like a blessing *and* a curse. Now that I've recognized it I can't turn it off. I felt the emptiness you felt that your mother was not there to enjoy last night. I also felt the sense of guilt on your part. Don't buy into that, whatever you do. You have the right to enjoy life. She gave up her own so you could do just that. You're free to take control over your life now."

Later that morning they set out on the road, heading straight to Milan, bypassing Venice. In Milan Dan parked the Land Rover in a garage at Milan Linate Airport. Then they took a taxi to the Milano Centrale train station, an imposing, bombastic structure begun in the early twentieth century. The roof stretched over the equivalent of ten soccer fields providing cover for the largest flow of trains in Europe. Muscular statues adorned the façade with winged horses predominant. The building was a mix of baroque, classical, and art deco. A repeated adornment was the bundle of rods and axe, a symbol of ancient Rome which Mussolini adopted for his fascist logo. The effect was one of intimidation more than grandiosity.

The walls of the main gallery presented large murals on the wall depicting various cities in Italy and the rest of Europe. There were art deco mosaics that depicted the artist's interpretation of the wonders of rail travel. From this six hundred by sixty-foot space you descended a grand staircase onto the boarding platform. Light streamed in from the curved glass skylights set in the ceiling of the main gallery and the boarding platforms.

The pomposity of the building was lost on both Dan and Evangeline. He was on full alert for threats and she had seen it before and had very little interest in its history. From Milan it was a three-hour ride to Rome. They could relax.

Once in Rome, Dan rented a car under his alias and, as they were leaving the station, called Jane.

"I'm on the ground," she said after answering. "Where should we meet?"

"Do you have a car?"

"Yes."

"Meet me on *via della Travicella*. It's southwest of Roma Termini near *Parco Regionali Appia Antica*." Dan had worked out a secluded place to meet.

"How the hell am I supposed to find that?"

"Look it up on your GPS. It's a small cobblestone road with walls on each side in an empty industrial section. No one can see what's on the road because of the walls. We can meet and you can take Evangeline. Tell me what you're driving."

Jane told Dan and they agreed to meet in a half hour.

When Jane turned onto the *della Travicella* she saw Dan's car pulled up close to the wall on the right side of the road. She parked behind him and walked to the car.

"Right on time," Dan said. "Jane, meet Evangeline. Evangeline this is Jane." He spoke Italian which Evangeline and Jane both understood.

"So, you're the girl who's causing such a stir."

Evangeline looked at Jane with a critical eye. She saw a good looking, mature woman who had an air of competence and success about her. She took an instant dislike to her, instinctively thinking of her as a rival, one of two women with whom Dan was connected. As she was evaluating her assets against Jane's, Dan spoke up.

"Ladies I want you to get along. Things are too critical and too dangerous for any spats."

"I apologize," Jane said. "I didn't mean any criticism by my comment. But Dan's rescuing you did seem to stir up a firestorm of activity."

"It's not my fault." Evangeline replied with some snippiness in her voice. "In fact, I didn't want him to help me at first." Then she smiled and put a hand on Dan's shoulder, claiming her territory. "But now I realize that he's helped me recover my life. I don't know how to thank him."

"That was the one good thing Dan mentioned to me before I authorized the operation. If nothing else, he could save a teenager's future."

Dan interjected. "Now we're entering a new phase. Evangeline, you're going to go with Jane. You'll be safe and I need you to tell her everything you can about Aebischer's activities." He pointedly did not call him her father. "You can trust her. Everything you told me you can tell Jane. She'll listen and understand. She won't judge you. It will all help."

Evangeline started to shake her head in the negative.

"If you don't want to go into some of the details, that's fine. No one knows about them but me. But you need to make it clear to Jane who Aebischer is and his role in your...mother's death."

"What are you going to do?" Evangeline asked.

"I'm going to meet with Conti. We're going to have a talk and then I'm going to turn him over to Jane."

"Who are you?" Evangeline asked. "And who is this woman? She is your boss?"

"She's my boss, and my helper. Who we are is not important. That we can help you that we can stop Aebischer and bring him to some justice. That is what is important."

"You can't arrest him. My testimony won't stand in the face of his money and bribes. I told you he's built up a case against me for mental instability, even insanity."

"Don't worry, we won't be arresting him."

"Then what...?" Evangeline stopped mid-sentence. She began to suspect Aebischer's fate might be worse with these people.

"We better wrap this up. I don't want to stay here too long," Dan said. "Where are you going to go?"

"We've got a place north of Milan. We'll drive there this afternoon." She gave Dan the address.

The two women got out and walked back to Jane's car.

"You don't have any change of clothes," Jane noted.

Evangeline shook her head. "We never had a chance to get any."

Jane slipped her arm through Evangeline's, "Then we'll do some shopping before we leave for Milan."

Evangeline started to smile at the thought of new clothes.

Dan watched the women drive off. He was about to get into his car when he saw an old man coming down the road. He was pushing a cart filled with junk. He looked like someone collecting other people's trash to try to find something of small value that he could use or sell.

But Dan noticed something else. The man made direct eye contact with him, unusual for a street person; they did not look for confrontation. An enemy in disguise? Dan thought not. The old man had that intensity he'd seen in other places. In Mexico City and most recently in St. Mark's Plaza in Venice. Dan hesitated outside of his car.

"Who are you?" He asked as the man stopped beside the car.

He had the dark, intense eyes of the woman in Venice. "Who I am is not important. You know what I am."

He spoke in a thick, Sicilian accented Italian.

"You have something for me?" Dan asked.

The man nodded.

"You're going to meet Pietro Conti—"

"How did you know?"

"Always the unimportant questions. What is important is for you to know he will try to double cross you, to ambush you. He has sent for some men to help him."

"But I still need to meet with him."

The man nodded. He reached into his pocket. Dan stiffened but didn't move. The man pulled a piece of paper out and handed it to Dan. There were two addresses on it.

"Meet him here." He pointed to the first address. "It is a good spot."

"And the second address?"

"You watch from there. You can get to the roof and deal with the men who will try to kill you. But remain vigilant. Pietro may have a final surprise for you. Be ready."

He turned to go.

"How did you find me here? This is a secluded spot. I picked it for that purpose."

The man turned back to Dan. "A Watcher knows. We are watching...helping...where we can."

With that he shuffled off pushing his cart.

Dan marveled at this network of people. They lived on the margins of society, humble, ignored by most, avoided by others. But they had a gift and used it to help him. That gift could probably make them fortunes but they didn't pursue gain in the material world. They pursued success on the spiritual side of reality and he was somehow part of their plans.

He got into his car and punched in Pietro Conti's number.

"*Signore* Conti," Dan said when he answered. "I have the girl and it's time to make the exchange."

Pietro's eyes widened. He couldn't believe his luck. There was no way he was going to find such a secretive man, a man whose face he was not even sure of, but here he was, on the phone, wanting to make the exchange. Pietro felt he had been given a new opportunity to complete what had become a failed mission.

"*Sì, sì*, we can make the exchange. When you didn't show up I was worried. I heard through the news about the attack at Feriz's compound, but nothing from you."

"You seem to have a leak in your organization, and someone who doesn't want me to succeed. We ran into some trouble."

"Trouble?" Conti played dumb. He wanted to find out what had happened.

"Just something that delayed me a bit. The important thing is I have the girl and she is in good condition, healthy."

"*Bene, bene*. Where should we meet?"

"I will tell you just before we do the exchange. How soon can you be in Rome?"

"Tomorrow."

"I'll call you tomorrow and let you know what to do."

"I don't even know your name. What do I call you?"

"You don't have to call me anything. Just answer when I call. Don't forget the money. And Pietro...remember this will be a dangerous time for you."

Dan hung up. He would tell Pietro the address later, after he had checked everything out and set up his counter strike.

Pietro Conti sat back in his office in Zürich. His head swirled. Could he now finish what Herr Aebischer had charged him to do? The opportunity now presented itself, but there was something unsettling about the assassin's calmness. He should have been angry but he wasn't. He should have accused Conti of a double cross; that was what the assassin had to think. The men Conti sent were supposed to kill him. Pietro had by now learned that instead, both were dead. And the man had acted as if nothing important had happened and that it was not connected to Pietro. Was the assassin setting him up?

Dan drove around the ring road to the address given him by the Watcher. He turned off onto A90 and into an industrial and warehouse section of the city. He drove around in the late afternoon until he found the spot. It could not be seen from any drivers passing by. The warehouses were older; not in neat, orderly rows, which resulted in small, semi-closed courtyards. The warehouses surrounding the meeting point had flat roofs where Dan suspected Pietro would position shooters. The Watcher spoke of a double cross. Pietro was going to try to kill him...again.

The second address was an unfinished apartment building with a high, flat roof on two levels that could be accessed from stairs leading up from the top parking level. It looked like the developer had planned to use the roof as part of the amenities of the building. From the upper one he had a good view of the roofs surrounding the courtyard where he would meet Conti.

If Conti posted shooters on the roofs, Dan would see them from his vantage point. Because of this information from the Watcher, Dan could neutralize the ambush before he drove into the courtyard.

Chapter 31

Jane took Evangeline into the historic center of Rome. The Galleria Alberto Sordi was a luxurious shopping mall, six stories set in a beautiful old building. It was located on the east side of the *Piazza Colona*, a plaza with a Doric column honoring the emperor Marcus Aurelius which had stood since AD193. They spent over two hours lost in shopping amidst the high-end shops, struggling to find more practical clothes among the fashion items in the stores.

They stopped at one of the many eateries in the shopping galleria for lunch. After leaving, Jane led them through some side streets, being careful to check for tails, where they found a more practical sports-oriented shop to complete Evangeline's new wardrobe. With the shopping complete, Jane headed north to Milan, her relationship with Evangeline considerably improved.

Pietro Conti called his employer, Jan Luis Aebischer.

"Herr Aebischer, the assassin called me. He wants to make the exchange. He says he has Evangeline and she is in good health."

There was a pause on the line. "He wants his final payment. Did you get the other information I asked of you?"

"Not yet Herr Aebischer. I'm working on it. But don't you want me to get this situation resolved?"

"Yes. Make sure you close the trail down. Bring Evangeline to Zürich, to the residence. It will be good to have her home again."

"*Jawohl.*"

When the phone went dead, Pietro punched in another number.

"*Am fluss Alte Bücher*," Old Books by the water, the voice said. The speaker spoke German with an Austrian accent.

"I'm not looking for a book, but I have a cleaning project in a private library. Do you have an opening in your schedule?" Pietro asked.

"How many do you need?"

"Three should be enough. Have them bring all their tools. I'll go over the work with them and they can choose what to use."

"When do you need the work done?"

"Later this week. I'm waiting for a call."

"You know there will be a surcharge for expedited services."

"I understand. How much will the bill come to?"

The man on the other line answered in code, dropping off two zeroes from his pricing.

"Three men, rush service…that will come to one thousand Euros."

"That is fairly steep," Pietro replied.

"You're free to hire anyone you like. Thank you for calling."

"*Nein, nein.* Don't hang up. The price is fine. I'm sure I can convince my employer."

"I don't reserve rush work. You accept now or find another service provider. If you accept, I'll expect a fifty percent deposit within twenty-four hours. Otherwise, I will not hold the schedule open. You know where to send it." The man hung up.

Pietro stared at his phone. This adventure of rescuing Evangeline was getting expensive. Of course, if the cleaners did their job, the assassin's half of the payment could be used to pay them and Herr Aebischer would be money ahead. Pietro knew his employer thought about such matters.

He put those thoughts aside and started arrangements for the money transfer of 50,000 Euros to an address in Munich. The address housed a small used book store that eked out a living in a city known for its publishing industry. There was an abundance of books expressing a conservative political theme but the proprietor, a solidly built compact man, seemed to hold no prejudices in either direction. Max Richter always expressed his love of the art of the book, its printing and binding. He could be relied on to recount interesting stories about many of the older books in his shop. The stories were always entertaining, if sometimes fanciful.

In the store there was a small backroom where Max's main work was done. It was done without drama, with the greatest security, and made him quietly rich. He kept his wealth hidden behind the persona of a musty book lover making a modest living involved in what he loved...books.

That afternoon the book seller logged into a Swiss bank account under one of his aliases. He checked the balance and noted that 50,000 Euros had been transferred to his account. The instructions on the account caused it to immediately be split up and moved into three different banks under different accounts for various front companies. The funds were for organizing and arranging meetings and presentations for corporate clients and their guests. He smiled.

Max picked up his phone and called three men. He explained he had a job for them in Rome and they should be ready to depart within an hour's notice. There would be fifteen grand in it for each of them. He would be calling them in the next twenty-four hours to send them on their way. They were to drive together, but stay in separate hotels if an overnight stay was required. They were to bring all their tools which meant sniper rifles, submachine guns like the MP5 along with semi-automatic pistols. The details of the job would dictate the tools used.

Dan called Conti to tell him they would meet on Saturday. He'd call the day of the meeting to give him the time and place. Pietro felt frustrated. He couldn't set up any trap ahead of time. He'd have to improvise, or rather the men the book seller sent would have to improvise. They were professionals, though, and could do the job, even without advance planning. One nagging worry was that the two men he had sent to Austria were also professionals. *Let's hope the book seller's men are better.* He would be glad when all this was behind him.

In the three days Dan had to wait, he picked up his car in Milan and drove back to Venice to collect more gear. On Saturday morning, already in his observation spot on the roof of the apartment building, Dan called Conti and gave him the address. He instructed him to meet at noon. At 10:00 am he watched as a car drove into the courtyard. Three men got out including Conti. They engaged in animated discussion with much pointing in different directions. The trunk was opened and the two men pulled long guns out. They had scopes and looked to Dan like sniper rifles. The two left and each went to a nearby warehouse and forced open the door. *Headed to the roofs.* He would have eyes on them from his vantage point two blocks away, just as the Watcher had implied.

Conti pulled what looked to Dan like an MP5 submachine gun out of the trunk. He opened the rear passenger door and laid it inside. Then he got back into the driver's seat. The windows were tinted dark enough that Dan couldn't see inside.

The watcher said to be careful of a surprise. Was there another shooter inside the car?

Within ten minutes the men appeared on their separate roofs. The courtyard was now quiet with only Pietro's car sitting there, waiting for Dan to arrive.

Dan relaxed. It was only 11:00 am. *Let them stew for an hour. The tension will only fatigue them.* Pietro Conti had set him up in Austria and was now trying to do it again. *He probably didn't bring the money with him.* Dan allowed a cold, grim smile to cross his face. *You've tried to double cross me once too often and now you will pay the price.*

He relaxed, keeping a loose eye on the two men set up on the rooftops. His ribs still hurt and he stiffened up when he was still for too long. The men were professional. Dan could see them sighting in the rifles, adjusting their scopes, and making sure they were concealed from anyone looking up. The men on the roofs had radios and Dan noted that they had checked in fifteen minutes ago. Suddenly the driver's door opened. Conti got out and ran over to the side of one of the warehouses and stood facing the wall. *He's relieving himself. Must be nervous.* Conti kept looking over his shoulder and when finished ran back to get into the car.

At five minutes to noon, Dan tightened up the bullet proof vest he had brought, ignoring the pain it set off in his rib cage, and slipped his M110 sniper rifle over the parapet wall. He had loaded the magazine with subsonic rounds. With the suppressor, no one would hear it in the courtyard. The men on the roofs had finished a check in with their radios. Dan assumed it was Conti they were calling.

When they were done, Dan put his sights on the farthest sniper. He settled his breathing in the familiar pattern. There was only Dan, his rifle, and the target. The deadly connection formed; the sense of a link between him and the target grew strong and solid. There was almost a Zen-like quality to the task, an unconscious process that involved a deadly art as well as mechanical technique. His hand closed and he squeezed the trigger. The rifle fired with a muffled *whoomp* and kick. The sniper had been sitting up, his head just above the edge of the roof wall. His head exploded and the body dropped back to the roof.

Dan barely noted the kill and turned his rifle to the second target. The connection came quicker this time but the results were the same.

After taking out the second target, Dan hurried down the stairs, put his rifle in the back seat of his Peugeot and gunned the car down the ramp to the street. He pulled slowly into the courtyard. Conti's car was sitting there. Dan stopped a hundred feet away. He waited. A minute later Conti opened the door and got out. He walked to the front of his car and stood there. Dan noted that Pietro was standing so he wouldn't block anyone shooting from the back seat. *Conti's surprise will be coming out of the rear on the passenger side.* That was good; nothing between either of them. *We'll both have a clear shot.*

Dan got out. He had his M4 slung over his shoulder at low ready. It was set on full auto but it was no match in rate of fire to the Heckler and Koch MP5. However, Dan had the advantage of a vest. He hoped the HK MP5 was chambered in 9mm, not .40 caliber; his vest would stop a 9mm round. Even so, he didn't look forward to an automatic weapons shootout.

"Do you have the girl?" Pietro shouted.

"Yes. Do you have the money?"

Pietro shouted he did.

"Get it out," Dan directed.

"Where's Evangeline?"

"When I see the money," Dan responded.

"You can put away your gun. I'm not armed," Pietro shouted.

"That's smart of you, but I'll hold on to it just the same. Show me the money."

Dan didn't move. If he had to trade shots with the man in the back, he wanted some distance between them. His M4 fired a 5.56 mm high velocity round that was very accurate. He would have a slight chance of hitting his target more accurately than his opponent.

The day was getting hot. Sweat started beading on Dan's forehead. He resisted the urge to wipe it down. It would all come down to timing just like a fast-draw contest in the old west, although this one done with far more deadly weapons. The .44 revolvers of the old west were not known for their accuracy, nor were the shooters. Many shots would often be fired before one opponent dropped.

Pietro looked up, wondering when his snipers would finish the job. Nothing came from the roofs.

“Are you looking for divine intervention? There’s no help from above. Just do what I say and you’ll be fine.”

Pietro turned to go back to the car. Dan watched him in his peripheral vision. His eyes were fixed to the rear door. As Pietro pulled open the driver’s door the rear door started to open. Dan brought up the carbine and leveled it at the door. The MP5 poked out first and the shooter let off a burst that missed Dan. He responded with a burst at the door window. The man must have ducked. He lurched out and fired a second round simultaneously with Dan. Dan’s burst hit the man in the chest and head. He flopped back against the door frame and dropped to the ground.

One of the 9 mm round slammed into Dan’s vest punching him hard to the ground. He fought blacking out. Pietro started to get back into the car. From the ground Dan fired off a long burst through the windshield on the driver’s side. Pietro didn’t finish climbing in. He had just escaped being torn up by multiple rounds. He stepped back and put up his hands.

“Don’t shoot me,” he cried out.

From the ground, struggling to get his breath back and remain conscious, Dan swung the carbine towards Pietro.

“Come forward...get on the ground...face down.” Dan squeezed out the word in a hoarse, raspy voice.

Pietro heard him and obeyed.

“I didn’t want to do this.” He was beginning to whine. “It was my employer. He wouldn’t let you just do your job and get paid. I warned him not to try to double cross you.”

Dan was getting his breath back. Now his whole rib cage was on fire. “Shut up.” Dan struggled to his feet. “If you open your mouth before I tell you, I’ll hurt you.”

Dan walked over to the shooter. He was bleeding out from multiple wounds to his torso. He looked up at Dan. Dan would get nothing out of him. Blood was seeping out of his mouth and he could hear the sucking sound in his chest from a bullet wound. As Dan looked at him, the man eyes went sightless and his head slid sideways. He walked back to Pietro.

"Get up." Dan motioned for him to walk to Dan's car. Once at the car, Dan had him lay face down on the pavement with his hands behind his head. Dan reached into the back seat and pulled out a roll of duct tape. He put the M4 inside the car and took out his 9 mm.

"Put your hands behind your back. If you move, I'll shoot you in the ass and you'll never sit comfortably again."

Pietro began to shiver but did as ordered. Dan secured his wrists behind him. He told him to get up. Pietro struggled and Dan finally had to help even though it ignited the pain in his chest. When upright, Dan wrapped tape around Pietro's mouth and eyes. He led him to the trunk of the car and pushed him inside. After closing the lid, Dan walked back to Pietro's car. The briefcase was inside but the money was faked, stacks of cut paper with a few one hundred Euro notes on the top and bottom of each stack. He'd make Pietro pay for that conceit.

Dan left the briefcase in the car. With a last look around he climbed in and drove away. The authorities would find the bodies by Monday; there would be no leads. With the briefcase, it would look like a drug deal gone bad.

Chapter 32

Use of the safe house outside of Milan was arranged in Langley by Henry through the Technical Services Division. Even so, Jane received a call from the Chief of Station in Rome asking how long she was going to be at the house and what she was doing. She told him to contact Henry back at Langley. If he wanted him to know more, Henry would inform him. Henry called her an hour later.

"Jane, how long are you going to be using the house? I've got a call from Springhouse, the Chief of Station."

"What did you tell him?"

"I told him he wasn't cleared to know and really didn't *want* to know. He only needed to know I'm using the house," replied Henry.

"Did he back off?"

"Of course, but the sooner you get done with things the better. He may start snooping around."

"I've got the girl here. We're debriefing her about her father. There's some interesting stuff coming out."

"Where's Dan?"

"He's meeting the contact. I haven't heard back yet. It's a dangerous situation. The contact tried to have him killed before."

"He's meeting him alone?"

"He works alone. He'll be okay." Jane said the last mostly on faith. She was worried.

Henry sighed. "Keep me posted."

"Will do, and Henry?" Jane paused for emphasis. "Tell Springhouse if he knows what's good for him, he'll stay far away from this place."

Dan drove north. He called Jane.

"I'm so glad to hear your voice," Jane said when she answered.

"I've got Conti in the trunk of the car. We're on our way to the safe house. There are three bodies back in Rome. The authorities will assume it's a drug gang killing."

"Conti tried to set you up again."

"Yeah. He wasn't very smart about it either. Listen, this guy's got to have a lot of information that could help us. I'm going to stop on the way to see what I can get out of him."

"Don't do what I think you're going to do."

"He'll arrive safely. But he might be a little worse for the wear. Remember he's tried to kill me twice."

"Don't do anything rash. When should I expect you?"

"I'll call you when I'm close. How's Evangeline?"

"She's doing well. We're getting along. She's started to open up. She's also worried about you. I think she has a major crush on you."

"No thinking about it. She wants me to run away with her and live happily ever after."

Jane sighed into the phone. "Ahhh, if it only worked that way."

On the way to Milan, Dan turned off on a small side road and drove until he came to a wooded spot off the back road. He parked the car out of sight of the road and got out, carefully stretching his body which was growing stiff from the cracked ribs and bruising through the bullet-proof vest.

He opened the trunk. Pietro lay in a heap inside. Dan bent down and grabbed him under his armpit and pulled him into a seating position. He swung the man's legs over the trunk sill and pulled his upper body free. Pietro tumbled to the ground with a muffled grunt. Dan bent over him and grabbed his arm again.

"Get up," he said. His voice was tired, his body was tired, and his mind was tired.

Pietro struggled to his feet. Dan led him into the woods. He stopped at a large tree and pushed Pietro up against it. He pulled the tape off of his mouth. Pietro let out a sharp yelp as the tape tore at his face. Next, he pulled the tape over his eyes which produced the same outburst. Pietro blinked and tried to rub his eyes with his wrists still taped.

"*Signore* Conti, you have made me very angry. I warned you to not do that but you've tried to double cross me and kill me. Twice."

"I was told to do that. I didn't want to, believe me. I had no choice."

"Shut up. I don't want to hear your excuses. I'm tired. I've been shot twice and I'm in no mood to listen to crap from you."

Pietro stopped talking. Dan took out his 9mm with its suppressor attached.

"I'm going to ask you some questions. If you don't answer me and answer truthfully, I'm going to respond by putting a bullet through your foot. You will feel a great deal of pain and you may never walk properly again. Each time I ask a question, if I don't think you're being honest, I'll shoot you higher. I'll go from your feet to your knees to your hands and arms. I'll riddle your limbs with bullets. You won't die but you'll be a cripple for the rest of your life. *Capische?*" Pietro looked at him, his eyes wide with fear? "*Verstehen Sie?*" Pietro finally nodded.

"Please, can you free my wrists? My circulation is cut off, I can't feel my hands." He held up his hands which were purple and swollen.

Dan took out a knife and sliced through the tape. Pietro peeled the rest from his wrists and began to massage his hands.

"Now, who do you work for?"

"He doesn't want me to divulge his identity. He insists—"

Dan fired a shot into the ground next to Pietro's foot.

"Herr Aebischer," Pietro shouted. "Jan Luis Aebischer."

"That's better. Now who is he? What does he do?"

Pietro swallowed hard and hesitated.

"No more warning shots. The next one goes straight into your foot."

Pietro lunged at Dan. He was solidly built and although shorter than Dan probably weighed the same. He grabbed Dan's right arm and pulled the pistol to one side. His head hit Dan in the chest and drove them both backwards. Dan fought to keep to his feet. Pain from his ribs and chest shot through him almost causing him to pass out. His gun dropped from his hand. Pietro swung his right hand at Dan's face in an awkward overhand punch. Dan countered, raising his left arm. He twisted to his left, letting Pietro's thrust go past him and tried to trip him as the man's momentum carried him forward.

The trip didn't work and Pietro turned to renew his attack. Dan knew Pietro would attack his wounded chest and rib cage. He knew he was vulnerable with such fresh wounds. Pietro lunged forward, trying to tackle Dan who danced sideways, grunting from the pain of the movement. Pietro's body missed its target and Dan brought a hard righthand down on Pietro's head. The man staggered back. This time Dan closed, shooting a left-hand punch straight into Pietro's nose, smashing it flat. Blood spurted out. Pietro threw two ineffective punches at Dan which were easily deflected.

Dan closed in. He needed to end the fight before Pietro could hurt him or pick up the gun. He had no illusions as to the results if Pietro got the upper hand. He sent a decoy jab at Pietro's head with his left and as Pietro put both arms up to shield himself, Dan swung his right hitting Pietro in the side just below his rib cage. The man bent over in pain. Dan swung a hard overhand-left down on his face. A sharp pain came from his fist as he felt Pietro's cheek bone crack.

Dan's anger now overflowed, masking his own pain. He followed up with more lefts and rights, striking Pietro in the face and torso. The man kept staggering but remained on his feet. Dan rained blows and finally, his face bloody and his eyes puffed almost closed he collapsed to the ground. Dan gave him a last kick in the chest and stepped back to retrieve his pistol.

He flicked the safety on and stuffed the gun into his belt. Pietro was twisting on the ground, struggling to regain his breath from Dan's beating. Dan stood there panting. The pain now returned as the adrenalin stopped flowing. He turned to the car and retrieved the duct tape.

Pietro was still on the ground when Dan returned. Dan prodded him with his foot.

"No, no more," Pietro said in a hoarse voice.

"Turn over," Dan said.

Pietro turned over and Dan pulled his arms behind him and taped his wrists together.

"Get up," Dan commanded.

Pietro struggled but could not regain his feet with his arms tied behind him. Dan reached over and helped pull him erect.

"We start again. I enjoyed pounding you and will enjoy it again, almost as much as shooting you, if you don't answer properly. Now, who is Aebischer and what does he do?"

Pietro spoke in a muffled voice. His cheekbone was cracked, his nose still bled down over his lips and onto his shirt. His eyes were almost swollen shut.

"He is a banker."

"Be specific."

Pietro took a deep breath. "He'll have me killed for saying more."

"I'll cripple you and then kill you for saying less. Either way you lose. Your game is over, it's my game now."

"You don't understand. There's a very dangerous man out there. Aebischer will send him after me."

"The man who sent those three I killed today?"

Pietro nodded.

"We'll get to that later. But now I want an answer or I start shooting.

The fight seemed to have gone out of Pietro. He sagged back against the tree.

"Herr Aebischer is an expert at hiding money, where it comes from and where it goes. He is very skilled at this. As a result, certain groups use his services to move large amounts of money. They pay large fees to do so but their anonymity is assured."

"Who are these groups?"

Pietro shook his head. "You can shoot me, but that's just it. I don't get to know. It is all very compartmentalized. I can't tell you because I don't know."

Dan put the pistol up against Pietro's knee. "I'm going to start at your knee because you tried to fight me."

"Please, I don't know. But I do know that he keeps records...in his mansion. He's meticulous about that." Dan pulled back to watch Pietro's bruised and swollen face.

"Where is that?"

"Zürich. But you'll never get in. It's heavily guarded."

"But you've been inside."

Pietro nodded.

"You'll draw me a layout later. What groups is he working with?"

"I don't know who they are. there are gun dealers, drug dealers, I think, and possibly terrorist organizations. But as I said, I have no details."

"Quite a collection of associates. What's his history? How did he get into this work?"

"I don't know his background except that his father was a banker and was suspected of being a Nazi sympathizer. He's very private. And he's not a person you want to cross."

"We'll see. Now who sent those three men? Did you call them?" Dan's voice had gotten lower, more dangerous. His anger started to well up again. This man had sent men to kill him. Dan wanted to know who operated these men. If it was Pietro, his life was forfeit. If someone else, they were going to receive Dan's vengeance.

"I placed a call, at Herr Aebischer's direction, believe me. There's a man in Munich. He is a book seller. I don't know his name. I don't even know where his shop is located, only that it's in Munich and probably along the Isar River. He calls it "*am fluss Alte Bücher*". He arranges everything. He hired the men and sent them."

"How much did you offer to pay him to kill me?"

Pietro flinched at the tone of Dan's voice.

"One hundred thousand Euros. Fifty down."

Dan thought for a moment. He'd gotten what he needed and Pietro was now beaten into submission. He'd let Jane and the others finish milking him for information.

"You're going back into the trunk, mouth taped. I'm taking you to a place where others will interrogate you further. If they don't get your cooperation, if they suspect you are trying to deceive them, and they are good at figuring that out, they will turn you over to me again. And I will be very happy to inflict more pain on you. Do you understand?"

Pietro nodded. After stuffing him back into the trunk, Dan settled himself into the driver's seat and started out for Milan again.

Chapter 33

Dan arrived in the early evening. He pulled into the garage, and after the door was closed, opened the trunk. Two large men pulled Conti out and took him into the house.

"What did you do to him?" Jane asked when she saw Pietro.

"He tried to get away and we had it out. He'll be all right, but he came close to getting parts of him shot."

Just then Evangeline walked into the room. She gasped as she saw Pietro and stepped back. Jane left the room to keep her from coming back inside.

"He looks like someone beat him up. What happened?" she asked.

"He tried to get away from Dan...after he tried to have him killed."

"*Oh mein Gott!*" she exclaimed. "Is Dan all right?"

Jane nodded her head. "He's fine. But I don't want you to go in the room."

"Don't worry. I don't want Pietro to see me. He works for Aebischer. I don't like him."

"Did he do anything to you?"

"No, but he supports my father's business."

"We're going to find out more about that. You can help in that area."

Jane went back into the room where Dan and the others were standing. "Take Conti down to the basement, to the interrogation room. Check his injuries and clean him up,"

"May I have some water, please?" Pietro asked in Italian. His words were slurred with his broken and swollen jaw.

Jane gave him a stern look. "When I'm ready," she replied in German. "If you're cooperative, you'll be treated well. If you're not, things will not be good for you. I will personally see to it."

Pietro looked at her face. It was set hard and uncompromising. He nodded. The two men shuffled him downstairs.

"How are you?" Jane asked Dan when they were gone.

"Sore as hell, but I'll survive. I could use a large glass of water and a good whiskey."

"I'll get it for you." Jane pointed to the front room. "Go wait in the living room. There's someone who wants to see you."

When Dan entered the room, he saw Evangeline sitting in one of the overstuffed chairs. She jumped up when she saw him and ran across the room. She leapt on him wrapping her arms and legs around him like a child. Dan grimaced but didn't make a sound. He tried to ignore the pain while he held her as she hugged him.

"I'm so happy you're here. I was worried. Jane told me you were going to meet with Pietro. I told her he could not be trusted. I wanted to call you to warn you but Jane said you knew and would handle the situation. And you did. You're here!"

She dropped to the ground much to Dan's relief.

"Are you okay? You look a little pale?"

He smiled. "I'm okay. I had some trouble which made my ribs hurt some more. I'll be fine though. I'm glad to see you are doing well."

"Oh, I'm so sorry. I shouldn't have jumped up on you, but I'm so glad to see you. I've worried so much for the past three days." She stepped back. "Sit down, here on the couch. I want to sit next to you. I won't hurt you I promise."

Jane came in with a tray and glasses. She had water, two whiskeys and a lemonade for Evangeline. Dan took the water glass and drained it. Then he picked up the whiskey and took a large sip.

"Ahh. That makes the day better."

"Don't I get something to drink?" Evangeline asked.

Jane pointed to the lemonade. "No alcohol now but we'll have wine for dinner."

Evangeline pouted for a moment and then smiled again. She seemed happy that Dan was back. They spent a half hour in casual conversation which included Dan complimenting Evangeline on her new clothes and asking how everyone was getting along. Fred and Warren came in and greeted Dan.

"You took these guys into the field with you? You must like living dangerously," Dan said with a smile.

"Don't be mean. They're doing a great job and we're going to need their skills. Evangeline has helped us fill in some gaps about Aebischer, but we'll need these guys to give us a more complete picture."

Jane got up to prepare something for the group to eat. "Evangeline, show Dan his bedroom. He needs to clean up and there's a change of clothes for him. Dinner in a half hour."

In Dan's bedroom, Evangeline reached up and kissed him full on the lips.

"Easy girl," he said. "I'm pretty sore and we're still just close friends."

She looked up at him, her eyes filled with longing, "I'm going to change your mind about that. Once we've taken care of Aebischer, things will be different."

"Who said anything about 'we' taking care of him?"

"Well, I can't live a normal life until he's out of the picture, so I should help."

"Evangeline, just help Jane with information and leave the rest to me...and the others on this team. It's what we do and I don't want you to be a part of it. It's not part of your life or your world."

"But you're part of my life and world...and I know more about dangerous people than you might imagine."

Dan smiled at her. "You may, but I must insist you leave this to me. You help with the information. Help Jane and the others find out everything they can. Now let me get a shower and change. I'll see you downstairs."

Evangeline gave him a pouty look and left the room.

In addition to Fred, and Warren, Jane had brought two field agents with her. When they came upstairs after locking Conti in room in the basement, Jane introduced them to Dan.

"This is Marcus and Roland. I brought them over to help us."

The two men nodded to Dan. They were both big, each over six feet tall and burly. They moved with an athlete's grace, showing an economy of motion for such large bodies. Even under loose clothing, one could see their strength. They were polite but could not hide the clues that they were tough men, men who did not shrink from doing hard things.

"Where did you guys serve?" Dan asked.

"Delta Force," Marcus said. "Does it show?"

"Like a billboard," Dan replied.

Roland just stared at Dan.

"How 'bout yourself?" Marcus asked.

"Army sniper."

"The guys that get to hang out on rooftops while the rest of us do the real fighting," Roland said.

Dan looked at the man, who stared back at him, giving no hint of his thoughts.

"The guys that cover your ass while you're down in the street," Dan said.

"Be nice boys," Jane said. "We all have different parts to play."

"You're right," Dan said. He got up with a smile and went over to shake hands with the two men. "Glad to have any help I can get." The last was said without much conviction.

"Are you going to feed Pietro?" Dan asked after dinner. They were relaxing in the living room. Dan was on the couch with Evangeline snuggled up against him. She would not be denied a prime spot close to his side. Jane sat on one of the chairs, with Fred and Warren across from her. The latter two didn't contribute to the conversation, knowing it was out of their area of expertise. They just wanted to absorb and learn.

"He can wait. I know you softened him up, that he capitulated, but I don't want him to get a second wind and try being a tough guy again. It's better not to have to break him a twice. It just wears down the body."

She put her drink down on the coffee table. "He can sit the night and get very uncomfortable. I'll talk to him tomorrow."

"He's probably got this macho idea that a woman isn't to be considered a threat. He may not react to you like he did me."

"Marcus and Roland will take care of any attitude that comes up."

"So, what's the plan for Aebischer? I'm sure he's the one the Watcher was talking about."

"Kill him," Evangeline said. Everyone looked at her. Warren's mouth dropped open. She looked around. "He's a monster." Looking back at Dan she said, "I told Jane what happened. He deserves to die. He killed family and who knows who else."

Dan looked back at Jane. "She has a point. He must not get off."

"I agree," Jane responded. "But we need to know what he knows. I want to capture him and take him somewhere, not here, but somewhere more private and get everything he knows."

"What's Henry say?"

"That's what Henry wants as well."

Chapter 34

Jan Luis Aebischer sat in his study. Pietro had not called in. He had arranged to meet Evangeline's rescuer yesterday to exchange the money for her. He should have reported back by now. Aebischer knew Conti had used the services of the book seller from Munich. The man had access to the best in the business. With his services it should have been easy to take this man down. He wanted the additional money; he would hope the other attack had not been orchestrated by Conti. Aebischer had confidence the man's greed would overcome his sense of caution. It would only take one shot when he stepped out of his vehicle and it would be all over. Yet, no phone call.

Finally, Aebischer called Pietro. His phone rang and then went to voice mail. He hung up. Something was very wrong. He punched in the number for the book seller. He loathed making direct contacts with the operatives he had to use. It could create dangerous trails back to him. But he needed information and Pietro was out of communication...or worse.

"*Am fluss Alte Bücher,*" a man said upon answering the phone.

"Have you heard back from the work *Signore* Conti assigned you?" Aebischer asked.

There was a long pause on the other end. "This is highly irregular. I do not speak about client's work to others."

"*Signore* Conti works for me and I haven't heard back from him about the cleaning project."

"Neither have I. Don't call me about this again."

The phone went dead. Herr Aebischer looked across the room. Rarely did anyone talk to him that way. The book seller's name was Manfred Fraczek but Aebischer suspected that was not his real name. He knew where his shop was located, near the Isar River, but that was all. He forced himself to remain calm and think through the problem. That's what it was in the end, a problem, one to be solved.

Fraczek hadn't heard back either which was unusual. Aebischer assumed the book seller would be informed about the job when it was completed. And now that Aebischer had called, the man was sure to be worried.

He took inventory of the recent past events. Two hit men were dead in Austria, the authorities wondering who they were and asking questions. They wouldn't find anything. The men couldn't be linked back to him...except for Conti? That might be a problem. Now Conti was missing and, presumably, the men sent to kill the assassin were dead. Was Conti dead? If not, was he in the hands of the assassin? That would lead the killer back to him. Aebischer did not like the prospect of that.

Events had gotten complicated. Even if he could stay insulated from any investigation, there was an assassin loose, a man who probably wanted revenge and who probably knew where to go to get it.

And in the middle of this mess, Evangeline was still not under his control. He recalled her image, long blonde hair, beautiful blue eyes, well developed even as a teenager. She had grown into such a beautiful young woman. He wanted her back. He wanted her, like he had wanted her sister. If he could get her back, she could be such a pleasure to him in his old age. He felt a stirring in his loins, something that had been lacking since her sister died and she ran away. The child knew too many secrets as well. Getting her back solved so many issues for him.

He shook his head. *Time for day dreaming later*. Now he had to deal with Rashid as well as an assassin. Unfortunately, he couldn't just disappear for a while. He had to wait for Rashid's funds to be transferred and then go to work to split it up and move it around. Then the funds had to be paid out at the right moment, before his work was fully complete. It was too rich a deal to let it go; and his reputation would be badly damaged.

No, he had to wait for now.

He picked up his phone again and called Conti. It went to voice mail again. Next, he called the captain of his yacht in Villefranche-sur-Mer.

"How soon can the *Nordstern* be ready to depart?"

"I am installing a new generator. It will be a week before she's ready to go. Do you have a destination?"

"No. I will contact you later. A week is just about right. Then I want to go off on a long cruise. I'll tell you where later."

The next day, Jane spent hours downstairs accompanied by Marcus and Roland. Pietro was not resistant, now looking to save himself from what he suspected could be his death. His details about Aebischer's mansion and work habits corroborated what Evangeline had told them. He confirmed a journal that chronicled the various clients Aebischer dealt with over the years and promoted himself as one who could interpret the meaning of the coded entries, a reason for Jane to keep him alive.

Still, it was surprising to Jane how many gaps there were in Pietro's information. Aebischer kept his life very private, even from his closest assistant.

Jane made copious notes on the transactions and activities which Conti could remember. The yacht and its location were confirmed. Jane called James Springhouse, the Station Chief, and asked him to have someone keep an eye on the yacht. She didn't want Aebischer sailing off one night, never to be found.

After a grinding day of grilling Pietro, Jane came upstairs. Dan had started making dinner for everyone. Evangeline was trying to help out. She was happy to do anything if it kept her close to Dan. Jane smiled and poured herself a whiskey.

Dan put the large pan in the oven and wiped his forehead. Both he and Evangeline looked frazzled but satisfied. Dan grabbed a beer from the fridge and popped the cap. He took a long swig.

"How did it go?" He asked. "You really put in some hours downstairs."

"It was productive. That's what it takes. Grind it out. Get all the information while the client is cooperative. When they're fatigued, you sometimes get more insights. Their guard is down."

"I'm not sure I've got the patience for that."

Jane smiled and lifted her glass to Dan. "That's why we do different jobs."

"Okay, what's the plan?" Dan asked.

Evangeline stopped what she was doing to listen to the answer.

"Later, after dinner. We'll discuss it and then I'll call Henry and wake him up." Jane looked at the stove. "Smells good, what are you making?"

"*Lasagna alla Bolognese.* It's genuine, with ground beef and pork, good pasta, a ragù I've been cooking for most of the day, and a *besciamella* that Evangeline helped with." Both Dan and Evangeline beamed at Jane.

"Well, this calls for a bottle of good wine." She turned to Fred. "See if there is a Sangiovese downstairs." Turning back to Dan, "Are you going to feed Conti any of your culinary delight?"

"*Absolut nicht!*" Evangeline exclaimed. "He doesn't deserve such good food. Not when I have something to do with it."

"I guess that settles it," Dan said.

The meal was sumptuous. No one talked about Conti or Aebischer or any plans. They kept the conversation light and social. Later that evening, everyone retired to the living room. Dan had told Evangeline earlier that she couldn't be in on the planning, but she refused to be excluded.

"I have things to contribute," she told him.

"Didn't you tell Jane everything?"

"There are a few things I know that will help in your preparation, if you're planning what I think you are."

Dan gave her a steady look. She stared right back at him, her eyes bright and shining with affection, excitement? A mix of both it seemed to Dan.

"You are quite the schemer, aren't you?"

She just smiled at him. "So, I need to be in the room. And don't worry about secrets. I'm good at keeping them. I've kept one for years." Her voice and smile faded at the thoughts stirred up in her mind.

Dan relented.

The others sat down and pulled their chairs close together. Evangeline claimed her spot snuggled up against

Dan on the couch. The conversation took place in English. Evangeline could speak and understand both English and Italian along with her native Swiss German.

"As I said, Henry wants to capture Aebischer. The Swiss authorities won't help for obvious reasons. We're not supposed to operate in their country and Aebischer is too rich and connected. Claiming he broke laws won't help. We don't have direct evidence to connect him. Evangeline is right when she says her accusations wouldn't help either."

"It has to be undercover then," Dan said.

"What have you found out about security at the mansion?" Jane asked Warren Thomas. He was the tech wizard who had been snooping through Aebischer's electronic accounts and files for most of the day.

"It's pretty sophisticated. It has a strong firewall. The weak link is the wireless connection to get out to the internet. Someone made the mistake of using the same pathway for his security and his work, connecting with his office downtown and various banks as well as the general internet. That's protected but I was able to crack it after five hours of work. I've been in and set up a bug that will recognize my computer as part of the network, but it won't show on the network diagram."

"You can turn off his security?" Dan asked.

"Better than that. I can keep it running but blind it. I can loop the videos so everything looks normal. It won't be hard. The external view really doesn't change much. When you go in, no one will see you."

"There's a better way in," Evangeline spoke up.

Everyone turned to look at her.

"Aebischer has a secret tunnel that goes out to the back of the property. There's a cover hidden in a planting bed in the foliage just inside the fence. The trees screen the property from the road. It's dense inside the foliage. The top looks like a sewer cover.

"The tunnel leads into the basement of the building. There are hidden elevators from Aebischer's bedroom and office to the basement so he can leave undetected if there is a break-in."

She smiled at everyone with satisfaction at offering a game changing piece of information.

"You didn't tell me everything," Jane said. Her voice was tense.

"It's okay," Dan interjected. "She's being helpful, even if on her own terms."

"Can it be opened from the outside?" Jane asked.

Evangeline shook her head. "I don't know. We, my s...s...mother and I explored it from the inside. I suppose you can pry it open."

Jane turned to Warren, "Can you tell if the cover is alarmed?"

He nodded. "I can check on that. That wasn't a focus on my exploration of the system. Give me some time tonight and I'll have an answer for you in the morning."

They talked late into the night. The plans were set. Henry would be appraised. Fred would remain behind. Warren would monitor the security from a van nearby the mansion. Marcus would join Dan in the kidnapping while Roland stayed behind, much to his frustration, to keep an eye on Pietro.

The van would be outfitted with the electronic gear Warren needed to monitor and control the security system. He immediately set out to make a list of what to bring with them. Jane would drive the van which would be parked near where the Aebischer's escape tunnel emerged. Evangeline loudly insisted on going with them and Jane finally relented after Dan gave his support. She would allow the girl to ride with her in the van.

Chapter 35

Rashid made five wire transfers, from five different companies he controlled, to five separate accounts owned by Herr Aebischer, the amounts, all different, totaled twenty million Euros. Aebischer's work would be to run the funds through shell companies until the trail was lost in a maze of transfer records. It would finally end up in three legitimate "front" companies controlled by Aebischer.

One account would be used to pay the Russian mafia boss, Kuznetsov, for one hundred and fifty kilos of C-4 plastic explosive along with ten cases filled with the German Panzerfaust 3 anti-tank grenade launchers with their attendant warheads. The weapon could be operated by one man and fired indoors, unlike many rocket launchers, due to its minimal back blast. The armaments would be distributed to six different terror cells throughout Europe.

Another payment was destined for Bulat Zakayev, the Chechen gun dealer. He was to provide a fresh supply of AK47 rifles, MP5 machine guns, and pistols, along with ammunition, and hand grenades to the terrorist cells.

The third payment would be dispersed amongst the terror cells to supply them with support funds to carry out the planned attacks.

Rashid smiled. The planning had taken a year and a half. The cells did not know their targets or their exact roles and wouldn't until days before the attacks were to begin. Leaders were instructed to train their groups on the Panzerfaust 3 but did not know where the weapon would be used. Similarly, the assault teams were readied and prepared to use the AK47 and MP5 automatic weapons but were not informed where or when an attack would take place.

When Jane last talked with Henry, she told him about Aebischer's involvement in money laundering, not for just tax cheats but for various underworld groups, some of them possibly connected to terrorists.

"We've seen an uptick in internet traffic hinting at a large operation in Europe, either one large attack or a series of coordinated attacks. Aebischer might be involved in this." Henry said.

"It could be. How soon do you expect the attacks to take place?"

"That's just it. We don't know enough to say. We've alerted the governments involved but they're reluctant to raise the threat profile without some idea of how imminent the threat is.

"If we can get our hands on Aebischer's ledgers, we might find out more. If it's a large operation it will take a large amount of money and planning."

"The agency is monitoring known arms dealers," Henry said. "That might give us a clue. When are you going in?"

"A few more days. I'll alert you when we depart for Zürich. The plan is to transport Aebischer back here to

Italy. Here we can find out what he knows without any interruption."

"We can't spend too much time at the safe house. We'll have to find another place."

"You work on that, I'll work on getting him and his ledger out of Zürich."

Aebischer's nervousness increased with each passing day. He had received the funds from banks in Cypress, Beirut, Malta and Gibraltar, all known havens for hiding funds and doing anonymous transfers. Aebischer had done his part and moved the money through his myriad accounts until the funds were parked and ready to disperse. Now he had to wait for Rashid to authorize the release. Aebischer didn't know exactly when he was to disperse the payments. He could be waiting for a week or more. Meanwhile, there was an assassin loose.

The planning went on back at the safe house. Conti was kept in the basement's secure room. He complained only mildly. A doctor had visited him; there was not much to do about his broken jaw. It would heal. He was still working to make himself important enough to keep alive. Between Conti and Evangeline, the team assembled a clear picture of the security around the mansion.

"The front gate is strong and heavily guarded. Like most he thinks an assault would come from the front. People forget about attackers just going around the obstacle," said Marcus as they went over the security picture. "Even with Warren's help to neutralize the cameras, the guards make infiltrating from any direction difficult."

The consensus was the tunnel that Evangeline spoke of was the best way inside.

"I can neutralize the alarm on the cover in the system," Warren said with pride. "The more complex problem will be the cameras inside the mansion. There are cameras throughout the interior."

"Can you create loops for them as well?" Jane asked.

"Yes, but there's more activity inside. Someone would more easily see a repetition of a pattern or not sec an expected activity like security making the rounds."

The discussions went on as the team gnawed away at the problem. They were determined to come up with a workable plan. Dan's frustration grew. He wanted to get on with the mission. He usually worked alone in a much looser environment where had to improvise. The planning was starting to seem obsessive.

"How many security personnel are we talking about, inside and outside?" he asked.

Warren answered, "I've recorded one at the main gate, two going around the house outside and three or four men inside. I can't be sure.

"Why so few outside?" Marcus asked.

"He's relying on the cameras," Dan answered. He turned to Warren, "Why aren't you sure of the inside number?"

"Two of the men inside seem to roam randomly, so it's hard to pin them down. There's definitely one at the monitors, but there may be more in the rotation. I haven't been able to single each one out to be sure."

"Seven men at the most. We can eliminate them," Dan said.

"We don't want to do that," Jane said. "We're not in the countryside of Croatia. This is Zürich and the police will come quickly if an alarm is triggered."

"I can keep that from happening...at least from being transmitted," Warren said.

"All right. That helps." Dan ignored Jane's reference to his attack on Feriz's mansion. "If Marcus and I can locate the inside guards, we can neutralize them. With suppressed weapons the guards outside may not hear what's going on." He turned to Warren, "Do they interchange between inside and outside?"

Warren frowned. "I don't know. I haven't seen it, but I can't say it doesn't happen."

"All right, we go in, find the inside security, take them out, grab Aebischer and get out via the tunnel," Dan said.

"And Aebischer will depart via the same tunnel when he hears a shot inside, even if it's not heard outside," Jane said.

"And you'll be at the exit to grab him," Dan responded.

"But if an alarm is triggered," Jane said, "the exterior guards will come running and now you have a full-fledged gun battle, something we need to avoid."

Dan got up and paced the room. His frustration showed. If it were him alone, he'd go in and take out the inside security, then grab Aebischer and leave either with him going willingly or knocked unconscious and over his shoulder.

Evangeline watched Dan as he paced. She followed the conversation and was getting increasingly worried. These people didn't realize how methodical and ruthless her father was.

"You must not underestimate Aebischer," Evangeline said. "He will have backups in place. I hope you find them all. You said you could stop his wireless alarm from going out, but what if he has a wire connection? Is that possible?"

"Yeah, it is. I can't see that from my equipment, though."

"We'll have to find the phone lines going to the property and cut them," Dan said from across the room.

"Do we just cut all the power lines?" Warren asked. "That would simplify all the other issues."

"And alert him to an attack. No, if he has multiple ways to communicate, we don't want to alert him. Let him think the phone lines are working. It will give him a sense that help is coming. Help that will never arrive."

Evangeline still worried. Aebischer would have a backup, maybe more than one. He would not rely on just one or even two systems to protect him. He had too many secrets.

Chapter 36

Dan went downstairs after leaving one of the long sessions discussing all the facets of capturing Aebischer. He unlocked the door, and leaving his weapon outside, went in to talk to Pietro.

The prisoner gave him a wary look as Dan entered. He was sitting on a mattress on the floor. There was a single chair in the room along with a bucket for taking care of his business in an emergency. When used, Roland had the unenviable task of emptying it, which he protested strenuously about, until Marcus agreed to share the onerous chore. There was nothing else in the room. Pietro was led to a washroom daily which, hopefully, negated the need for the bucket.

Dan took the one chair as Pietro moved to get up off the mattress.

"Sit," he said.

Pietro sat back down. His face still showed bruises from the beating Dan had delivered.

"You're making a big deal about this ledger and how it's in code. I'd think you were making it up just to save your ass. However, Evangeline has confirmed what you said." Pietro's face showed his relief. "Now I need to know where to find this ledger. I won't have much time to go looking for it."

"I told the woman I wasn't sure—"

"That's not good enough." Dan leaned forward. He could see the fear in Pietro's eyes.

"You saw it. Otherwise, you can't say it exists. Where did you see it?" Dan's eyes bore into the man. He wanted nothing more than to pound him again. His anger rose again at the thought of what Pietro had done and how close to getting killed he had come.

Pietro swallowed hard. "In the office. It was on his desk. I am pretty sure it was the ledger book."

"Tell me in detail what you saw, the circumstances around it, everything."

Pietro recounted how once when he came to see Herr Aebischer the book was on his desk. He had been making entries. He closed it when Pietro came in and put it in his safe. Aebischer, noticing Pietro's interest, told him the book was an insurance policy, for the two of them.

"We have to crack a safe to get the book."

Pietro nodded. "If he hears you coming, he'll bolt but he'll lock the ledger in his safe."

From Pietro's description, Dan knew the safe was too heavy to move. Blowing the door would destroy the ledger, wiping out the information they were seeking. And there wasn't going to be enough time to drill it open or crack the code on the lock. In any case they didn't have a safecracker on the team.

Dan would have to get Aebischer to give him the combination. He could do that, but it would take time. From what Conti and Evangeline had told him, Jan Luis Aebischer could be a tough man to crack.

It was Thursday. The team had been developing its plans for two days. Dan could wait no longer. It was time to act. He pointed out that Aebischer knew Conti was missing and so would presume the assassin was still alive and might now know who he was. Aebischer would not want to just sit around and wait for Dan to show up. And the threat of a massive terror operation was not going away. If Aebischer was involved then the best chance of interrupting the operation was to remove him. Taking him out of the picture could stall any funds transfers and that could interrupt supplies needed for an attack.

Fred had discovered that a large amount of money had flowed into Aebischer's accounts, millions of dollars from suspect banks. He could not uncover the source of the funds, nor could he follow the subsequent transfers. He couldn't even be sure if they were still in Aebischer's control. The lack of clear information and timeline called for acting now, even if all the details had not been worked out.

Thursday night the team left the safe house, Dan, Jane, Marcus, Warren, and Evangeline. They drove through the night towards Zürich in three vehicles. Jane and Warren were in the van posing as security trade show participants on their way to another event with their electronic gear to demonstrate to corporate purchasers. Dan and Evangeline were tourists. She had been given a new passport indicating she was from Freiburg, a town in southern Germany, but had been raised in Switzerland, which would explain her Swiss German accent. Dan was her uncle from America, over on holiday. She was taking him back to see the family. Marcus had a U.S. passport and was a tourist exploring the Alps.

Since Switzerland had joined the Shengen agreement, a treaty that largely abolished border checks, there were no stops at the border crossings unless you had something to declare. All the vehicles had *vignette* stickers on their windshields indicating they had prepaid for the toll roads. Jane expected all the vehicles to just make a slow pass through the border control along with all the other non-commercial traffic.

The drive would take about three and a half hours. They would stay in three different hotels near the Zurich airport used for business travelers on budgets. Aebischer lived in a large estate house a half hour north of downtown Zürich, just outside of Embrach. The home was located on twenty partly wooded acres in a hilly section outside of the suburb. A single road ran through the area servicing the few wealthy estates on the hillside. They would find a location on the backside, near the escape tunnel's exit where Jane could park the van.

The next morning, Friday, dawned cool and cloudy. The team met after breakfast in a parking lot on the northeast side of the airport, near the executive jet terminal. The two cars were left in the lot and the team transferred into the van and drove north to the mansion to scout the property while waiting for dark.

Evangeline seemed excited as if they were on a great adventure. The others were more somber, knowing how many ways the operation could go wrong. Warren sat fidgeting with his fingers, lacing and unlacing his hands. Marcus sat back with his eyes closed, not asleep but almost in a meditative state. Dan kept an alert posture, watching through the outside mirror for any tail.

In fifteen minutes, they were in Embrach. From there they changed to a small road that wound through the forest on the hillside overlooking the town. They passed the entrance to the mansion. Evangeline leaned over Dan's shoulder to get a good look. He could hear her labored breathing in his ear as she saw the property, filled with so much trauma, that she left two years ago.

"Tell me where the escape tunnel comes out," Jane said over her shoulder.

Evangeline studied the side of the road as the van slowly drove on. When they passed another estate, Jane stopped.

"It seems we've gone beyond the property at this point. We're about to head down the other side of the hill."

"It looks so different from the street side," Evangeline said. "I'm not sure I can identify the spot."

Dan turned to her, "You have to try again. We can drive back, more slowly, but we can't go poking around the fencing for hours. This is not a neighborhood where strangers go unchecked."

"Does he have something like a getaway car stashed near the tunnel exit?" Marcus asked. "If he just climbs out of the tunnel, he's got a long walk to get anywhere and he'd be vulnerable."

"I don't know," Evangeline said.

"Good point," Dan added. "Let's watch the turnouts while Evangeline studies the grounds."

Halfway around the property Evangeline spoke up. "I think this may be the spot."

At the same time Dan touched Jane's arm. "Look to the right. There's a car hidden in the woods. Turn here."

There was a narrow path leading off the road. Only about twenty yards into the woods, the path turned to the right and opened up. An SUV was parked there, facing out for a quick exit.

"There we are," Jane said. She backed the van up and turned it around next to the other vehicle. "We can park here during the operation and wait for all of you to exit."

Dan looked at Marcus. "Let's check out the exit. We'll have to pry it open tonight."

Marcus nodded and they both got out.

"Be careful," Jane called out. "You stay here!" She commanded Evangeline who was getting up to go with Dan.

"No you don't," Dan said. "You're part of the team, so you follow orders. Just me and Marcus for now."

He closed the door. They walked to the edge of the road and crouched behind a bush.

"We can get into the cover just off the road before we come to the fence. It's ideal for us." Dan said.

They sprinted across the quiet road and disappeared into the woods. Within twenty feet they came to the fence. It was made of black painted iron, about eight feet high with sharp spikes on top of the uprights. Both men carefully examined the material, trying to find any alarm triggers or evidence of electrification. The fence seemed to serve only as a mild notice of the privacy of the property.

"He's probably relying on his security. This fence wouldn't stop anyone."

Marcus nodded and quickly climbed up and threw himself over, landing on his feet. Dan followed him.

"We'll split up. Go about fifty feet, turn and come back," Dan said.

Ten minutes of walking a grid through the undergrowth, Dan heard a whistle. *He must have found it.* He went towards the sound and found Marcus standing on the cast iron plate. It did look like a sewer cover.

"The girl said it was latched with a wheel she and her mother had to turn. The wheel probably opens and retracts pins locking the plate in place," Marcus said. "That won't be easy to just muscle open. There's only two of us and we'd need a hell of a pry bar."

"We can't hammer on it from the outside either. That will ring through the tunnel and someone will notice."

Marcus stared at the cover and scratched his head. "Maybe we can dig around the edge. There has to be a tube forming the exit. It's probably made of concrete. Chipping that away won't make so much noise and then we can get to the mechanism from below the lid."

Dan thought for a few minutes. "That's going to be a crap load of work, but looks like it's the only way."

Marcus smiled. "Afraid of getting some blisters on your hands?" He flexed his large arms. "I grew up doing construction while going through college. I'm not worried about a little digging."

"Wow, look at those guns. Tell you what, you dig, I'll supervise."

"Not on your life, buddy. We're in this together. If I've got your back, you gotta help shovel. Let's get going. I'll make a list of what we need on the way back. We don't have much time to waste."

Chapter 37

Back near the airport, they stopped at a hardware store. Marcus had a list of tools: shovels, a digging bar, two pry bars, two cold steel chisels along with a file to sharpen them and two hammers. He included a stout, thick wooden dowel rod and a pair of bolt cutters. Dan went in to make the purchase. His German accent was good enough to not raise any questions with the clerk.

"Can you get this done today?" Jane asked.

"Have to," Dan replied. "We can work into the night with our headlamps."

"But someone could see the lights from the road, even through the brush."

"We'll need you to give us an alert. If a car comes, just tell us, we'll turn the lamps off until it's clear."

"Let's hope it doesn't go that long."

Dan's face was set in a grim stare. "This is how things go. We improvise and make the plan work...somehow."

The team grabbed a carryout lunch in Embrach. Evangeline went into the restaurant and ordered for the group. They ate in a hurry while driving up into the wooded area. After Jane parked the van, Marcus and Dan got out and collected their tools. They jogged across the road and disappeared into the brush.

"Now we just sit around and wait?" Evangeline asked.

Jane nodded. "Much of this work is waiting."

"Are you all spies? Do you work for the CIA or something? Is that what Dan is, a spy?"

Jane looked at the girl. She was smart as well as beautiful. She seemed to Jane to have courage, or what might be called pluck. What her mother had experienced with Aebischer, and what he was capable of, seemed to be the only things that struck terror in her.

"You should not ask too many questions, especially questions I can't answer."

Evangeline looked back at Jane, unafraid. "Why, you'll have to kill me then?"

"This is not something to joke about. Those two men are going into a deadly situation. We don't have all the possible outcomes covered. One or both may not survive. You can tell we're not normal thieves or intruders but I can't tell you anything more. It's partly for your protection and partly for ours."

"What will happen afterwards, if Dan is successful?"

"We'll bring Aebischer out and put him into the van. We'll take him out of the country to interrogate him about the terror operation that is being planned. Hopefully we won't be too late to interrupt it."

"So you work for the U.S. government. You're some sort of anti-terrorist group."

Jane didn't respond to Evangeline's question. "Are you going to be okay with Aebischer in the van with you?"

She saw a brief look of fear cross the girl's face. "I'll be okay. He'll be tied up won't he?"

Jane nodded.

"And now I'm not defenseless, I have friends, you and Dan as well as Marcus and Warren." She turned to Warren and smiled at him.

Jane smiled at her. “Good. I don’t want you to be fearful. If we’re successful in capturing him, Aebischer won’t be able to hurt you.”

“You might not be successful?”

Jane shrugged. “There’s always a chance things can go wrong.”

“If you are successful, what will happen to him? What will happen to me?”

“I can’t answer either of those questions at this point. This operation is far looser and dangerous than any I have undertaken before.”

“That makes me feel good,” Warren said. “I’m nervous enough without you making comments like that.”

“You just do your part. That will give us time to complete the operation. You can’t let any communications get out.”

She turned back to Evangeline. “I understand Dan gave you a pistol, let me see it.”

Evangeline took the Glock 19 out of her jacket pocket. She started to hand it to Jane barrel first.

“Stop!” Her voice was sharp. “Turn it around and hand me the grip,” Jane said. “I don’t approve of you having a weapon. I don’t know why he would give it to you, it could endanger the mission.”

“He showed me how to use it.”

“Do you know how to empty it?”

Evangeline nodded. Jane handed the gun back to her. “Show me,” she commanded.

Evangeline pushed the release button and ejected the magazine, then she worked the slide back to clear the chamber.

“Now show me how to put the safety on as if there is a round in the chamber.”

Evangeline looked at the weapon and then back at Jane. "There's no safety lever. Dan said that the weapon won't go off if dropped. The trigger has to be pulled."

"That's correct. But you made a basic mistake. Your weapon shouldn't have a round in the chamber until you're ready to use it. You empty the gun, pull the trigger, it won't re-cock, then put the loaded magazine back in. Now the trigger will be un-cocked and you'll have to work the slide before your first shot. Got it?"

Evangeline nodded. Her face was serious. She didn't seem reluctant to handle the gun and acted like she wanted to do it properly.

"You practiced with it?"

"*Ja*," we spent an hour shooting trees in the woods."

Jane gave her a sour look. "Just remember, if you have to use it in close quarters think of the gun as an extension of your finger. Just point like that and you'll probably hit your target. This would be a last resort. I don't expect you to get involved and I don't expect you to use your weapon. Understand?"

Evangeline nodded solemnly.

Across the street Dan and Marcus got busy digging around the exit. In an hour they dug down three feet around the concrete tube forming the vertical tunnel.

"Now we start chiseling," Marcus said. "Let's hope no one is close. The sound shouldn't carry since we're going into concrete and it's damped by the ground."

"Warren," Dan said into his throat mike, "We're going to start hammering. If you hear anything suspicious, let me know so we can stop."

"Roger that."

The two men started hammering away, first gently, and when that didn't produce much result, harder. Despite the cool, gray day, they were soon sweating profusely. After a half hour, Dan put down his hammer and chisel.

"We're getting in each other's way. Why don't we do this in short shifts and the one not hammering can sharpen the second chisel?"

Marcus smiled at him. "And I suppose you want me to take the first shift?"

"Of course I do," Dan replied with a smile. "I'm the ranking member of this team."

"In your own mind maybe."

Marcus adjusted his position to gain maximum effect from each blow to the chisel.

"Watch and learn," he said as he efficiently chipped away at the concrete.

Ten minutes later he stopped.

"Your turn."

Dan took up the sharpened chisel. They continued for the next hour, stopping only to cut the reinforcing rods. Two hours into the task and they had a crater two feet in diameter sloping to about six inches in depth at the center.

"How thick is this wall?" Dan asked.

"A foot thick, maybe less. We're making good progress."

The deeper they went, the more they worked to widen the hole. Finally, Marcus poked through and almost dropped the chisel into the shaft.

"Breakthrough!"

"Congratulations," Dan said.

"Now we widen the hole." Marcus peered through the hole with his flashlight. "I can see the wheel."

"I'm guessing the dowel is to turn it?"

"You got it. The wheel probably has spokes. We can hammer them with the dowel and turn it from outside."

"Clever man."

"My dad was an engineer. I guess I absorbed some of his knowledge."

"Master engineer and combatant. We make a good team."

"I'm not as good at being as invisible as you. I stand out too much."

"It could be the fact that you're over six feet tall, north of two hundred pounds, and have a short, military haircut. Other than that, you blend in quite nicely."

"Funny man," Marcus replied with a snort. "I also don't work as loosely as you." He turned back to the shaft. "Let's make this hole wider."

An hour later, they could see the wheel and the spokes.

"Warren," Dan called out, "We're ready to try to unlock the cover. You neutralized the alarm?"

"Yes. Go ahead."

"It's most likely to turn counter-clockwise to retract the pins," Marcus said.

Dan poked the dowel through the hole and after a bit of adjusting, had it firmly against one of the spokes. Marcus gave the dowel a whack with the hammer. Nothing moved.

"Wait," Dan said. Let me get it up against the spoke again. "Don't miss or you'll smash my hand."

"That's why I want to do the hammering."

"Go ahead hot shot."

Marcus struck the dowel again.

"Reset," Dan said. "Okay go."

It went on like that with Marcus taking ever increasing harder blows. Each blow produced a dull ring. The wooden dowel helped to deaden the sound. Still, Dan worried about how long it was taking to make the wheel budge.

Finally, with a loud squeak, the wheel turned.

"Yay, we got motion," Dan said.

"I could feel that through the hammer."

They worked the wheel around with repeated blows. Every quarter turn they had to set on another spoke.

“We’ll get it unlocked and wait until we come back to lift the lid. The pry bars will make it easy to open.”

“Don’t want to try it now?” Marcus asked.

Dan shook his head. “We’ve made enough noise. Let’s wait until we’re going in. I don’t want someone exploring the tunnel before we’re in and realizing a breech is occurring. We come back, get in and deal with whatever crap comes at us.”

“We got to talk through this, you and me, so we’re on the same page.”

“We will, but it will be loose, you know that. Improvising is what we’re going to be doing after we enter.”

“At least let’s talk about key objectives along the way.”

After the wheel had been fully turned the men packed their tools and laid some brush over the dirt trench and the hole in the concrete. Five hours had passed since they had started. They were dirty and sweating but happy to have crossed this first hurdle.

“You boys need to wash up. We’ll go back to the airport area and you can clean up. Then Evangeline and I will do some shopping for food and drinks and we’ll review the plans again,” Jane said after the men came back to the van.

She started the vehicle and drove out over the hill and back to the airport.

Chapter 38

Before it gets dark we need to locate the phone lines so we can cut them," Dan said. They were in the van eating carryout food Jane and Evangeline had purchased in a supermarket.

"Warren, how do you tell the phone line from the power line? I don't want Marcus to electrocute himself," Dan asked.

"We're lucky the lines are above ground," Warren replied. "It's simple, really. When you look at the multiple lines on the pole, electric power is on top, cable, the thick tube is in the middle and phone is on the bottom. Since the house is fairly far from the road, all the lines probably run down from the pole and go underground to the junction box on the side of the building. You just track the line from the lower run on the pole and cut it before it goes underground."

"But don't cut the wrong one," Marcus said.

"Yeah. That'll give you a kick...probably kill you," Warren said.

"How about we let you cut the line?" Dan asked with a smile.

Warren's eyes got big. Jane laughed. "Don't worry, Dan or Marcus will do the job."

Warren exhaled a long breath in relief. "I'm okay in the van, but this is as close to field work as I want to get."

"Warren, my boy, you're in the middle of field work and if it gets messy, you'll be in the middle of that as well," Dan said. "So make sure you do your part and give us enough time to do ours."

"Don't panic him," Jane said. "He'll be okay here in the van."

When they were finished eating, Jane headed back to the mansion. They drove slowly past the gate and noted the utility pole a hundred yards from the driveway.

"Mark the distance," Marcus said.

They drove to the parking area and stopped.

"How far back to the pole?" Marcus asked.

Jane looked close at the odometer. "Looks like half a kilometer."

Marcus looked down the road. "Maybe I better wait until dark, do it just before we go in. After I cut the line, I'll jog back to the tunnel and we can go."

Dan nodded and opened the passenger door. "Let's go outside," he said to Marcus.

The two men stepped out and walked a few paces from the van. Jane watched as they huddled together. She knew they were going over what details they had to work with and pin down hard objectives in what could develop into a confused mess. It was something they needed to do together. They needed to be on the same page and understand their next steps in the middle of what was going to be a chaotic situation. It also helped to bond them together. They were going to rely on each other to stay alive.

When they returned to the van, Marcus lay down in the back and promptly closed his eyes. Dan got back into the passenger seat and leaned back to do the same.

"Are you going to sleep?" Evangeline asked.

"Resting. Centering. Getting mentally prepared," Jane said and put her finger to her lips. She touched Dan's shoulder and gestured for him to come outside with her.

The two of them walked away from the van.

"How do you feel about this?" Jane asked.

"About as good as any other operation."

"How are you physically? You've been shot twice now."

"My side and chest are sore, but that won't keep me from functioning. Hell, I had a bullet go through my leg in Mexico and still managed to get into Jorge's mansion and kill him. I'll be all right."

"It worries me. I worry about you." She put her hand on his arm.

"Don't. Just make sure Warren jams the signals so no alarms are transmitted. If the ledger is in the safe, I have to get Aebischer to open it."

"You can do that?"

"I'll have to be brutal. It won't be pretty since I won't have much time. He'll think he can delay and help will come. I have to make him realize that it won't and he'll suffer badly from my hand if he doesn't open the safe."

"What about the guards? Are you going to take them out?"

"Marcus and I agree that the best thing to do is to take them out as quietly as we can. We'll use our hands or knives so we don't alert Aebischer, but if we have to, we'll use our M4s. They're loaded with subsonic rounds since this is close work, and with the suppressors, they won't make much noise. I'm just worried about whether we're looking for three or four inside men."

"And the outside guards?"

"Once we've neutralized the ones inside, they shouldn't be hard to deal with. The guard at the gate may never get involved."

"Just bring Aebischer out, even if you can't get the ledger. With him gone, the money won't move and we can get what he knows out of him later. I'll bet he has most of the ledger in his head."

Dan nodded. "We'll get him out. He may not be in good shape, but he'll be alive."

Evangeline had leaned forward in the van watching their discussion with great interest.

"Don't forget," Dan said, "We've got a date after this is over." He touched her cheek and they turned back to the van.

Jane smiled at him as they walked back.

When they got in the van, Evangeline asked, "What now?"

"We wait, we rest. You should too. We're going to be up late tonight. You don't want to be sleepy."

He looked over his shoulder at Warren who was monitoring his electronic equipment. His four monitors were showing video from both inside and outside the house. He switched through the cameras steadily. "You going to be okay without rest? It's going to be a late night and we'll need you giving us advice in real time once we're inside."

"I'm all right. I'm trying to find out whether or not there's a fourth man inside."

"Maybe give it a rest. After you jam the wireless signal going out, you have to help us navigate around the guards and find Aebischer."

Warren nodded and leaned back. He stretched his arms out over his head, brushing the roof of the van. "I got it. I'll be your extra eyes inside."

Chapter 39

Just before midnight Marcus stirred and went over his gear. Both he and Dan would be wearing tactical vests. They would carry M4 carbines with suppressors attached. In addition, they both carried 9mm handguns with suppressors. Each man had an MK 3 knife, the one issued to the SEALS, attached to their vests. The M4s were equipped with thirty-round magazines and they carried three extra mags. They both had two extra magazines for their 9mm pistols.

With their black vests, black, tactical pants, and boots, they were an intimidating sight. They didn't bring their night vision goggles. They would rely on the house lighting. They had throat mics and ear pieces to allow them to communicate with Warren back in the van. Warren would let them know where the interior guards were and allow the men to ambush them silently.

Evangeline watched the preparations with wide eyes. The level of tension increased in the van as the men checked their equipment. There was a sharp odor of nervous sweat, mostly coming from Warren who also watched in fascination, turning his attention back and forth between the activity in the van and the monitors.

"Ready?" Marcus asked when he had finished.

Dan nodded. He looked over at Jane who was staring back intently at him. "We'll be fine. When we're in, you should take your weapon and stand watch over the exit. Warren can alert you if someone other than us is coming. Put your suppressor on and take out anyone who isn't us or Aebischer."

Jane nodded. Dan reached up and patted her cheek. As he turned to go Evangeline reached over the passenger seat and wrapped her arms around his neck and hugged him tight, her face pressed against his.

"Please don't get killed. Please come back. I love you," she whispered in his ear.

"I'll be fine. You just wait here and do what Jane says. It's important that you don't create an issue back here. It will jeopardize our safety, understand?"

She nodded. Dan kissed her cheek and stepped out into the dark.

The two men grabbed the pry bars and sprinted across the road. Once on the other side, Marcus headed off to the utility pole. When he got there, he realized that, while he could see the wires at his level, he could not see which level of line above they connected to.

"Warren, can't see which level the lines come from. Any way to identify them at my level? I'd like to not have to climb the pole."

"That's tricky. The communication lines will be larger, especially if there is cable communication connected to the house. The power line will have a metal insulating cover around it from about 8 feet above the ground. It keeps anyone from getting shocked. With 230-volt systems in Europe, that's a big deal."

"This is like playing Russian roulette. Pick a wire and cut. I could be a hero or fried."

"If you can shine a light for just a moment, you will see where each line comes from. The upper one is power. It will have an insulator at the connecting point."

"Can't do that. I'm too close to the gate. Even a quick flash will be seen and someone might investigate."

"Tell me what you see at your level. Do you see the metal cover around one of the lines?"

There was a pause. "Yeah. There's definitely a metal cover around one of the lines, going into the ground."

"The other one just is a cable?"

"Yep. You're one hundred percent sure the one not covered is the communication line?"

"I'd bet on it," Warren said.

"Thanks, but I'm the one betting on it...betting my life. Here goes."

Everyone in the van held their breath.

A moment later Marcus announced, "I'm still alive, so I guess I cut the right one."

There was a big exhale from everyone.

"On my way back," Marcus said.

When he rejoined Dan at the tunnel exit, they put the pry bars between the cover and its surrounding ring. "Watch close, Warren, we're going to lift the cover," Dan said.

There was a screeching sound as they pried on the lid. It came up. Marcus slid his bar underneath it and the two men grabbed the cover and pivoted it on its hinges. Once it had been lifted above its seat, it made little noise as it was pulled the rest of the way open.

"Cover's open," Dan said. "Heads up Warren, we're going in. Keep us updated on any activity."

"Let's take a pry bar with us," Marcus said. Dan looked at him wondering how it could help. "We may have to pry the door at the end of the tunnel open. It may not unlock from the inside."

"Good point."

The two men climbed down the ladder. Once on the bottom, Dan checked in with Warren. "Can you hear me? We're in the tunnel."

"Hear you just fine," came the reply.

The two men walked through the dark tunnel, feeling their way along the walls. At the end, they found a light switch and flipped it on.

"We turned on the lights. You see anything outside?" Dan asked.

Jane shook her head and Warren relayed the message. "No light showing on this end. There's no one in the basement from my videos, so you're good to open the door."

The door was locked and needed a key to open.

"Damn. I was hoping for a latch to turn." Dan said.

It was a wooden door, stout; made of oak. Marcus studied it for a moment.

"I can dig away at the wood around where the deadbolt slides through, or I can try to dig open the key slot from this side. Then we can make the mechanism work without a key."

"Let's do that."

Marcus began to thrust the pry bar at the lock. The bar had weight to give force to his efforts, but only a dull blade. The blows came over and over with only little progress. Dan kept checking in with Warren; the strikes would obviously be echoing in the basement hallway outside of the door. Finally, Marcus was able to break off the bezel and expose the innards of the lock. He slipped his knife inside and shoved the deadbolt back. The door opened.

"We're inside the basement," Dan said into his mic.

"Tell them to go to the right," Evangeline said. "The stairs are at the end of the corridor."

When they got to the stairs, Dan whispered to Warren. "Where are the guards? We're about to go onto the main floor."

Both men had a diagram of the floor plan in their heads. Their first objective was to find and eliminate as many inside guards as possible on their way to Aebischer's office. Warren had confirmed Aebischer was working there, even at this late hour.

"When you get to the top of the stairs, there's one in the front foyer of the house. He's sitting near the front door."

"Put that camera on a loop, we're going up."

"Give me a minute," Warren replied.

Dan turned out the light in the basement and he and Marcus crept up the stairs. At the top, Dan slowly turned the door knob, then applied a slight pressure to the door. It cracked open an inch without a sound. The door was well used as the basement housed the wine cellar and other rooms used by Aebischer; some that brought terror to Evangeline whenever she thought about them.

He put his eye to the crack but couldn't see the front door. He would have to open the door further. He pulled his head back and turned to Marcus. They whispered together.

"Got to open wider. If the guard sees me, I'll rush him. Watch my back for anyone else."

"How far away is he?" Marcus asked.

"Can't tell yet. It could take me a couple of seconds to reach him."

"I'll follow you out. If he gets ready to fire, stay low and I'll take him out."

Dan nodded.

Inch by inch pushed the door open. The guard was sitting at a table, facing the front door. He looked relaxed but not asleep. Dan crept through the opening. *Hope the floor doesn't squeak.* He stepped forward, his knife out, not making a sound. He muffled his breathing even as his heart rate accelerated.

When he got within ten feet, the guard, sensing a presence, turned. Dan sprang forward, launching himself over the last few feet. The guard stood up from his chair, turning to face the intruder. Before he could pull up his weapon, an HK M5, Dan was on him. He slammed into his chest, pulling his left arm around the man, trapping the guard's right hand and weapon against their bodies. At the same time Dan thrust his knife into the left side of the man's neck. He rocked the blade back and forth, searching for the carotid artery. The knife sliced through the artery and Dan held the man tight against him, muffling his mouth as his life spurted out of him. In seconds his body sagged against Dan and he gently let him collapse to the ground.

Marcus had come up behind Dan. "We should put him someplace in case someone comes looking for him, better to be missing than lying here dead."

"Basement," Dan said.

Marcus nodded and they picked up the body and carried it back down the stairs, putting it in a corner at the bottom of the steps.

"We still have the blood all over the floor," Dan said.

"But not on the table, so it's not as obvious. It's the best we can do for now."

"What's the guard situation?" Dan asked Warren.

"Outside guards are not alerted. Activity normal. We have one in the kitchen. Looks like he's taking a break. One moving through the lower halls. He's back in the library now, opposite side of the house from the kitchen. There's one outside Aebischer's office upstairs and one still in the monitor room."

"Take out the kitchen first?" Marcus asked.

Dan nodded. He spoke into his mic. "Start a loop in the kitchen, we're going in."

"Roger," said Warren.

Both men moved down the side hall towards the kitchen. The door was open. Dan lay down on the floor and peeked around the opening. The man sat eating a sandwich. He was watching television with his back turned to the opening. Dan moved forward while Marcus stepped to one side for a clear shot with his 9mm out. Before Dan could close the man noticed a reflection in the kitchen window and turned towards the door, pulling his side arm out of its holster.

Dan ran forward. As the man raised his pistol, Marcus fired. The round hit him in the chest and he fell back against the large kitchen table. Dan reached him and used his knife to finish him off with a slash to his neck artery.

He pulled the guard off the table and both men dragged him to the wall and stuffed him into a pantry. They put his pistol and M5 machine gun in with him. Except for the blood on the floor there was no evidence of the guard's demise. Dan went to the sink and wet a dish towel and tried to mop up the blood as best he could. He threw the bloody towel into the pantry closet with the body when he finished.

"Are we still clear?" Dan asked.

"Clear. Outside and inside normal."

"Are you going to take out the third guard downstairs?" Jane asked.

"Not sure," replied Dan. "Where is he?" He asked Warren.

"He must be moving. Can't see him right now. He's in between monitors."

"Can't spend time on a cat and mouse when he disappears," Dan said. He turned to Marcus. "Let's go get Aebischer."

"Roger that. We can hold off any attack from the office and we have Aebischer's own escape route ready and waiting."

The two headed back down the hall to the front foyer. They moved up the stairs which were covered in a thick, silent carpet.

"Take the hallway to the right. There's a second corridor halfway down going to the left. Aebischer's office is at the end. The guard is sitting at a desk outside the door. It's like a receptionist's station," Warren said.

"Got it. Keep a watch out for the roving guard."

Before they got to the top of the stairs Dan and Marcus huddled together.

"We won't have the element of surprise this time. He'll see us coming down the hall."

Marcus nodded.

"You take him out with your 9mm. It's quieter than the M4. I'll go straight to the door and keep Aebischer from using the elevator."

"If it's locked?"

"I'll shoot it open and shoot Aebischer if he's about to leave." Marcus gave Dan a sharp look. "It'll be a non-lethal shot."

Jane along with Warren and Evangeline listened intently as the two men planned the next engagement. Dan had to get into the office quickly enough to keep Aebischer from descending the elevator, or else Jane would have to backstop the banker's escape.

They padded down the carpeted hall, moving slowly and quieting their breathing. At the corner, both men stopped. They had their 9mms out and ready.

Dan nodded. Marcus stepped into office hallway and took aim at the guard. His shot hit the man in the chest. Dan ran down the hall and grabbed the office door. Marcus ran up to the man and put another shot into his head.

Chapter 40

Inside the office, Aebischer heard the shot and with only a moment's hesitation, pushed the panic button under the center section of his desk. The button was to alert his guards to an intrusion and signal the local *polizei*. What he didn't know was that those two signals were not going to get through.

He then got up from his desk and started for the elevator just as Dan burst into the room.

"*Halt*," Dan said in German.

Aebischer looked at Dan. His eyes wide with surprise. "Who are you? What do you want?"

Dan didn't hesitate at the door but continued across the room at a run after shouting to Aebischer. Before the banker could open the elevator door, he grabbed him and pulled him back away from the wall. Without a word, he threw the older man to the floor and grabbed his arms, pulling them behind his back. He took a pair of plastic handcuffs and zip-tied them around Aebischer's wrists. When he stood up, Marcus was in the room.

"Go outside and keep watch," Dan said. "I'm going to talk with Herr Aebischer. Hopefully, this won't take long. How are we doing with the guards?" He asked Warren.

"All looks normal except that I've lost the signal in the monitor room. Not sure what's causing that."

"Can you still see the guard in there?"

"Never could directly but I could see he was working the monitors."

"Still see that?"

"Affirmative."

Marcus went back outside. Dan yanked Aebischer to his feet and shoved him into a chair which he pulled into the middle of the room.

"Who are you?" the banker asked again.

"The man you hired and then tried to kill," Dan replied.

Aebischer gave Dan a dark look. He sat in the chair, facing the man who would want revenge, but showed no fear.

"I don't have a lot of time, so I want you to know that your panic button signal didn't transmit. The wireless is blocked and the phone line is down. You're cut off. The men outside don't know what's going on and anyone coming down the hall is going to get killed by my friend outside your door."

He paused for Aebischer to absorb what he had just said. "So I have you all to myself."

"What do you want? I can pay you what you're owed...and more. I want to keep my involvement in the rescue quiet, so I'm happy to pay you more, a lot more. Just name your price."

"I want something else." Dan put his face close to Aebischer. "I want the ledger book you keep here in the office."

"I don't know what you're talking about."

Dan stood up and swung his open hand across Aebischer's face with a violent whack. The blow split the banker's lip open.

"I know about the book. Both Pietro and Evangeline confirmed it. Let's not play around, it will only mean more pain for you."

Aebischer shook his head. "They don't know what that book is about. It is of no use to you. It's just some accounting records."

Dan smacked him across the face again, this time from the other direction. Aebischer's head flopped to one side.

"Here's what's going to happen. You're going to produce the ledger for me, quickly, or I'm going to start shooting you, first in the foot, then knee, then hands and elbows. By the time I'm done you will be crippled for the rest of your life and I'll have the book. So, if you'd like to not be crippled, produce the book."

Aebischer glared at Dan. His face twisted into a hateful look. "It's in the safe which has a time lock on it. I can't open it until tomorrow."

"Dan pulled out his 9mm and put it to Aebischer's foot. "Last chance."

"I'm telling the truth, you—"

Dan pulled the trigger and Aebischer screamed out in pain. The bullet went through his left foot and lodged in the floor. Dan grabbed a roll of tape from his vest.

"I'll gag you and continue shooting you until you override the system. I'm sure you have a way to do that, so don't try to give me any stupid story otherwise."

Aebischer cried out in pain but Dan could see he was working to control it, not wanting to appear weak.

"I can make you experience more pain than you ever caused others. Dan grabbed him by his throat and looked close into his pale blue eyes. His voice was low and deadly. "I'd rather kill you than mess with you anymore, but there are people who want the information you have. If you think you won't give it, you're wrong. Everyone gives up what they know at the end. It's only a matter of time. If you don't give it to me tonight, I'll turn you over to people who will take all the time they need to get it out of you. It will be very painful and go on as long as you want to hold out. You won't die. They'll make sure of that, but you'll want to die."

"You don't scare me. I'm not one easily scared." Aebischer's voice was shaky but he was trying to control it.

"I'm not trying to scare you. I'm just letting you know what's coming. The choice is yours. No one is coming to rescue you."

As Dan and Marcus stormed the office, the guard in the monitor room called the kitchen guard. He didn't get an answer. He next called the man roving the first floor.

"Go check the kitchen. My monitor shows Franz sitting there, but there's something wrong. He's been eating his sandwich for ten minutes. It looks odd."

"Okay, on my way," came the reply.

Two minutes later the guard called back to the monitor. "I don't see Franz anywhere. Is he still showing on the monitor?"

"*Ja*. Something's wrong. Check the front foyer."

"Should we call Herr Aebischer?"

"Not yet, I don't want to disturb him in case it's just something wrong in the system."

Less than a minute later the guard came over the intercom. "Hermann is missing as well."

"Head to the office, I'm activating the internal alarm."

The guard in the monitor room activated the alarm key but again, unbeknownst to him, no alarm rang outside. He left the monitor room and headed to the office.

"The monitor guard has left his room, he may be headed to the office," Warren shouted over the intercom.

Marcus went to full alert with his M4 at ready. The monitor watchman met up with the first-floor guard in the upper hall. They ran around the corner. Marcus opened fire. The monitor room guard fell with multiple rounds hitting him in his chest. The other guard dropped to the ground and returned fire with his HK M5. Before Marcus could turn his fire to the man on the ground, he was hit in the torso. He flew back, dropping his carbine.

The guard ran forward just as Dan, crouching, opened the door. When he saw Dan's head, he instinctively kicked out with his foot, not waiting to swing the M5 down. Dan rolled to one side stunned by the kick to his temple.

Aebischer shouted out, "Don't kill him!"

Dan was reaching out to grab the man's legs and pull him down when the guard reversed his weapon and struck Dan behind his ear. Dan's vision went black and he collapsed unconscious.

Chapter 41

Back in the van, Warren relayed what had happened to Jane.

"I'm going in," she called back to Warren as she left the van.

Evangeline pulled the side door open and jumped out after her.

"Stop!" shouted Warren.

"*Nein*," Evangeline replied. "They need me in there. I know the house better than anyone."

She sprinted across the road and through the brush. Jane was just disappearing down into the tunnel. Evangeline followed.

"Go back," Jane ordered. "This is no place for you."

"It's my home. I know it best. I can help."

Jane shook her head. At the bottom of the ladder, she adjusted her M4. Evangeline came down the ladder behind her. "You'll jeopardize the mission."

"But I can help. I know the layout better than anyone. And I know this man. He won't expect me to be here, it will throw him off."

Jane waved her arm in dismissal, "I don't have time to argue. Stay behind me and don't get in my way."

The two women felt their way down the dark tunnel. When they came to the door, Jane turned to the right.

"The stairs will take you to the front foyer. If anyone comes in from outside you can shoot them. You go up the steps and to the right to Aebischer's office."

Jane nodded and moved forward. Evangeline turned left. She hunted along the wall. She was looking for a hidden latch. It opened a panel to reveal an elevator door. The elevator came out in Aebischer's office.

The guard ran over to Aebischer and cut his cuffs. Then he dragged Dan to the chair Aebischer had vacated. The banker hobbled back to his desk and sat back against it. His face was contorted in a mixture of pain and rage. The guard tied Dan's hands behind him. Dan regained consciousness and looked up at a face full of hate and fury.

"Now mister assassin, we shall see how tough you are. You talked about pain? I am an expert at it, although in quite a different context. Still, what I've learned can be translated to you. In the end you will lose your manhood as well as be crippled, similar to what you threatened me with."

"And you expect me to tell you something?"

Aebischer shook his head and let out a harsh laugh. "No, I expect you to suffer and me to enjoy your torment. It will be for my pleasure, a measure of compensation for the trouble you've caused me. And when I'm tired of it, you will die." He leaned forward, close to Dan's face. "You will not be able to relieve your torment. There will be nothing you can give me or tell me to make it stop. It is for my pleasure only. You have no hope." He leaned back with a gleam in his eyes. "You have entered hell, my hell."

Aebischer nodded to the guard who swung his fist into Dan's face. He began to pummel him on his head and torso. The pain in his ribs lit up causing him to cry out.

"Ah it seems we've found a sore spot on your body. Wounds from your previous encounters? We will exploit that as we go forward."

Aebischer turned to the guard. "How many guards are left?"

"I think they killed Franz, Hermann, and Max along with Nils outside your office."

Aebischer just nodded.

"Should I call in the guards from outside?"

"No. We don't know if there are any others trying to get in. Tell them to be on full alert. I don't know how these two managed to get past them."

"I think the security system is compromised, maybe jammed. Max said there was something not right about the video links."

"This man said our communications are cut off, so we're on our own. We will take him down to the basement. I have a special room for him. After you secure him, go help the other guards and all of you keep watch. Have you tried your phone?"

The guard nodded. "I'm not connecting although the system says there is a signal."

"That indicates it's jammed. When morning comes, we'll leave with the cars and gather some men to clean up."

"What about your foot?"

"I have bandages downstairs. It will be okay until tomorrow. Right now, I want to introduce my assassin to his future. Soften him up."

The guard hammered more blows on Dan who grunted with the intense pain. It was worse when the blows landed on his torso than on his face.

"Now I'm taking you down to your hell."

He turned to limp over to the wall that concealed his elevator when the panel opened. Evangeline stood in the opening. She had a wild look in her eyes and a 9mm in both hands pointed in front of her.

Aebischer stood there, too stunned to move.

"Evie," he said in surprise.

The guard was bending over Dan to drag him to the elevator. He stood up and reached for his machine gun which was on the desk. Evangeline saw the movement and swung in his direction. She held the pistol out in front of her, remembering Jane's words about pointing it like a finger. Her eyes closed involuntarily as she pulled the trigger twice. The guard fell back against the desk and hit the floor as the rounds hit him in the chest and arm.

Aebischer stepped forward.

"*Halt*," Evangeline said as she swung the pistol back to him. He stopped.

"Evie, you've come home. I've missed you so much. Please put the gun down. You're back now where you belong."

"I'm not back. Do you think I would come back to a monster like you?"

"Evie, please. I sent this man to rescue you. Then he didn't return you. I was trying to find out what happened. But you're here. We can make this right. You belong home, with me. We belong together."

"You killed my mother...my sister. You made me a freak and then you killed the only person who loved me."

"*I* love you. I'll take care of you. You'll never want for anything. Just come back to me. Let us be together."

"You can't give me what I want. You can't give me my mother back."

"Your mother was unstable. She wanted to expose us all. It would have led to you being taken away from me. I couldn't allow that. Sophia was suicidal. You know what she did."

Evangeline was shaking at this point. Dan watched carefully not wanting to divert her attention. Aebischer was close enough to reach her if she shifted her gaze away from him.

"I was there that night. I saw you. You did things to her while she was tied up on the bed. Now I know what those were. I've learned all about those dirty things. But then you smothered her."

Evangeline's voice began to break. Dan kept thinking, *don't break down, don't give him the opening. Our lives depend on that.*

"And then," she paused to get control over her emotions without much success. "And then...you hung her up!"

Evangeline began to sob. Aebischer lunged forward. Evangeline pulled the trigger and a bullet slammed into his shoulder spinning him sideways to the ground. Just then Jane burst through the door in a crouch. She immediately took in the scene, two men down, one was Aebischer, Dan tied up in a chair, and Evangeline sobbing with a gun in her hand.

"Evangeline put down your gun," she ordered. "I've got everyone covered. Go untie Dan."

Evangeline set the gun carefully on the floor. She went over to Dan.

"You're hurt," she said through her sobs.

"The knife. Cut the rope," Dan said between gasps. It was hard to breathe and harder to talk.

Jane cleared away the weapons.

"The guards outside are moving. They're coming into the house, the front door." Warren's voice came over the com link. "They must have heard the shots."

"Can you watch Aebischer?" Jane asked Dan.

"Yeah." His voice was barely audible. She gave him the 9mm.

"I'm going to take out the guards."

"Wait until they're all in the front hall, then use full auto. You don't want any of them sneaking around to come at us from another entrance."

Jane nodded and ran from the room.

Dan turned to Evangeline who was standing in shock. She stared at her father, the man of her nightmares, the man she shot.

"He's not dead?"

"No. But you saved us all by not letting him get your gun. Now I need you to do something."

Evangeline walked over to Dan.

"Take my knife, go out in the hall and find Marcus. If he's alive, cut some cloth, from the other guard's shirt, and stop his bleeding. We have a chance to save him if he's still with us. Can you do that?"

Evangeline nodded.

Jane waited at the top of the stairs. She lay on the floor looking around the corner and over the edge of the steps. Her M4 was cradled in her arms. *Let them all get inside.*

"How many are outside?" She whispered to Warren.

"Three of them. The two at the house and the front gate guard. He's running up to the door. They're waiting for him to enter."

Jane calmed her breathing. She had not been involved in field work for over a decade, but she kept herself current with weapons. She had not killed before, but now it was time to use those skills in a life-or-death situation. Dan was injured, Marcus might be dead; it was now up to Jane to give them a chance to evacuate the house with their prize.

The front door opened. No one appeared. Then a head showed around the corner of the doorway, down low. Jane held still. She knew they couldn't see her at the top of the stairs. One man came through in a crouch and took up a defensive position to the right. The next one went to the left. They both scanned the area on the main floor with an occasional glance up the stairs. The third guard entered and all three advanced towards the steps.

Now was the time. Jane slid her rifle forward and opened fire on full automatic. She moved the rifle from left to right, sweeping across the men. They were separated but the confines of the room meant they were still close to one another. One of the men returned fire, the shots going high into the ceiling. Then it was quiet.

Her magazine was empty. Jane immediately ejected it and pulled another one from her vest. She inserted it and ran down the stairs. Two of the men were moving. Without pausing to let herself think about, least she shrink from the task, she fired a short blast into each of the downed men. Then she turned and ran back up the stairs.

Evangeline was clamping a shirt over Marcus' wound. He had been hit in his side and shoulder. Jane looked at him. He was conscious with labored breathing.

"We've got all the guards and Aebischer. Now we're going to get out of here with you and get you some help. You hang on."

Marcus gave a nod of his head. He looked at her. His eyes gave away nothing. He didn't look panicked, just fatalistic, as if accepting that he might have bought the farm this time.

"Please don't die. You have to stay alive until we can get you to a hospital," Evangeline said, her voice pleading with him.

"Stay with Marcus and keep pressure on the wound. Don't worry about the shoulder, it's not dangerous, but we have to keep him from losing too much blood from the lower wound."

Jane ran into the office.

"Can you walk?" She asked Dan.

"Yeah. Help me up."

Aebischer lay on the floor. He was wounded in his left foot and shoulder. He would need help walking. Marcus might not be able to walk at all.

"Warren," Jane called. "We need you in here right now. Everything's secure but we've got to get Marcus and Aebischer out and they need help. Dan's injured but he can walk but he won't be much help in carrying anyone out."

She heard Warren take a deep breath. "On my way.

Jane stripped the belts off the two guards, the one injured in the office and the one dead outside in the hall next to Marcus. Next, she shoved the injured guard on his side and cut off his shirt.

"*Werden Sie mich töten?*" the guard asked.

"Are you going to kill me?" Evangeline translated.

"Not unless you make me," Jane answered in German. "Can you walk?"

The guard struggled to his feet in answer.

"You and I are going to help my man outside. If you do anything I don't like. If you try to stop or slow us down, I'll shoot you. Help me out and you'll save your life. *Verstehen Sie?*"

The man nodded.

Warren arrived at the office out of breath. His face pale, his eyes wide with fear or excitement.

"Warren, you help Aebischer walk. His foot is shot as well as his shoulder. Hold him on his right side. Evangeline you lead the way. Warren and Aebischer will follow. I'll go next with Marcus and the guard. Dan you follow. If the guard tries anything shoot him."

"With pleasure," Dan said, his voice a barely audible rasp.

"Now did you get the ledger?" Jane asked.

"No. I was working on that when I got taken out."

"Can you get it out of Aebischer?"

"It'll take some time."

"Marcus can't wait. We have to get him to a hospital, one outside of Switzerland."

Dan thought for a moment. "We can go. The ledger will stay in the safe."

"Okay, let's go," Jane said.

"We can't all get in the elevator, we'll have to go down the stairs," Evangeline said.

"Lead the way," Jane said.

The unlikely parade of wounded made their way down the stairs, down into the basement, and into the tunnel. They emerged after some effort from the manhole cover and limped across the road. It was 2 am. Low clouds scudded along covering and uncovering the three quarters moon; the air was chilly and the breeze had a bite to it.

Once in the van, Dan helped Jane secure the captives. Then Jane opened the emergency field kit. She took out the clotting bandages and applied them along with disinfectant, first to Marcus' wounds and then to Aebischer and the guard.

"Time to go," she said. She maneuvered the van back on the road and down the hill, heading back to the airport parking area.

Chapter 42

The van stopped at the airport parking lot. It was 3:00 am. They worked without lights, not wanting to attract any attention from airport security.

"Can you drive?" Jane asked Dan.

"Yeah. I hurt but I can drive. Let's put Marcus in my car. He can be 'asleep' in the back seat when we drive through the border control. It should just be a slow pass through. They don't even need to look for the *vignette* since we're leaving Switzerland."

"Good. I'll drive the van. We'll put the guard in your trunk," she said to Dan. "Warren you take the other car. We'll put Aebischer in your trunk."

"He won't get loose will he?" Warren asked.

"No." Jane replied. "It locks from the outside. We'll caravan. No one will know the vehicles are connected," Jane said.

The sky was thickening; the moon was becoming hidden behind an increasing cloud cover. The night was getting darker which suited Dan just fine. The three vehicles pulled out.

They headed towards the city and connected to the expressway going around the top of Zürich. They stayed on the toll roads, making connections as they headed south to Lugano. They were headed to Como where they would cross into Italy, an hour from Milan. Jane called ahead to alert the consulate office about Marcus's condition.

Then she called Henry. It was 10:30 pm back in Washington.

"We have the goods. You'll need to send a cleanup team to Zürich. There's collateral damage to remove."

"Anyone on the team hurt?" Henry asked.

"Marcus. We're going to have to get him to a hospital. It could be touch and go with him."

"Dan?"

"He's beat up but otherwise okay. You have the address of the mansion. I wouldn't wait too long."

"I'll have a team from Germany in there in the morning. How many bodies?"

Jane took a quick mental count. "Six or more."

"This wasn't supposed to be an all-out gunfight."

"It couldn't be helped, believe me. Just get the place cleaned up. And Henry, send in a locksmith. There's a safe in the office that we need opened. It has the ledger in it."

Evangeline climbed into the back seat and helped Marcus drink some water. Dan watched in his mirror. She was attentive, checking to see that his bleeding hadn't started again. She tried to make him as comfortable as she could, until Dan suggested that she climb back up front and just let him rest.

They crossed at 6:30 am, just before the sun came up. An hour later they were entering the consulate grounds. The physician checked Marcus and said they had to take him to the hospital. James Springhouse called one of his contacts in the *Agenzia Informazioni e Sicurezza Esterna* or AISE. He assured the man that the U.S. was not conducting any covert actions on Italian soil but one of his investigators, working on uncovering a gun smuggling operation in France, was ambushed and shot. The story had been worked out by both Jane and James. The embassy doctor worked on Aebischer whose wounds were not life threatening.

With Marcus in good hands, the team headed back to the safe house. After putting Aebischer and the guard in separate, locked rooms, Jane, Dan, Warren, Roland, and Evangeline sat down. Jane poured everyone a double shot of whiskey, even Evangeline.

"Marcus going to be all right?" Warren asked.

"We'll know more in the morning. It's best we leave things in the embassy's hands at this point. I don't want to get on AISE's radar, and Dan certainly can't." Jane continued as they sat in the living room.

"Do we go back? We don't have the ledger." Roland said.

"Henry will take care of it with the cleanup crew," Jane said.

"Aebischer says it's all in his head, and he might be right," Dan said.

Jane took a sip of her whiskey. "Or he could be trying to convince us to keep him alive...for the information. He'd probably dole it out slowly in any case."

"He could decode it on a similarly slow rate. He doesn't know we have Pietro, who may or may not be lying about his ability to decode the book. In any case, I agree that Aebischer will want to make a case for us needing him."

"Along with Pietro," Jane said.

Evangeline was silent through much of the conversation. She barely sipped her whiskey. Warren watched her intently. She noticed his focus and smiled at him.

"Fred," Jane turned to her researcher who had stayed behind, "How's our friend Pietro doing?"

"He complains about the accommodations and keeps telling me how important he is going to be to our operation."

"But he doesn't know what that is," Jane said.

"Yeah, but he's sure it has something to do with terrorists and he'll be key to unlocking the ledger. He's a bit of a bore, frankly."

"Boring's good sometimes," Warren said.

He went on to describe the operation and spoke glowingly of Evangeline's role in turning the tables on a desperate situation. The girl blushed at Warren's effusive comments. Dan could tell he was smitten by her.

"She arrived at the right time, that's for sure," Dan said. "If Aebischer had gotten me in the elevator before Jane got upstairs, things would not have worked out so well."

"I didn't know I could do that," Evangeline said. She looked at Dan. "But seeing you, and remembering what you and Jane told me about shooting...it all happened so fast—"

"The important thing is that you did the right thing," Jane said.

"I've never shot a gun before. It's odd, but it doesn't scare me. And I don't feel bad about shooting the guard or my father."

"He would have hurt you to save himself," Dan said.

"I know that. I know what he's done, what he's capable of still doing." She looked back and forth between Jane and Dan. "What will you do with him? Will you kill him?"

There was silence in the room. Finally, Dan spoke.

"He deserves that, from what he did to your mother and what he's done with his funding work for terrorists and criminals." He shook his head. "I just don't know at this point."

"Let's all sleep on it. We've been up all last night. Let's talk later this afternoon," Jane said.

As the team started to leave, Jane signaled Dan to wait behind. Evangeline caught the sign and held back but Dan told her to go and get some rest.

"We not only have to go through the ledger," Jane said, "But we have to deal with the pending terror threat. That's got to be the first priority. We have to find a way to interrupt that operation. Later we can dig for all of Aebischer's information about who the groups are and how the money flows."

"I can do that if you let me get rough with him. He knows I'd like to kill him. I already told him that I would cripple him to get him to talk."

"Does he think we'd hold you back?"

Dan shook his head. "I told him that you would arrange for him to be worked over for as long as it took to get the information we need."

"Is there any way we can do this without getting too brutal?"

Dan looked at Jane. "You don't want to go there?"

"Not if there's another way."

Dan studied the carpet for some moments.

"Here's what I'd like to do. I have an interest in Evangeline. I rescued her, got her to tell me her story. She's gotten to me. We've got a connection between us and I feel responsible to make sure things come out well for her." He shifted in his seat as if coming to a conclusion. "It helps balance the ledger for me."

"You have a crush on her? I can see she has one on you."

“It’s not that,” Dan shook his head. “I feel affection, for sure, but there’s something more. I need to make sure that this ends well for her.”

“Your soft spot…for women and children.”

“If you say so. I’ll deny it all.”

He got up and grabbed Jane’s glass.

“Another round?”

Chapter 43

The next morning Dan went into the room where Aebischer was being kept. The man was lying on a mattress on the floor. He struggled to sit up when he saw Dan. He looked wary. His arm was in a sling and his foot was bandaged and in a soft cast.

Dan sat on a chair facing him.

"The doctor says your shoulder will heal. You'll have some limited motion but the joint will work." He spoke in German. "The foot is going to be more of a problem. It will heal but you will have a permanent limp."

Aebischer looked nervously at Dan. He had been given some relief from the pain. Dan knew that had worn off by now and guessed Aebischer didn't want him to inflict more.

"You know that I'd like nothing more than to take you out and execute you. Leave you in the foothills to be eaten by the wild boars, never to be found. It's what you deserve. Your career is over. The only thing for you to decide is how it ends."

He leaned forward towards the man. Aebischer couldn't help himself. He flinched, leaning back from the intensity that Dan knew was on his face.

"Against my strong objections there is a scenario where you may get to live, not as a free man, but one alive instead of dead. Are you interested in hearing it, or do you want me to carry out my sentence?"

"They wouldn't let you just execute me. I'm too valuable."

Dan smiled. "Are you willing to bet your life on it?" He could see the doubt on Aebischer's face.

"What do you want?"

"Two things. First you will sign a document declaring that you've decided to retire and go into seclusion and you are turning over all your assets to your daughter, Evangeline. She is going to take over all the wealth you've accumulated, the money, the hard assets, the real estate—all of it. Second, you're going to tell me everything you know about the upcoming terrorist operation. Who the groups are, where they are, what they're planning? They won't get their funding, but I want more than that. I want to stop them from trying something now and you're going to help me do that."

"I don't—"

Dan put his finger to his lips. "Don't speak yet. If I don't like the information you give me, if I don't think it's honest or helpful enough, I'll execute you like I described. So weigh what you tell me carefully."

Aebischer swallowed. He spoke carefully. "I have much of what you're asking, but not all of it. I made a point of knowing enough to understand my exposure, but not enough to be complicit."

"You are complicit. You're just fooling yourself. But we're going to start with your declaration. I will have someone from our legal department come over and draw it up. It will be notarized and witnessed, all very legal. And, it will be done today. We don't have much time."

"Why should I turn over everything I've worked for, everything I've accumulated? Will you leave me destitute? I'm a man of substance, a man of means," he continued. "What right do you have to do this?" His face grew red and a look of rage replaced the one of caution. "I worked hard. I was thorough in doing my job, that's why I got wealthy. So what if some of my work enabled terrorists? They were only working against the Jews who are trying to control the world's finances. They were a blot on our European cultures, even before the war and it hasn't gotten any better."

His voice rose as his rant increased. Dan sat there watching the hate spew out of his mouth.

"Don't try to sound so virtuous. You abused your elder daughter, had a daughter by her, killed her, and then were going to start abusing the younger daughter." Dan spit on the floor. "You disgust me."

"What do you know? I wanted to keep my blood line pure. Not let my daughter couple with some low bred scum. It's better to keep it in the family."

Dan only shook his head. The man was not sane. No one would penetrate his rationalizations for what he had done.

"None of that matters now and I don't want to hear you try to justify your disgusting actions. You ruined two lives, maybe three. Who knows what happened to your wife? Right now, you need to understand that your old life is over. It's gone. Your wealth is gone. You will never see or touch it again. But if you cooperate to my satisfaction, you may keep your life."

Dan stood up. "Here's a chance to do right by Evangeline. You will never touch your wealth and so you have to leave it to her. Do that and you take one step to keeping your life."

Aebischer looked up at Dan. There was a calculating tone in his voice.

"You guarantee you will not kill me if I do what you ask?"

Dan shook his head. "No guarantees. But you avoid a sure bet I will kill you. It's a step in saving your sorry ass."

Aebischer looked long and hard at Dan. There was no softness, no give in Dan's expression. He looked at Aebischer like something to be eliminated, disposed of. The man finally sighed and nodded in assent.

The embassy sent over a lawyer who only knew that a Swiss banker wanted to help the CIA and needed to turn over all his assets to his daughter since he was going to disappear into the U.S. protection system. The document spelled out numerous bank accounts. The real estate consisted of the Zurich mansion, a villa in Locarno on *Lago Maggiore*, an ancient townhouse in Florence, and a ski lodge in Zermatt with a view of the Matterhorn. The luxury yacht, *Nordstar*, was included in the document. Catchall phrases, "including, but not limited to..." were put into all the listings since no one wanted to leave any items in doubt.

When it was done the attorney left. Dan and Jane were given a copy to read, yet unsigned.

"I can hardly believe you got this. Evangeline is now a very wealthy woman," Jane said after reading through the document.

"Probably three to five hundred million dollars."

"Can she handle all of that?"

Dan smiled. "I don't know. What I do know is that Warren would like to help her. Did you notice him? He's in love."

"A man's fantasy. An angel with a hot body who fights like a tiger."

"Maybe not every man's fantasy."

"She's the perfect waif, and the perfect temptress. I know about these things."

"You do?" Dan leaned over to her and whispered into her ear. "Are you one of those?"

Jane laughed and shoved him away. "You know better than that." She flexed her biceps. "This is not waif material." Then she turned serious. "She's in love with you. And now she's worth millions of dollars. Is this where you get off the train?"

Dan looked thoughtful. He suspected an ulterior motive in Jane's question. "It could be enticing, but I'm not ready to get off yet. I still feel like this is my calling for the present. Besides, she only thinks she's in love because I was the first man to really help her, not try to take advantage of her."

"I don't know. She's a powerful combination, especially now with all that money."

"Well, we'll just have to help her stay on an even path, won't we?"

Jane changed the subject.

"What about point number two?"

"We get this signed and then we'll get what he knows out of him. I want you to help me debrief him. When this is signed," Dan waived the document, "he's close to being irrelevant. We can get into the safe and we have Pietro."

"Who may or may not know anything about the codes."

"It will help pressure Aebischer."

Two notaries were called to the house, one Italian, one from the U.S. embassy, along with several witnesses, all part of the embassy staff. They watched Aebischer sign four copies of the document and attached their signatures to it as well. When the papers were signed and sealed, they left with no knowledge of what was going on beyond what they witnessed.

Chapter 44

While the cleanup crew descended on the Zürich mansion, Jane and Dan grilled Aebischer for nine hours. After some resistance, he capitulated and gave Jane all the information he had. There were terrorist cells located in Frankfort, Paris, and London. He had address information on the Frankfort cell only. It was the main one that directed the others. The existence of the cells was not news, but Aebischer gave them the bank accounts they accessed, one's that he had set up. These three cells were going to coordinate all the attacks but Aebischer didn't know the date.

Fred and Warren went to work immediately to find the other addresses. Jane communicated all her information back to Henry who passed it to his boss, Roger Abrams, head of SAD who discussed it with his boss, Garrett Easton, the Deputy Director of Operations. Easton contacted his counterparts in Frankfort, Paris, and London. Now with more detailed information those agencies agreed to put together an intervention plan including U.S. operatives.

Henry called Jane back after arrangements had been agreed to.

"Jane, I want you to send Dan to Frankfort to make sure this cell is taken down. From what Aebischer said, this is the key cell. The ranking ISIS operative works from that location."

Jane took Dan outside to be alone. "Henry's worried that the *Bundesnachrichtendienst,* the *BND,* won't act in time. He wants you to go to Frankfort and see what you can do."

"You going to let them know about me?"

"The *BND*?"

Dan nodded.

"Not directly. Henry's going to let them know we'll be monitoring the situation and will inform them of any new information we develop."

"What about the money? It won't be passed through. That should shut the cells down."

"Maybe, maybe not. Some of them may have the resources to put part of the plan into action. Take Roland with you. He's itching to get into action, sort of payback for babysitting Pietro."

"You know I work alone."

"Yes, but a backup will help this time. You don't know how many operatives there are in the Frankfurt cell and you won't be able to cover everyone. Roland's solid. He'll be an asset."

Dan gave her a sour look but agreed. They walked through the backyard. It was a mix of badly kept grass and overgrown planting beds.

"Are you going to tell Evangeline about her inheritance?"

"I don't know. It's earth-shaking news, even if she doesn't realize it at first. Maybe you should sit down and have a woman-to-woman talk with her."

"Chicken." Jane said as she smiled at him.

"I admit it. She might convince me to live a life of leisure with her millions while she makes it her mission to keep me satisfied." He smiled back.

"You're still sure you don't want to get off the train?"

Dan looked thoughtful. "I've been given a gift and I've begun to see it in action. I can read people now in a way I couldn't before, see into them, so to speak. I don't know how, but I *feel* what they're feeling and can sense the truth or falseness of what they're saying."

They walked in silence. Jane waited for Dan to elaborate. "That sensitivity tells me I'm supposed to use this gift for the missions you give me." He shook his head. "So, no, it's not time to get off the train. Not yet."

"You're on a different path than Evangeline."

"I don't know what her path is. She certainly doesn't know...yet. But I do think our paths will cross now and again. That's probably all it will be, crossing paths."

"Does your gift enable you to see the future?"

"No, definitely not. But I can sense things." He kicked a stone in the drive. "Hell, I don't know much about this and don't know where it will end. But I'll continue to do my job, especially if some good comes out of it beyond killing the bad guys."

Jane put her hand on Dan's arm. She looked into his eyes. "Thank you for that. I want to run this mission with you, not without you. I'll talk to her."

They turned to go back into the house. Evangeline watched them from an upstairs window.

After dinner that night, Dan took Roland aside while Jane sat down to talk with Evangeline.

"I want to commend you again on how you handled yourself in the mansion."

"Thank you." Evangeline gave Jane a curious look. Like seeing an odd stranger for the first time. "How do you do it? I mean how do you kill so easily? I just reacted by instinct almost, and to try to protect Dan. But you...you killed three guards. Doesn't it bother you?"

Jane smiled and looked into her eyes. "You have been through a lot for your age. You are a brave woman. From what you've told me about your mother, I think you must have inherited her courage. But you're not a warrior. I can see that."

"And you are? What's the difference?"

"A warrior first chooses to go into battle. A warrior is one who sees their calling to help to fight the enemy, directly, and on the front lines. I was a fighter all through my life growing up, defending my little brother and sister. What I do is my choice. I gave up a normal life to do this, similar in some ways to Dan. He gave up a normal life when he chose to make the men who killed his wife and child pay for their actions. We just linked our paths together on this shared pursuit.

"You are a fighter," Jane continued, "But you fought for survival. You have courage, but you didn't choose a life of being a warrior, a fighter. You're not one to run to the sound of gunfire. There's another role in life for you. And believe me you have been given an incredible opportunity to do some good with it."

"Instead of being a drugged-out porn star?"

"Instead of that, yes."

"How do you know I have an opportunity?"

Jane took Evangeline's hands in hers. "We have worked out a deal with your father. He understands that his old life is over. There's no chance of him going back to that. Dan convinced him to do one good thing in his life. He has signed over all his assets, all his wealth to you. You are his only surviving relative." She smiled at Evangeline. "You are now a wealthy woman."

Evangeline looked at Jane. Her face was blank. It was as if she didn't understand Jane's words.

"He's giving everything to me? Why?"

"Maybe there's a small spark of contrition in his evil heart. Or maybe he's trying to make us think better of him."

"What did you promise him?" Evangeline's voice was full of suspicion.

"Nothing direct. He's hoping this act will save him in the end."

"Don't."

"Don't what?" Jane asked.

"Don't save him. He killed my mother." Tears began to form in her eyes. She leaned forward, her voice harsh and choked. "No amount of money pays for that." She pulled her hands back. "If he can buy his life with his money, I don't want it."

"It's yours. The documents establish that. You can do with it what you want."

"I'll give it all away. It would be like taking blood money."

Evangeline stood up.

Jane looked up at her. "Think about it what it means. It is a fortune of three to five hundred million dollars. You don't have to decide or do anything for a while. Take as long as you need to think about what you want to do." She paused, and then added, "Talk to Dan if that will help."

Later that night Evangeline pulled Dan aside. "You promised Aebischer his life for turning his money over to me? "

Dan looked surprised. “I didn’t promise him anything. I told him it was not in my hands. And if it was, I would be inclined to execute him.”

“That’s what you should do. I don’t want his money, his blood money.” Her voice was sharp. There was a fierce look in her eyes. “He killed my mother. He can’t get away with that.”

Dan sighed. “Evangeline, I agree with you, but the world is more complicated. If the higher levels of authorities agree he has value to them, he’ll be kept alive. Their interests are not the same as yours...or mine, in this matter.”

She shook her head, her hair flying. “That’s not right.”

“Agreed.”

They were sitting in the kitchen. The others had retired for the night. Dan touched her arm to get her to look at him.

“You should not renounce this inheritance, even though it comes from Aebischer. It’s not blood money as you called it. Whether Aebischer lives or dies has nothing to do with him turning over his fortune to you. It’s not in our hands.” She looked at Dan with a mixture of anger and affection. “There are good things you can do with the wealth, things that may take time for you to figure out. I’ll be around to help and Jane will be available. We won’t leave you without support. A fortune of this size requires careful consideration and handling.” He smiled at her. “But don’t reject it. Consider it a gift your mother fought for.”

Evangeline looked into Dan’s eyes. “I’d welcome it if you would stay with me. If I’m going to be such a wealthy woman, you could join me. We can do things with the money together, good things, fun things. I can’t do this alone," she reached up to touch Dan's cheek, "And you're the only one I want to be with."

She paused as if gathering her courage. "Don't you see, I love you? You saved me and opened me up to a new life. And now with all that money we can live it together. You don't need to keep doing what you're doing."

Dan grabbed her hands and put them into his. He leaned close to her. "I don't do this for the money. I have been given a gift, from the shaman. I don't know how, but I'm to use it on these missions."

"Is it Jane? Are you in love with her? Is that why you reject me?" Evangeline's lips trembled.

"No. If anything it's Rita. I'm still not over her death. We were a perfect fit, hand-in-glove. I still have a hole in my heart from her death." Dan knew his face betrayed his grief. "It's a wound not yet healed. It will someday, just as this mission will end someday. But that day is not now."

"So, I won't see you anymore? This is it?"

Dan's smile returned. "No. You'll see me. I have a clear sense our paths will cross, maybe many times." He turned serious. "But I also see that we have different paths, different stories for our lives."

Evangeline looked sad; she lowered her eyes. Dan cupped his hand under her chin. "But that doesn't mean we won't see each other. You have many here, not just me, who want you to succeed. I think you've won the hearts of all of us. You have that gift."

"I only want your heart...and you won't let it go."

"It still belongs to Rita. But you have found a place there now, a place forever."

She reached forward and hugged the man who had rescued her and saved her from her captivity.

Chapter 45

Roland and Dan went to visit Marcus in the hospital where he was recovering from surgery. The bullet had hit one of his kidneys which had to be removed. He would heal just fine but there would be some convalescent time involved.

"Hey slacker," Roland said when they entered the room.

"Fuck you," Marcus replied.

"That's original," Roland said.

"You're just jealous because you had to stay behind and babysit while Dan and I did men's work."

"If I had gone, I might not have gotten shot. I hear you missed the shooter and he was only twenty feet away."

"He ducked."

Roland smiled and said, "How you doing, buddy?"

"I'm gonna be fine. Just be light one kidney."

"That mean you're gonna piss a lot more?"

"No stupid. That's the bladder. I still got a good one. The doctor says I should watch my intake of salt and not drink too much."

"Damn, that's going to cramp your lifestyle," Roland said.

Marcus looked over at Dan. "How did things shake out?"

Dan told him what had transpired since they had gotten back.

"Roland and I are going to go to Frankfort to make sure the cell leader, Jabbar Khalid, gets killed. He has a lot of influence over the other cells in Europe."

"What's up?" Marcus asked.

"Aebischer confirmed that the intel we have about an attack coming is correct. An Arab financier named Rashid al-Din Said recently moved millions into Aebischer's accounts to fund a coordinated attack on airports in Europe."

"Are you going to go after Said?"

Dan shook his head. "Don't know where he is. Fred hasn't found anything on him yet, but Aebischer may be able to help us. We're just trying to intercept the pending operation."

"Killing Khalid and interrupting the money, should disrupt the attacks," Roland added.

"Damn. I'd like to go with you, but I'm going to be stuck here for a few more days and then have about six weeks of rehab."

"We'll send pictures," Roland said with a grin on his face.

Marcus gave him the finger. "Go kick some ass."

"You got it, buddy," Roland said.

"We gotta go," Dan said. "Lots of planning to do."

Marcus and Roland were cut from the same cloth. They had become friends in Delta Force. Dan had reluctantly come around to accept Roland coming with him. He, like Marcus, had the warrior spirit and looked forward to engaging the enemy with no quarter asked or given.

Back at the safe house Jane gave Dan the address of an apartment that Fred had rented under Dan's alias. It was located on the intersection of Glauburgstrasse and Lenaustrasse. The rooms had a view of the intersection and the apartment building across the street where the terror cell was located. They could surveil the terrorists from the apartment. Jane gave them the best pictures Warren could find of Jabbar Khalid. They were to track him while Jane kept them updated on the progress of the *BND.* If the intelligence unit failed to take down the terrorists, or if Khalid escaped, Dan and Roland were to provide the backup to insure he did not survive.

Roland loaded their gear while Dan said goodbye to Evangeline.

"Please stay safe," she said as she hugged him.

"I will. Don't make any decisions until I come back, promise?"

She nodded.

Jane walked out to the car with Dan.

"Keep checking in and I'll update you on the *BND.*"

"What are you going to do about Pietro?" Dan asked.

"I don't know. I'm about to punt him to Henry. He's going to want to bring Aebischer back, along with the ledger. What he'll do with Pietro remains to be seen."

"I warned Evangeline that people above us were going to make the decision on Aebischer. I think I've prepped her for the fact that he may not be executed."

"Is she okay with that?"

Dan shook his head. "Of course not. But maybe you can assure her that Aebischer, should he live, will never be a free man."

"I'll do that."

"Now about Pietro. Remember he tried to have me killed twice. I don't want him running loose and messing with Evangeline."

"He was ordered to do what he did. He's also terrified of you and what you might do to him if he's out from under my protection."

"Good. Keep him worried about that. It'll make him more pliant." Dan paused for a moment. "I don't want him loose. He could be trouble for Evangeline."

"We'll deal with that later. Right now, I'll have an embassy staff person drive you to Marseille. From there each of you purchase an older car and drive separately. If you need to split up, you'll both have transportation. And you can leave them anywhere."

"Buy a beater, right? No luxury sedan."

"Right." Jane reached up and gave Dan a hug. Take care of yourself. You and Roland get this done and get back here so we can wrap this mess up and close the operation."

Dan gave her a mock salute. "Yes ma'am."

He got into the car with Roland and they headed for Marseille.

They arrived at their apartment in Frankfurt late that evening at different times and checked in. It had two bedrooms with a living room, bath, and eat-in kitchen. The first thing Dan did was to unpack their surveillance gear and set it up.

They had a camera with a telephoto lens aimed at the windows of the target apartment. Hopefully, they would see evidence of Khalid there. They could easily monitor the comings and goings of the apartment residents.

"What's the plan?" Roland asked.

"We play it as it develops."

"Do you always do things like this? No planning and hope for the best?"

Dan nodded. "That's how it generally works. You have to improvise."

“Precise planning prevents piss-poor performance.”

“In a perfect world. I work in a very imperfect world...lots of gray.”

Roland shook his head. “Do we follow anyone if they leave the apartment?”

“Yes and no. If they’re leaving to carry out a mission, they’ll probably leave together, unless they have more than one vehicle. We’ll try to determine that right away. If Khalid leaves, I’ll tail him. You stand out too much.”

“I doubt he’s a professional in uncovering tails.”

“I agree but you’d make it easier for him.”

“So I just sit around?”

“We take turns monitoring. We’ll do it 24/7 so there’s no gaps. If we have to do a takedown, we’ll do it together.”

After discussing their tactics, however thin, Dan left to purchase some groceries to hold them for a few days.

Chapter 46

Rashid al-Din Said was worried. His calls to Herr Aebischer were not answered or returned. He didn't leave any messages. His number was blocked from Aebischer's phone but Aebischer always took his calls and now he wasn't. Rashid also knew that when Aebischer saw a blocked number he knew it was one of his more important clients. Something was wrong.

He was sitting in his office in Riyadh in one of the high-rise buildings along King Fahd Boulevard. It was a block from the Saudi Stock Exchange which suited Rashid's purposes just fine. Ten days had gone by since he had visited Herr Aebischer. His calls to tell the Swiss banker to disperse the funds were not answered. Now he was being held up.

After two days with no reply, Rashid placed a call to Jabbar Khalid in Frankfort.

"Jabbar, something is not right. I haven't heard back from our banker. The funds haven't moved yet."

"What do you want us to do, *Sayyid*?"

"What tools do you have in your possession to do the task?"

"We have side arms, automatic weapons, but only one rocket launcher."

"Ammunition?"

"We have enough." Jabbar paused before adding, "But the other groups have only their individual weapons and some grenades. There are no explosives."

Rashid thought about what Jabbar had told him. His grand plan was in danger of becoming a small terrorist attack. The cells could do some damage but his vision was for something much larger. What had gone wrong?

"I will call you back. Put everyone on alert. The plans may be compromised and we may have to act quickly." He ended the conversation.

Rashid sat down and poured himself a cup of tea. He had a calculating mind. He was analytical and thorough. That was how he had made more millions out of the millions he had inherited. He was faced with a problem. He needed to solve it.

He picked up his phone again.

"*Da*," said a guttural voice on the other end in Russian.

"Hello, Yevgeni Kuznetsov?"

"Who wants to know?" The man answered in English.

"My name is Rashid. I sent some funds to our Swiss contact, Herr Aebischer. I can't reach him and I'm trying to determine if you received the payment."

"*Nyet*. I have assembled the list of what was ordered but have not received any funds."

"Herr Aebischer is out of communication at the moment. I would like you to release the order and I will personally see that the funds are transferred to your account."

"It is not possible. I don't work like that."

"I assure you I am good for the money, many times more than the funds required."

"That is not the issue. I don't move product without payment. If I do, I may be out the product *and* the money. If I hold on to the product at least I'm not out of both."

"This is for a very important cause Yevgeni Kuznetsov. The goods must be delivered without delay."

"Rashid, I don't know you or your cause. I also don't care to know about your cause. It is not mine. My cause is getting paid for what I deliver...before I deliver."

"I can transfer the funds you ask for today. Just give me the bank numbers."

"No, no. That is foolish and you should know it. Direct transfer of large amounts will set up a clear trail between you and me. I am not eager for that to happen. Herr Aebischer is a middle man for a reason. If he is not available then find another one who can establish himself with me and we can do business. Otherwise, we have nothing to talk about."

"You would turn your back on millions of dollars?"

Kuznetsov sighed. "I will sell the goods to someone, probably sooner than later. I am turning my back on the complications of acting foolishly as you request. Call me when you have found Herr Aebischer or his replacement." He ended the call.

Rashid sat with a scowl on his face. He was not accustomed to insubordination, to people not deferring to his wishes. The Russian was direct and rude. It was something Rashid disliked. They were so uncultured, the Russians, especially the gangsters.

Back in the States, the NSA computers, coded to detect keywords, spit out the transcription of the phone call. The words "automatic weapons" and "rocket launchers" triggered the action. The computer further analyzed the text and the algorithm decided a human should review the conversation.

The information was forwarded to the CIA and the name "Jabbar" cross -referenced to the terrorist in the

Frankfurt cell. The NSA was asked to monitor both phone numbers and pull any calls made on them.

Rashid's second call was then intercepted and the CIA now was alerted to the names, "Rashid" and "Yevgeni Kuznetsov".

The DDO was alerted and passed the information down to Henry Mason's boss who called Henry into his office.

"You've got an operation going on to try to interrupt a pending terror operation." He said to Henry. "We've just intercepted two phone calls from a Rashid. One to Jabbar in Frankfurt and one to a Yevgeni Kuznetsov in Russia. The good news is it looks like you've successfully interrupted the money. The bad news is that this Rashid may be ordering the cells to attack with what weapons they already have. How much damage can they do?"

Henry lifted his palms in the air. "Who knows? We've alerted the Brits, the French and Germans to the pending operation. I've got an operative in Frankfurt to disrupt any attack by Jabbar. But I can't cover all the possible targets."

"Nor should you have to."

"I just want to make sure that Jabbar is taken down. That will set back future operations for some time, if nothing else."

"You've got a full green light on that. Just stay below the radar so we don't ruffle German feathers. If they can do the job, so much the better."

"I've instructed my operative to do that."

Henry went back to his office to call Jane with an update.

Chapter 47

Jabbar Khalid had no illusions. Every action he took might be his last. It was what was expected of a jihadist. He didn't expect to live a long life, but he did hope it would be glorious with victories for Allah against the infidel. He trusted in Rashid's vision of Europe falling to Islam. It was soft, corrupt, and lazy. The leaders would not defend their people and only made excuses which made Jabbar's work easier. Now the time had come to improvise. Something had gone wrong. Maybe the financier had been captured. If so, no one could feel secure. They all might be exposed.

Jabbar called his men together. There were six of them in the apartment. They never went out together, only in twos or threes. Each of them had connections to three or four other men giving Jabbar a team of twenty to set up an attack.

"We will not be getting the weapons we were promised. The money man has been compromised." Jabbar paused for effect. "We all may have been compromised."

"What do we do?" One of the men asked.

"We will act with what we have. I will use the rocket launcher and attack the planes. The rest of you must organize your men to attack the terminal and kill as many as you can. Leave yourself an escape route, but know that you are mujahideen and must be willing to die for your faith."

"I have enough explosives to make two vests," another said.

"Do that. Use two of your men."

"Will their families be taken care of, *Sayyid*?"

"Yes. I will see to it. You must prepare them for their sacrifice. We will honor them before they set out."

The man nodded. Jabbar could see that he felt the weight of his task. He also guessed the man was privately glad to not be asked to make the immediate sacrifice. Attacking the terminal was risky enough and would probably get most of them killed, but at least a warrior had a chance to escape or to go down fighting. The suicide bombers could not get lost in the adrenaline rush of battle. They could only take heart in knowing that they would produce many casualties, maybe more than those who attacked with machine guns.

A day later Jabbar received a call from London. The caller told him that the police had raided the terror cell. They hit two apartments and one house in London's East End. Some of the men were captured; the caller had just managed to escape and was now on the run and in hiding.

"They knew where we were," he complained to Jabbar. "There must be an informant."

"Maybe. Our banker has been compromised, so the information may have come from him."

After encouraging the man, Jabbar hung up. He turned to the others in the apartment.

"We must go into action now. The London group was just raided. We may be next. We have to assume the authorities know about us and are ready to act. We leave tonight. You must disperse and collect your men. We will attack tomorrow in the middle of the morning. The airport will be busy, many people, and planes on the runway waiting to take off. We will make a big strike. It will be a glorious blow for Allah."

The six men were to divide up between Terminals One and Two. The two suicide bombers would go to Terminal Two, the smaller one, and separate in the lobby. They would trigger their vests at 10:30 am. The other four teams would infiltrate the lobby of Terminal One and at 10:30 open fire on the crowds. Drivers would wait at the drop-off level to give the shooters a chance to escape after they had emptied their magazines. Once their automatic weapons, shortened AKs-47s, were out of ammunition, they would drop them and rely on their hand guns to fight their way out of the terminal to the waiting cars.

Jabbar would go to the west end of the airport on the *Airportring Strasse*, if the wind was from the north or east. The planes would be stacking up on that end and there was an open parking area for plane enthusiasts. He could wait there to attack. He had a driver with him and if their escape was compromised, there were hundreds of acres of woods behind him that they could get into and make their way unseen to the south. They could go for miles in the forest. Even without a car, they would have a good chance to escape.

Roland was on watch late that night when he saw two of the men leave. He woke Dan.

"We got some of the marks leaving. It's late. Something's up."

Dan was instantly awake. He watched with Roland as the men scanned the street and then slipped out of the doorway, trying to keep in the shadows. There were no lights on in the apartment, but the two men could see occasional flashes of light.

"Flashlights. Something's up for sure," Dan said. "You follow those two."

Just then two more men eased out of the building's front entrance.

"I don't think any of them are Jabbar," Dan almost to himself. "I'm going down on the street."

Dan and Roland grabbed their gear bags containing their weapons and headed downstairs. Both carried side arms under their jackets. The bags held their M4 carbines with silencers and 1x4 30mm tactical scopes mounted along with extra magazines. The weapons would allow for accurate shooting up close and out to 300 meters.

At the doorway they split up. Roland turned left and hurried to follow the first group that had departed the building. Dan waited in the shadows of the doorway for a couple of minutes. When no more came out, he walked across the street and ducked down the alley between apartment buildings. *Might be a back door and Jabbar may be extra cautious.* Sure enough, at the back of the building Dan peeked around the corner and saw two men leaving. They walked away from him down the alleyway. Dan followed quietly.

Chapter 48

Under the street light Dan recognized Jabbar Khalid. After noting the make and color of the car, he retraced his steps and got into his own vehicle. Dan had no idea whether or not the BND was aware of the movement of the terrorists. He had seen the surveillance car at the end of the block. Would they call in the activity? Would they follow one of the pairs that left the apartment? He was sure that they weren't aware of Khalid who left via the alleyway. It was going to be up to Dan to keep track of the man.

Roland followed the two men on foot for three blocks. They got into a red Opel sedan and headed east on Glauburgstrasse. He noted the license number and ran back to get his own car. He drove as fast as he dared while watching the parked cars. Thankfully, it was 3:00 am and there was little traffic on the roads. At the intersection with a grand boulevard, the Nibelungenallee, he spotted the red Opel in front of a Moroccan restaurant. Roland breathed a sigh of relief and turned the corner, slipping into a parking place along the boulevard. He adjusted the mirror on his car and sat back to wait.

Unbeknownst to both Dan and Roland, the *BND* did notice the third pair of men leaving in a battered VW and, after calling in to their headquarters, they began following them. The two men stopped at another apartment building and one of them got out and disappeared inside using a door key. The other drove off. The BND agents followed the car and called in the address where the passenger got out.

The local commander of the TE Directorate, which covered terrorism and organized crime, monitored the calls from the surveillance team. He thought about calling Deputy Director of the Directorate but it was late at night. There didn't seem to be an operation going on. He only knew of two men who left the building on Glauburgstrasse. It could just be the men moving into different apartments. He would monitor the activities and update the Directorate office in the morning.

The man entered the apartment building and looked back through the side window at the street. He saw the surveillance car pull out to follow the VW as it drove off. He took out his phone and made a call.

"Ahmed, you are being followed."

The driver acknowledged the call. "I'll go to pick up the others, but we'll go out the back and use another car. We'll leave them watching the VW until we have completed our mission. Hakim, you make sure the two bombers are ready and continue as planned."

Dan followed Khalid through Frankfurt. He stopped at a nondescript warehouse and went in. A few minutes later he came out with a case. It looked like it held a large weapon. The other man followed with an armload of cases. *A reusable rocket launcher with multiple rounds?* That had been one of the words picked up by the NSA. Dan thought about that for a moment. *Going to hit the planes lining up to take off? If the others attack the terminals, he'll be all alone out near the runways.* It looked like Aebischer's information was correct; this cell was going into action.

He pulled out his phone.

"Roland," he said after placing the call, "What do you have?"

"Waiting at the curb. They're in a restaurant. Maybe picking up weapons or extra men. Can't tell yet."

"I'm on Khalid. He's just picked up what may be a rocket launcher with multiple rounds. I'm thinking he'll go after the planes on the runway while the rest are attacking the terminals."

"I'll try to follow these guys and intercept them before they can get into action."

"I'll do the same with Khalid. One worry is that we don't have eyes on two of the men."

"Yeah. Hope the *BND* are on that," Roland said.

"I'm going to call Jane and alert her. Maybe she can make sure the BND goes into action."

"Roger that. Stay in touch."

"You too."

Dan hung up and called Jane. Once she woke up and listened to him, said she would have Henry call the head of the TE Directorate in Germany. He was not someone who would listen to Jane. That fact irritated her, not so much personally, but professionally. It was inefficient.

Khalid drove off and Dan started following. It was now 4:30 am. The two terrorists drove around Frankfurt in a random pattern. *Probably killing time until daylight. They could be checking for tails as well.* It was too risky to keep following with such little traffic to conceal his tail.

Have to risk that they'll be after the planes, not the terminals. He dropped off and headed for the airport.

He had memorized the layout and knew there was a car park on the perimeter road, at the end of the runway. It was a place where people could watch the planes take off and land. He would position himself along the route, concealed, and wait for the car to drive by. Starting so early, hours before dawn, Dan was certain the attack would occur in the morning. *Not too early. They'll wait for the crowds to build up.*

The *BND* assured Henry that they had the terror cell under surveillance. What they neglected to tell him was that they had only two of the six men under watch and were soon to find they were watching an empty apartment.

The terrorists had now split up into more groups. Hakim sat with the two suicide bombers, Omar and Rafik. As dawn broke through the clouds, they performed their ablutions and said their prayers. Hakim helped them into their vests and showed how to trigger them. They talked about the timing. They would exit the car at Terminal Two. After entering, they would separate and move into the crowds. At 10:30 am they would trigger their vests and be transported to heaven. Dying in jihad would mean instant access to paradise with all its attendant pleasures.

The two men were somber. They came from the slums of Baghdad and had few prospects for a better life. They had been promised money for their families. With their acts, they would secure their salvation and help for their impoverished families. Still, one of them seemed to Hakim to be more nervous, even reluctant.

"Do not fear, *al'akhu al'asghar,"* little brother, Hakim said. He put his arm around Omar. You will feel nothing.

One moment you will be in the airport, the next in paradise. Instant. Painless. I will attack with my machine gun when I hear you have departed and continue to kill the enemy. I may be killed myself and will probably die painfully. But I will be happy knowing you are well."

He smiled at the man who gave him a half smile back.

"We will leave at 9:30 by the back door just in case the Germans put a watch on the apartment. We will use your car. I will drop you both off at 10:15 which will give you time to get through the crowds and as deep inside the terminal as you can."

With the simple plans set the men made small talk. Hakim prepared tea and a simple meal. The men had little appetite however. It would be two hours before they had to leave. Hakim wanted to keep their minds off what was going to happen. He wanted to make sure they would be able to press the triggers when the time came.

Ahmed pulled up to a rundown apartment building. There were few in Frankfurt, a very upscale city. It was in the Nordend-Ost and could probably be considered more bohemian than old and seedy. He got out and noticed the car stopping at the beginning of the block. *Let them wait. They will be sitting here when hell's fire erupts at the airport.* He smiled and went into the apartment building. Jabbar was right to have the six men split up and gather their separate men. Even if some were captured or compromised, the rest could still carry out the attack.

There were three men in the apartment. They were armed with Romanian versions of the AK-47, a short barrel variant designed for close quarters. They had pulled together all the ammunition they had and each man carried three extra thirty round magazines for a total of one hundred, twenty rounds each. They could do a lot of damage.

The men went through their morning prayers before sitting down to strong coffee and pastries. This could be their last meal. They were somber but committed. They were fighters getting ready to go into battle.

Ahmed smiled at the thought of what the teams could accomplish. They would have eight shooters in total with automatic weapons and two drivers who would also be armed. Some of the terrorists had only two magazines but it would be enough. Allah willing, they would kill many and be able to fight their way out and escape in the panic and confusion they would sow.

Dan called Roland. It was now 8:00 am. "Any movement?"

"Coming out now, how'd you know?"

"Psychic, I guess. Are they still together?"

Roland counted the figures. "There's three of them. Not sure if the same two are in the group."

"They've split up. There's probably another two or three leaving from somewhere in the back. Just follow the group you've got eyes on. We know where they're going."

"When do you think it's going down?"

"My guess is mid-morning. Let's hope Jane got the *BND* on the alert."

Roland thought about that for a moment. "I can follow them. They won't know I'm here. I'd worry about losing them except that we know where they're headed. My worry is getting shot by the *BND*. Except for the long coats, these guys look pretty regular, not like terrorists."

"The coats are probably hiding machine guns."

"Yeah. And I'll have my M4 which may put me in the same class as them as far as the police go."

"I know it's a problem. You have to be careful."

"Thanks. But that's not very helpful. You're out on the perimeter and I'm going to be in the thick of it."

"If you see the police, just alert them. They're probably not wearing suicide vests so the cops can take them down at any time...the sooner the better."

"Good point. Talk to you later, buddy, gotta go."

Chapter 49

Dan called Jane and told her about Roland's concerns. She agreed to have Henry contact his counterpart in the *BND* and make sure they knew about both Dan and Roland.

Upon hearing back from Henry, Jane called Dan.

"The *BND* says that Roland should stay away from the airport. They will handle things on their end."

"But Roland has eyes on one of their cars. There will be multiple cars arriving, maybe at the same terminal. It will be a blood bath if they can get inside. Did Henry tell them about the rocket launcher?"

"He did. The *BND* doubts that's what you saw. They don't think the group could have such a weapon, but they'll have the police do regular patrols along the perimeter road."

"People park there to watch the planes take off. The plane enthusiasts will provide Jabbar with some cover."

Jane sighed. "That's what they told Henry. They don't want you to endanger civilians."

"You want me to stay on this? I can interrupt the attack. Jabbar will simply wait for the patrols to go by. He'll have no lack of targets. The planes will be steadily lining up."

"Yes. But be discrete. What about Roland?"

"He'll follow the one car into the terminal. He can try to attract the police when it stops. Maybe they can get to the terrorists before they get into the terminal."

"Roland speaks only a little German and if he gets a stubborn cop, they'll be inside while he's trying to get through to the guy."

"I know. It's a tricky situation."

"He needs to do the best he can." She paused. "And then both of you need to get out of there, no matter what else happens. I don't want a spotlight shining on you or the operation."

"Why the hell are we here then?"

"To take Jabbar down...and to contain casualties, if we can."

"Okay, I'll buy that." He hung up the phone.

There were now eight shooters armed with automatic AK-47 rifles and two suicide bombers, all in four cars, driving around Frankfurt with a morning rendezvous at the two main terminals. In addition, Jabbar was going to be using the rocket launcher to attack the planes on the runway. Roland was following one of the cars with shooters while Dan was positioning himself to intercept Jabbar. The men from the *BND* were dutifully watching the Volkswagen parked in front of one of the apartment buildings that had housed some of the terrorists.

Roland followed the Opal as it made its way to the airport. Just before 10:00 am the car pulled into a parking area off the road to Terminal One used for drivers waiting for pickup calls. *Perfect. I can wait here with them and not be suspicious. Bet the others will show up as well.* Roland called the news to Dan.

"That's good. Let me know if the others show up and call me when they head out," Dan said. "I'll update Jane."

"Tell her to get the *BND*'s ass in gear. I can't do this alone and don't want to get shot by the police."

"I hear you. I'll pass it on."

Within minutes Roland saw two other cars pull in that looked suspicious. They had young men, some with beards, in the vehicles and everyone was wearing long coats. The men were on their phones.

Roland called Dan. "We have three cars of attackers. I count eleven including the drivers." He described the three vehicles.

"Roger that. Let me call Jane."

Dan punched the number on his phone and Jane answered on the first ring. "Roland's identified three cars with eleven terrorists in them. They're waiting at a cell phone pull-over. The attack is imminent." Dan passed the descriptions to Jane.

"I'll call Henry's counterpart at the *BND*. Henry told him he'd hear from a female who's in touch with what's happening on the ground. He doesn't know who I am but he'll take my call."

"Let him know that Roland will be following them to the terminal." Dan gave her Roland's car information.

"The *BND* will contact the airport police. Tell Roland to hold back and let them make first contact."

"Unless they don't get there in time and the terrorists start for the terminal. You said to try to minimize casualties."

Jane sighed. "Yeah. That's what we do. We engage and not just defer to the locals. We try to do more."

"And maybe pay a price for that. I'll let you know when the cars leave." Dan looked up in his mirror and saw Jabbar's car go past. It was headed for the pull-off at the end of the runway. "Gotta go, my target just drove by. That confirms a rocket attack on the planes as well."

"Go. I'll pass that along."

Dan pulled out and drove up to the viewing area. Thankfully, there were a few other cars there, even in the morning. It made taking Jabbar down more dangerous but gave Dan some cover. He parked thirty yards away from Jabbar's car. He pulled out his binoculars and started looking at the planes.

Roland sat at the car park. He was nervous. The enemy was in three cars, there were going to be civilians all over the field of engagement, and the police would be involved and might see him as one of the bad guys. It seemed like a recipe for disaster...disaster for him.

At 10:15 am he called Dan.

"They're on the move. Terminal One. I'm following."

"Roger."

Dan passed the message on to Jane and then put his phone away. There would be no more calls. It was time for action. He watched Jabbar's car carefully. The man would need some time to set up the launcher. Dan assumed that the driver would help load, so Jabbar could fire the launcher faster.

Chapter 50

Roland pulled out to follow the three cars. The road was packed with traffic; Roland was a couple of cars behind the group.

Traffic slowed.

The line was creeping forward in a stop-and-go fashion when the lead terrorist car jumped out of line and accelerated ahead. The two others followed. Roland cursed. *Acting like they have a deadline. Coordinating the timing? Maybe an attack on the other terminal?* There was no time to call anyone. He pulled out amidst much angry honking and followed. The three cars pushed ahead and muscled back into line before getting to the harried airport policeman who was trying to keep things moving.

Roland was able to force his way to the curb three cars back. He took a deep breath and slid his M4 carbine, covered with his jacket, from the passenger seat onto his lap. He waited. *Let the locals handle it...if they come in time.* He was happy to do that, but if they didn't come in time, he would not let the terrorists simply walk into the terminal and begin killing innocents.

He waited, body tense, his eyes darting around. Where were the police? Would they get there in time? Would he be caught up in their response?

It was 10:20 am. The car doors opened.

At Terminal Two the two suicide bombers stepped out of their car.

"*Allah maeak*," God be with you, Hakim said to Omar and Rafik. They nodded and started for the terminal. They stood out with no luggage and coats which hid their vests, making them look thicker than they really were. The passengers who hurried towards the terminal, however, paid little attention.

"Don't walk so close," Rafik said to Omar.

"I'm afraid," Omar replied. "Let me walk near you on this last journey."

Rafik shook his head in derision. "If you must, but don't speak loudly in Arabic. It will draw attention to us."

Back at Terminal One Roland stepped out with his M4; it was time to act. He ducked around the back of his car, looking at the men over the trunk. He was twenty yards away. As the men began to step out, he shouted in Arabic, "*Waqf!*" Stop!

The men looked in his direction as Roland brought his carbine up. When they saw the weapon, one of the men pulled his AK out from under his coat. That was all the confirmation Roland needed. He fired a short burst at the three men, still grouped close together. One terrorist's head exploded. His rifle dropped from his hands as he collapsed to the ground. The other two were hit in the chest and flung back off their feet. One reflexively fired his AK, the rounds spraying the concrete as he fell. People near Roland ran for cover behind the line of cars. Those on the sidewalk screamed and began running in different directions away from the fallen men.

In the next instant the driver of one of the terrorist's cars closest to Roland jumped out and began firing at him. Some of the rounds shattered his windshield and some flew over his head. Roland ducked. A civilian fell from one of the bullets, others dropped to the ground or scrambled away in panic. The panic was spreading to the larger crowd going in and out of the terminal. Roland moved to the front where the engine would shield him. He leaned around the front bumper and fired a short burst, at the driver who was walking towards him. The man was hit in the chest and face. Brains and blood erupted from the back of his head; his body collapsed to the pavement.

By then the men from the first two cars had exited. Three started running for the terminal while the other two fired at Roland. He dove to the rear of the car in front for cover.

He was crouched behind the car and not easily seen when the two of the traffic *polizei* ran up. They saw the terrorists and focused on them. There were shouts to stop and get on the ground in German. The terrorists fired at the arriving *polizisten*. Both men were hit in the chest and fell to the pavement.

Roland could hear sirens approaching. The rest of the terrorists started for the terminal, following the first three. The crowds now had parted from the center of the shooting. There was a flurry of bodies running, stumbling over each other. They parted like a wave from the advancing terrorists. The crowd collided with many that were fleeing the shooting coming from Roland which led to people being knocked down and trampled. Some of the people just dropped to the ground and lay still.

This parting of the crowds left Roland with a clear line of fire. He switched to single-shot mode and fired after the running terrorists hitting two of them solidly in the back.

They fell to the ground, dead or too wounded to fight. The three others didn't stop to return his fire, much to his frustration. They kept going towards the doors.

Just then two guards came rushing out of the terminal doors. The terrorists, without breaking stride, opened fire on them before they could get off any shots. The guards went down in a lethal flurry of rounds. Roland got off two more shots, one of which hit one of the terrorists in the shoulder and spun him sideways. The remaining two terrorists disappeared into the terminal.

It had only taken a few minutes. Sirens sounded and a dozen anti-terrorist police, the GSG9, jumped out of four SUVs. At that moment the drivers of the two lead cars tried to force their way out. The GSG9 ordered them to stop; when one of the drivers pulled his pistol out the police opened fire on both cars, killing the drivers. Two of the police stopped to check the fallen terrorists; the others ran for the terminal.

The cavalry had arrived. There was no more for him to do. Roland knew the GSG9 could take care of things. He was relieved. He had not been caught in a crossfire, and had not been seen by the police. He put his carbine under his jacket and turned away, leaving his car. There was still a crush of people trying to leave the area. He joined the throng and fled the scene. Once clear of the area, Roland commandeered a vehicle and drove off to rendezvous with Dan.

The two suicide bombers were at the front doors when they heard the sound of gunfire. Omar shuddered. Rafik grabbed him and shoved him through the door.

"We have to split up now. It has started," Rafik whispered in a harsh voice. He started away from Omar.

"Rafik," Omar shouted. "I'm afraid. I can't do it."

Rafik turned and shouted for him to be quiet. The commotion caused a security guard to approach them. Omar turned and ran for the door. The guard hesitated, not sure whether to pursue the runner or interrogate his friend. Both men looked and acted suspicious.

In that moment Omar ran back out the entrance and tripped. He fell to the ground as the guard called out to him to stop and Rafik pushed his button. There was a roar and a lethal spray of round shot cutting through the crowd near the bomber. Rafik disappeared into pieces but the damage was done. Dozens of people fell, wounded or killed by the metal balls propelled by the explosives.

Outside, Omar got up and ran for the car with tears in his eyes. His coat flew open revealing his vest. A GSG9 officer shouted for him to stop. The crowd gave way, running from the blast which had torn out the terminal windows. Omar ignored the officer who, after a moment of hesitation, leveled his carbine and shot him. The terrorist hit the ground, his hands fumbled for the button, but he couldn't find it. A moment later two officers grabbed his arms and secured them as Omar gasped his last breath.

Jabbar and the driver got out of their car parked at the observation lot. Jabbar was on the far side of the car from Dan's position. He had the rocket launcher in his hands. There were three cars with plane watchers between Dan and the terrorist. Dan slipped out of his car with his M4 and crept around to the back side. He could not see Jabbar or the driver.

Dan heard gunfire in the distance. The others in the parking area might not know what had happened, but Dan knew that Jabbar would. A moment later there was a larger explosion.

The driver went around to the back of the car and opened the trunk. He took out what looked like a rocket. Dan sighted the driver and pulled the trigger. The single shot rang out and the man's head exploded. He dropped to the ground. Dan continued to fire at the car, trying to hit Jabbar, who was on the far side. Glass flew and two tires were flattened. As Dan was firing, Jabbar launched the rocket. It flew towards the first plane that was sitting parallel to the road. The shot was errant and hit the tail of the plane, ripping it off.

Both Dan's shooting and Jabbar's rocket launch caused the occupants in the other three vehicles to panic. Two of them had the presence of mind to start their vehicles and race out of the lot. Jabbar reached around the back of his car and grabbed the second rocket from his dead driver.

Dan didn't have a shot. He waited, wishing the third car would leave. The occupants had dropped below the window lines and seemed to be afraid to move. Through the rear glass and side window of his car, He saw Jabbar swing the rocket launcher over the hood towards him. Dan didn't have a clear shot. He fired and missed; the glass deflected the rounds.

As he dove for the ditch behind him to get another position, Jabbar fired. The rocket hit the car shattering it and lifting it up off the ground.

Dan's ears rang from the explosion. Shrapnel flew across the ditch. He would have been killed except for the protection the gully provided. Dan lay there disoriented and dazed. When he looked over the edge of the depression Jabbar was diving over the fence and running to the woods.

Dan crawled out of the ditch. *Got to go after him. Take Jabbar down.* He stumbled to the fence and climbed, falling to the ground on the other side. He got up and set off towards the tree line, fifty yards away. His head was clear by the time he reached the woods. He knew the woods went miles to the south. *Must find him before he gets too far.* As his senses returned, he began to course back and forth, like a dog hunting for a scent. He needed a trail to follow. Once he had a trail, he knew he was equal to or better than Jabbar in the woods.

Chapter 51

Dan found Jabbar's footprints in the soft ground along with broken branches. It was enough to give Dan the trail and direction. Now he had to get moving. He took out his phone and called Roland.

"Where are you? You okay?" Dan asked.

"I'm fine. I couldn't stop them all but I was able to minimize the damage. The police have taken the rest of the shooters down."

"Did you get out of there?"

"Yeah. I had to leave the car and commandeered another one. Where are you?"

"I'm in the woods on the southeast side of the airport. It goes for miles to the south. I've picked up Jabbar's trail. I've got to catch him before he crosses the road to the south and commandeers a car. If he does we won't catch him."

"What do you want me to do?"

"Get to the road to the south. You can work your way north through the woods. We'll try to pinch him between us. Keep your phone on."

"Leave your car where it is?"

"It's blown up. Almost got killed by a rocket. My ears are still ringing."

Dan ended the call and set out at a trot. He ran for a few minutes and then stopped to listen. He needed to close on Jabbar but didn't want to run into an ambush if Jabber thought to stop and wait for him. Adrenaline flowed through his body dampening the aches he felt from his cracked ribs and bruised chest.

It was about the hunt now. Dan was the predator, Jabbar was the prey. But an armed human was the most dangerous of prey. He didn't have the luxury of just tracking the man. He knew the opportunity for Jabbar to disappear lay ahead if he didn't catch him. *Maybe he doesn't know about the road*. That was not something Dan wanted to pin his hopes on. He kept up a fast pace in his pursuit.

After destroying the car, Jabbar grabbed his AK-47 and launched himself over the fence. He didn't know if he had killed the shooter. His ears rang from the explosion. If he stayed, there would be multiple *polizei* arriving and he would be killed. Aiming the rocket launcher proved harder than he had imagined. And if the shooter were still alive, he would attack Jabbar from the rear. Without his driver's help he could not cover his backside and fire at the planes. He only hoped the other men had been successful in their attacks.

He ran through the woods at breakneck pace, branches whipping at his face and arms. He nearly tripped multiple times over sticks and roots. Finally, out of breath, he slowed down. *Break a leg or twist an ankle and it will be all over*.

The woods held the promise of escape. It was unique, consisting of so many acres this close to town. It was a wild place. Inside you could not tell you were near a metropolitan area unless you listened closely for the background noise of traffic. But now with the airport closed down, there was an odd stillness to the forest.

Jabbar's mind raced with confused thoughts. How had he been compromised? Who had found out about the operation, the site of the attack and the rocket launcher? His mind went over all the men in the Frankfurt cell starting with his inner circle of the five men. Was there a traitor amongst them? He came up with no conclusions.

Rashid's call may have held the clue. He had said the Swiss banker had been compromised and that the additional arms and explosives were not coming. Perhaps that is how the authorities found out. Still, there was something odd about his encounter. No uniforms, no police cars. If the police knew, why hadn't they descended in numbers? There should have been a caravan of police cars roaring to the parking area, overwhelming any opposition. But there had been only one person who apparently knew what he was doing. Jabbar hoped his rocket had killed him.

He kept moving generally south. He could not be sure in the dense woods. He kept his pace just short of a run, not wanting to risk a fall. He was an urban bred man from the poor neighborhoods of Baghdad. He could navigate the alleyways and narrow passages in the dense warrens that confused and obstructed those not brought up in such areas. But the forests? They were foreign territory. His mind went back and forth; should he stop to make sure he wasn't being followed or keep going? Jabbar settled on keeping moving; it was important to put as much distance between him and the airport as possible. He was determined to escape to fight another day. Rashid would understand. Soldiers might be killed in this battle, but leaders were critical and Jabbar considered himself a leader.

Dan stopped at a creek. It was not large but it created an open area where he would be vulnerable to being targeted. He was in the brush cover just short of the two-foot-high bank. He could see what looked like footprints going up the far side—two prints that slid in the mud. His eyes searched the undergrowth on the far side, looking for any sign of an ambush. In nature there are no straight lines. That was his first check. Shapes or colors other than what the forest showed naturally were another check.

Seeing no signs of anyone, he took a deep breath and rushed across the creek. On the other side, he checked for signs of the trail and started jogging, his eyes darting back and forth, looking for the enemy as well as for signs of his passage. Occasionally he would have to stop and start a zigzag pattern, back and forth, to pick up the trail again. It was going to be hard to close the distance on his prey, but it was necessary to stay on course.

He was the hunter; he would get his prey.

Jabbar reached a cleared area roughly thirty meters in width. It ran west to east. In the middle he spotted a raised concrete tube with a metal manhole cover on top. It looked like a sewer line and was the reason for the cleared pathway. He ran across the uneven ground and hid in the dense brush on the other side. This was the place to wait to check on any pursuit. If there was one, he could shoot the pursuer when he was out in the open. If there wasn't any pursuit, he could continue south in more confidence. Eventually he would reach a road and would hijack a car and drive into Frankfurt. There were people there who would hide him until he could get out of the country. He would go to Marseille. He had connections there, people who would get in touch with Rashid. And Rashid would help him get back to the mid-East where he would wait for a new mission. The fight would not end. Jabbar readied his AK and waited.

Roland moved through the forest. He had no idea if he was on an intercept course. There were too many acres to cover. He moved slowly, using his ears to help him "cover" more ground. Finally, he came to the open sewer line. He stopped in the brush. *No sense in going further. If Jabbar is to the north, I'll intercept him when he gets here. If he's to the south, I've already missed him.* He settled quietly into the bushes and waited. After a few minutes, he decided to move laterally along the edge of the clearing. He could watch the open area while also looking for any sign that Jabbar had passed. If he had gone past Roland, he would need to head south as fast as he could to try to keep Jabbar from taking a car. He knew the man would have no compunction about killing a civilian.

As much as he tried, it was impossible to move with absolute silence through the dense growth near the edge of the clearing. No matter how carefully he tried, he was making noise as he worked his way through the thick cover.

Jabbar heard the sounds. He knew enough to realize that a deer would not make them. They picked their way delicately through the woods, only making noise when they burst into a run to escape a predator. *Who was this?* Someone had come across the clearing before him? Jabbar turned towards the sound.

After a few moments he saw a vague shape, almost a shadow. It showed itself and then disappeared as it moved through the cover. He brought his rifle around. There was no clear shot. The shape appeared for a moment, about fifty meters away. Jabbar fired off a short automatic burst in the direction of the movement. Then...nothing. Did he hit whatever was moving through the woods?

Roland hit the ground without thinking at the sound of the gunfire. It was an automatic response drilled into him through years of training and a full understanding that one's reaction speed meant the difference between life and death. The rounds whistled overhead with their sharp, deadly snapping sound. This was what he had trained for. The enemy spotted; the enemy engaged.

He smiled and raised his head slightly to peer through the leaves. He didn't move. The shooter, most likely Jabbar, hadn't fully seen him and had taken a sound shot, just shooting in the direction of the noise he had been making. Now he would wait and let his opponent make the next move and therefore the next sound.

Dan heard the burst of automatic fire. It was a heavier sound than the M4 made. *Jabbar's weapon!* He must have encountered Roland. Dan began to run at a faster pace. *Now we can catch him and take him down.*

Jabbar waited and watched for a minute. No sound, no movement came from the direction of his shot. Did he connect? He decided not to investigate. If anyone was following, they would have heard the shots and would be coming faster. It was time to get out. He began to crawl south. He would move carefully until he had put some meters between his position and where he thought the other person had been.

Roland heard the soft rustle of brush but could see nothing. Jabbar was on the move. He waited a moment and then began to crawl on an intercept direction. Suddenly he saw a body rise and run off. It was lost from view in the trees. Roland jumped up and ran after the figure. Another short burst of automatic fire caused him to drop to the ground again and crawl to the cover of a large tree. When he peeked around the trunk, he saw nothing, but he could hear someone crashing through the woods.

As Roland rose to run after the fleeing figure, he heard sounds of movement behind him. Instantly he dropped behind a tree, now watching to the north, rifle ready. A figure showed itself pushing through the cover. Roland took aim but waited.

When it emerged briefly, Roland saw it was Dan.

"Over here," he called out.

Dan stopped and then shifted directions, running towards Roland's voice.

"Jesus, I almost shot you," Roland said as Dan ran up to him.

"Where's Jabbar?"

"Going south. He's probably a hundred yards ahead. I heard you and stopped to watch my six."

"Let's go. The road's the next escape option for him," Dan said.

They set off running through the woods.

Chapter 52

Jabbar ran as fast as he could. There must be a road ahead; that was how the other man got into the woods. He would stop a car and escape. Panting and nearly out of breath, he burst onto the road and stopped. He looked around. There was a car on the side of the pavement, probably the one the other man came in.

Maybe he could hot wire it. As he started across the road, he heard a car coming. When it got near, Jabbar stepped back into the road and pointed his AK at the driver. He put up one hand indicating for the man to stop. The car's tires squealed as the driver mashed down on the brake pedal. Jabbar ran up to the driver's door.

"Get out!" He yelled in heavily accented German.

The man looked at him with eyes wide in fright and shook his head. "What do you want?" he asked.

Jabbar pulled the trigger and the window shattered along with the man's head. The dead man's foot slipped off the brake pedal and the car started rolling forward. Jabbar reached in and yanked open the door. Pulling the man out of the vehicle, he jammed himself into the driver's seat and stepped on the accelerator. The car lunged forward just as Dan and Roland emerged from the woods. They began firing at the fleeing vehicle. The rear window shattered but the car kept going. The Mercedes was out of sight before the two got into the car Roland had driven.

"We can't just chase him into Frankfurt, or wherever, this is a stolen car," Roland declared.

Dan pounded the dash in frustration. "Just go. We'll catch him."

Roland started the car and accelerated away. "This is a little Skoda. That's a Mercedes he's in. We won't catch it."

Dan didn't reply. He just stared ahead his fists clenched. In a mile they came to a four-way stop. There was nothing to see in any direction.

"We've got a one in three chance of picking the right direction," Roland said, "Maybe one in two assuming he wouldn't go straight." He paused. "But we're still not going to catch him."

"Go left. Towards downtown. He wants to get back and hide out in a friendly neighborhood. There have to be people who will hide him."

Roland shook his head. "Okay, but remember, this is a stolen vehicle."

He turned left and accelerated.

"Still not going to catch him," he muttered to himself.

"You so ready to give up?" Dan asked. There was anger in his voice.

Roland caught himself before answering. "Look, I know you're frustrated," he said as he pushed the little Skoda for all it was worth. "We were told to take Jabbar down. He got away. But we were also told to disrupt the attack. We did that. Saved a lot of lives."

"You saved a lot of lives."

"And you're pissed because you didn't get Jabbar? Like that was your sole responsibility? Fuck man, don't take this personally. We did most of the job we were sent to do.

You'd have done what I did and I could have missed Jabbar as well. It ain't your fault."

All Dan could do was growl to himself in frustration. Five more miles down the road and Roland spoke up again.

"We're not catching him or he went a different way. This is crazy to put ourselves in a position to get arrested."

Dan sighed. "You're right. We don't want to be caught up in the mess."

"Now you're thinking, buddy." Roland slowed and made a U-turn on the road to head back from the direction they came, away from the city. "We'll change out this car for another one as soon as we can and get the hell out of Germany."

"Head to Limburg. We'll ditch the car there and catch a train to Brussels. From there we can go south through France and get back to Milan. We'll have to ditch our weapons and just take our packs."

"Don't like doing that," Roland said. He headed for the main road into Limburg. Dan went over the route in his memory and gave Roland the directions.

An hour later they were in Limburg. They parked in the large lot at the main train terminal, separated and purchased tickets for Brussels. The train was due to arrive in a half hour. The two men sat apart both appearing calm. Dan pretended to read a German newspaper while Roland watched the news on the overhead TV screen. There were updated reports of the attack at the Frankfurt airport. All airports in Germany and nearby countries were closed. The two men were relieved to see that train travel had not been interrupted or stopped. While they waited, they noticed an increase in armed police presence patrolling through the terminal. Both men were relieved to hear the train announced. They casually got up and proceeded to board.

Once the train started moving Dan began to relax. He was still frustrated, but knew Roland had been right. What he was feeling was as much personal as professional. He didn't think he had held up his end of the mission. Missing Jabbar seemed like a failure to him and Dan racked his brain to think of how he could find and intercept the man again. For now, a mission to Frankfurt was out of the question.

He walked to the back of the car and called Jane.

"We're seeing the news feeds. Sounds like you were able to prevent huge losses. One bomber was able to trigger an explosion in Terminal Two. There was a second bomber, but he panicked and the police were able to keep him from setting off his vest."

"I missed Jabbar," Dan said.

There was silence on the phone, then Jane spoke, "He got off only one rocket. It hit the tail section. No one was killed."

"But he got away."

"That's okay. You managed to avert a huge disaster."

"Has anything occurred anywhere else?" Dan asked.

"The French police intercepted attackers attempting to assault Gare du Nord. All the terrorists were killed but seven civilians were wounded. Nothing's happened in London so far."

"I think Jabbar was the leader. The other cells were probably less well organized or supplied. That's what the money from Aebischer was to do, provide them with weapons and training."

"Agreed. Where are you now?"

"We're on a train to Brussels. From there we'll head south into France."

Jane thought for a moment. “Go to Lyon. I’ll have a car meet you there and drive you to Milan. I don’t want any record of tickets going into Milan.”

“Got it. Better send them on the way soon. You know how well the trains run.” He paused for a moment as Jane waited. “And, Jane, I’m sorry I didn’t get Jabbar.”

“Don’t be. I’m glad the two of you made it out unhurt and without getting caught. That was not easy.”

“I’ll make it up to you,” Dan said as if he hadn’t heard her.

Chapter 53

Jabbar abandoned the stolen car on the outskirts of Frankfurt near a subway station. He took the underground train to the Nord Ost district and walked to the apartment of a sympathizer. Once inside the apartment he began to relax. The owner of the apartment had the news on his television.

Jabbar watched intently as the announcers went over the events. To his frustration, he learned that only one of the bombers had successfully detonated his vest causing an estimated twenty or more casualties. The machine gun attacks were even less successful. The police mentioned an unknown shooter who had initially engaged the terrorists, stopping them from advancing and allowing precious time for the *polizei* to arrive. No one knew who the person was. It seemed that he had commandeered a car and fled the scene. Jabbar's less-than-successful rocket attack was also talked about. He sat with hands clenched. His attacks had failed on all fronts.

The apartment's owner offered Jabbar some tea. Later there was a meal which was eaten in silence. The owner, seeing Jabbar's anger and frustration, asked no questions and Jabbar offered no information. It was better that way.

After eating, Jabbar called Rashid. They did not talk directly about the events. Rashid indicated he knew what had happened from the news feeds.

"There were only two people involved in countering our efforts," Jabbar said.

"You're sure of this?"

"*Na'am sayyid.* I am sure."

"There must have been some support behind them. They were just the front end of the effort. I told you that our banker has been compromised along with his assistant, the spineless Italian."

"Who could do such a thing?"

"They must have been from the U.S. The European nations do not have the spine or interest in working so hard against us. They hope to appease and we will take advantage of that. Now it seems the United States has made it their mission to intervene, even in our work on the continent."

"That will make our work harder."

"Never fear, my soldier. It may be harder, but we will succeed, both in taking down the Europeans and in taking our fight to the Americans." Rashid paused. "But for now we must get you out of the city. Wait until the tensions have died down and then go to Marseille. You will wait there and I will arrange passage on a freighter going to the Lebanon."

"Yes, *sayyid.* I will go there and await further instructions."

"In the meantime, I will try to find the identity of these two men. Maybe you can remove them for us."

The argument was energetic and went late into the night. Roland insisted that he go with Dan to Marseille. NSA phone intercepts, now cued to Jabbar's and Rashid's names had produced some evidence that Jabbar Khalid had gone to that city to await transportation back to Lebanon. The information was passed on to the CIA. Dan declared he had unfinished business and would go there to kill Jabbar.

"You need someone to back you up," Roland kept insisting.

"I work alone on this one. I needed more people to deal with the assault but this is better with just me," Dan replied. "I'll get into disguise and work the neighborhoods until I locate Jabbar. Then I can take him down. It's what I'm trained to do. You'll just stick out too much."

"Hell, I can get into disguise as well."

Dan shook his head. "No offense, but you'll still stand out too much. I'm glad you were with me in Frankfurt," he turned to Marcus and added, "And I'm glad you were with me in Zürich, but neither of you would blend in, even in disguise. You'd still look too Delta Force."

"And that disqualifies me?" Roland said. As a warrior, he was angry at being left behind and he was insulted that his military presence, a deep part of who he was, disqualified him for a clandestine operation.

"You're a fighter. I'd want you by my side anytime there's a firefight. No question. But this is more undercover. I have to try to find this man in a closed community that doesn't speak to outsiders much. I'm going to have to craft a persona and become that person. It's more than just putting on a physical disguise." Dan leaned over at Roland. "I have to become a mid-Eastern immigrant, looking to join the jihad." He sat back. "That's a whole different challenge."

At this point, Jane could see both Roland and Dan digging in their heels.

"I have to agree with Dan here," she said.

Roland turned to her, his eyes flashing, still angry. "You think I can't do this?"

Jane returned Roland's aggressive stare. She wouldn't back down. "No, not this part. Leave it to Dan."

Roland looked away, still angry.

"Look, after Dan identifies his target, if he needs help, you'll be the one I send. But this is what Dan is trained for. I have to let him do this."

"So he doesn't feel he failed. He gets to try this on his own."

Jane hardened her voice. "Dan gets to try this on his own because he's the best we have to do this successfully. End of story. Now I don't want to hear any more grousing about this. We each have a role on this team and yours is not the same as Dan's in all situations."

Marcus talked to Roland later but he couldn't get Roland to see the situation from Jane's point of view.

"He's going to be pissed for a while, but he'll get over it," Marcus said.

Two days later, Dan had a new identity. He was now Abdullah ben-Wassal, related to a minor Bedouin tribe in the Sinai that held a small territory. It was not a prominent tribe. It would be disastrous for Dan to run into someone from the same tribe. He would never get through the flurry of family connections that would surely result from such a meeting.

He dyed his hair black and worked a darkening agent into his skin, all over his body. He grew a short beard, mostly untrimmed. The look, when finished was unkempt and down and out.

His story was that he was born in Italy of immigrant parents. He rebelled against their strict upbringing and rejected their old ways. He never learned to speak Arabic properly beyond the few words Dan knew. He was westernized but marginalized and ready to do battle against the oppressive Europeans who he now saw as his enemy and the reason for his lack of success in the world.

He would be looked at as cannon fodder by someone like Jabbar. Dan hoped the man would be interested enough to recruit him and assign him to the cell in Marseille. Dan just needed to connect with Jabbar; the rest would then play out to its deadly conclusion.

Chapter 54

Dan checked into a seedy hotel in the *quartiers nords* area of Marseille. It was the low-income area of the city and filled with drugs and associated crime. The landmarks consisted of block-long high-rise apartment buildings. They looked like the ghetto apartment structures all over major cities in the west. Dan wondered why anyone would plan and build such structures for the poor. They always seemed to collect crime and violence. They were stark, unattractive, and inhuman in scale, cramming too many people into their dreary spaces.

The city was a simulating mix of cultures with a large Corsican population who didn't think of themselves as very French, a large contingent of North African immigrants of Muslim background and the continental French who prided themselves on being the keepers of the culture in the city. The gangs were run by all three groups, each vying for dominance.

The *quartiers nords* neighborhood was also not far from the port area. Part of Dan's cover would be he was looking for work on the docks, not wanting to get involved in the more dangerous drug trade. He spent the first week looking for work being careful not to create too positive an impression since he didn't want to get hired, just to be seen trying.

Dan spent his nights in various bars working his way through the network of patrons dropping hints that he wanted to get involved with some sort of militancy. Most times he was rebuffed. Much of the poor were looking to just get by using foul means or fair.

The neighborhoods near the high-rise tenements were run by the local mafia crime syndicates. The police were mostly ornamental and didn't intrude much beyond the main thoroughfares. Dan knew he was on his own.

He had finished nursing a beer in a rundown bar. It was late. His inquiries with the bartender resulted in stony looks and a statement of ignorance, feigned or otherwise. Dan got up; there was nothing more to accomplish this evening. He stepped outside and started down the side street. On this road, like many others in the poor districts, the street lamps were far apart and some did not work.

It was dark. The night was heavy with the smell of the sea. The air was cool indicating the coming of fall. Dan shrugged inside his jacket and trudged down the sidewalk. He was soon aware of two men who came out of the shadows and started following him. A third man appeared in front and started walking towards him. Were they together? Dan tensed.

The man approaching from the front stopped and spoke to Dan.

"Can you help me out? I need some money for the bus."

Dan stopped and eyed the stranger. He could hear the two from behind approaching. Dan stepped to the side so he could see the men coming from behind. In a moment the three were in a semi-circle standing around Dan.

"Your money and phone and you won't get hurt," the first man said.

"Just move on and *you* won't get hurt," Dan replied.

"Smartass," said one of the others in a thick, northern African accented French. "Maybe we teach you a lesson."

With that he pulled out a club. It was wooden and looked heavy. He swung it at Dan's head. Dan leaned back; the blow went past him. He grabbed the striker's arm and pulled him through the arc of his swing. The man's momentum helped to carry him along. Dan threw him into the first man and stepped forward towards the third attacker who was just processing what had happened. Dan brought up his leg in a powerful kick to the man's groin. The man cried out and bent over. As he did, Dan scissored his left leg and kicked the man in the face, sending him to the concrete with a broken jaw.

At that moment the other two had disentangled themselves and both squared away at Dan.

"You bastard!" The man with the club shouted and stepped forward again. As he raised his arm to strike again, Dan spun counter clock-wise and lashed out his left foot as he completed his turn, striking the man at the side of his left knee. He could hear the crack as the knee joint buckled from the side impact. The man went down like a felled tree, dropping his club and grabbing at his leg.

Only a few seconds had passed and now the last man standing, the one who had approached from the front, pulled out a knife.

"I'll cut you to pieces," he said in a low guttural voice.

Dan said nothing but slipped off his jacket and wrapped it around his left arm. It would serve as a shield from the knife until he could close on his attacker. He waited, centered, ready to counter strike. The man shuffled around making sham thrusts that didn't come close to connecting, hoping Dan would commit. Dan waited.

Suddenly the man rotated the blade with the sharp edge facing upright in his hand and lunged forward, looking to stab him in the gut and slice upward. Dan stepped to the left and the blade thrust found only air. The man's momentum carried him forward. Dan grabbed the attacker's knife arm and looped it under his own and behind the man's back with a violent wrench that dislocated the attacker's shoulder.

The knife dropped to the ground. Dan completed the move with a strike to the man's neck and he went down, writhing in pain, semi-conscious. It was all over in less than thirty seconds. Dan stepped back. The attackers were not going anywhere soon. The only one who could pose a threat was the first man, now recovering from the kick to his groin. His jaw was broken, but his limbs were intact.

Dan kicked the knife away and stepped over to the attacker. He bent down close to the man's face. The attacker looked at him with fear in his eyes.

"Do you want to live?" Dan asked in a low voice.

The man just looked at him and then slowly nodded a yes.

"If you don't want to get killed or maimed, do not try to follow me, understand?"

The man nodded.

"And don't ever come near me again. Next time I'll kill you."

Dan stood up. The man just watched from the sidewalk where he lay as Dan turned and walked away.

Two nights later, Dan was in another bar, asking the same questions with similar results. It was beginning to look like the community was too closed to penetrate, or the local criminals didn't know much about the Islamist element. He was at the bar when two large men sat down on either side. One of them leaned toward Dan and spoke.

"There is someone who wants to speak to you. Come with us."

"And where would we be going?" Dan asked.

"To meet this person."

"Who is he?"

"He'll tell you if he wants you to know."

"Why should I go with the two of you?"

"You don't want to say no."

"I'm looking for work, can this person help me?"

"Maybe. He's the one to help, if he decides to."

Dan thought for a moment. These men were large. They were calm, matter-of-fact in their manners, acting confident in their ability to handle trouble. Quite unlike the three street thugs that had tried to rob him. They would not go down easily. Still, there was one less to deal with. Dan liked his chances.

"Okay, but if this is a setup, one or both of you will get hurt."

"Just come with us. It's for real," the man replied. He stood up indicating they should leave.

They walked out of the bar with one in front and one behind. Not the best position tactically, but what he expected. They walked for three blocks in silence before entering an apartment building. It was smaller than the block-long monstrosities that scarred the neighborhood; much more on a human scale.

The trio climbed three flights of stairs and knocked on a door. It was opened and Dan was shuffled inside between the two men. The living room opened at the rear to the kitchen and dining area. There were three other men in the room, all armed with automatic weapons,

MP5s. Sitting at the dining table, farther into the apartment, was a large, fat man. He was eating from a platter of pasta and thick sausages. There was a large glass of red wine next to the platter.

He didn't look up. He kept busy wielding his knife and fork on the sausage. Dan stood at the entrance to the dining area, between the two men who had brought him. Everyone waited for the fat man to acknowledge them. Finally, the man looked up after washing down a huge mouthful of food with a large swallow of wine.

"I'm French," he said in a thick, raspy voice, "But I love Italian food. It's a shame we didn't invent Parmigiano cheese. We created so many other cheeses, but we missed it with that one." His French was heavily accented. Dan guessed he might be from Corsica. His hair was black and combed straight back. He had puffy cheeks in keeping with his corpulent physique. The eyes were black and set deep in his fleshy face. "And olive oil. But we use it so much we may as well have invented it."

His expression grew serious as he focused a sharp stare at Dan. "You're the man who took out three punks on the street two nights ago, are you not?"

Dan returned the man's stare. "That's me. Did they belong to you?"

The man shook his head. "Amateurs. Mostly a bother to me, but not important."

"Why am I here if it's not about that?"

The man studied Dan for a moment. He pushed his plate away, wiped his face with a large napkin, and took another sip of wine. "We still make the best wine." He wiped his face with a large cloth napkin. "I have been informed that you are asking around for work. Plus, you say you want to be a soldier, maybe a jihadist? How you handled those punks the other night indicates you can take care of yourself and could be useful to the right person. Stand over there," he pointed to a ceiling light that spilled a large pool of illumination on the floor. The men moved Dan into the brighter light.

The fat man stood up. He approached Dan who tensed himself, ready to strike if attacked although he didn't think he had much of a chance with all the armed men around.

The man studied Dan closely. "You're not an Arab," he said with finality. Stepping back from his examination, he continued, "You look like one. And you could pass for one ninety-five percent of the time, but you're not. I've been around middle-Easterners most of my life, living here in Marseille. I've fought with them and worked with them. You have something usually missing from them. You have a presence about you, the way you carry yourself. Now, here, in what might be considered a dangerous situation, you aren't panicked. The middle-Easterners I've been around would also not panic but they would show much more suspicion and tension...you don't. You're quite calm in fact." He paused for a moment. "Plus, your eyes are not quite the right color."

The man turned and walked back to his seat.

"Sit down." He gestured to a chair on the side of the table. Dan went to it and sat down.

"I'm Gaspard. What is your name?"

"Abdullah," Dan replied.

The fat man produced a smile which quickly faded. "Don't waste my time. You are not an 'Abdullah'. What is your real name?"

"That's not really important, is it? What do you want of me? Or more importantly, what can you do for me?"

"A bold answer. No, I don't need to know your name. I'll lay my cards on the table. This neighborhood is mine. I'm in charge. Nothing happens here unless I authorize it.

I answer to higher ups, but here my word is law. Business is done with my approval. Actions are taken only with my approval. So, what you do comes under my authority. As you can imagine, I need strong men to carry out my orders. You, my mysterious friend, could be helpful to me." He pointed to Dan with his finger. "Would you like a glass of wine?"

"*Non, merci,*" Dan responded.

"So, if you are not a middle-Easterner, who are you and what are you after? You're not the type who wants to go on a jihad. I don't see any 'true believer' in you. Tell me what you're after."

"I'm not after work as you describe it."

"What then?"

Dan took a breath. The man had nailed him. He was one of the few who could see through his disguise. No disguise was perfect and Dan knew he always had to rely on no one being able to examine him in detail. He had placed his trust in others being more interested in what he could offer and therefore would not look too closely at his cover, either his disguise or his story. He had nothing to lose at this point. With this man, his cover was blown, even as he tried to keep up the charade.

"I'm looking for a man, a man in the Arab community, a jihadist."

"Now that's interesting. We have those sorts in Marseille. They are scum as far as I'm concerned. They only want to kill civilians and are not interested in proper criminal enterprises. They interfere with our markets. I won't have anything to do with them."

"But you know of them. You run this part of the city and I bet you know what's going on in much of the rest of it."

Gaspard didn't answer but just looked at Dan.

Dan continued, "Can you help me find this man?"

Gaspard's face broke into a broad grin. "That *is* bold. I brought you here to explore hiring you and now you want to hire me." He smiled. "Just why should I help you?"

"I can pay you well for your help, if that's what you mean."

"Maybe you can, maybe you can't. Maybe you can do something for me in return, if I help you."

Dan shook his head. "I don't want to get involved in your affairs. I'm not that person and I don't go after civilians."

"But you're willing to go after jihadists, killers of civilians. You'll even pursue them into strange cities. You have the look of a hard man. I expect you have killed before. What I might ask of you is not that hard and it doesn't involve civilians. I, too, respect them if they don't interfere with my business."

Dan could see he was not going to buy this man's help. What might he want in return for helping Dan find Jabbar?

"What would you want me to do in exchange for your help?"

"There's a man making a try for my territory. The bosses won't put a stop to him. They haven't disciplined him. He has a relative higher up who protects him. Not close, an older second cousin, but close enough to allow him the freedom to hound my operations. I can't take him out directly. That would bring the bosses down on me, but an outsider could do it. And he could just disappear back from wherever he came. My men, my operation would be clean."

"And if he goes, his threat goes?"

"Precisely."

"How do I know you can help me?"

"Who are you looking for?"

"An Arab named Jabbar Khalid. He would have arrived here from Frankfurt. He was in charge of the attack on the airport."

"And you followed him here? I suspect there is more to you than just a street tough. Are you with a government agency?"

"I'm on my own."

"But on the trail of a jihadist. I think you are some sort of assassin, so what I want you to do will be exactly what you are experienced at doing. Do we have a deal?"

Dan looked back at Gaspard. Thoughts swirled in his head. Should he turn this offer down and ask Jane to find Jabbar? He doubted the CIA could locate him before the terrorist left for the mid-East; that was the only reason Jabbar was in Marseille, to get back there. Did killing a gangster at another's request cross a line that shouldn't be crossed? What would Jane or Henry say about it? He had no answers, but a conviction arose in his mind. A sense that he should go ahead. It was what he did, improvise. He made a decision.

"Find Jabbar first."

Chapter 55

It only took Gaspard a few days to locate Jabbar. His men connected with Dan in the same bar as before. They took him to Gaspard's apartment.

"You have the information on Jabbar?"

"I'll give it to you after you do the job for me."

"How do I know I can trust you?"

The man shrugged. "I'm a man of my word and always pay my debts. I have no love for this Jabbar. He's not worth my helping to remain alive. I would welcome you killing him just as I welcome you killing Léon, the man trying to take my territory."

Dan's newly sharpened senses flooded him. His mind sifted the information he was receiving. He had a strong sense the man could be trusted. Dan marveled at how clear this intuition was. Could he trust it? Everything he was sensing told him Gaspard would keep his word.

Gaspard gave Dan the address where Léon lived. It was another apartment building similar to the one Gaspard lived in. After checking it out, Dan located a building two blocks away. He found a back door that was locked. It was one he could pick. Dan spent one morning going through the building, still in disguise, locating the roof access. It was a little used stair, almost a ladder, at the end of the top floor hallway. At the top was a landing with a locked door. Dan successfully picked this lock as well. He pushed the door. After some effort with the door scraping across accumulated dirt and debris, it opened and Dan stepped out onto the roof. He found a spot at the far corner that had a good sight line to the front door of Léon's apartment building.

With his sniper location selected, Dan had to establish Léon's pattern. He had his M110 sniper rifle used in Evangeline's rescue. With the silencer the direction of the bullet would not be easily determined and he would be long gone before anyone figured out where the shot had come from.

Dan had no connection to the target. He couldn't care less about the man's fate. He was another gangster. They all had blood on their hands just like the mob in Brooklyn. *Live by the sword, die by the sword.* The maxim may not have been a perfect fit, but it was close enough. These men lived in a violent world, outside the law. They knew what they were doing and what the consequences of mistakes were. It didn't matter to Dan whether Gaspard or Léon ran the neighborhood; someone would. What mattered to Dan was that he find Jabbar before the man left Marseille.

It was the end of August. Dan waited three days while an early-appearing mistral blew through Marseille. Wind speeds could get up to fifty miles an hour or more with a strong one and Dan didn't want to try a shot from two full blocks distance in such a wind. It was funneled through the streets by the huge apartment buildings, creating a shifting confusion of direction that made a long shot almost impossible.

Finally, the evening of the third day, the wind subsided. It usually diminished at night, but this evening held the promise of a quieter day to follow. He set out before sun up and entered the apartment using the rear door. Once on the roof, Dan set up his rifle. He would be shooting to the north, north east. The sun would be on his right, but not in his eyes. He was using the .300 Win Mag rounds.

He settled into the familiar routine of waiting. He had checked the distance earlier and now, after factoring the early morning breeze, made his final scope adjustments. Gaspard had no clue that today was the day Dan would take his shot. As a precaution, Dan had made sure that his activities after making the deal were not known to Gaspard or his men. He would do the job and then visit Gaspard to collect his payment.

The sun came up as Dan waited. Léon generally went out for breakfast and coffee, often meeting others in coffee shops and small restaurants. Dan hoped today would be no different. Striking from a distance was the way Dan liked to operate. Lately that had not always been possible. Today felt more comfortable and familiar.

People had been leaving the building singly and in small groups all morning. Dan watched them all through his scope. Gaspard had given Dan pictures of the man he was going to kill. In his reconnoitering he had seen the target leave the building more than once. He felt comfortable that he would be able to spot him in his sights.

At 9:30 am the door opened. Dan watched through the scope. Two men stepped out and looked around. There was a large BMW at the curb; its rear door opened. The men nodded and a third figure went through the door followed by two more men. It was Léon. Dan centered his scope on the man's head. Leon paused for a moment to take in the day. It was a fatal move. Time stood still; Dan's breathing and heart rate slowed. He squeezed the trigger and the rifle bucked in his arms. The bullet entered Leon's left temple. His head flopped sideways, blood and brains erupting from his right side. He slumped to the ground.

Dan didn't watch as the bodyguards drew their weapons and looked around for the shooter. It was a futile effort. There was nothing to see. He quickly disassembled the M110, packed it in his bag and crawled to the roof access door. Once downstairs and in the alley, Dan walked to the next street and away from the scene two blocks behind him. He kept walking until he saw a bus coming.

Dan ran to the nearby stop and boarded the bus. In minutes he was blocks away. In a half hour he was back at his apartment. He spent the day inside. If there was going to be a blowback in Gaspard's direction, Dan didn't want to be in the middle of it. He placed a call to Gaspard to let him know the task was completed. It would give the man notice in case Léon's men came after him.

Dan knew the situation between Gaspard and Léon's crew would be tense. Gaspard would have his tracks covered but he had no doubt that the man was in for a rough ride in the aftermath.

He waited one more day and then went to visit the man, taking care to be certain he was not followed. True to his word Gaspard gave Dan all the information he had come up with on Jabbar. The terrorist was holding up in a safe house closer to the waterfront. It was near the *Font Vert cité* or housing complex. He was in a row of townhouses that sat across the Rue Font Vert from some of the huge apartment buildings that populated the area. It was located just off the Rond Pointe Pierre Parraf, a circle going over the railroad tracks and surrounding an ugly dirt construction site and a crumbling, abandoned bridge that crossed over the tracks.

In his disguise, Dan spent a few days walking the area. He maintained a low profile, looking like a strung-out bum, and being careful to not trigger any confrontations. He was scouting shooting or ambush sites and escape routes. It was going to be harder this time. Dan didn't hold out much hope of using nearby apartment buildings. They were too high and much too hard to get in and out of without being challenged. He resigned himself to the fact that the job would have to be done up closer than he would like.

Chapter 56

The townhouse held ten men, as near as Dan could count. He didn't know where they all would sleep. He had seen Jabbar only once but that was enough. The man didn't go out. Dan would have to go in. The hit would have to be done late at night in the deep hours before sunrise. People generally entered their soundest sleep after 3:00 am. And someone waking from a deep sleep was likely to be too confused or disoriented to react quickly. The advantage would be on the attacker, who would be fully awake.

Still, Dan had to stack the odds further in his favor. He knew he might have to take out all the men in the apartment to insure he got Jabbar and to eliminate pursuit. He would purchase an older car and just abandon it if he couldn't get back to it after the hit. It would be stolen before the police found it.

Dan found a beat up, Citroën Jumpy panel van. It was cheap, only five hundred Euros and looked it. The motor burned oil and made some unhealthy sounds but it would be highly desirable to anyone doing business in the city. Someone could probably get another two or three years of hard work out of the beast before it died and, with an engine swap, maybe double that life span. He purchased the van as Abdullah ben-Wassal. If the vehicle was traced to that name, the police would never find the person.

The night of the operation, Dan dressed in black. He wore a bullet proof vest and brought along a lightweight, black balaclava to cover his face. His tactical knife was sheathed and on his belt. He reluctantly left his M4 behind and took his CZ 9mm with a suppressor. In addition, Dan packed a Walther PPK .22 semi-automatic pistol with a suppressor, shooting sub-sonic rounds. Such a weapon would be hard to hear, even in an adjacent room. Dan took the two long guns, disassembled them, packed them in a bag, and put them in a rented locker at the Gare de Marseille Saint Charles train station.

Next Dan paid up his room through the following day. He didn't plan to return but wanted no troubled raised about the bill. He lay down that afternoon and tried to rest. Sleep wouldn't come; it never did before an operation. But just laying still on the bed letting his mind go over the operation enabled his body to get the rest it needed. That evening he went out to eat, getting some food at a street vendor selling falafel. Dan washed it down with just water.

At 1:30 in the morning he slipped out of his hotel room and drove off. The Jumpy was not a quiet vehicle so Dan had to park it a couple of blocks away from the target. He pulled into an empty lot in front of a row of three businesses: an auto repair shop, a laundromat, and a small grocery store. Next to the row of shops was a medium-rise apartment building. Across the street a five-foot high wall ran along the road. Dan vaulted over the wall and was now concealed in a green area choked with overgrown bushes. It represented an attempt by the city to break up the bleakness of the apartments with green spaces. Fortunately for Dan, the city neglected to keep up with the landscaping. They had become thickets which hid his presence.

He moved to his right along the wall fully concealed. When he got to the row of apartments Dan paused and waited. An occasional car drove up and parked, with the occupants quickly going into one of the townhouses. By 2:30 a.m. that traffic had ended; everyone was in bed. The night was still. Dan continued to wait in the cover of the brush, biding his time. He would have to walk down the townhouse row to get to his target. Jabbar was in the second to last unit.

Just beyond the row were train tracks. They were down in a gully with the streets running over them. The tracks went from northwest to southeast, ending in the Gare de Marseille Saint Charles, the major terminal for the Paris to Marseille run. A couple of kilometers to the northwest there was a freight terminal which was working that night. Dan could hear the low rumble of switching engines as they formed up the freight cars that had been loaded from the docks. Just before 3:00 am a train from the station came by. Dan waited for it to pass and then stepped out onto the street.

He walked casually on the sidewalk, as if he belonged. If seen, he hoped he would not be of any interest. At the door, Dan readied his .22 pistol and started to pick the lock. The tumblers fell into place and Dan opened the front door with light click. He stepped into the room and closed the door behind him. Standing still, he let his eyes adjust to the dark. The entrance had a closet on the left and a short wall on the right. The wall ended opening to a living room on the right. It was faintly lit from the street lighting filtering through the blinds on the front windows. Just beyond the opening, stairs ascended upward into more darkness. The hallway at the front ran back into what Dan guessed was the dining room and kitchen. All the bedrooms would be upstairs.

He peeked around the corner. One figure was on the couch, another lying on a pad on the floor. Dan unsheathed his knife. He slowly stepped into the living room, his eyes darting from one sleeping form to the other. He picked up a pillow from a chair he passed. The man on the floor was lying on his right side with his face buried into a pillow, his back to Dan. His neck was exposed. Dan knelt down behind him. He put the pillow on the side of his head, pressed his body over him, and plunged his knife into the man's neck severing his carotid artery. There was a soft moan which Dan muffled with the pillow and his body as the man jerked and spasmed. In ten seconds, the man grew still and there were no more sounds from him. Dan felt the body go limp. Blood soaked the pillow.

He got up and stepped back, taking stock of the room. The man on the couch had not stirred. He was lying more face up, his head tilted slightly towards Dan. There was a low coffee table between Dan and the couch. He reached down and picked up the blood-soaked pillow. Then he backed up and stepped inside the low table. Two steps and he would be at the man's face. Some sleepers could sense a presence, even in their sleep. Dan had learned to do this during his training in the military and his experiences in the field. He would need to move swiftly.

He stepped forward, pillow in his left hand, knife in his right. The man stirred and mumbled something unintelligible as Dan reached him. His eyes opened as Dan shoved the pillow on his face and fell forward, pinning him down. His knife found the man's neck. He gave out a muffled yell and twisted sideways violently. The pillow slid off of his face.

The man yelled out, "*Saeidni! Qutil!*" Help me! Murder!

Dan's knife found his artery. Dan slid the knife from the side of his neck to his throat and the man's words died in a gurgle of blood. Dan got the pillow back over the man and held it tight until he felt his body go limp. He stood up. He was panting, his heart was racing. He got back up and went to the entrance of the room so he could watch the stairs and hallway. He waited with his .22 pistol drawn. His breathing slowed as his heart rate came down. All was quiet. The cries of the dying man did not seem to have disturbed the sleepers on the second floor.

After waiting for two minutes with nothing stirring, Dan began climbing the stairs. He stepped near the edges of the steps knowing that putting his weight there would create less chance of a step creaking. At the top, there was a short hallway going forward with one door, probably a bedroom at the front of the building. Towards the rear of the building there were three doors indicating two more bedrooms and a bathroom.

Dan turned to the front of the building. He would check this room first. It was a bit more separated from the others and his chances of neutralizing the occupants without waking the others were good. He padded the few steps from the stairs to the door. With his .22 in his right hand, he slowly turned the door knob. Once the bolt had fully retreated into the door, he gave the door a gentle push with his shoulder. It opened with a soft creak as it cleared the door frame.

Dan slipped inside and partly closed the door behind him. He didn't want to risk making any additional noise by trying to latch it. He stood still, controlling his breathing, making no sound. He was a shadow, a ghost. There was a dim glow coming through the curtains from the street outside. Dan could see two beds with two bodies in each of them. One man was snoring loudly. They were all partially dressed, pants, undershirts, but no shoes or socks. The air was dense with the strong odor of unwashed bodies.

He took a step forward and raised his pistol. Four *thwacks* came from the suppressed weapon. The sound was hardly louder than the click of a door latch. Four holes appeared in the heads of the sleepers. They would never awake. *If my count is correct, that's four down and maybe six to go.* Dan listened at the door and then stepped back into the hall.

He padded slowly down the hall to the second bedroom door. This room was in the center of the building. Dan turned the knob and pushed gently against the door. It held for a moment and then gave way with a louder squeak than the first door. Dan stepped inside. Two men were in separate beds. They both sat up, one was rubbing sleep from his eyes the other was reaching for his gun on the night stand next to the bed. Dan shot him and swung the weapon back to the other man as he switched on a light. It was Jabbar.

Dan paused. Here was his target, he should shoot and leave, but he hesitated.

"Do you know who I am?" Dan asked speaking German in a low voice.

Jabbar looked at him, now fully awake. Then his eyes turned to the pistol on his side table.

"You'll never get to it," Dan said.

"Who are you?" Jabbar finally asked.

"Frankfurt Airport. I'm the one who ruined your plans. Your suicide bombers failed. Your assault teams were intercepted and your rocket only hit the tail of the plane." Dan paused for a moment. "And you didn't get away. I tracked you here."

"So now you kill me?"

Dan nodded. "I am the angel of death…for you and all of your kind."

With that Dan pulled the trigger and Jabbar fell back with a hole in his forehead. Dan stepped forward and put two more rounds into the terrorists.

He opened the door and entered the hall. A man from the last bedroom was standing outside his door, his pistol in his hand.

"Who are you?" He asked in Arabic.

Dan fired his .22 and the man jerked. His 9mm went off into the ceiling as he fell back. Dan put two more shots into his torso, sending him to the ground. There were shouts in the back bedroom. Dan ran for the stairs as two more men burst into the hall. They saw their comrade on the floor and someone running. They opened fire as Dan turned and raced down the stairs, taking the steps three at a time. He pulled the front door open and dove through it as shots flew over his head.

The shots and sounds of the men shouting and running down the stairs were loud. Lights started going on in the adjacent apartments. He would never make it down the long drive illuminated by the street lights. Getting back to the wall and his van was not an option. He made the calculation in an instant and turned left towards the railroad tracks.

He sprinted across the street trying to reach the cover of the embankment when a flurry of shots rang out. A bullet slammed into his back, like a huge fist had pounded him. His vest stopped the round, but Dan was thrown to the ground. He didn't stop, but scrambled on his hands and knees and dove into the brush. He tumbled down the embankment. When he hit the bottom, he got up, fighting for breath as he forced his body to move forward towards the train station. He had to put some distance between himself and his pursuers. There was excited shouting in Arabic going on above him as neighbors joined the men from the apartment. They would all be armed.

Chapter 57

Dan stumbled down the tracks. He kept his .22 in his hand. He heard men coming down the embankment. They would fan out, not knowing which direction Dan went. He knew he could not outrun them in his condition. In addition to his older rib injuries, the shot to his back, while stopped by the vest, had bruised him to the point that he could only take shallow breaths. A deep breath caused his back to spasm and his lungs to empty. No, there would be no running. He just needed to keep moving. Even hidden in the thickets along the embankment, he didn't stand much of a chance remaining concealed from a thorough search. And if he counter-attacked, he would give away his position to all the others involved in the pursuit.

For all Dan knew the whole townhouse row was now out looking for him. Word of the shootings and Jabbar's execution would now be emerging, incensing the crowd above to find the assassin. Dan's options were limited. He didn't see any viable way out.

Then he heard and felt the rumble of a train approaching. It came from his left, heading towards the Gare de Marseille Saint Charles; a passenger train. Dan pushed into the thicket and turned left to watch. The light appeared illuminating the track and some men searching the brush. They were working their way carefully in both directions. *Probably got others above watching for any movement.* They also would man the overpasses as well, trying to pen him in. He couldn't make any progress while in the thick brush on the slope, and if he dropped down to the tracks he would be seen.

He had one chance, which might not work, but presented at least one course of action. Dan lurched out from the brush just before the train reached him and stumbled across the tracks in front of the engine. A shout went out from above but before anyone could fire, the train went by, shielding him from view. He continued across the next set of tracks. As soon as the train was past, he would be exposed again. Dan moved towards the station. He had no other options. Climbing out on the far side would just put him back on the streets in what was now an enemy neighborhood. There would be no place to hide up there.

Then he saw it. Another headlight. A train was coming from the station and heading his way. Would it get to him in time? Dan crouched in the brush on the far side of the tracks. He took a quick inventory of his body. He could move, but it was painful. It was too painful to take deep breaths. He kept breathing in a rapid, shallow manner to avoid throwing his back into a spasm.

The inbound train finally passed. Dan was exposed. The shouting increased on the other side. Some shots rang out but Dan could tell they hadn't zeroed in on him. The outbound train approached; the shots came closer to Dan's position in the brush. If he moved, he'd be spotted and most likely shot. The train rumbled past. It was moving at a jogging pace, still picking up speed.

Dan waited for ten cars to go by. He studied them as best he could. At the back of each car were rungs attached to the side of the car. There was almost no space between cars but Dan could see rungs on the rear. If he could grab the ones on the side, he could swing around and hold on to the ones in the rear. He didn't know if he could enter the cars, but he could ride for a short distance if he could find some footing. Dan stuffed his pistol in his pocket; after the tenth car had gone by, he sprang from his cover. Almost holding his breath, he began to run along the side of the tracks. A set of rungs started to slide past him, the train was accelerating, in a moment he would not be able to keep up with it. He reached up and grabbed a handhold with his left hand. With one more thrust of his legs, he swung his body towards the rungs. His feet scrambled to find footing; he reached out with his right hand.

He was panting with shallow breaths as he worked his way around to the rear of the car. His feet found purchase as he clung to the metal rods forming the ladder rungs. The coupling holding the cars together was next to his feet, the large metal connection moving and swaying as the two cars lurched back and forth. He flattened himself against the back of the car. There was no cover. He knew his pursuers were watching; some of them had probably seen him run for the train. He only hoped the acceleration would keep them from following him onto one of the cars. In the next minute the train was going too fast. They were out of the immediate area. He had escaped the trap.

Dan had no idea where the train was headed. It was not one of the modern ones used on the Paris-Marseille route. It was older, probably a local that worked its way through the smaller towns. Starting in the morning, it was mostly empty as it headed out. After a few kilometers the train began to slow. *What the hell*? He was not far enough out of the area to feel safe if the train stopped. His pursuers, if convinced he had jumped the train, would follow it hoping to find him when it stopped. He was not yet safe.

The train did stop. Dan could see the lights of the freight terminal on the far side of the tracks. A train was backing into the siding, putting together a long string of cars before heading out. Apparently, the passenger train had to stop to allow the freight locomotive to switch to the siding.

Dan eyed the cars. There were piggy-back cars made up of sea containers stacked on rail car frames. At the back of each there was a small platform. Dan could see what looked like a depression. Perhaps he could hide there. He stepped across the coupling and looked to the front and rear. Seeing no one standing on the tracks, he gingerly let himself down and shuffled across the tracks. Dan pushed through the brush separating the main line from the siding. The siding area was lit so he had to be careful. If anyone saw him and caught him, he would be arrested and that would be the end of the game. Any basic police inquiry could link him to the killings, if anyone cared.

He watched for a minute. The freight locomotive, with fifteen cars already attached to it, backed into the long line of assembled cars. There was now a train of probably fifty or sixty cars. Dan didn't see anyone along the side of the train. It was twenty yards away. He could hear the passenger train begin to accelerate again. When it had passed, the freight locomotive powered up. There was sequential banging as the couplings tightened in a new direction, like a metallic snake uncoiling.

Dan broke from the cover and ran to the cars. He grabbed one halfway back on the train and clamored up on it. As he had hoped, there was a depression. It wasn't much, probably only twenty inches deep, but he could lie flat and had a chance of not being seen. The train slowly gathered speed. When the car Dan was riding on rolled out of the yard and onto the main track, it passed out of the lit area. Dan began to relax. He would ride this until far from Marseille and jump off as it slowed. The terrorists and their neighbors would be looking and following the local passenger train. He had escaped.

Chapter 58

Dan sat in the safe house with Jane and Evangeline. Marcus and Roland had flown back to the States with Pietro Conti and Jan Luis Aebischer. Evangeline was coming to grips with the fact that political and security considerations had trumped her wishes and her abusive father, who had committed murder, would be allowed to live. Jane had impressed upon her that it would not be a life of ease or influence. He would not be free and would be milked for all the information he had about his dealings with terrorists and those who supplied them. Such information would result in more targets for Dan to go after.

"I still don't want his money." Evangeline said. She remained firm in her decision.

Jane had not been able to convince her that accepting her inheritance didn't make her complicit in her mother's death.

Dan sat quietly. He was still sore from his injuries, but was recovered enough to restart his routine of running and exercising. It felt good to be out on the back roads, thumping along, eating up the kilometers, his mind refreshed by the passing scenery. Jane and Evangeline enjoyed more relaxing mornings in the kitchen or on the back patio.

"I'd like to take both of you on a short trip," Dan said after returning from a morning run. He had showered and dressed and was eating some breakfast while Jane drank her second cup of coffee. Evangeline was sitting close to Dan, as she did every chance she got.

"Where to?" Jane asked.

"Let's drive to Venice. I want to show you something in the city."

"I'm not sure we have time. I should be getting back to Washington. Henry will be calling for me before too long."

"We have time. It's important to me."

Evangeline had no comment. She would go anywhere with Dan even back to the mansion in Zürich.

"We can pack up after I eat. We'll take the embassy Mercedes they loaned you. Just pack some things for an overnight in case we stay too long. It's only a three-hour drive so we can be back this evening if we want."

Three and a half hours later, Dan pulled into the parking garage at the end of the causeway. They walked to the canal and hired a speed boat. Dan told the pilot to take them to Piazza San Marco. Once there, they got out and walked the plaza. It was a fresh, fall day the breeze was invigorating, the crowds of summer had thinned. They ate lunch at the outdoor table of one of the restaurants lining the plaza.

"This is lovely, but what did you want to show us?" Jane asked.

Dan, as always, was looking around, checking the groups of pedestrians that flowed around them.

"Just wait. I hope I can show you what we came for," he replied.

"What's the mystery about?" Evangeline asked. "You wouldn't even give us a hint on the drive."

"It's my surprise," Dan smiled at her. "I think today may help both of you."

He scanned the plaza. On the far side he located the scarf kiosk. He focused on it. The woman was there. She turned, as if compelled by Dan's stare. Their eyes met. Even across the distance, Dan could feel the connection, the energy.

"Let's go, he said, standing up.

"I'm not finished with my lunch," Evangeline said.

"Doesn't matter," Dan replied. "This is more important." He put a fifty Euro note on the table to cover the meals and hurried the two women out onto the plaza.

"Follow me," he said.

He walked over to the stall. The woman held his eyes as he approached.

"*Signora*," Dan said as he reached the kiosk, "If you have time, I would like to talk with you and have you meet these two women with me."

The woman turned to her daughter who was standing behind the kiosk. She spoke to her in a language that was not Italian.

Turning back to Dan, she said. "She will watch the stand while we go to speak. But I already know who these women are."

"Then you must know why I want them to meet you and speak with you."

The woman nodded. "Follow me," she said as she turned to go.

As before, she walked off into one of the small pedestrian side streets. Dan and the women followed. She made two more turns and then stopped at the door to a smaller house.

"We can talk here without worry about interruptions," she said as she unlocked the door.

The four of them entered the home and walked back into the kitchen. They sat at a large table. Jane looked at the woman carefully. She did not look old but Jane could not begin to guess her age, somewhere in the middle part of life. She wore a full skirt and loose shirt. Her thick, dark hair pushed out from under her scarf. It was her eyes that held Janc’s attention. They were black, intense, and seemed to look through her when the woman returned her gaze.

“My name is Palmira. It means ‘pilgrim’ in your language.” She spoke in heavily accented Italian dialect which Jane couldn’t place.

“You are Jane,” she said. She turned to the girl, “And you are Evangeline.”

“How do you know who we are?” Evangeline asked. “Did Dan tell you?”

The woman smiled without replying.

“I know why Dan brought you here. You are both important...in ways you do not grasp.”

“And you will enlighten us?” Jane asked.

The woman looked at Jane. Her eyes seemed to examine the meaning of Jane’s question.

“If you let me,” she replied.

Jane waited. Dan had arranged this meeting. There was something he wanted her to gain from it. They hadn’t driven three hours for a casual encounter with a local Venetian scarf vendor.

“You are the woman who directs Dan in his battles. I understand he has already told you of his encounters in Mexico and here in Venice. I am that encounter here, a Watcher. But you don’t see the value of us. You are still locked in your rational mind. I understand that is the world you must live in, to operate in, but it limits you.

"I hope you will allow your mind to be enlarged even as you have to work with those more shut off to this other part of reality. You will benefit from knowing more, and from using that knowledge."

"How will you help me?" Jane asked.

"I cannot show you the same way Tlayolotl showed Dan. I do not have the Shaman's power. But you must look back to what Dan told you about his experiences. You say you accept what he says yet I see your mind is still unconvinced. You ignore the obvious."

"And what is that?"

"That Dan is alive. Someone, something saved him from dying, twice as he recounts. What more evidence do you need?" The woman's eyes began to glow with the intensity of her words.

Jane didn't flinch but the argument drilled into her rational mind, creating confusion. Dan's surviving the journey he spoke of was irrefutable, but his explanation was hard to accept. It created a conflict that Jane could not resolve.

"Now more recently, I told Dan to accept the job offer he was given by the man, Pietro. Dan understood that I could see more than what was on the surface. You have now seen that he was right. His actions have saved this girl," she gestured to Evangeline, "And given her a new chance in life. And he exposed the larger darkness I spoke of and broke its power. It may rise up again, but for now it is defeated."

"I accept that Dan was correct. And you're one of the Watchers he talks about. How many of you are there?"

The woman just smiled but didn't answer.

"Are you suggesting that I accept every paranormal story that I come across? There are a lot of crazy people out there."

The woman's face grew hard. Jane could barely return her intense gaze. "Do not speak foolishly to me. You have too important a part to play. Just as Dan needed a greater insight, so do you. Watchers are trying to help. We see farther than you see, deeper, and so can guide you if you let us. You need to trust Dan's insights, especially his encounters with other Watchers. He brings you here so you can better understand. It is up to you."

She turned to Dan, dismissing Jane for the moment. "You must not give up. Help her where you can. She may yet begin to understand; the battle is too important for her to remain ignorant."

The woman now focused on Evangeline. Jane could see her dark eyes boring into the young girl who shrank from the sharp look.

"I know why you are here, even if you do not."

Evangeline could only stare back at the woman, afraid to speak.

"Dan saved you from captivity: to drugs, to pornography, and to your fears. I know what happened to you. I couldn't see it at first, the darkness was too thick, too dangerous. But Dan pierced it and then I saw. And with that seeing I saw your mission."

Evangeline mustered the courage to speak. Jane could see the effort it took.

"Y...you can see my future?"

"Not completely. One's future is never fully written until one lives it. We always can change it. But I can see your destiny, the direction you should go, even if you cannot. You can choose not to go there. That is always open to one...to not choose their rightful destiny."

Evangeline spoke in a small voice. "What is my destiny?"

The woman's face softened. Her eyes lost some of their fearsome intensity.

"Do you know what your name means?"

Evangeline shook her head.

"Your mother gave you that name, over the objections of your father. He wanted to name you Hilda. It was one of the few times your mother was able to prevail over her father." She took the girl's hand in hers.

Evangeline could feel her energy. It flowed over her causing the hair on her arms to stand up. She shivered; something was going through her body, an energy she had no control over.

"Your name means 'light bearer'. It is your destiny."

"I don't understand."

"You will, if you accept it. You will learn how to live into your name."

"But what does that mean, 'live into my name'?"

"You are to use what you have been given to bring light to dark souls, others who have been damaged by the darkness of evil. Others like you. You have been given great assets. They should not be despised or refused. Accept them. They are your birthright. Your mother died protecting you. Dan nearly died saving you and arranged for all the wealth to be in your hands. You can do much good with it. It is not something to renounce."

"I should accept his wealth, his blood money?"

The woman kept Evangeline locked in her stare as she kept her hands locked onto Evangeline's hands.

"It is the first step in following your destiny. Do not be afraid. You have time to go slow, to find your path. Dan will be there when you need him as will others."

"I want him to stay with me." Evangeline's voice came out in a timid whisper. "I need his help, especially if I'm going to accept this wealth."

"We each have our own story. His story is different from yours. But your stories intersect at times. Be thankful for that." She turned to Jane again. "And this woman," her voice was calm and full of affection. "She will come to understand, even if it is hard for her. And her story will intersect with yours as well. You have strong friends to help along the way."

"Will you help?" Evangeline asked.

"I already have. I sent Dan on his path to rescue you. You do not need me anymore. The others will help. I am a Watcher who can see a little into the future, that is all."

She stood up indicating it was time to go. Jane noticed they had been sitting for two hours. It had seemed like only a few minutes. She had many more questions but she knew they would not be answered. Enough explanations had been given; full understanding was now up to her.

The four of them got up and left the apartment. Back in the piazza the woman took Jane's hands in hers. They were warm as if heated by an inner fire, a fire reflected in her eyes. Jane felt the intensity of her grasp. Energy surged through her body. *Where was that coming from*?

The woman leaned close to Jane and whispered in her ear. "You play an important part in Dan's success, in his survival. Your relationship will be stormy and confused at times. I cannot see how it works out, but I see your stories are intertwined. You are linked to one another. He is the tip of the spear in this battle and you are part of that spear. You need to seek a deeper understanding."

She released Jane's hand, turned, and walked back to her kiosk.

"She didn't say goodbye to you," Evangeline said.

"She didn't have to," Dan replied.

The three of them walked to the waterside and hired a boat to take them back to the causeway. They drove back to Milan that same night, each lost in their own thoughts.

Chapter 59

Henry, I'm going to be gone another week. I know I've been away a long time but you wanted me to have a serious conversation with Dan." Jane was calling on her secure phone from Milan. "We've got things pretty well wrapped up now. Evangeline has moved back to Zürich. You got Roger to work on the State Department to help Evangeline get her finances under control. Both Fred and Warren are looking out for her from a distance. She's in contact with one or both almost daily. There's nothing left but to have that talk with Dan."

"You haven't done that yet? How long does this take for God's sake?"

"I've been a bit busy. I had a lot of tracks to cover up and I've learned some new things that I need time to process. Plus, this is not a typical debriefing conversation. I remember that you as much as threatened to have Dan taken out if he 'turned rogue' as you said. I'm thinking about that and don't want to let that possibility become a reality."

"I was speaking a bit hastily, I admit. But the principle still stands."

"I know it does. That's why I want to take the time to make sure it never comes up again."

Henry sighed. "I hope your feelings aren't compromising your judgment."

"My feelings all contribute to how I judge, but they don't stand in the face of facts. And the fact is Dan was right. The Watcher in Venice was right. And it's time for you to accept that there is something else going on with what Dan does and how he does it."

Henry was silent for a moment, then in a quiet voice, "I admit something else was going on, some insight we didn't have...or we missed." His voice became stronger. "But I'm not ready to sign on to some paranormal theory about spirits guiding our assassin."

"Okay Henry. Look, I admire you more than you might guess, but in this case, I've got to tell you to keep an open mind. You don't have to use any words that offend your sense of rationality, but something else was going on here to make the connection between Evangeline and the huge network of terror operations we uncovered." She paused, "Just keep an open mind, please?"

The next day Dan and Jane drove to Porto Santa Margherita. They boarded Dan's catamaran and put out to sea on a fresh northwest wind. The yacht was forty-five feet long and twenty-five feet wide. Four cabins were nestled in the two hulls. The connecting bridge deck, above the hull cabins, housed the galley, eating saloon and navigation station. Behind the bridge deck cabin was a broad, open cockpit with twin helm stations on either side of the boat. Clearing the harbor, they raced downwind towards the Dalmatian coast at twelve knots. Dan had set one reef in the main sail and flew the working jib.

The yacht could go much faster, but Dan had no desire to drive her near her limits, especially sailing short-handed. The ride, while lumpy at times was under control.

Jane spent some time sitting forward, in front of the bridge deck cabin. Ahead of her was a woven netting strung between the two hulls that extended from where she sat to the bows. You could see the bows going through the water which flowed under the netting. She was mesmerized by how they plunged through the waves, sometimes piercing them with a shower of water thrown up and sometimes riding up their backs to then surf downward, the yacht accelerating and both bows hissing with spray flying.

After watching the show for an hour, she worked her way back to the bridge deck, behind the cabin. The auto pilot was doing a good job of keeping up with the yacht's motion. Dan poured Jane a cup of coffee.

"Aren't you going to get tired?" She asked.

"This invigorates me. A sailor doesn't want to waste such a fair wind. We can be down to the islands off Croatia before dawn. Stay up tonight and enjoy the downhill ride and we can sleep in tomorrow."

"If the boat drives itself, do you need to stay up?"

Dan gave her a questioning look. "You can't leave the boat alone, someone always has to keep watch, even if it steers itself."

Jane studied him. "You really do love this don't you?"

"I feel alive out here, safe and alive. I can turn off my constant surveillance mode and relax." He looked around. "See any threats?"

Jane scanned the horizon. "Nothing, Captain," she replied.

"That's the point."

"What if a boat comes in sight?"

"There's a system called AIS. All commercial boats have them, as do many private yachts. It's built into the marine radios now. It broadcasts the identity of a vessel.

If one comes in sight, I turn on the AIS and can see what it is, how large it is, it's bearing and speed, and even where it's headed."

"And if a boat doesn't have it?"

"Then I go into caution mode. My street instincts kick back in. But mostly, I can let that part of me relax."

Jane smiled at him. She was beginning to understand the sailing just might be one of the things that would keep Dan sane in his work. He really couldn't relax in his Venice estate as nice as that was. Someone could always uncover who he was and where he lived. But out here? If Dan didn't register a destination, no one would know where he went. He could sail away into privacy and security, at least for a while.

"I'll make us something to eat," she said to Dan as the sun dipped in the west.

Dan smiled at her as he sat at the helm. He didn't have to steer. The auto pilot kept the yacht on the compass course Dan had set. He did keep a relaxed watch, checking the wind and scanning the horizon every few minutes. The AIS system showed only two freighters heading north to Venice and one passenger ship heading south. Both were well to the west. Dan could barely see them with his binoculars. He turned the system off. The weight of the past months began to drain out of him. He was sailing away to hide from the world with a woman he admired and, if he was honest, had much affection for. He savored the moment.

A half hour later, Jane came out from the galley with a plate of scrambled eggs. They were mixed with sausage and vegetables.

"I made a one plate meal like you suggested. I call it 'Eggs with Stuff in Them'."

Dan laughed. "It'll never be popular with that name. You need to come up with something more exotic." He thought for a moment. "How about '*Eggs al Forno con Verdure*'?"

"That should make it taste better."

They drove on through the night. Dan walked around the decks occasionally but always returned to the seat at the helm. The large steering wheel moved obediently to the commands of the auto pilot, keeping the yacht on its set course. Jane helped by bringing him snacks and drinks—coffee and juices. By 1:00 am Jane was asleep on the padded bench seat in the saloon inside the bridge deck cabin. Dan could see her from his helm position. He liked the fact that she was there. He liked the fact that she wasn't sea sick. The ride was enough to affect anyone sensitive to motion sickness but Jane seemed blissfully free of symptoms. She was enjoying the adventure and now had relaxed enough to fall fast asleep.

At 3:00 am they were off Cape Kamenjak. Dan cut close to the island Otok Fenoliga and headed across the sound, keeping a close eye out for the Venice-Rabac ferry. Two hours later they crossed the north cape of Otok Unije and a half hour later were headed up a narrow bay to a sheltered anchorage.

Jane awoke when Dan got to work starting the auxiliary motors and furling the sails.

"Are we there?"

"Another half hour of motoring and we'll anchor."

The sun was just coming up when Dan dropped anchor. They were alone. The bay was a half mile wide and five miles long, running south to north. The headlands gave it great protection from the northerly winds. It was quiet and still.

Dan stretched and yawned. "Time for some sleep, at least for me."

"I think I'm going to watch the sun come up, then I'll take another nap," Jane replied.

As Dan turned to go down into the cabin inside the hull, Jane grabbed his arm and turned him around. She reached up and kissed him.

"Thank you for taking me out. This is very special."

"You are very welcome. You seem like a natural. No sea sickness."

He headed down to one of the cabins to sleep. Jane wrapped a blanket around her and went forward to sit on the trampoline and watch the colors slowly change off the starboard bow as the sun rose.

Dan slept until noon. The two enjoyed a leisurely lunch on deck. There was little wind in the anchorage and the early September sun was warm. After lunch Dan said he was going for a swim.

"So soon after you ate? Didn't your mother tell you you'd get a cramp?"

"We grew up in Brooklyn. Nobody in my family knew about that old wives' tale. Besides, I'm not going to swim across the bay, just around the yacht."

He found his swim trunks and put on some fins, a mask, and snorkel.

"May as well check the hulls for barnacles and other growth while I'm in the water."

He jumped in. Jane watched him glide around the hulls and disappear between them. She ran down into the cabin and put on a suit she had purchased before they left. She stood on the rear beam that formed the back of the cockpit in the stern. It was just over three feet high. One could sit on it. It spanned the width of the catamaran and held the winches and control lines for the sails. She stood up on the beam and executed a perfect swan dive into the clear, blue water.

When she came up to the surface, Dan was treading water and clapping.

"I give you a 9.5."

"Only 9.5? I thought it was a 9.8 at least."

"Degree of difficulty held you back, dear."

He took a breath and dove under the water. Jane watched him swim with powerful strokes and glide along the bottom of the starboard hull, running his hand along it. She swam between the hulls and was at the bow when Dan came back up.

"Everything good down there?"

"Yep. The underwater parts of the two hulls are pretty clean. They're painted with a special paint that restricts marine growth, but they still have to get scraped occasionally."

They swam around for some time with Dan occasionally disappearing and then coming up from below to grab her toes. The first time Jane legitimately squealed in fright, not knowing if some sea creature was attacking. After that it was just to give Dan the expected reaction.

Later they were relaxing in the sun again, each with a glass of wine. Dan couldn't help noticing Jane's athletic figure. Her legs were sleek and well formed, like a distance runner. Her upper body also showed her athleticism. The effect on Dan was strong. Jane was physically a trim, fit, and sexy woman. She coupled that with a strong, intelligent personality. It was much the way he remembered Rita.

"Dan, we have to talk about your improvising. Henry is worried. He said some things about the danger of field agents going rogue—"

"Is Henry worried about me going rogue?"

"The worry did cross his mind."

"But I was right about this operation. The Watcher was right."

"I know that now...and Henry knows it. But he gets worried."

"I like Henry, but it isn't right for him to sit back in DC and second guess me."

"He's had to do that for all his field agents. And he wasn't always in DC. Henry ran operations from Vienna, Moscow, and Beirut. He's experienced in field work. He's seen agents go off the reservation, so to speak."

"And he's had to take care of them, I'm guessing. Is that what he threatened?"

Jane reached over to take Dan's hand.

"He just mentioned he's had to do it before. And he finished by saying he hoped he wouldn't have to do it...with you."

Dan scowled.

"He really has your best interests at heart."

"I'm not so sure about that."

Jane's fingers intertwined with Dan's. He made no attempt to pull his hand back.

"Look how am I supposed to operate? I'm not a regular agent you keep on a short leash with a specific task to follow, a specific script. I'm supposed to be out there, freelancing. That's going to look a lot like 'going rogue'."

Jane took back her hand and sipped her wine.

"Tell me," Dan continued, "How do I do what you called me to do? You now know that you and I are part of a larger battle going on. I hope the Watcher impressed that upon you."

Jane nodded. She was staring into Dan's eyes.

"Well, Henry is part of that as well. He has to let me have the freedom to work however I need to. Hell, if I'm caught or compromised, I don't get any backup. I'm on a tightrope without a net. Now Henry wants to impose some limitations. Like asking me to jump through a hoop while balancing on that rope."

Jane kept looking at him.

"Don't you see the dilemma?" Dan asked.

"I do."

"How do I get out of it?"

"When I get back, I'll have a heart-to-heart with Henry. It's his operation after all. I'll let him know I'm adamant that he trust you and put aside any worry about you going rogue. I'll put my job on the line."

"You'd do that for me?"

Jane nodded. "Yes. I believe in you, now more than ever."

"There'll be some in the agency who'll try to turn Henry's head. There's some who, if they knew about the program, wouldn't like it and would look for any reason, any way to shut it down."

"I know that. It is going to be part of my job going forward, watching your six back at headquarters."

"Thank you."

Chapter 60

Dan reached out his hand and touched Jane's cheek. Jane couldn't tell who moved first, but their heads moved towards each other and the next thing she knew they were kissing. It was tentative at first then rose in intensity. Her lips opened and she felt their tongues meet. An electric energy flowed through her body. She pulled Dan against her and wrapped her arms around him.

Then in a moment it was over. Their lips parted. Dan leaned back to look at her, his eyes searching her face. His countenance held a slightly bewildered expression.

"I...I'm sorry," he stammered.

"That was nothing to be sorry about," Jane said in a low voice that evidenced her arousal.

Dan looked uncomfortable. He got up and went over to the table to grab the bottle of wine. It was a fruity, local white wine made from the Zelen grape. Few people outside of wine enthusiasts had experienced it, but it was known throughout the northern Adriatic. He came back and refilled their glasses.

"Maybe we shouldn't drink too much, we might get into trouble," Jane said with a wry smile on her face.

"It's a nice bottle and we can't let it go bad. Besides, Henry's not around to watch."

Jane chuckled. The tension of talking about Henry had passed, as had the awkwardness of their kiss. What it meant; Jane understood. What it would lead to, she had yet to process.

The two, slightly tipsy from the wine, started working on dinner. Dan had brought along fresh shrimp. He boiled some pasta and began to heat up a marinara sauce for a shrimp and pasta bowl dinner. Jane rummaged through the galley stores and put together a salad for the meal.

They made small talk while working together. To Dan it was eerily similar to meals he had enjoyed making with Rita. They had often cooked together before starting their restaurant. While Dan was not a chef, he was a passable cook and enjoyed it. He opened a bottle of a Slovenia cabernet sauvignon from the *Slovenska Istra* region near the Adriatic. It was considered one of Slovenia's best wines.

"You seem to be an expert on Slovenia wines," Jane remarked.

"Not really, but someone told me about how underrated they were and when I tried some, I liked them." He took a sip. "I like wine, but I think in the end, I'm a beer guy."

"Even with the good whisky I introduced you to?"

"You did indeed. I like your choice of bourbons as well, but I'm not a connoisseur, even of beer. I'm like that guy who says, 'I don't know much about art but I know what I like'."

"That's such a cliché. It's beneath you."

"There's always an element of truth to a cliché, that's how it becomes one. But in my defense, I try to learn...about what I'm drinking as well as art."

He raised his glass to Jane and took a sip.

After dinner had been cleaned up, they sat on the long, padded bench in the bridge deck cabin savoring small glasses of bourbon, Jane's choice of Knob Limited Edition. Light from the setting sun played on the banks of the bay with steadily changing hues. They spoke little and watched it turn, finally, to purple and then the dark blue of night. There were no sounds except for the occasionally screech of a gull.

"I love the stillness. It's something you can't get anywhere near a city...always a background noise there."

"It is peaceful," Jane said. She snuggled close to Dan as the cool of the evening descended.

In a moment their heads turned to one another again and they were kissing. This time it was soft, tender. Then it began to build. Jane reached up and pulled Dan's shirt over his head. They kissed again as she ran her hand over his chest and shoulders.

Dan unbuttoned Jane's shirt. She slipped it off her shoulders. He ran his hand over her back and unclasped her bra. She moaned her approval and quickly shrugged it off. She lay back as Dan caressed her breasts and the rest of her body. Her breath came in sharp pants. She wanted his hands all over her.

Without a word he stood up, took her hand, and led her down into the hull to the master cabin which held a queen-size bed. They both slipped off their shorts and lay against one another, their upper bodies naked. She could feel his arousal against her, hard and insistent.

Their kissing became more impassioned. Dan covered her breasts and torso with kisses. He marveled at her athletic body and her well rounded breasts. As he kissed them Jane held his head in her hands. She wanted more of him, all of him.

And then the passion collapsed. It was like a sailboat surging along on a stiff breeze that suddenly sailed into a wind hole with the sails going limp and the boat's speed dropping to zero. Dan rose up over her, panting. He looked strange, almost disoriented. She felt the deflation as well and just stared back up at him. She waited. She didn't want to be the one to break the moment. But it was already broken.

"Jane..." Dan didn't complete the sentence. "What just happened?"

"We want each other," Jane replied gently. She reached up and stroked Dan's face.

"Yes, but something else. You felt it just as I felt it. Something broke the mood, the energy."

She nodded.

"Maybe we should go slow. Not do this too fast."

"Is that what you want?"

Dan looked perplexed. "I don't know. Part of me wants you. Now, tonight, completely. But there is something else, a caution? Something broke the mood for both of us."

"Don't go all psychic on me," Jane said.

"No, no. But I know what I felt and I know you felt it too. My new sensitivity tells me that."

"The gift from Tlayolotl? He's the one who interrupted our moment?"

"No, nothing like that. I'm just saying that I know what you felt at the same time I felt it. Like a cool wind flowing over us both. It wasn't a bad feeling, but it swept away the passion of the moment."

He looked thoughtful, still leaning over Jane who stared back into his face. She was struck by how exactly he described what she had felt. He really did seem to have an increased empathetic sense.

Dan continued, “You are so beautiful. I admit that I want you very much. I want to make love to you so naughty it’ll make you weak in the knees.”

Jane, despite herself, burst into laughter. “You are a goof ball.”

“I mean it. But there was something else that flowed over us. Something that had to do with waiting.”

“Was it Rita?” Jane had to ask.

“No. I got no sense of that. It was something more diffuse, but still strong. It’s more of a waiting and enjoying one another on different, deeper levels. I never felt this before.” He suddenly looked concerned. “You’re not upset, are you?”

Jane pulled him down onto her and kissed him fully. It was a strong, loving kiss, one that hinted of ‘you’re my man’.

“No, I’m not upset. I felt it too. You described it perfectly.” She reached over and gathered her blouse and shorts. “Tonight’s not the night. I guess a girl can’t get lucky each time she tries.”

“Now you make me feel bad.”

“I’m just kidding you,” Jane said as she punched him in the shoulder. “Let’s go watch the stars.”

They went out to the trampoline up at the bows and lay down. Without city lights, the sky sparkled. It was as sharp as in the desert. They talked late into the night. Jane told Dan about her life and family and Dan was able to explain to Jane how important Rita was and how devastated he was at losing her. Later he brought out blankets and pillows and they fell asleep on the trampoline.

Dawn found them completely huddled under the blankets to ward off the dew. They spent that day swimming and relaxing. Neither talked about the night before but there was an increased familiarity and closeness between them.

"Will Henry notice how we are with one another? He's sharp enough to pick up on things like that," he asked.

"So what? We care for each other. That's a good thing." Jane didn't go further. She would deal with Henry. She would make sure he was supportive in the end.

They began their return trip the next morning. Both were relaxed and pensive. Dan was focused on sailing the yacht. He thought about where he was in life. He had done some good on this latest mission and felt good about that fact. Still, he worried about Henry and others back at the CIA. There were many possible and actual enemies in Langley and he could be marked as a problem, a loose end to be tied up despite Jane's efforts. It seemed to be a precarious position. *I'm a maverick, no doubt.* The thought wasn't comforting, knowing the CIA. Still, his sense of mission remained, along with his attraction to Jane. Working with her made it easier. And the Watchers only reinforced his conviction that he was doing the right thing.

Dan smiled as he steered his yacht. He'd keep playing the game out, all while watching for any signs of disaffection out of Langley telling him it was time to go underground.

Jane spent hours thinking about what had almost happened. She sat for long periods watching the boat surge through the waves. She could feel the power of the sails, now going more into the wind instead of with the wind, thrusting the yacht forward through the waves. She marveled at how the sails could develop so much energy.

Where their relationship would go in the end, Jane had no clue. She might be falling in love with an assassin, and one who worked for her. *Didn't see that coming,* She lied to herself. She was not sure what she should do. For the moment they had avoided crossing a line but she knew that could easily change. What to do for now? Jane didn't know and didn't want to set any plans or limits. What did the Watcher say? Their lives were going to be intertwined going forward. Maybe that was enough for now.

The End

Afterword

The Captive Girl is the third book in the Dan Stone series. I have stepped ahead in time with this story in order to get Dan to Europe. The next tale is titled "The Assassin and the Pianist". It's a story I've had in mind for a couple of years but had to wait to write it.

If you enjoyed this story, please consider writing a review on Amazon. Reviews do not have to be lengthy and are extremely helpful for two reasons: first, they provide "social proof" of a book's value to the reader unfamiliar with the author, and second, they help readers filter through thousands of books in the same category to find ones that are worthy of their time investment. You provide an essential service to other Amazon readers with a solid review. I very much value your support.

Other novels published by David Nees:

Payback; Book One in the Dan Stone Series
The Shaman; Book Two in the Dan Stone Series
The Assassin and the Pianist; Book Four in the Dan Stone Series
Death in the Congo; Book Five in the Dan Stone Series

After the Fall: Jason's Tale; Book One in the After the Fall Series
Uprising; Book Two in the *After the Fall* series
Rescue; Book Three in the *After the Fall* series
Undercover; Book Four in the After the Fall series

For information about upcoming novels, please visit my website at *https://www.davidnees.com* or go on Facebook to find my page, *facebook.com/neesauthor*. Also, you can sign up for my reader list on my website to get new information. No spam; I never sell my list and you can opt out at any time.

The following is an excerpt from my next novel, *The Assassin and the Pianist*.

The Assassin and the Pianist
Excerpt from Chapter 1

He sat in the upstairs room looking out at the hedges lining the gravel drive. The pale winter light softly illuminated the room. The south-facing bank of the driveway hungrily drank in the weak warmth from the sun, eager to leave behind the hard freeze of winter. Downstairs a Chopin Étude was being played on a piano.

The precise cadence of the notes was only slightly tattered on their journey from the piano to his room upstairs. As he absorbed the music, the vise that held his mind in its painful grip, slowly, almost imperceptibly, began to relax. The music had its restorative effect on him, as it always did.

It was during these times, when his brain was released from the fierce clamp of pain, that he could go over the events, as best as he could remember them, that had occurred to bring him to this stone house with a woman playing the piano downstairs.

He remembered again the car journey on the icy roads, through the hills. He was in the back seat with his hands tied. Next to him sat a large man. The man's partner was driving. They were hurrying to...where? He didn't know.

The car sped around a turn and started to slide on the frozen road. The man in the backseat said something in Russian. Dan could understand most of it.

"Slow down or you'll kill us," The man's voice was low and thick.

"We were told to hurry. Not let anything distract us. The boss is eager to talk with him," the driver replied.

He assumed they were talking about him, but he had no idea why someone would want to talk with him, let alone tie him up. His head throbbed with a fierce pounding. His vision alternated between blurry and clear. Nothing made sense. Why was he bound? Who wanted to talk to him? Who were these men?

He was vaguely aware that the men had been with him for some time, holding him captive. They had asked questions. They had beaten him. They had injected him with chemicals that had made him confused and disoriented, sometimes causing him to lose consciousness. Now he could barely function and only in the present. And the present was a confusing puzzle.

On the next turn the car hit black ice and slewed sideways. The driver flailed away at the steering wheel trying to control the vehicle, but there was no traction. The captive instinctively ducked his head between his legs and the car slammed into the guard rail, spun back onto the pavement, and flipped on its side.

The burly man sitting next to him was thrown against the side window, smashing it with his head. The driver flew against the steering wheel and slammed his forehead into the car's windshield.

The bound man sat back up. For the moment the other two were stunned from the blows they had received. He reached for the man's pocket. The man had pulled a folding knife from it earlier to pick at his nails. He grabbed the knife and cut his wrists free. He pushed against the door. It was jammed. Panic rose like a black cloud to engulf him. He slammed his shoulder into the door again and again. The blows only ignited the pain from his other wounds. He leaned back and brought his legs up and kicked against the window until it cracked open.

He threw himself out of the now broken window and rolled onto the icy ground. The shock of the frigid air convulsed his chest causing him to almost choke. Looking back into the car, he saw his two captors stirring. Without hesitation, the man climbed over the guardrail and skidded down the frozen slope to the river below. It was shallow and moving fast over the boulders as the water sped down out of the mountains.

He didn't hesitate. The terror he felt came from above. He needed to get far away from it. He splashed into the frigid waters, straining for the other shore and the cover of the trees. Half way across, he slipped on a rock and fell into the water. Coming up he gasped for breath. There was a shout from above and a shot rang out. He heard the bullet strike the water to his right. The shot sent him scrambling to the shore and into the trees.

More shouts came from above. More shots flew into the woods after him. There was splashing from behind. They were coming.

I hope you will enjoy this next story. Thank you for reading my book. Your reading pleasure is why I write my stories.

Made in United States
Orlando, FL
24 May 2024